IRISH TALES OF TERROR

IRISH TALES OF TERROR

Edited by Peter Haining
Introduction by Ray Bradbury

WINGS BOOKS
New York • Avenel, New Jersey

Originally published as *The Wild Night Company: Irish Tales of Terror*.

Copyright © 1970 by Peter Haining.
Foreword copyright © 1970 by Ray Bradbury.

This edition is published by Wings Books,
distributed by Random House Value Publishing, Inc.,
40 Engelhard Avenue, Avenel, New Jersey 07001,
by arrangement with Peter Haining and
Euro-Features Limited.

Random House
New York • Toronto • London • Sydney • Auckland

Printed and bound in the United States of America

Library of Congress Cataloging-in-Publication Data

Wild night company
      Irish tales of terror / edited by Peter Haining.
          p.   cm.
      Originally published as: The Wild night company: Irish tales of
terror.
      ISBN 0-517-12245-6
      1. Horror tales, English—Irish authors. 2. Ireland—Fiction.
I. Haining, Peter. II. Title.
PR8876.5.H67W55 1995
823'.08738089415—dc20   94-31456
                                                              CIP

10 9 8 7 6 5 4 3 2 1

CONTENTS

ACKNOWLEDGMENTS

The Editor wishes to extend his sincere thanks to the following authors (or their executors, trustees or agents) and publishers for permission to include copyright material in this book; Messrs. William Heinemann Limited for 'Julia Cahill's Curse' by George Moore from *The Untilled Field;* Macmillan and Company Limited for 'The Crucifixion of the Outcast' by W. B. Yeats from *Early Poems and Stories;* the executors of the estate of A. E. Coppard for 'The Man from Kilsheelan' by A. E. Coppard from *The Black Doll;* Messrs. Jonathan Cape Limited tor 'Hell Fire' by James Joyce from *A Portrait of the Artist as a Young Man;* Messrs. Jarrolds Limited for 'Witch Wood' by Lord Dunsany from *The Fourth Book of Jorkens·* Messrs. Hollis and Carter for 'The Coonian Ghost' by Shane Leslie from *Shane Leslie's Ghost Book;* the executors of the author's estate for 'The Haunted Spinney' by Elliott O'Donnell; Messrs. C. J. Fallon Limited for 'The Fairies' Revenge' by Sinead de Valera from *The Stolen Child;* The Scott Meredith Literary Agency for 'The Moon Bog' by H. P. Lovecraft; the author and A. D. Peters and Company Limited for 'A Wild Night in Galway' by Ray Bradbury. Finally, I should like to express my deep appreciation to Ray Bradbury for both his continuing interest in my work and the magnificent foreword he has contributed to this volume.

'In "The Parochial Survey of Ireland" (1814) it is recorded how the story-tellers used to gather together on a wild evening and all tell their tales. And if any had a different version from the others, they would all recite theirs and vote and the man who had varied would have to abide by their verdict. In this way stories have been handed down with great accuracy.'

W. B. YEATS.

FOREWORD

There are times when we long for an interval, some respite, when the Irish would no longer surprise us.

They are much too clever, move quickly on their feet, vanish here to reappear there, and they write so well suicide seems most appealing.

My adventures with the Irish, which is why I am up front here in a Foreword, are no different than anyone else's. They may vary somewhat in detail, but the end result is the same. I was walking along, minding my own business, ignoring Ireland, when an avalanche fell on me. That is to say: the Irish.

Before I go any further, let me give you my background. I was born and raised in Waukegan, Illinois in the middle of, if you please, prejudiced America. I was raised with an amiable disregard, if not outright contempt, for the Irish, by a loving father who simply knew no better. It was the thing to do. Everybody did it. Contempt and disregard are a way of life, conveniences; they save thinking.

So while I did not actively practise contempt, I was perhaps guilty of disregard after I grew up. Then, two things happened to me. A woman named McClure crept up on me and married me and gave me four daughters; what a collision *that* was!

And another Irishman, named John Huston, hailed me from a boat and asked if I might help harpoon some Whale or other named MOBY DICK. The next thing I knew, aged 33, I was off to Dublin in the morn, and lost seven months in and out and around the Royal Hibernian Hotel, getting to know every banjo-plucker and squealing tenor beggar in the street and the candy-butcher lady across the street from the Gaiety Theatre,

7

and the actors back-stage at the Abbey, and a taxi-driver named Nick who drove me every night and every night from All Souls until Lent, back and forth from Kilcock, along the Liffey to Dublin, philosophising as he drove.

I would have nothing to do with it all. It began to charm me, of course, but I told my wife and friends, never never would I write so much as a jot or tittle about Eire. It was not my country, nor my customs, nor my people. The weather was inadmissable, the Church unforgiveable, the politics confusing; and the poverty beyond the pale. As soon as I could get off the Island before it sank, the better for Anglo-Saxon Waukegan me.

Well, the rest is easily told. I got out of Ireland, but the Irish refused to get out of me. They began to talk in old tongues late at night inside my head, and one noon lying in the sun of California I heard Nick driving around a long curve of fog outside Maynooth, and I wrote a story about him. And another voice got up in my mind and cried, if you write of Nick, you must write of *me*! Me, me! cried other voices.

Jesus, I thought, I don't love *one* Irish woman, but the whole damn Team, the Isle and all its wild inmates, up to and including the little lady who insisted on playing the harp around the corner from my hotel, even in the falling rain.

So I simply gave up, tossed in the sponge, let my reason crumble, forgot the old contempt, abandoned the ignorant pose, and wrote twelve one-act plays, one three-act comedy, fifteen short stories, and twenty-nine poems and essays about the Irish.

I have been lost ever since, God help me. The awful teasing fools have lugged my soul away. I know they lie. I know they think me worse fools than they. I admit it. But I am in love and I suppose no week will pass in the

8

rest of my life I will not hear their voices raising and falling in that beautiful lilt somewhere off thousands of miles away.

Enough of my being sunk in love. If I go on much longer, my old self from the Illinois days will suffer a severe depression just above my right eye.

I have been conned into writing this Foreword because I know the people here, in this book, also, by their many writings. And if the Irish are fiercely patriotic, they are even more fiercely individual. Here in this collection you will find not only the great roaring pack, but the lone singing person. They may march by in an army, but, look close! everyone dances to a different tune!

I will not pick favourites. Just about everything in this book pleases me, and for different reasons. Here the happy sad and the sad happy commingle and make do. Here shadows run over Galway hills, and there the sun breaks through in Grafton Street like a spotlight outside the Four Provinces pub. No story is like any other; the authors would rather be nailed-up-dead than assume similar attitudes or expressions.

Be warned. If you have ignored the Irish, or held some small contempt for them, in your past, that all is over now. And over as soon as you finish this and begin. If you would not lose your soul, man, slam this book shut now. Throw it in the trash. But, because of what I've already said, I think it's too late. You're already hooked. Give up. Lick your finger. Turn the page. There's the Mob, terrible, loveable, seizing at your elbow, telling what must be told. God help you in the first dread moments of Change. After that, it's all love.

Ray Bradbury

INTRODUCTION

Fantasy has been an integral part of Ireland and the Irish since time immemorial. Any casual traveller journeying through the country's dark valleys and across the sombre grey mountains, where progress has yet to set its untidy footsteps, can soon appreciate why the people have such an instinctive eye and ear—and wariness, too —for the forces of the unknown. Civilisation has made few inroads here on superstition; legends and myths are a part of the fabric of life, and no amount of 'rational explanation' will drive away the Irishman's caution where the unknown is concerned, or his respect for the beings 'not quite of this earth'.

Writing some eighty years ago in her magnificent study of Irish folk lore, *Ancient Legends*, Lady Wilde (mother of Oscar) said of the 'strange and mystical superstitions of the Irish' that they were 'brought thousands of years ago from their Aryan home but still, even in the present time, affect all the modes of thinking and acting in the daily life of the people'.

She went on: 'The superstition of the Irish peasant is the instinctive belief in the existence of certain unseen agencies that influence all human life; and with the highly sensitive organisation of their race, it is not surprising that the people live habitually under the shadow and dread of invisible powers which, whether working for good or evil, are awful and mysterious to the uncultured mind that sees only the strange results produced by certain forces, but knows nothing of approximate causes.'

The basic superstition of the Irish, then, is not unlike that of much of humanity, except that here so much of life and of what is unusual is attributed to the unseen and the power of the invisible. In a word, the fantastic has no more established domain than in Ireland.

11

Under these circumstances, it is small wonder that these forces take on many more guises than in other cultures. There are the *Denee Shee* (the fairies), the *Leprechauns, Cluricauns* and *Far Darrigs* (the solitary mischievout little people), the *Thevshi* (ghosts), witches and warlocks, werewolves, vampires and demons, *Banshees* (Women of the Fairies), *Merrows* (Mermaids), the *Pooka* and the legendary giants—not to mention all manner of other phantoms and night shapes impossible to describe. (Some of these are common to all peoples, of course, but the Irish seem to have by far the largest share of the supernatural.)

With all this 'raw material' to draw from there is obviously much to attract the professional writer and teller of fantasy stories, but the Irish themselves—those that *know*, that is—do not easily impart their experiences, and over the years collectors have had to tread carefully and patiently to win the confidence of the inhabitants. For isn't it a fact that the little people can hear everything that is said and will punish those who speak lightly of them?

In this anthology I have attempted to assemble those stories which, I consider, best capture the fantasy side of Ireland. They are taken from many periods and are of many strange things. The contributors fall into two categories: those famous Irish authors who have shown a penchant for the dark side of their country, and those distinguished English and American writers who have likewise been drawn to the supernatural in Ireland and written of it with understanding and skill. Both groups have set out—and to some measure succeeded—in capturing that which is mystical and magical in the land. While the items are predominantly fiction, I have included a number of factual reports by authors whose scholarship and research in the fields in which they write make their opinions ones to be valued and not lightly dismissed. I hope that by employing this combination of fact and fiction the reader will come to appreciate not only how firmly entrenched the popular figures of terror are, but also to realise that what he may at first— unwary sceptic!—be inclined to dismiss as fiction could so easily be fact.

The reader will note also how many of the 'beings of the unseen' recur from the earliest tales to those written quite recently. Our first contributor, the twelfth century Norman-Welsh historian, Giraldus Cambrensis, for instance, records a strange tale of half-humans, and his words are almost re-echoed in the uncanny events described by the Irishman Elliott O'Donnell in 'The Haunted Spinney' eight centuries later. Other authors write of devils from prehistory, fairies going about their timeless errands and dark fears that have no face and no date. Fantasy and the figures of fantasy have always been a part of Irish life, and this is what this book sets out to show.

My only disappointment in assembling the material has been the sparseness of modern Irish writers contributing to this area of their nation's literature from whom one could draw material. I researched in vain for stories among the present generation, and time and time again met with the statement that today writers are 'all bothered about sex and such things and have no time for the ghosts and little people'. By and large what new material is being created comes from visiting authors who, holidaying in Ireland, find their imaginations stirred by the beauty and mystery of the countryside. More power to them and their ilk, but where have all the Irish storytellers gone that they remain unmoved by the romance around them?

Ireland's great poet, W. B. Yeats, has already defined the Irish absorption with superstition and fantasy, and in doing so honed down to a few lines what I have

13

inexpertly been trying to say here. It makes a fitting conclusion, then, to end with the words he wrote nearly a century ago and which remain every bit as true today: 'The Celt, and his cromlechs, and his pillar-stones, these will not change much—indeed it is doubtful if anybody at all changes at any time. In spite of hosts of deniers, and asserters, and wise-men, and professors, the majority still are averse to sitting down to dine thirteen at table, or being helped to salt, or walking under a ladder, of seeing a single magpie flirting his chequered tail. There are, of course, children of light who have set their faces against all this, though even a newspaperman, if you entice him into a cemetery at midnight, will believe in phantoms, for everyone is a visionary, if you scratch him deep enough. *But the Celt, unlike any other, is a visionary without scratching.*'

PETER HAINING

THE MAN-WOLF

by Giraldus Cambrensis

GIRALDUS CAMBRENSIS (*c. 1147–1223*) *wrote one of the earliest and still most famous works on the history and people of Ireland, the* Topographia Hibernica. *Born in Wales, he entered the church as a young man and earned rapid recognition, becoming first royal chaplain and later preceptor to Prince John. In 1185 he accompanied the Prince to Ireland and there began work on his study of the island. He observed and recorded many of the strange customs, and also briefly skirted the areas of fantasy and myth. However, from the weight of his scholarly tome I have been able to select this strange episode which must undoubtedly qualify as one of the very first recorded tales of Irish fantasy in either fact or fiction.*

About three years before the arrival of Prince John in Ireland, it chanced that a certain priest, who was journeying from Ulster towards Meath, was benighted in a wood that lies on the boundaries of Meath. Whilst he, and the young lad his companion, were watching by a fire they had kindled under the leafy branches of a large tree, there came up to them a wolf who immediately addressed them in the following words: 'Do not alarm yourselves and do not be in any way afraid. You need not fear, I say, where there is no reason for fear.' The travellers none the less were thrown in a great fear and were astonished. But the wolf reverently called upon the Name of God. The priest then adjured him, straitly charging him by Almighty God and in the might of the

15

Most Holy Trinity that he should do them no sort of harm, but rather tell them what sort of creature he was who spake with a human voice. The wolf replied with seemly speech, and said: 'In number we are two, to wit a man and a woman, natives of Ossory, and every seven years on account of the curse laid upon our folk by the blessed Abbot S. Natalis, a brace of us are compelled to throw off the human form and appear in the shape of wolves. At the end of seven years, if perchance these two survive they are able to return again to their home, re-assuming the bodies of men, and another two must needs take their place. Howbeit my wife, who labours with me under this sore visitation, lies not far from hence, grievously sick. Wherefore I beseech you of your good charity to comfort her with the aid of your priestly office.' When he had so said, the wolf led the way to a tree at no great distance, and the priest followed him trembling at the strangeness of the thing. In the hollow of the tree he beheld a wolfen, and she was groaning piteously mingled with sad human sighs. Now when she saw the priest she thanked him very courteously and gave praise to God who had vouchsafed her such consolation in her hour of utmost need.

The priest then shrived her and gave her all the last rites of Holy Church so far as he was able. Most earnestly did she entreat him that she might receive her God, and that he would administer to her the crown of all, the Body of the Lord.

The priest, however, declared that he was not provided with the holy viaticum, when the man-wolf, who had withdrawn apart for a while, came forward and pointed to the wallet, containing a mass-book and some consecrated Hosts which, according to the use of his country, the good priest was carrying suspended from his neck under his clothing. The man-wolf entreated him not to deny them any longer the Gift of God, which it was

16

not to be questioned, Divine Providence had sent to them. Moreover to remove all doubt, using his claw as a hand, he drew off the pelt from the head of the wolfen and folded it back even as far down as the navel, whereupon there was plainly to be seen the body of an old woman. Upon this the priest, since she so instantly besought him, urged though it may be more by fear than by reasoning, hesitated no longer but gave her Holy Communion, which she received most devoutly from his hands. Immediately after this the man-wolf rolled back the skin again, fitting it to its former place.

These holy rites having been duly rather than regularly performed, the man-wolf joined their company by the fire they had kindled under the tree and showed himself a human being not a four-footed beast. In the early morning, at cock-light he led them safely out of the wood, and when he left them to pursue their journey he pointed out to them the best and shortest road, giving them directions for a long way. In taking leave also, he thanked the priest most gratefully and in good set phrase for the surpassing kindness he had shown, promising moreover that if it were God's will he should return home (and already two parts of the period during which he was under the malediction had passed) he would take occasion to give further proof of his gratitude.

As they were parting the priest inquired of the man-wolf whether the enemy (the English invader) who had now landed on their shores would continue long to possess the land. The wolf replied: 'On account of the sins of our nation and their enormous wickedness, the anger of God, falling upon an evil generation, hath delivered them into the hands of their enemies. Therefore so long as this foreign people shall walk in the way of the Lord and keep His commandments, they shall be safe and not to be subdued; but if—and easy is the downward path to iniquity and nature prone to evil—it comes

17

to pass that through dwelling among us they turn to our whoredoms, then assuredly will they provoke the wrath of the Lord upon themselves also.'

TEIG O'KANE AND THE CORPSE

(Traditional)

IRELAND abounds in traditional tales—both oral and recorded—dating from antiquity and endlessly retold over town and countryside hearths. Many of these stories are stiff with warning, retribution and moralising, making good use of the fear of the unknown to discourage drinking, wenching, thieving and all manner of wayward activities. This particular tale of a wild young roué whose life is changed by a 'visitation' is typical of the entire tradition and introduces us, for the first time in this collection, to the half-world of fairy spells.

There was once a grown-up lad in the County Leitrim, and he was strong and lively, and the son of a rich farmer. His father had plenty of money, and he did not spare it on the son. Accordingly, when the boy grew up he liked sport better than work, and, as his father had no other children, he loved this one so much that he allowed him to do in everything just as it pleased himself. He was very extravagant, and he used to scatter the gold money as another person would scatter the corn. He was seldom to be found at home, but if there was a fair, or a race, or a gathering within ten miles of him, you were dead certain to find him there. And he seldom spent a night in his father's house, but he used to be always out rambling, and, like Shawn Bwee long ago,

18

there was 'the love of every girl in the breast of his shirt', and it's many's the kiss he got and he gave, for he was very handsome, and there wasn't a girl in the country but would fall in love with him, only for him to fasten his two eyes on her, and it was for that some-one made this *rann* on him—

'Look at the rogue, its for kisses, he's rambling,
    It isn't much wonder, for that was his way;
He's like an old hedgehog, at night he'll be scrambling
    From this place to that, but he'll sleep in the day.'

At last he became very wild and unruly. He wasn't to be seen day nor night in his father's house, but always rambling or going to his *kailee* (night-visit) from place to place and from house to house, so that the old people used to shake their heads and say to one another, 'it's easy seen what will happen to the land when the old man dies; his son will run through it in a year, and it won't stand him that long itself'.

He used to be always gambling and card-playing and drinking, but his father never minded his bad habits, and never punished him. But it happened one day that the old man was told that the son had ruined the charac-ter of a girl in the neighbourhood, and he was greatly angry, and he called the son to him, and said to him, quietly and sensibly—'Avic', says he, 'you know I loved you greatly up to this, and I never stopped you from doing your choice thing whatever it was, and I kept plenty of money with you, and I always hoped to leave you the house and land, and all I had after myself would be gone; but I heard a story of you today that has disgusted me with you. I cannot tell you the grief that I felt when I heard such a thing of you, and I tell you now plainly that unless you marry that

19

girl I'll leave house and land and everything to my brother's son. I never could leave it to anyone who would make so bad a use of it as you do yourself, deceiving women and coaxing girls. Settle with yourself now whether you'll marry that girl and get my land as a fortune with her, or refuse to marry her and give up all that was coming to you; and tell me in the morning which of the two things you have chosen.'

'Och! *Domnoo Sherry!* father, you wouldn't say that to me, and I such a good son as I am. Who told you I wouldn't marry the girl?' says he.

But his father was gone, and the lad knew well enough that he would keep his word too; and he was greatly troubled in his mind, for as quiet and as kind as the father was, he never went back of a word that he had once said, and there wasn't another man in the country who was harder to bend that he was.

The boy did not know rightly what to do. He was in love with the girl indeed, and he hoped to marry her sometime or other, but he would much sooner have remained another while as he was, and follow on at his old tricks—drinking, sporting, and playing cards; and, along with that, he was angry that his father should order him to marry, and should threaten him if he did not do it.

'Isn't my father a great fool,' says he to himself. 'I was ready enough, and only too anxious, to marry Mary; and now since he threatened me, faith I've a great mind to let it go another while.'

His mind was so much excited that he remained between two notions as to what he should do. He walked out into the night at last to cool his heated blood, and went on to the road. He lit a pipe, and as the night was fine he walked and walked on, until the quick pace made him begin to forget his trouble. The night was bright, and the moon half full. There was not a breath of wind blowing, and the air was calm and mild. He walked on for nearly three hours, when he suddenly remembered that it was late in the night, and time for him to turn. 'Musha! I think I forgot myself,' says he; 'it must be near twelve o'clock now.'

The word was hardly out of his mouth, when he heard the sound of many voices, and the trampling of feet on the road before him. 'I don't know who can be out so late at night as this, and on such a lonely road,' said he to himself.

He stood listening, and he heard the voices of many people talking through other, but he could not understand what they were saying. 'Oh, wirra!' says he, 'I'm afraid. It's not Irish or English they have; it can't be they're Frenchmen!' He went on a couple of yards further, and he saw well enough by the light of the moon a band of little people coming towards him, and they were carrying something big and heavy with them. 'Oh, murder!' says he to himself, 'sure it can't be that they're the good people that's in it!' Every *rib* of hair that was on his head stood up, and there fell a shaking on his bones, for he saw that they were coming to him fast.

He looked at them again, and perceived that there were about twenty little men in it, and there was not a man at all of them higher than about three feet or three feet and a half, and some of them were grey, and seemed very old. He looked again, but he could not make out what was the heavy thing they were carrying until they came up to him, and then they all stood round about him. They threw the heavy thing down on the road, and he saw on the spot that it was a dead body.

He became as cold as the Death, and there was not a drop of blood running in his veins when an old little grey *maneen* came up to him and said, 'Isn't it lucky we met you, Teig O'Kane?'

Poor Teig could not bring out a word at all, nor open

his lips, if he were to get the world for it, and so he gave no answer.

'Teig O'Kane,' said the little grey man again, 'isn't it timely you met us?'

Teig could not answer him.

'Teig O'Kane,' says he, 'the third time, isn't it lucky and timely that we met you?'

But Teig remained silent, for he was afraid to return an answer, and his tongue was as if it was tied to the roof of his mouth.

The little grey man turned to his companions, and there was joy in his bright little eye. 'And now,' says he, 'Teig O'Kane hasn't a word, we can do with him what we please. Teig, Teig,' says he, 'you're living a bad life, and we can make a slave of you now, and you cannot withstand us, for there's no use in trying to go against us. Lift that corpse.'

Teig was so frightened that he was only able to utter the two words, 'I won't'; for as frightened as he was, he was obstinate and stiff, the same as ever.

'Teig O'Kane won't lift the corpse,' said the little *maneen*, with a wicked little laugh, for all the world like the breaking of a *lock* of dry *kippeens* (twigs) and with a little harsh voice like the striking of a cracked bell. 'Teig O'Kane won't lift the corpse—make him lift it'; and before the word was out of his mouth they had all gathered round poor Teig, and they all talking and laughing through other.

Teig tried to run from them, but they followed him, and a man of them stretched out his foot before him as he ran, so that Teig was thrown in a heap on the road. Then before he could rise up the fairies caught him, some by the hands and some by the feet, and they held him tight, in a way that he could not stir, with his face against the ground. Six or seven of them raised the body then, and pulled it over to him, and left it down on his back. The breast of the corpse was squeezed against Teig's back and shoulders, and the arms of the corpse were thrown around Teig's neck. Then they stood back from him a couple of yards, and let him get up. He rose, foaming at the mouth and cursing, and he shook himself, thinking to throw the corpse off his back. But his fear and his wonder were great when he found that the two arms had a tight hold round his own neck, and that the two legs were squeezing his hips firmly, and that, however strongly he tried, he could not throw it off, any more than a horse can throw off its saddle. He was terribly frightened then, and he thought he was lost. 'Ochone! for ever,' said he to himself, 'it's the bad life I'm leading that has given the good people this power over me. I promise to God and Mary, Peter and Paul, Patrick and Bridget, that I'll mend my ways for as long as I have to live, if I come clear out of this danger—and I'll marry the girl.'

The little grey man came up to him again, and said he to him, 'Now, *Teigeen*,' says he, 'you didn't lift the body when I told you to lift it, and see how you were made to lift it; perhaps when I tell you to bury it you won't bury it until you're made to bury it!'

'Anything at all that I can do for your honour,' said Teig, 'I'll do it,' for he was getting sense already, and if it had not been for the great fear that was on him, he never would have let that civil word slip out of his mouth.

The little man laughed a sort of laugh again. 'You're getting quiet now, Teig,' says he. 'I'll go bail but you'll be quiet enough before I'm done with you. Listen to me now, Teig O'Kane, and if you don't obey me in all I'm telling you to do, you'll repent it. You must carry with you this corpse that is on your back to Teampoll-Démus, and you must bring it into the church with you, and make a grave for it in the very middle of the church,

23

and you must raise up the flags and put them down again the very same way, and you must carry the clay out of the church and leave the place as it was when you came, so that no one could know that there had been anything changed. But that's not all. Maybe that the body won't be allowed to be buried in that church; perhaps some other man has the bed, and, if so, it's likely he won't share it with this one. If you don't get leave to bury it in Teampoll-Démus, you must carry it to Carrick-fhad-vic-Orus, and bury it in the churchyard there; and if you don't get it into that place, take it with you to Teampoll-Ronan; and if that churchyard is closed on you, take it to Imlogue-Fada; and if you're not able to bury it there, you've no more to do than to take it to Kill-Breedya, and you can bury it there without hindrance. I cannot tell you what one of those churches is the one where you will have leave to bury that corpse under the clay, but I know that it will be allowed you to bury him at some church or other of them. If you do this work rightly, we will be thankful to you, and you will have no cause to grieve; but if you are slow or lazy, believe me we shall take satisfaction of you.'

When the grey little man had done speaking, his comrades laughed and clapped their hands together. 'Glic! Glic! Hwee! Hwee!' they all cried; 'go on, go on, you have eight hours before you till daybreak, and if you haven't this man buried before the sun rises, you're lost.' They struck a fist and a foot behind on him, and drove him on in the road. He was obliged to walk, and to walk fast, for they gave him no rest.

He thought himself that there was not a wet path, or a dirty *borreen* (lane) or a crooked contrary road in the whole country, that he had not walked that night. The night was at times very dark, and whenever there would come a cloud across the moon he could see nothing,

24

and then he used often to fall. Sometimes he was hurt, and sometimes he escaped, but he was obliged always to rise on the moment and to hurry on. Sometimes the moon would break out clearly, and then he would look behind him and see the little people following at his back. And he heard them speaking amongst themselves, talking and crying out, and screaming like a flock of sea-gulls; and if he was to save his soul he never understood as much as one word of what they were saying.

He did not know how far he had walked, when at last one of them cried out to him, 'Stop here!' He stood, and they all gathered round him.

'Do you see those withered trees over there?' says the old boy to him again. 'Teampoll-Démus is among those trees, and you must go in there by yourself, for we cannot follow you or go with you. We must remain here. Go on boldly.'

Teig looked from him, and he saw a high wall that was in places half broken down, and an old grey church on the inside of the wall, and about a dozen withered old trees scattered here and there round it. There was neither leaf nor twig on any of them, but their bare crooked branches were stretched out like the arms of an angry man when he threatens. He had no help for it, but was obliged to go forward. He was a couple of hundred yards from the church, but he walked on, and never looked behind him until he came to the gate of the churchyard. The old gate was thrown down, and he had no difficulty in entering. He turned then to see if any of the little people were following him, but there came a cloud over the moon, and the night became so dark that he could see nothing. He went into the churchyard, and he walked up to the old grassy pathway leading to the church. When he reached the door, he found it locked. The door was large and strong, and he did not know what to do. At last he drew out his knife with

25

difficulty, and stuck it in the wood to try if it were not rotten, but it was not.

'No,' said he to himself, 'I have no more to do; the door is shut, and I can't open it.'

Before the words were rightly shaped in his own mind, a voice in his ear said to him, 'Search for the key on top of the door, or on the wall.'

He started. 'Who is that speaking to me?' he cried, turning round; but he saw no one. The voice said in his ear again, 'Search for the key on the top of the door, or on the wall.'

'What's that?' said he, and the sweat running from his forehead; 'who spoke to me?'

'It's I, the corpse, that spoke to you!' said the voice.

'Can you talk?' said Teig.

'Now and again,' said the corpse.

Teig searched for the key, and he found it on top of the wall. He was too much frightened to say any more, but he opened the door wide, and as quickly as he could, and he went in, with the corpse on his back. It was as dark as pitch inside, and poor Teig began to shake and tremble.

'Light the candle,' said the corpse.

Teig put his hand in his pocket, as well as he was able, and drew out a flint and steel. He struck a spark out of it, and lit a burnt rag he had in his pocket. He blew it until it made a flame, and he looked round him. The church was very ancient, and part of the wall was broken down. The windows were blown in or cracked, and the timber of the seats was rotten. There were six or seven old iron candlesticks left there still, and in one of these candlesticks Teig found the stump of an old candle, and he lit it. He was still looking round him on the strange and horrid place in which he found himself, when the cold corpse whispered in his ear, 'Bury me now, bury me now; there is a spade and turn the ground.'

26

Teig looked from him, and he saw a spade lying beside the altar. He took it up, and he placed the blade under a flag that was in the middle of the aisle, and leaning all his weight on the handle of the spade, he raised it. When the first flag was raised it was not hard to raise the others near it, and he moved three or four of them out of their places. The clay that was under them was soft and easy to dig, but he had not thrown up more than three or four shovelfuls, when he felt the iron touch something soft like flesh. He threw up three or more shovelfuls from around it, and then he saw that it was another body that was buried in the same place.

'I am afraid I'll never be allowed to bury the two bodies in the same hole,' said Teig, in his own mind. 'You corpse, there on my back,' says he, 'will you be satisfied if I bury you down here?' But the corpse never answered him a word.

'That's a good sign,' said Teig to himself. 'Maybe he's getting quiet,' and he thrust the spade down in the earth again. Perhaps he hurt the flesh of the other body, for the dead man that was buried there stood up in the grave, and shouted an awful shout. "Hoo! hoo! hoo!!! Go! go!! go!!! or you're a dead, dead, dead man!' And then he fell back in the grave again. Teig said afterwards, that of all the wonderful things he saw that night, that was the most awful to him. His hair stood upright on his head like the bristles of a pig, the cold sweat ran off his face, and then came a tremor over all his bones, until he thought that he must fall.

But after a while he became bolder, when he saw that the second corpse remained lying quietly there, and he threw in the clay on it again, and he smoothed it overhead, and he laid down the flags carefully as they had been before. 'It can't be that he'll rise up any more,' said he.

He went down the aisle a little further, and drew near

to the door, and began raising the flags again, looking for another bed for the corpse on his back. He took up three or four flags and put them aside, and then he dug the clay. He was not long digging until he laid bare an old woman without a thread upon her but her skirt. She was more lively than the first corpse, for he had scarcely taken any clay away from about her, when she sat up and began to cry, 'Ho, you *bodach* (clown)! Ha, you *bodach*! Where has he been that he got no bed?'

Poor Teig drew back, and when she found that she was getting no answer, she closed her eyes gently, lost her vigour, and fell back quietly and slowly under the clay. Teig did to her as he had done to the man—he threw the clay back on her, and left the flags down overhead.

He began digging again near the door, but before he had thrown up more than a couple of shovelfuls, he noticed a man's hand laid bare by the spade. 'By my soul, I'll go no further, then,' said he to himself; 'what use is it for me?' And he threw the clay in again on it, and settled the flags as they had been before.

He left the church then, and his heart was heavy enough, but he shut the door and locked it, and left the key where he found it. He sat down on a tombstone that was near the door, and began thinking. He was in great doubt what he should do. He laid his face between his two hands, and cried for grief and fatigue, since he was dead certain at this time that he never would come home alive. He made another attempt to loosen the hands of the corpse that were squeezed round his neck, but they were as tight as if they were clamped; and the more he tried to loosen them, the tighter they squeezed him. He was going to sit down once more, when the cold, horrid lips of the dead man said to him, 'Carrick-fhad-vic-Orus,' and he remembered the command of the good people to bring the corpse with him to that place if he should be unable to bury it where he had been.

He rose up, and looked about him. 'I don't know the way,' he said.

As soon as he uttered the word, the corpse stretched out suddenly its left hand that had been tightened round his neck, and kept it pointing out, showing him the road he ought to follow. Teig went in the direction that the fingers were stretched, and passed out of the churchyard. He found himself on an old rutty, stony road, and he stood still again, not knowing where to turn. The corpse stretched out its bony hand a second time, and pointed out to him another road—not the road by which he had come when approaching the old church. Teig followed that road, and whenever he came to a path or road meeting it, the corpse always stretched out its hand and pointed with its fingers, showing him the way he was to take.

Many was the cross-road he turned down, and many was the crooked *boreen* he walked, until he saw from him an old burying-ground at last, beside the road, but there was neither church nor chapel nor any other building in it. The corpse squeezed him tightly, and he stood. 'Bury me, bury me in the burying-ground,' said the voice.

Teig drew over towards the old burying-place, and he was not more than about twenty yards from it, when, raising his eyes, he saw hundreds and hundreds of ghosts —men, women, and children—sitting on top of the wall round about, or standing on the inside of it, or running backwards and forwards, and pointing at him, while he could see their mouths opening and shutting as if they were speaking, though he heard no words, nor any sound amongst them at all.

He was afraid to go forward, so he stood where he was, and the moment he stood, all the ghosts became

29

quiet, and ceased moving. Then Teig understood that it was trying to keep him from going in, that they were. He walked a couple of yards forwards, and immediately the whole crowd rushed together towards the spot to which he was moving, and they stood so thickly together that it seemed to him that he never could break through them, even though he had a mind to try. But he had no mind to try it. He went back broken and dispirited, and when he had gone a couple of hundred yards from the burying-ground, he stood again, for he did not know what way he was to go. He heard the voice of the corpse in his ear, saying 'Teampoll-Ronan,' and the skinny hand was stretched out again, pointing him out the road.

As tired as he was, he had to walk, and the road was neither short nor even. The night was darker than ever, and it was difficult to make his way. Many was the toss he got, and many a bruise they left on his body. At last he saw Teampoll-Ronan from him in the distance, standing in the middle of the burying-ground. He moved over towards it, and thought he was all right and safe, when he saw no ghosts nor anything else on the wall, and he thought he would never be hindered now from leaving his load off him at last. He moved over to the gate but as he was passing in, he tripped on the threshold. Before he could recover himself, something that he could not see seized him by the neck, by the hands, and by the feet, and bruised him, and shook him, and choked him, until he was nearly dead; and at last he was lifted up, and carried more than a hundred yards from that place, and then thrown down in an old dyke, with the corpse still clinging to him.

He rose up, bruised and sore, but feared to go near the place again, for he had seen nothing the time he was thrown down and carried away.

'You corpse, up on my back,' said he, 'shall I go over again to the churchyard?'—but the corpse never answered him. 'That's a sign you don't wish me to try it again,' said Teig.

He was now in great doubt as to what he ought to do, when the corpse spoke in his ear, and said 'Imlogue-Fada'.

'Oh, murder!' said Teig, 'must I bring you there? If you keep me long walking like this, I tell you I'll fall under you.'

He went on, however, in the direction the corpse pointed out to him. He could not have told himself, how long he had been going, when the dead man behind suddenly squeezed him, and said, 'There!'

Teig looked from him, and he saw a little low wall, that was so broken down in places that it was no wall at all. It was in a great wide field, in from the road; and only for three or four great stones at the corners, that were more like rocks than stones, there was nothing to show that there was either graveyard or burying-ground there.

'Is this Imlogue-Fada? Shall I bury you here?' said Teig.

'Yes,' said the voice.

'But I see no grave or gravestone, only this pile of stones,' said Teig.

The corpse did not answer, but stretched out its long fleshless hand, to show Teig the direction in which he was to go. Teig went on accordingly, but he was greatly terrified, for he remembered what had happened to him at the last place. He went on, 'with his heart in his mouth', as he said himself afterwards; but when he came to within fifteen or twenty yards of the little low square wall, there broke out a flash of lightning, bright yellow and red, with blue streaks in it, and went round about the wall in one course, and it swept by as fast as the swallow in the clouds, and the longer Teig remained looking at it the faster it went, till at last it became like a bright ring of flame round the old graveyard, which no one could pass without being burnt by it. Teig never saw, from the time he was born, and never saw afterwards, so wonderful or so splendid a sight as that was. Round went the flame, white and yellow and blue sparks leaping out from it as it went, and although at first it had been no more than a thin, narrow line, it increased slowly until it was at last a great broad band, and it was continually getting broader and higher, and throwing out more brilliant sparks, till there was never a colour on the ridge of the earth that was not to be seen in that fire; and lightning never shone and flame never flamed that was so shining and so bright as that.

Teig was amazed; he was half dead with fatigue, and he had no courage left to approach the wall. There fell a mist over his eyes, and there came a *soorawn* (vertigo) in his head, and he was obliged to sit down upon a great stone to recover himself. He could see nothing but the light, and he could hear nothing but the whirr of it as it shot round the paddock faster than a flash of lightning.

As he sat there on the stone, the voice whispered once more in his ear, 'Kill-Breedya'; and the dead man squeezed him to tightly that he cried out. He rose again, sick, tired, and trembling, and went forward as he was directed. The wind was cold, and the road was bad, and the load upon his back was heavy and the night was dark, and he himself was nearly worn out, and if he had had very much farther to go he must have fallen dead under his burden.

At last the corpse stretched out its hand, and said to him, 'Bury me there'.

'This is the last burying-place,' said Teig in his own mind; 'and the little grey man said I'd be allowed to bury him in some of them, so it must be this; it can't be but they'll let him in here.'

The first faint streak of the *ring of day* was appearing in the east, and the clouds were beginning to catch fire, but it was darker than ever, for the moon was set, and there were no stars.

'Make haste, make haste!' said the corpse; and Teig hurried forward as well as he could to the graveyard, which was a little place on a bare hill, with only a few graves in it. He walked boldly in through the open gate, and nothing touched him, nor did he either hear or see anything. He came to the middle of the ground, and then stood up and looked round him for a spade or shovel to make a grave. As he was turning round and searching, he suddenly perceived what startled him greatly—a newly-dug grave right before him. He moved over to it, and then looked down, and there at the bottom he saw a black coffin. He clambered down into the hole and lifted the lid, and found that (as he thought it would be) the coffin was empty. He had hardly mounted up out of the hole, and was standing on the brink, when the corpse, which had clung to him for more than eight hours, suddenly relaxed its hold of his neck, and loosened its shins from round his hips, and sank down with a *plop* into the open coffin.

Teig fell down on his two knees at the brink of the grave, and gave thanks to God. He made no delay then but pressed down the coffin lid in its place and threw in the clay over it with his two hands; and when the grave was filled up, he stamped and leaped on it with his feet, until it was firm and hard, and then he left the place.

The sun was fast rising as he finished his work, and the first thing he did was to return to the road, and look out for a house to rest himself in. He found an inn at last, and lay down upon a bed there, and slept till night.

Then he rose up and ate a little, and fell asleep again till morning. When he awoke in the morning he hired a horse and rode home. He was more than twenty-six miles from home where he was, and he had come all that way with the dead body on his back in one night.

All the people at his own home thought that he must have left the country, and they rejoiced greatly when they saw him come back. Everyone began asking him where he had been, but he would not tell anyone except his father.

He was a changed man from that day. He never drank too much; he never lost his money over cards; and especially he would not take the world and be out late by himself of a dark night.

He was not a fortnight at home until he married Mary, the girl he had been in love with; and it's at their wedding the sport was, and it's he was the happy man from that day forward, and it's all I wish that we may be as happy as he was.

THE FRIENDLY DEMON

by Daniel Defoe

DANIEL DEFOE *(1660-1731), whose place in English literature is assured with* Robinson Crusoe, *was actually a man of many and varied interests—not the least of these being the occult and the 'unseen world'. His famous ghost story* The Apparition of One Mrs. Veal *has stood the test of time admirably and students of the supernatural will find much of value in his* Essay on the History and Reality of Apparitions. *In this work he states categorically: 'I must tell you, good people, he that is not able to see the devil, in whatever shape he is pleased to appear in, he is not really qualified to live in this world, no, not in the quality of a common inhabitant'. Bear this in mind as you read the rare little item here, for while it has elements of whimsy there is much of the sinister, too.*

A gentleman in Ireland, near to the Earl of Orrery's house, sending his butler one afternoon to a neighbouring village to buy cards, as he passed a field, espied a company in the middle thereof, sitting around a table, with several dishes of good cheer before them. And moving towards them, they all rose and saluted him, desiring him to sit down and take part with them. But one of them whispered these words in his ear, 'Do nothing this company invites you to'. Whereupon, he refusing to accept of their kindness, the table and all the dainties it was furnished with immediately vanished, but the company fell to dancing and playing upon divers musical instruments.

The butler was a second time solicited to partake of their diversions, but would not be prevailed upon to engage herself with them. Upon which they left off their merrymaking and fell to work, still pressing the butler to make one among them, but to no purpose. So that, upon his third refusal, they all vanished and left the butler alone, who in a great consternation returned home without the cards, fell into a fit as he entered the house, but soon recovering his senses, related to his master all that had passed.

The following night, one of the ghostly company came to his bedside and told him that if he offered to stir out the next day, he would be carried away. Upon his advice he kept within till towards the evening, and, having occasion to make water, ventured to set one foot over the threshold of the door in order to ease himself, which he had no sooner done but a rope was cast about his middle in the sight of several passers-by and the poor man was hurried from the porch with unaccountable swiftness, followed by many, many persons.

But they were not nimble enough to overtake him, till a horseman, well mounted, happened to meet him upon the road, and seeing many followers in pursuit of a man hurried along in a rope without anybody to force him, catched hold of the cord and stopped him in his career, but received for his pains, such a strap upon his back with one end of the rope as almost felled him from his horse. However, being a good Christian, he was too strong for the devil, and recovered the butler out of the spirits' clutches, and brought him back to his friends.

The Lord Orrery, hearing of the strange passages, for his further satisfaction of the truth, thereof, sent for the butler, with leave of his master, to come and continue some days and nights at his house, which, in obedience to his lordship, the servant did accordingly. Who after his first night's bedding there, reported to the earl in the morning that his spectre had again been with him and assured him that on that very day he should be spirited away, in spite of all the measures that could possibly be taken to prevent it. Upon which he was conducted into a large room, with a considerable number of holy persons to defend him from the assaults of Satan, among whom was the famous stroker of bewitched persons, Mr. Greatrix, who lived in the neighbourhood, and knew, as may be presumed, how to deal with the devil as well as anybody. Besides, several of eminent quality were present in the house; among the rest, two bishops, all waiting the wonderful event of this unaccountable prodigy.

Till part of the afternon was spent, time slid away in nothing but peace and quietness but at length the enchanted patient was perceived to rise from the floor without any visible assistance, whereupon Mr. Greatrix and another lusty man clapped their arms over his shoulders and endeavoured to weigh him down with their utmost strength, but to no purpose. For the devil proved too powerful and, after a hard struggle on both sides, made them quit their hold; and snatching the butler from them, carried him over their heads and tossed him in the air, to and fro like a dog in a blanket, several of the company running under the poor wretch to save him from the ground. By which means, when the spirits' frolic was over, they could not find that in all this hurry scurry the frightened butler had received the least damage, but was left in *status quo* upon the same premises, to prove the devil a liar.

The goblins, for this bout, gave over their pastime and left their May-game to take a little repose. That he might in some measure be refreshed against their next sally, the lord ordered the same night two of his servants to lie with him, for fear some devil or other should come and catch him napping. Notwithstanding which, the butler told his lordship the next morning that the spirit has again been with him in the likeness of a quack doctor, and held in his right hand a wooden dish full of grey liquor, like a mess of porridge, at the sight of which he endeavoured to awake his bedfellows.

But the spectre told him his attempts were fruitless, for that his companions were enchanted into a deep sleep, advising him not to be frightened, for he came as friend and was the same spirit that cautioned him in the field against complying with the company he there met, when he was going for the cards; adding that if he had not refused to come into their measures he had been forever miserable; also wondered he had escaped the day before, because he knew there was so powerful a combination against him; that for the future there would be no more attempts of the like nature; further telling the poor trembling butler that he knew he was sadly troubled with two sorts of fits; and as a friend he had brought him a medicine that would cure him of both, beseeching him to take it.

Then the spiritual doctor asked his patient if he knew him. The butler answered no. 'I am,' says he, 'the wandering ghost of your old acquaintance John Hobby, who has been dead and buried these seven years; and ever since, for the wickedness of my life, have been lifted into the company of those evil spirits you beheld in the fields, am hurried up and down in this restless condition, and doomed to continue in the same wretched way till the day of judgement'—adding that 'had you served your Creator in the days of your youth, and offered up your prayers that morning before you were sent for the cards, you had not been treated by the spirits that tormented you with so much rigor and severity.'

After the butler had reported these marvellous passages to my lord and his family, the two bishops that were present, among other quality, were thereupon consulted, whether or no it was proper for the butler to follow the spirit's advice in taking the plantain juice for cure of his fits, and whether he had done well or ill in refusing the liquid dose which the spectre would have given him. The question at first seemed to be a kind of moot point, but after some struggle in the debate, their resolution was that the butler had acted through the whole affair like a good Christian for that it was highly sinful to follow the devil's advice in anything, and that no man should do evil that good might come of it.

So that, in short, the poor butler, after his fatigue had no amends for his trouble, but was denied, by the bishops, the seeming benefit that the spirit intended him.

THE PARRICIDE'S TALE

by Charles Robert Maturin

CHARLES ROBERT MATURIN *(1782-1824) was an Irish
clergyman who moved in Dublin society circles,
dressed outlandishly, constantly courted rumour
and speculation and was said by his literary ad-
mirers to have the 'madness of genius.' He frequently worked, we are told, in a room full of
people, his mouth covered with a paste made of
flour and water to prevent himself joining in the
conversation. This love of flamboyance and exag-
geration is much evident in Maturin's work, particularly the famous* Melmouth the Wonderer *from
which the following grim story of two immured
lovers is taken. 'Melmouth', the immortal man, is
certainly one of the greatest of all Irish fantasy
characters and in his creator's extravagant life we
can see a pattern of behaviour emerging which has
since become almost the style for Irish writers.*

It was in the midst of one of his most licentious songs
that my companion suddenly paused. He gazed about
him for some time; and faint and dismal as the light
was by which we beheld each other, I thought I could
observe an extraordinary expression over-shadowed his
countenance. 'It was indeed a horrid night,' said he, un-
consciously advertising to some circumstance in the narrative; and his voice sank into mutterings, and he for-
bore to mention the subject further.

I rose and entreated my companion to relate the circumstance he had alluded to. His excessive good nature

40

acceded to this request in a moment; and he prepared himself with a kind of grim alacrity for the effort. He was now in his element. He was enabled to daunt a feeble mind by the narration of horrors, and to amaze an ignorant one with a display of crimes; and he needed no more to make him commence. 'I remember,' said he, 'an extraordinary circumstance which I did not recollect immediately; so many strange thoughts have crossed my mind every day, that events which would make a life-long impression on others pass like shadows before me, while thoughts appear like substances. *Emotions are my events;* you know what brought me to this cursed convent; well, don't shiver or look *paler,* you were pale before. Be that as it may, I found myself in the convent, and I was obliged to subscribe to its discipline. A part of it was that extraordinary criminals should undergo what they called extraordinary penance; that is, not only submit to every ignominy and rigor of conventual life (which, fortunately for its penitents, is never wanting in such amusing resources), but act the part of executioner whenever any distinguished punishment was to be inflicted or witnessed. They did me the honour to believe me particularly qualified for the species of recreation, and perhaps they did not flatter me. I had all the humility of a saint on trial; but still I had a kind of confidence in my talents of this description, provided they were put to a proper test; and the monks had the goodness to assure me that I could never be long without one in a convent. This was a very tempting picture of my situation, but I found these worthy people had not in the least exaggerated. An instance occurred a few days after I had the happiness to become a member of this amiable community, of whose merits you are doubtless sensible. I was desired to attach myself to a young monk of distinguished family who had lately taken

41

the vows and who performed his duties with that heart-less punctuality that intimated to the community that his heart was elsewhere. I was soon put in possession of the business: from their ordering me to *attach* myself to him, I instantly conceived I was bound to the most deadly hostility against him. The friendship of convents is always a treacherous league; we watch, suspect, and torment each other, for the love of God. This young monk's only crime was that he was suspected of cherishing an earthly passion. He was, as I have stated, the son of a distinguished family, who (from the fear of his contracting what is called a degrading marriage, i.e., of marrying a woman of inferior rank whom he loved and who would have made him happy, as fools, that is, half mankind, estimate happiness) forced him to take the vows. He appeared at times broken-hearted, but at times there was a light of hope in his eye, that looked somewhat ominous in the eyes of the community. It is certain that hope, not being an indigenous plant in the parterre of a convent, must excite suspicion with regard both to its origin and its growth.

'Some time after, a young novice entered the convent. From the moment he did so, a most striking change took place in the young monk. He and the novice became inseparable companions; there was something suspicious in that. My eyes were on the watch in a moment. Eyes are particularly sharpened in discovering misery when they can hope to aggravate it. The attachment between the young monk and the novice went on. They were forever in the garden together; they inhaled the odours of the flowers; they cultivated the same cluster of carnations; they entwined themselves as they walked together; when they were in the choir, their voices were like mixed incense. Friendship is often carried to excess in conventual life, but this friendship was too like love. For instance, the psalms sung in the choir sometimes

42

breathe a certain language; at these words, the young monk and the novice would direct their voices at each other in sounds that could not be misunderstood. If the least correction was inflicted, one would entreat to undergo it for the other. If a day of relaxation was allowed, whatever presents were sent to the cell of one, were sure to be found in the cell of the other. This was enough for me. I saw that secret of mysterious happiness, which is the greatest misery to those who never can share it. My vigilance was redoubled, and it was rewarded by the discovery of a secret; a secret that I had to communicate and thereby raise my consequence. You cannot guess the importance attached to the discovery of a secret in a convent (particularly when the remission of our own offences depends on the discovery of those of others).

'One evening, as the young monk and his darling novice were in the garden, the former plucked a peach, which he immediately offered to his favourite; the latter accepted it with a movement I thought rather awkward; it seemed like what I imagined would be the reverence of a female. This young monk divided the peach with a knife; in doing so the knife grazed the finger of the novice, and the monk, in agitation inexpressible, tore his habit to bind up the wound. I saw it all—my mind was made up on the business—I went to the superior that very night. The result may be imagined. They were watched, but cautiously at first. They were probably on their guard; for, for some time, it defied even my vigilance to make the slightest discovery. It is a situation incomparably tantalising, when suspicion is convinced of her own suggestions, as of the truth of the gospel, but still wants the *little fact* to make them credible to others. One night when I had, by direction of the superior, taken my station in the gallery (where I was contented to remain hour after hour, and night after night,

43

amid solitude, darkness, and cold, for the chance of the power of retaliating on others the misery inflicted on myself)—one night I thought I heard a step in the gallery—I have told you that I was in the dark—a light step passed me. I could hear the broken and palpitating respiration of the person. A few moments after, I heard a door open, and knew it to be the door of the young monk. I knew it; for by long watching in the dark, and accustoming myself to number the cells, by the groan from one, the prayer from another, the faint shriek of restless dreams from a third, my ear had become so finely graduated that I could instantly distinguish the opening of *that door,* from which (to my sorrow) no sound had ever before issued. I was provided with a small chain, by which I fastened the handle of the door to a continuous one, in such a manner that it was impossible to open either of them from the inside. I then hastened to the superior, with a pride of which none but the successful tracer of a guilty secret in convents can have any conception. I believe the superior was himself agitated by the luxury of the same feelings, for he was awake and up in his apartment, attended by *four monks,* whom you can remember.' I shuddered at the remembrance. 'I communicated my intelligence with a voluble eagerness, not only unsuited to the respect I owed these persons, but which must have rendered me almost unintelligible, yet they were good enough not only to overlook the violation of decorum which would in any other case have been severely punished, but even to fill in certain pauses in my narrative, with a condescension and felicity truly miraculous. I felt what it was to acquire importance in the eyes of a superior, and gloried in all the dignified depravity of an informer. We set out without losing a moment. We arrived at the door of the cell, and I pointed out with triumph the chain unremoved, though a slight vibration perceptible at our approach showed the wretches within were already apprised of their danger. I unfastened the door—how they must have shuddered! The superior and his satellites burst into the cell, and *I* held the light. You tremble. Why? I was guilty, and I wished to witness guilt that palliated mine, at least in the opinion of the convent. I had only violated the laws of nature, but they had outraged the decorum of a convent, and, of course, in the creed of a convent, there was no proportion between our offences. Besides, I was anxious to witness misery that might perhaps equal or exceed my own, and this is a curiosity not easily satisfied. It is actually possible to become *amateurs in suffering*. I have heard of men who have travelled into countries where horrible executions were to be daily witnessed, for the sake of that excitement which the sight of suffering never fails to give, from the spectacle of a tragedy, or an *auto-da-fé*, down to the writhings of the meanest reptile on whom you can inflict torture, and feel that torture is the result of your own power. It is a species of feeling of which we never can divest ourselves, a triumph over those whose sufferings have placed them below us; and no wonder—suffering is always an indication of weakness—we glory in our inpenetrability. I did, as we burst into the cell. The wretched husband and wife were locked in each other's arms. You can imagine the scene that followed. Here I must do the superior reluctant justice. He was a man (of course from his conventual feelings) who had no more idea of the intercourse between the sexes than between two beings of a different species. The scene that he beheld could not have revolted him more if it had been the horrible loves of the baboons and the Hottentot women at the Cape of Good Hope; or those still more loathsome unions between the serpents of South America and their human victims, when they can catch them and twine round them in folds of unnatural and

45

ineffable union. He really stood as much astonished and appalled to see two human beings of different sexes, who dared to love each other in spite of monastic ties, as if he had witnessed the horrible conjunctions I have alluded to. Had he seen vipers engendering in that frightful knot which seems the pledge of mortal hostility, instead of love, he could not have arrested more horror; and I do him the justice to believe he felt all he attested. Whatever affection he might employ on points of conventual austerity, there was none here. Love was a thing he always believed connected with sin, even though consecrated by the name of a sacrament and called marriage, as it is in our church. But, love in a convent!—Oh, there is no conceiving his rage; still less is it possible to conceive the majestic and overwhelming extent of that rage, when strengthened by principle and sanctified by religion. I enjoyed the scene beyond all power of description. I saw those wretches, who had triumphed over me, reduced to my level in a moment—their passions all displayed, and the display giving me the position of a hero triumphant above all. I had crawled to the shelter of their walls a wretched and degraded outcast—and what was my crime? Well, you shudder; I have done with that. I can only say want drove me to it. And here were beings whom, a few months before, I would have knelt to as to the images round the shrine, to whom, in the moments of my desperate penitence, I would have clung as to the "horns of the altar", all brought as low and lower than myself. "Sons of the morning", as I deemed them in the agonies of my humiliation, "how were they fallen!" I feasted on the degradation of the apostrate monk and novice. I enjoyed, to the core of my ulcerated heart, the passion of the superior. I felt that they were all men like myself. Angels, as I had thought them, they had all proved themselves mortal; and by watching their

46

motions, and flattering their passions, and promoting
their interest, or setting up my own opposition to them
all, while I made them believe it was only theirs I was
intent on, I might make a shift to contrive as much
misery for others, and to carve out as much occupation
for myself, as if I were actually living in the world.
Cutting my father's throat was a noble feat certainly (I
ask your pardon, I did not mean to extort that groan
from you), but here were hearts to be cut, and to the
core, every day, and all day long; so I never could want
employment.'

Here he wiped his hard brow, drew his breath for a
moment, and then said: 'I do not quite like to go
through the details by which the wretched pair were
deluded into the hope of effecting their escape from the
convent. It is enough that I was the principal agent, that
the superior connived at it, that I led them through the
very passages you have traversed tonight, they trembling
and blessing me at every step.

'They were conducted *here*. I had suggested the plan,
and the superior consented to it. He would not be present, but his dumb nod was enough. I was the conductor
of their (intended) escape; they believed they were
departing with the connivance of the superior. I led
them through those very passages that you and I have
trod. I had a map of this subterranean region, but my
blood ran cold as I traversed it; and it was not at all
inclined to resume its usual temperament, as I felt what
was to be the destination of my companions. Once I
turned the lamp, on pretence of trimming it, to catch a
glimpse of the devoted wretches. They were embracing
each other. The light of joy trembled in their eyes. They
were whispering to each other hopes of liberation and
happiness, and blending my name in the interval they
could spare from their prayers for each other. That sight
extinguished the last remains of compunction with which

47

my horrible task had inspired me. They dared to be happy in the sight of one who must be forever miserable. Could there be a greater insult? I resolved to punish it on the spot. This very apartment was near—I knew it— and the map of their wanderings no longer trembled in my hand. I urged them to enter this recess (the door was then entire) while I went to examine the passage. They entered it, thanking me for my precaution—they knew not they were never to quit it alive. But what were their lives compared to the agony their happiness cost me? The moment they were inside, and clasping each other (a sight that made me grind my teeth) I closed and locked the door. This movement gave them no immediate uneasiness; they thought it a friendly precaution. The moment they were secured, I hastened to the superior, who was on fire at the insult offered to the sanctity of his convent, and still more to the keenness of his penetration, on which the worthy superior prided himself as much as if it had ever been possible for him to acquire the smallest share of it. He descended with me to the passage. The monks followed with eyes on fire. In the agitation of their rage, it was with difficulty they could discover the door after I had repeatedly pointed it out to them. The superior with his own hands, drove several nails, which the monks eagerly supplied, into the door, that effectually joined it to the staple, *never to be disjoined*; and every blow he gave, doubtless he felt as if it were a reminder to the accusing angel to strike out a sin from the catalogue of his accusations. The work was soon done—the work never to be undone. At the first sound of steps in the passage and blows on the door, the victims uttered a shriek of terror. They imagined they were detected, and that an incensed party of monks was breaking open the door. These terrors were soon exchanged for others, and worse, as they heard the door nailed up, and listened to our departing steps. They

48

uttered another shriek, but O how different was the accent of its despair—they knew their doom!

'It was my pretence (no, my delight) to watch at the door, under the pretence of precluding the possibility of their escape (of which they knew there was no possibility); but, in reality, not only to inflict on me the indignity of being the convent jailer, but to teach me that callosity of heart, and induration of nerve, and stubbornness of eye, and apathy of ear, that were best suited to my office. But they might have saved themselves the trouble. I had them all before ever I entered the convent. Had I been the superior of the community, I should have undertaken the office of watching the door. You will call this cruelty, I call it curiosity, that curiosity that brings thousands to witness a tragedy, and makes the most delicate female feast on groans and agonies. I had an advantage over them: the groan, the agony I feasted on, were real. I took my station at *the door*, that door which, like that of Dante's hell, might have borne the inscription, "Here is no hope", with a face of mock penitence, and genuine, cordial delectation. I could hear every word that transpired. For the first hours they tried to comfort each other—they suggested to each other hopes of liberation—and as my shadow, crossing the threshold, darkened or restored the light, they said, "That is he"; then, when this occurred repeatedly, without any effect, they said, "No no, it is not he," and swallowed down the sick sob of despair, to hide it from each other. Towards night a monk came to take my place, and to offer me food. I would not have quitted my place for worlds; but I talked to the monk in his own language, and told him I would earn a merit with God by my sacrifices, and was resolved to remain there all night, with the permission of the superior. The monk was glad to have a substitute on such easy terms, and I was glad of the food he left me, for I was hungry now, but I reserved the appetite of my soul for richer luxuries. I heard them talking within. While I was eating, I actually lived on the famine that was devouring them, but of which they did not dare to say a word to each other. They debated, deliberated, and, as misery grows ingenious in its own defence, they at last assured each other that it was impossible that the superior had locked them in there to perish by hunger. At these words I could not help laughing. This laugh reached their ears, and they became silent in a moment. All that night, however, I heard their groans—those groans of physical suffering that laugh to scorn all the sentimental sighs that are exhaled from the hearts of the most intoxicated lovers that ever breathed. I heard them all that night. I had read French romances, and all their unimaginable nonsense. Madame Sévigné herself says she would have been tired of her daughter in a long tête-à-tête journey, but clap me two lovers into a dungeon, without food, light, or hope, and I will be damned (that I am already, by the bye) if they do not grow sick of each other within the first twelve hours. The second day hunger and darkness had their usual influence. They shrieked for liberation, and knocked loud and long at their dungeon door. They exclaimed they were ready to submit to any punishment; and the approach of the monks, which they would have dreaded so much the preceding night, they now solicited on their knees. What a jest, after all, are the most awful vicissitudes of human life! They entreated now for what they would have sacrificed their souls to avert four-and-twenty hours before. Then the agony of hunger increased; they shrank from the door, and grovelled apart from each other. *Apart!* How I watched that. They were rapidly becoming objects of hostility to each other. Oh, what a feast to me! They could not disguise from each other the revolting circumstances of their mutual sufferings. It is one thing for lovers to sit

50

down to a feast magnificently spread, and another for lovers to crouch in darkness and famine—to exchange that appetite which cannot be supported without dainties and flattery, for that which would barter a descended Venus for a morsel of food. The second night they raved and groaned; and, amid their agonies (I must do justice to women, whom I hate as well as men) the man often accused the female as the cause of all his sufferings, but the woman never, never reproached him. Her groans might indeed have reproached him bitterly, but she never uttered a word that could have caused him pain. There was a change which I well could mark, however, in their physical feelings. The first day they clung together, and every movement I felt was like that of one person. The next the man alone struggled, and the woman moaned in helplessness. The third night—how shall I tell it?—but you have bid me go on. All the horrible and loathsome excruciations of famine had been undergone; the dissolution of every tie of the heart, of passion, of nature, had commenced. In the agonies of their famished sickness they loathed each other. They could have cursed each other, if they had had breath to curse. It was on the fourth night that I heard the shriek of the wretched female: her lover, in the agony of hunger, had fastened his teeth in her shoulder. That bosom on which he had so often luxuriated became a meal to him now.'

'Monster! and you laugh?'

'Yes, I laugh at all mankind, and the imposition they dare to practice when they talk of hearts. I laugh at human passions and human cares, vice and virtue, religion and impiety; they are all the result of petty localities, and artificial situation. One physical want, one severe and abrupt lesson from the colourless and shrivelled lip of necessity, is worth all the logic of the empty wretches who have presumed to prate it, from Zeno

51

down to Burgersdicius. It silences in a second all the feeble sophistry of *conventional* life, and ascetical passion. Here were a pair who would not have believed all the world on their knees, even though angels had descended to join in the attestation, that it was possible for them to exist without each other. They had risked everything, trampled on everything human and divine, to be in each other's sight and arms. One hour of hunger undeceived them. A trivial and ordinary want, whose claims at another time they would have regarded as a vulgar interruption of their spiritualised intercourse, not only by its natural operation sundered it forever but, before it ceased, converted that intercourse into a source of torment and hostility inconceivable, except among cannibals. The bitterest enemies on earth could not have regarded each other with more abhorrence than *these lovers*. Deluded wretches, you boasted of having hearts, I boast I have none, and which of us gained most by the vaunt, let life decide. My story is nearly finished. When I was last here I had something to excite me; talking of those things is poor employment to one who has been a witness to them. On the *sixth* day all was still. The door was unnailed; we entered. They were no more. They lay far from each other, farther than on that voluptuous couch into which their passion had converted the mat of a convent bed. She lay contracted in a heap, a lock of her long hair in her mouth. There was a slight scar on her shoulder; the rabid despair of famine had produced no further outrage. He lay extended full length. His hand was between his lips; it seemed as if he had not strength to execute the purpose for which he had brought it there. The bodies were brought out for interment. As we removed them into the light, the long hair of the female, falling over a face no longer disguised by the novice's dress, recalled a likeness I thought I could remember. I looked closer! she was my own *sister*—my

52

only one—and I had heard her voice grow fainter and
fainter. I had heard . . .'

And his own voice grew fainter—it ceased.

THE SOUL CAGES

by T. Crofton Croker

T. CROFTON CROKER (*1798–1854*) *is regarded as one
of the most distinguished of all Irish folklore
collectors, and during his lifetime he played a leading role in the founding of several important
historical societies including the Percy Society and
the British Archæological Association. He possessed an unrivalled knowledge of the Irish
countryside, spent a great deal of time among its
people, and drawing on this knowledge retold in
book form many of the nation's great legends and
tales. Probably his most famous work is* Fairy
Legends and Traditions of the South of Ireland
which was highly praised by Sir Walter Scott in his
Waverley Novels. *The following tale of the Irish
mermaids is taken from it. These beings are
apparently not uncommon on the wilder reaches
of the coast—so the locals say—and fishermen
believe to see one is a sign of a coming gale*

Jack Dogherty lived on the coast of County Clare. Jack
was a fisherman, as his father and grandfather before
him had been. Like them, too, he lived all alone (but
for the wife), and just in the same spot. People used to
wonder why the Dogherty family were so fond of that
wild situation, so far away from all human kind, and in
the midst of huge shattered rocks, with nothing but the

wide ocean to look upon. But they had their own good reasons for it.

The place was just the only spot on that part of the coast where anybody could well live. There was a neat little creek, where a boat might lie as snug as a puffin in her nest, and out of this creek a ledge of sunken rocks ran into the sea. Now when the Atlantic, according to custom, was raging with a storm, and a good westerly wind was blowing strong on the coast, many a richly-laden ship went to pieces on these rocks; and then the fine bales of cotton and tobacco, and such like things, and the pipes of wine, and the puncheons of rum, and the casks of brandy, and the kegs of Hollands that used to come ashore! Dunbeg Bay was just like a little estate to the Doghertys.

Not but they were kind and humane to a distressed sailor, if ever one had the good luck to get to land; and many a time indeed did Jack put out in his little *corragh* (which, though not quite equal to honest Andrew Hennessy's canvas life-boat, would breast the billows like any gannet), to lend a hand towards bringing off the crew from a wreck. But when the ship had gone to pieces, and the crew were all lost, who would blame Jack for picking up all he could find?

'And who is the worse of it?' said he. 'For as to the king, God bless him! everybody knows he's rich enough already without getting what's floating in the sea.'

Jack, though such a hermit, was a good-natured, jolly fellow. No other, sure, could ever have coaxed Biddy Mahoney to quit her father's snug and warm house in the middle of the town of Ennis, and to go so many miles off to live among the rocks, with the seals and sea-gulls for next-door neighbours. But Biddy knew that Jack was the man for a woman who wished to be comfortable and happy; for, to say nothing of the fish, Jack had the supplying of half the gentlemen's houses of the country

54

with the *Godsends* that came into the bay. And she was right in her choice; for no woman ate, drank, or slept better, or made a prouder appearance at chapel on Sundays, than Mrs. Dogherty.

Many a strange sight, it may well be supposed, did Jack see, and many a strange sound did he hear, but nothing daunted him. So far was he from being afraid of Merows, or such things, that the very first wish of his heart was to fairly meet with one. Jack had heard that they were mighty like Christians, and that luck had always come out of an acquaintance with them. Never, therefore, did he dimly discern the Merrows moving along the face of the waters in their robes of mist, but he made direct for them; and many a scolding did Biddy, in her own quiet way, bestow upon Jack for spending his whole day out at sea, and bringing home no fish. Little did poor Biddy know the fish Jack was after!

It was rather annoying to Jack that, though living in a place where the Merrows were as plenty as lobsters, he never could get a right view of one. What vexed him more was that both his father and grandfather had often and often seen them; and he even remembered hearing, when a child, how his grandfather, who was the first of the family that had settled down at the creek, had been so intimate with a Merow that, only for fear of vexing the priest, he would have had him stand for one of his children. This, however, Jack did not well know how to believe.

Fortune at length began to think that it was only right that Jack should know as much as his father and grandfather did. Accordingly, one day when he had strolled a little farther than usual along the coast to the northward, just as he turned a point, he saw something, like to nothing he had ever seen before, perched upon a rock at a little distance out to sea. It looked green in the body, as well as he could discern at that distance, and he would have sworn, only the thing was impossible, that it had a cocked hat in its hand. Jack stood for a good half-hour straining his eyes, and wondering at it, and all the time the thing did not stir hand or foot. At last Jack's patience was quite worn out, and he gave a loud whistle and a hail, when the Merrow (for such it was) started up, put the cocked hat on its head, and dived down, head foremost, from the rock.

Jack's curiosity was now excited, and he constantly directed his steps towards the point; still he could never get a glimpse of the sea-gentleman with the cocked hat; and with thinking and thinking about the matter, he began at last to fancy he had been only dreaming. One very rough day, however, when the sea was running mountains high, Jack Dogherty determined to give a look at the Merrow's rock (for he had always chosen a fine day before), and then he saw the strange thing cutting capers upon the top of the rock, and then diving down, and then coming up, and then diving down again.

Jack had now only to choose his time (that is, a good blowing day), and he might see the man of the sea as often as he pleased. All this, however, did not satisfy him—'much will have more'; he wished now to get acquainted with the Merrow, and even in this he succeeded. One tremendous blustering day, before he got to the point whence he had a view of the Merrow's rock, the storm came on so furiously that Jack was obliged to take shelter in one of the caves which are so numerous along the coast; and there, to his astonishment, he saw sitting before him a thing with green hair, long green teeth, a red nose, and pig's eyes. It had a fish's tail, legs with scales on them, and short arms like fins. It wore no clothes, but had the cocked hat under its arm, and seemed engaged thinking very seriously about something.

Jack, with all his courage, was a little daunted; but

56

now or never, thought he; so up he went boldly to the cogitating fisherman, took off his hat, and made his best bow.

'Your servant, sir,' said Jack.

'Your servant, kindly, Jack Dogherty,' answered the Merrow.

'To be sure, then, how well your honour knows my name!' said Jack.

'Is it I not know your name, Jack Dogherty? Why, man, I knew your grandfather long before he was married to Judy Regan, your grandmother! Ah, Jack, Jack, I was fond of that grandfather of yours; he was a mighty worthy man in his time: I never met his match above or below, before or since, for sucking in a shellful of brandy. I hope, my boy,' said the old fellow, with a merry twinkle in his eyes, 'I hope you're his own grandson!'

'Never fear me for that,' said Jack; 'if my mother had only rcared me on brandy, 'tis myself that would be a sucking infant to this hour!'

'Well, I like to hear you talk so manly; you and I must be better acquainted, if it were only for your grandfather's sake. But, Jack, that father of yours was not the thing! he had no head at all.'

'I'm sure,' said Jack, 'since your honour lives down under the water, you must be obliged to drink a power to keep any heat in you in such a cruel, damp, cold place. Well, I've often heard of Christians drinking like fishes; and might I be so bold as ask where you get the spirits?'

'Where do you get them yourself, Jack?' said the Merrow, twitching his red nose between his forefinger and thumb.

'Hubbubboo,' cries Jack, 'now I see how it is; but I suppose, sir, your honour has got a fine dry cellar below to keep them in.'

'Let me alone for the cellar,' said the Merrow, with a knowing wink of his left eye.

'I'm sure,' continued Jack, 'it must be mighty well worth the looking at.'

'You may say that, Jack' said the Merrow; 'and if you meet me here next Monday, just at this time of the day, we will have a little more talk with one another about the matter.'

Jack and the Merrow parted the best friends in the world. On Monday they met, and Jack was not a little surprised to see that the Merrow had two cocked hats with him, one under each arm.

'Might I take the liberty to ask, sir,' said Jack, 'why your honour has brought the two hats with you today? You would not, sure, be going to give me one of them, to keep for the *curiosity* of the thing?'

'No, no, Jack,' said he, 'I don't get my hats so easily, to part with them that way; but I want you to come down and dine with me, and I brought you the hat to dine with.'

'Lord bless and preserve us!' cried Jack, in amazement, 'would you want me to go down to the bottom of the salt sea ocean? Sure, I'd be smothered and choked up with the water, to say nothing of being drowned! And what would poor Biddy do for me, and what would she say?'

'And what matter what she says, you *pinkeen*? Who cares for Biddy's squalling? It's long before your grandfather would have talked in that way. Many's the time he stuck that same hat on his head, and dived down boldly after me; and many's the snug bit of dinner and good shellful of brandy he and I have had together below, under the water.'

'Is it really, sir, and no joke?' said Jack; 'why, then, sorrow from me for ever and a day after, if I'll be a bit

58

worse man nor my grandfather was! Here goes—but play me fair now. Here's neck or nothing!' cried Jack.

'That's your grandfather all over,' said the old fellow; 'so come along, then, and do as I do.'

They both left the cave, walked into the sea, and then swam a piece until they got to the rock. The Merrow climbed to the top of it, and Jack followed him. On the far side it was as straight as the wall of a house, and the sea beneath looked so deep that Jack was almost cowed.

'Now, do you see, Jack,' said the Merrow: 'just put this hat on your head, and mind to keep your eyes wide open. Take hold of my tail, and follow after me, and you'll see what you'll see.'

In he dashed, and in dashed Jack after him boldly. They went and they went, and Jack thought they'd never stop going. Many a time did he wish himself sitting at home by the fireside with Biddy. Yct where was the use of wishing now, when he was so many miles, as he thought, below the waves of the Atlantic? Still he held hard by the Merrow's tail, slippery as it was; and, at last, to Jack's great surprise, they got out of the water, and he actually found himself on dry land at the bottom of the sea. They landed just in front of a nice house that was slated very neatly with oyster shells; and the Merrow, turning about to Jack, welcomed him down.

Jack could hardly speak, what with the wonder, and what with being out of breath with travelling so fast through the water. He looked about him and could see no living things, barring crabs and lobsters, of which there were plenty walking leisurely about on the sand. Overhead was the sea like a sky, and the fishes like birds swimming about in it.

'Why don't you speak, man?' said the Merrow: 'I dare say you had no notion that I had such a snug little

59

concern here as this? Are you smothered, or choked, or drowned, or are you fretting after Biddy, eh?'

'Oh! not myself, indeed,' said Jack, showing his teeth with a good-humoured grin; 'but who in the world would ever have thought of seeing such a thing?'

'Well, come along, and let's see what they've got for us to eat?'

Jack really was hungry, and it gave him no small pleasure to perceive a fine column of smoke rising from the chimney, announcing what was going on within. Into the house he followed the Merrow, and there he saw a good kitchen, right well provided with everything. There was a noble dresser, and plenty of pots and pans, with two young Merrows cooking. His host then led him into the room, which was furnished shabbily enough. Not a table or a chair was there in it; nothing but planks and logs of wood to sit on, and eat off. There was, however, a good fire blazing upon the hearth—a comfortable sight to Jack.

'Come now, and I'll show you where I keep—you know what,' said the Merrow, with a sly look; and opening a little door, he led Jack into a fine cellar, well filled with pipes, and kegs, and hogsheads, and barrels.

'What do you say to that, Jack Dogherty? Eh! may be a body can't live snug under the water?'

'Never the doubt of that,' said Jack, with a convincing smack of his under lip, that he really thought what he said.

They went back to the room, and found dinner laid. There was no tablecloth, to be sure—but what matter? It was not always Jack had one at home. The dinner would have been no discredit to the first house of the country on a fast day. The choicest of fish, and no wonder, was there. Turbots, and sturgeons, and soles, and lobsters, and oysters, and twenty other kinds, were on the planks at once, and plenty of the best of foreign spirits. The wines, the old fellow said, were too cold for his stomach.

Jack ate and drank till he could eat no more: then, taking up a shell of brandy, 'Here's to your honour's good health, sir,' said he; 'though, begging your pardon, it's mighty odd that as long as we've been acquainted I don't know your name yet.'

'That's true, Jack,' replied he; 'I never thought of it before, but better late than never. My name's Coomara.'

'And a mighty decent name it is,' cried Jack, taking another shellful: 'here's to your good health, Coomara, and may ye live these fifty years to come!'

'Fifty years!' repeated Coomara; 'I'm obliged to you, indeed! If you had said five hundred, it would have been something worth the wishing.'

'By the laws, sir,' cries Jack, '*youz* live to a powerful age here under the water! You knew my grandfather, and he's dead and gone better than these sixty years. I'm sure it must be a healthy place to live in.'

'No doubt of it; but come, Jack, keep the liquor stirring.'

Shell after shell did they empty, and to Jack's exceeding surprise, he found the drink never got into his head, owing, I suppose, to the sea being over them, which kept their noddles cool.

Old Coomara got exceedingly comfortable, and sung several songs; but Jack, if his life had depended on it, never could remember more than

> '*Rum fum boodle boo,*
> *Ripple dipple nitty dob;*
> *Dumdoo doodle coo,*
> *Raffle taffle chittiboo!*'

It was the chorus to one of them; and, to say the truth, nobody that I know has ever been able to pick any particular meaning out of it; but that, to be sure, is the case with many a song nowadays.

At length said he to Jack, 'Now, my dear boy, if you follow me, I'll show you my *curiosities!*' He opened a little door, and led Jack into a large room, where Jack saw a great many odds and ends that Coomara had picked up at one time or another. What chiefly took his attention, however, were things like lobster-pots ranged on the ground along the wall.

'Well, Jack, how do you like my *curiosities*?' said old Coo.

'Upon my *sowkins* (soul) sir,' said Jack, 'they're mighty well worth looking at; but might I make so bold as to ask what these things like lobster-pots are?'

'Oh! the Soul Cages, is it?'

'The what? sir!'

'These things here that I keep the souls in.'

'*Arrah!* what souls, sir?' said Jack, in amazement; 'sure the fish have no souls in them?'

'Oh! no,' replied Coo, quite coolly, 'that they have not; but these are the souls of drowned sailors.'

'The Lord preserve us from all harm!' muttered Jack, 'how in the world did you get them?'

'Easily enough: I've only, when I see a good storm coming on, to set a couple of dozen of these, and then, when the sailors are drowned and the souls get out of them under the water, the poor things are almost perished to death, not being used to the cold; so they make into my pots for shelter, and then I have them snug, and fetch them home, and keep them here dry and warm; and is it not well for them, poor souls, to get into such good quarters?'

Jack was so thunderstruck he did not know what to say, so he said nothing. They went back into the dining-room, and had a little more brandy, which was excellent, and then, as Jack knew that it must be getting late, and as Biddy might be uneasy, he stood up, and said he thought it was time for him to be on the road.

'Just as you like, Jack,' said Coo, 'but take a *duc an durrus* (stirrup-cup) before you go; you've a cold journey before you.'

Jack knew better manners than to refuse the parting glass. 'I wonder,' said he, 'will I be able to make out my way home?'

'What should ail you,' said Coo, 'when I'll show you the way?'

Out they went before the house, and Coomara took one of the cocked hats, and put it upon Jack's head the wrong way, and then lifted him up on his shoulder that he might launch him up into the water.

'Now,' says he, giving him a heave, 'you'll come up just in the same spot you came down in; and, Jack, mind and throw me back the hat.'

He canted Jack off his shoulder, and up he shot like a bubble—whirr, whirr, whiz—away he went up through the water, till he came to the very rock he had jumped off, where he found a landing-place, and then in he threw the hat, which sunk like a stone.

The sun was just going down in the beautiful sky of a calm summer's evening. *Feascor* was seen dimly twinkling in the cloudless heaven, a solitary star, and the waves of the Atlantic flashed in a golden flood of light. So Jack, perceiving it was late, set off home; but when he got there, not a word did he say to Biddy of where he had spent his day.

The state of the poor souls cooped up in the lobster-pots gave Jack a great deal of trouble, and how to release them cost him a great deal of thought. He at first had a mind to speak to the priest about the matter. But what could the priest do, and what did Coo care for the priest? Besides, Coo was a good sort of an old fellow, and did not think he was doing any harm. Jack had a regard for him, too, and it also might not be much to his own credit if it were known that he used to go dine with Merrows. On the whole, he thought his best plan would be to ask Coo to dinner, and to make him drunk, if he was able, and then to take the hat and go down and turn up the pots. It was, first of all, necessary, however, to get Biddy out of the way; for Jack was prudent enough, as she was a woman, to wish to keep the thing secret from her.

Accordingly, Jack grew mighty pious all of a sudden, and said to Biddy that he thought it would be for the good of both their souls if she was to go and take her rounds at Saint John's Well, near Ennis. Biddy thought so too, and accordingly off she set one fine morning at day-dawn, giving Jack a strict charge to have an eye to the place. The coast being clear, away went Jack to the rock to give the appointed signal to Coomara, which was throwing a big stone into the water. Jack threw, and up sprang Coo!

'Good morning, Jack,' said he; 'what do you want with me?'

'Just nothing at all to speak about, sir,' returned Jack, 'only to come and take a bit of dinner with me, if I might make so free as to ask you, and sure I'm now after doing so.'

'It's quite agreeable, Jack, I assure you; what's your hour?'

'Any time that's most convenient to you, sir—say one o'clock, that you may go home, if you wish, with the daylight.'

'I'll be with you,' said Coo, 'never fear me.'

Jack went home, and dressed a noble fish dinner, and got out plenty of his best foreign spirits, enough, for that matter, to make twenty men drunk. Just to the minute came Coo, with his cocked hat under his arm. Dinner was ready, they sat down, and ate and drank

64

away manfully. Jack, thinking of the poor souls below in the pots, plied old Coo well with brandy, and encouraged him to sing, hoping to put him under the table, but poor Jack forgot that he had not the sea over his own head to keep it cool. The brandy got into it, and did his business for him, and Coo reeled off home, leaving his entertainer as dumb as a haddock on a Good Friday.

Jack never woke till the next morning, and then he was in a sad way. "Tis to no use for me thinking to make that old Raparee drunk,' said Jack, 'and how in the world can I help the poor souls out of the lobster-pots?' After ruminating nearly the whole day, a thought struck him. 'I have it,' says he, slapping his knee; 'I'l be sworn that Coo never saw a drop of *poteen*, as old as he is, and that's the *thing* to settle him! Oh! then, is not it well that Biddy will not be home these two days yet; I can have another twist at him.'

Jack asked Coo again, and Coo laughed at him for having no better head, telling him he'd never come up to his grandfather.

'Well, but try me again,' said Jack, 'and I'll be bail to drink you drunk and sober, and drunk again.'

'Anything in my power,' said Coo, 'to oblige you.'

At this dinner Jack took care to have his own liquor well watered, and to give the strongest brandy he had to Coo. At last says he, 'Pray, sir, did you ever drink any poteen?—any real mountain dew?'

'No,' says Coo; 'what's that, and where does it come from?'

'Oh, that's a secret,' said Jack, 'but it's the right stuff —never believe me again, if 'tis not fifty times as good as brandy or rum either. Biddy's brother just sent me a present of a little drop, in exchange for some brandy, and as you're an old friend of the family, I kept it to treat you with.'

'Well, let's see what sort of thing it is,' said Coomara.

The *poteen* was the right sort. It was first-rate, and had the real smack upon it. Coo was delighted: he drank and he sung *Rum bum boodle boo* over and over again; and he laughed and he danced, till he fell on the floor fast asleep. Then Jack, who had taken good care to keep himself sober, snapt up the cocked hat—ran off to the rock—leaped in, and soon arrived at Coo's habitation.

All was as still as a churchyard at midnight—not a Merrow, old or young, was there. In he went and turned up the pots, but nothing did he see, only he heard a sort of a little whistle or chirp as he raised each of them. At this he was surprised, till he recollected what the priests had often said, that nobody living could see the soul, no more than they could see the wind or the air. Having now done all that he could do for them, he set the pots as they were before, and sent a blessing after the poor souls to speed them on their journey wherever they were going. Jack now began to think of returning; he put the hat on, as was right, the wrong way; but when he got out he found the water so high over his head that he had no hopes of ever getting up into it, now that he had not old Coomara to give him a lift. He walked about looking for a ladder, but not one could he find, and not a rock was there in sight. At last he saw a spot where the sea hung rather lower than anywhere else, so he resolved to try there. Just as he came to it, a big cod happened to put down his tail. Jack made a jump and caught hold of it, and the cod, all in amazement, gave a bounce and pulled Jack up. The minute the hat touched the water away Jack was whisked, and up he shot like a cork, dragging the poor cod, that he forgot to let go, up with him tail foremost. He got to the rock in no time, and without a moment's delay hurried home, rejoicing in the good deed he had done.

But meanwhile, there was fine work at home; for our friend Jack had hardly left the house on his soul-freeing expedition, when back came Biddy from her soul-saving one to the well. When she entered the house and saw the things lying *thrie-na-helah* (higgledy-piggledy) on the table before her—'Here's a pretty job!' said she; 'that blackguard of mine—what ill-luck I had ever to marry him! He has picked up some vagabond or other, while I was praying for the good of his soul, and they've been drinking all the *poteen* that my own brother gave him, and all the spirits, to be sure, that he was to have sold to his honour.' Then hearing an outlandish kind of a grunt, she looked down, and saw Coomara lying under the table. 'The blessed Virgin help me,' shouted she, 'if he has not made a real beast of himself! Well, well, I've often heard of a man making a beast of himself with drink! Oh hone! Oh hone!—Jack, honey, what will I do with you, or what will I do without you? How can any decent woman ever think of living with a beast?'

With such like lamentations Biddy rushed out of the house, and was going she knew not where, when she heard the well-known voice of Jack singing a merry tune. Glad enough was Biddy to find him safe and sound, and not turned into a thing that was like neither fish nor flesh. Jack was obliged to tell her all, and Biddy, though she had half a mind to be angry with him for not telling her before, owned that he had done a great service to the poor souls. Back they both went most lovingly to the house, and Jack wakened up Coomara; and, perceiving the old fellow to be rather dull, he bid him not to be cast down, for 'twas many a good man's case; said it all came of his not being used to the *poteen*, and recommended him, by way of cure, to swallow a hair of the dog that bit him. Coo, however, seemed to think he had had quite enough. He got up, quite out of sorts, and without having the manners to say one word in the way of civility, he sneaked off to cool himself by a jaunt through the salt water.

Coomara never missed the souls. He and Jack continued the best friends in the world, and no one perhaps, ever equalled Jack for freeing souls from purgatory; for he contrived fifty excuses for getting into the house below the sea, unknown to the old fellow, and then turning up the pots and letting out the souls. It vexed him, to be sure, that he could never see them; but as he knew the thing to be impossible, he was obliged to be satisfied.

Their intercourse continued for several years. However, one morning, on Jack's throwing in a stone as usual, he got no answer. He flung another, and another, still there was no reply. He went away, and returned the following morning, but it was to no purpose. As he was without the hat, he could not go down to see what had become of old Coo, but his belief was, that the old man, or the old fish, or whatever he was, had either died, or had removed from that part of the country.

WICKED CAPTAIN WALSHAWE

by Joseph Sheridan Le Fanu

JOSEPH SHERIDAN LE FANU (1814-1873) is still one of the most widely read of the nineteenth century ghost story writers. He based many of his tales on actual occurrences and in so doing introduced the Irish people to not a few of their own legendary hauntings. He spent most of his life in Dublin, and was first contributor to, later editor and owner, of the Dublin University Magazine, *now a veritable treasure-trove for those interested in the macabre and the supernatural. In the phantom story which I have selected here from one of Le Fanu's volumes long out of print, we meet him at his best, writing with efficiency and chilling conviction.*

A very odd thing happened to my uncle, Mr. Watson, of Haddlestone; and to enable you to understand it, I must begin at the beginning.

In the year 1822, Mr. James Walshawe, more commonly known as Captain Walshawe, died at the age of eighty-one years. The Captain in his early days, and so long as health and strength permitted, was a scamp of the active, intriguing sort; and spent his days and nights in sowing wild oats, of which he seemed to have an inexhaustible stock.

Captain Walshawe was very well known in the neighbourhood of Wauling, and very generally avoided there. He had quitted the service in 1766, at the age of twenty-five, immediately previous to which period his debts had grown so troublesome that he was induced to extricate

69

himself by running away with and marrying an heiress. He was quartered in Ireland, at Clonmel, where was a nunnery, in which, as pensioner, resided Miss O'Neill, or as she was called in the country, Peg O'Neill, the heiress.

Her situation was the only ingredient of romance in the affair, for the young lady was decidedly plain, though good-humoured looking, with that style of features which is termed potato; and in figure she was a little too plump, and rather short. But she was impressible; and the handsome young English lieutenant was too much for her monastic tendencies, and she eloped. They took up their abode at Wauling, in Lancashire.

Here the Captain amused himself after his fashion, sometimes running up, of course, on business to London. He spent her income, frightened her out of her wits, with oath and threats, and broke her heart.

Latterly she shut herself up pretty nearly altogether in her room. She had an old, rather grim, Irish servant-woman in attendance, Molly Doyle. This domestic was lean and religious, and the Captain knew instinctively she hated him; and he hated her in return, and often threatened to put her out of the house, and sometimes even to kick her out of the window.

Years passed away, and old Molly Doyle remained still in her original position. Perhaps he thought that there must be somebody there, and that he was not, after all, very likely to change for the better.

He tolerated another intrusion, too, and thought himself a paragon of patience and easy good-nature for so doing. A Roman Catholic clergyman, in long black frock, with a low standing collar, and a little white muslin fillet round his neck—tall, sallow, with blue chin, and dark steady eyes—used to glide up and down the stairs, and through the passages; and the Captain sometimes met him in one place and sometimes in

70

another. But by a caprice incident to such tempers he treated this cleric exceptionally, and even with a surly sort of courtesy, though he grumbled about his visits behind his back.

Well, the time came at last, when poor Peg O'Neill—in an evil hour Mrs. James Walshawe—must cry, and quake, and pray her last. The doctor came from Penlynden, and was just as vague as usual, but more gloomy, and for about a week came and went oftener. The cleric in the long black frock was also daily there. And at last came that last sacrament in the gates of death, when the sinner is traversing those dread steps and never can be retraced.

The Captain drank a great deal of brandy and water that night, and called in Farmer Dobbs, for want of better company, to drink with him; and told him all his grievances, and how happy he and the poor lady upstairs' might have been had it not been for liars, and pick-thanks, and tale-bearers, and the like, who came between them—meaning Molly Doyle—whom, as he waxed eloquent over his liquor, he came to curse and rail at by name, with more than his accustomed freedom. And he described his own natural character and amiability in such moving terms that he wept maudlin tears of sensibility over his theme; and when Dobbs was gone, drank some more grog, and took to railing and cursing again by himself; and then mounted the stairs unsteadily to see 'what the devil Doyle and the other ——— old witches were about in poor Peg's room'.

When he pushed open the door, he found some half-dozen crones, chiefly Irish, from the neighbouring town of Hackleton, sitting over tea and snuff, etc., with candles lighted round the corpse, which was arrayed in a strangely cut robe of brown serge. She had secretly belonged to some order—I think the Carmelite, but I am not certain—and wore the habit in her coffin.

'What the d—— are you doing with my wife?' cried the Captain, rather thickly. 'How dare you dress her up in this—trumpery, you—you cheating old witch; and what's that candle doing in her hand?'

I think he was a little startled, for the spectacle was grisly enough. The dead lady was arrayed in this strange brown robe, and in her rigid fingers, as in a socket, with the large wooden beads and cross wound round it, burned a wax candle, shedding its white light over the sharp features of the corpse. Molly Doyle was not to be put down by the Captain, whom she hated, and accordingly, in her phrase, 'he got as good as he gave'. And the Captain's wrath waxed fiercer, and he plucked the wax taper from the dead hand, and was on the point of flinging it at the old serving-woman's head.

'The holy candle, you sinner!' cried she.

'I've a mind to make you eat it, you beast,' cried the Captain.

But I think he had not known before what it was, for he subsided, a little sulkily, and he stuffed his hand with the candle (quite extinct by this time) into his pocket, and said he:

'You know devilish well you had no business going on with y-y-your d—— witchcraft about my poor wife, without my leave—you do—and you'll please to take off that d—— brown pinafore, and get her decently into her coffin, and I'll pitch your devil's waxlight into the sink.'

And the Captain stalked out of the room.

'An' now her poor sowl's in prison, you wretch, be the mains o' ye; an' may yer own be shut into the wick o' that same candle, till it's burned out, ye savage.'

'I'd have you ducked for a witch, for twopence,' roared the Captain up the staircase, with his hand on the banisters, standing on the lobby. But the door of the chamber of death clapped angrily, and he went down to the parlour, where he examined the holy candle for a while, with a tipsy gravity, and then with something of that reverential feeling for the symbolic, which is not uncommon in rakes and scamps, he thoughtfully locked it up in a press, where were accumulated all sorts of obsolete rubbish—soiled packs of cards, disused tobacco-pipes, broken powder-flasks, his military sword, and a dusty bundle of the *Flash Songster* and other questionable literature.

Captain Walshawe reigned alone for many years at Wauling. He was too shrewd and too experienced by this time to run violently down the steep hill that leads to ruin. Forty years acted forcibly upon the gay Captain Walshawe. Gout supervened, and was no more conducive to temper than to enjoyment, and made his elegant hands lumpy at all the small joints, and turned them slowly into crippled claws. He grew stout when his exercise was interfered with, and ultimately almost corpulent. He suffered from what Mr. Holloway calls 'bad legs', and was wheeled about in a great leathern-back chair, and his infirmities went on accumulating with his years.

I am sorry to say, I never heard that he repented, or turned his thoughts seriously to the future. On the contrary, his talk grew fouler, and his fun ran upon his favourite sins, and his temper waxed more truculent. But he did not sink into dotage. Considering his bodily infirmities, his energies and his malignities, which were many and active, were marvellously little abated by time.

It was a peculiarity of Captain Walshawe, that he, by this time, hated nearly everybody. My uncle, Mr. Watson, of Haddlestone, was cousin to the Captain, and his heir at law. But my uncle had lent him money on mortgage of his estates and there had been a treaty to sell, and terms and a price were agreed upon, in 'articles' which the lawyers said were still in force.

I think the ill-conditioned Captain bore him a grudge for being richer that he, and would have liked to do him an ill turn. But it did not lie in his way; at least while he was living.

My Uncle Watson was a Methodist, and what they call a 'class leader'; and, on the whole, a very good man. He was now near fifty—grave, as beseemed his profession—somewhat dry—and a little severe, perhaps—but a just man.

A letter from the Penlynden doctor reached him at Haddlestone, announcing the death of the wicked old Captain; and suggesting his attendance at the funeral, and the expediency of his being on the spot to look after things at Wauling. The reasonableness of this striking my good uncle, he made his journey to the old house in Lancashire incontinently, and reached it in time for the funeral.

The day turning out awfully rainy and tempestuous, my uncle persuaded the doctor and the attorney to remain for the night at Wauling.

There was no will—the attorney was sure of that; for the Captain's enmities were perpetually shifting, and he could never quite make up his mind as to how best to give effect to a malignity whose direction was being constantly modified.

Search being made, no will was found. The papers, indeed, were all right, with one important exception: the leases were nowhere to be seen. My uncle searched strenuously. The attorney was at his elbow, and the doctor helped with a suggestion now and then. The old serving man seemed an honest, deaf creature, and really knew nothing.

My uncle Watson was very much perturbed. He fancied—but this possibly was only fancy—that he had detected for a moment a queer look in the attorney's face, and from that instant it became fixed in his mind

74

that he knew all about the leases. Mr. Watson expounded that evening in the parlour to the doctor, the attorney and the deaf servant.

Ananias and Sapphira figured in the foreground, and the awful nature of fraud and theft, or tampering in any wise with the plain rule of honesty in matters pertaining to estates, etc., were pointedly dwelt upon; and then came a long and strenuous prayer, in which he entreated with fervour and aplomb that the hard heart of the sinner who had abstracted the leases might be softened or broken in such a way as to lead to their restitution; or that if he continued reserved and contumacious, it might at least be the will of Heaven to bring him to public justice and the documents to light. The fact is, that he was praying all this time at the attorney.

When these religious exercises were over, the visitors retired to their rooms, and my Uncle Watson wrote two or three pressing leters by the fire. When his task was done, it had grown late; the candles were flaring in their sockets, and all in bed, and I suppose, asleep, but he.

The fire was nearly out, he chilly, and the flame of the candles throbbing strangely in their sockets shed alternate glare and shadow round the old wainscoted room and its quaint furniture. Outside were the wild thunder and piping of the storm, and the rattling of distant windows sounded through the passages, and down the stairs, like angry people astir in the house.

My Uncle Watson belonged to a sect who by no means reject the supernatural, and whose founder, on the contrary, has sanctioned ghosts in the most emphatic way. He was glad, therefore, to remember, that in prosecuting his search that day, he had seen some six inches of wax candle in the press in the parlour; for he had no fancy to be overtaken by darkness in his present situation.

75

He had no time to lose; and taking the bunch of keys —of which he was now master—he soon fitted the lock and secured the candle—a treasure in his circumstances; and lighting it, he stuffed it into the socket of one of the expiring candles, and extinguishing the other, he looked round the room in the steady light, reassured. At the same moment an unusually violent gust of the storm blew a handful of gravel against the parlour window, with a sharp rattle that startled him in the midst of the roar and hubbub; and the flame of the candle itself was agitated by the air.

My uncle walked up to bed, guarding his candle with his hand, for the lobby windows were rattling furiously, and he disliked the idea of being left in the dark more than ever.

His bedroom was comfortable, though old-fashioned. He shut and bolted the door. There was a tall looking-glass opposite the foot of his four-poster, on the dressing-table between the windows. He tried to make the curtains meet, but they would not draw.

He turned the face of the mirror away, therefore, so that its back was presented to the bed, pulled the curtains together, and placed a chair against them, to prevent their falling open again. There was a good fire, and a reinforcement of round coal and wood inside the fender. So he piled it up to ensure a cheerful blaze through the night, and placing a little black mahogany table, with the legs of a Satyr, beside the bed, and his candle upon it, he got between the sheets, and laid his red night-capped head upon his pillow, and disposed himself to sleep.

The first thing that made him uncomfortable was a sound at the foot of his bed, quite distinct in a momentary lull of the storm. It was only the gentle rustle and rush of the curtains which fell open again; and as his eyes opened, he saw them resuming their perpendicular dependence, and sat up in his bed almost expecting to see something uncanny in the aperture.

There was nothing, however, but the dressing-table and other dark furniture, and the window-curtains faintly undulating in the violence of the storm. He did not care to get up, therefore—the fire being bright and cheery—to replace the curtains by a chair, in the position in which he had left them, anticipating possibly a new recurrence of the relapse which had startled him from his incipient doze.

So he got to sleep in a little while again, but he was disturbed by a sound, as he fancied, at the table on which stood the candle. He could not say what it was, only that he wakened with a start, and lying so in some amaze, he did distinctly hear a sound which startled him a good deal, though there was nothing necessarily supernatural in it.

He described it as resembling what would occur if you fancied a thinnish table-leaf, with a convex warp in it, depressed the reverse way, and suddenly with a string recovering its natural convexity. It was a loud, sudden thump, which made the heavy candlestick jump, and there was an end, except that my uncle did not get again into a doze for ten minutes at least.

The next time he awoke it was in that odd, serene way that sometimes occurs. We open our eyes, we know not why, quite placidly, and are on the instant wide awake. He had had a nap of some duration this time, for his candle-flame was fluttering and flaring, *in articulo,* in the silver socket. But the fire was still bright and cheery, so he popped the extinguisher on the socket, and almost at the same time there came a tap at his door, and a sort of crescendo 'hush-sh-sh!' Once more my uncle was sitting up, scared and perturbed, in his bed.

He recollected, however, that he had bolted his door; and such inveterate materialists are we in the midst of

77

our spiritualism, that this reassured him, and he breathed a deep sigh, and began to grow tranquil. But after a rest of a minute of two, there came a louder and sharper knock at his door; so that instinctively he called out: 'Who's there?' in a loud, stern key. There was no sort of response, however.

The nervous effect of the start subsided; and after a while he lay down with his back turned towards that side of the bed at which was the door, and his face towards the table on which stood the massive old candlestick, capped with its extinguisher, and in that position he closed his eyes. But sleep would not revisit them. All kinds of queer fancies began to trouble him—some of them I remember.

He felt the point of a finger, he averred, pressed most distinctly on the tip of his great toe, as if a living hand were between his sheets, and making a sort of signal of attention or silence. Then again he felt something as large as a rat make a sudden bounce in the middle of his bolster, just under his head.

Then a voice said: 'Oh!' very gently, close at the back of his head. All these things he felt certain of, and yet investigation led to nothing. He felt odd little cramps stealing now and then about him, and then, on a sudden, the middle finger of his right hand was plucked backwards, with a light playful jerk that frightened him awfully.

Meanwhile the storm kept singing, and howling and ha-ha-hooing hoarsely among the limbs of the old trees and the chimney-pots; and my Uncle Watson, although he prayed and meditated as was his wont when he lay awake, felt his heart throb excitedly, and sometimes thought he was beset with evil spirits, and at others that he was in the early stages of a fever.

He resolutely kept his eyes closed, however, and, like St. Paul's shipwrecked companions, wished for the day.

78

At last another little doze seems to have stolen upon his senses, for he awoke quietly and completely as before—opening his eyes all at once, and seeing everything as if he had not slept for a moment.

The fire was still blazing redly—nothing uncertain in the light—the massive silver candlestick, topped with its tall extinguisher, stood on the centre of the black mahogany table as before; and, looking by what seemed a sort of accident to the apex of this, he beheld something which made him quite misdoubt the evidence of his eyes.

He saw the extinguisher lifted by a tiny hand from beneath, and a small human face, no bigger than a thumb-nail, with nicely proportioned features peep from beneath it. In this Lilliputian countenance was such a ghastly consternation as horrified my uncle unspeakably.

Out came a little foot then and there, and a pair of wee legs, in short silk stockings and buckled shoes, then the rest of the figure; and, with the arms holding about the socket, the little legs stretched and stretched, hanging about the stem of the candlestick till the feet reached the base, and so down the Satyr-like leg of the table, till they reached the floor, extending elastically, and strangely enlarging in all proportions as they approached the ground, where the feet and buckles were those of a well-shaped, full-grown man, and the figure tapering upwards until it dwindled to its original fairy dimensions at the top, like an object seen in some strangely curved mirror.

Standing upon the floor he expanded, my amazed uncle could not tell how, into his proper proportions; and stood pretty nearly in profile at the bedside, a handsome and elegantly shaped young man, in a bygone military costume, with a small laced, three-cocked hat and plume on his head, but looking like a man going to be hanged—in unspeakable despair.

He stepped lightly to the hearth, and turned for a few seconds very dejectedly with his back towards the bed and the mantlepiece, and he saw the hilt of his rapier glittering in the firelight; and then walking across the room, he placed himself at the dressing table, visible through the divided curtains at the foot of the bed. The fire was still blazing so brightly that my uncle saw him as distinctly as if half a dozen candles were burning.

The looking-glass was an old-fashioned piece of furniture, and had a drawer beneath it. My uncle had searched it carefully for the papers in the day-time; but the silent figure pulled the drawer quite out, pressed a spring at the side, disclosing a false receptacle behind it, and from this he drew a parcel of papers tied together with pink tape.

All this time my uncle was staring at him in a horrified state, neither winking or breathing, and the apparition had not once given the smallest intimation of consciousness that a living person was in the same room. But now, for the first time, it turned its livid stare full upon my uncle with a hateful smile of significance, lifting up the little parcel of papers between his slender finger and thumb.

Then he made a long, cunning wink at him, and seemed to blow out one of his cheeks in a burlesque grimace, which, but for the horrific circumstances, would have been ludicrous. My uncle could not tell whether this was really an intentional distortion or only one of those horrid ripples and deflections which were constantly disturbing the proportions of the figure, as if it were seen through some unequal and perverting medium.

The figure now approached the bed, seeming to grow exhausted and malignant as it did so. My uncle's terror nearly culminated at this point, for he believed it was drawing near him with an evil purpose. But it was not so; for the soldier, over whom twenty years seemed to have passed in his brief transit to the dressing-table and back again, threw himself into a great high-backed arm-chair of stuffed leather at the far side of the fire, and placed his heels on the fender.

His feet and legs seemed indistinctly to swell, and swathings showed themselves round them, and they grew into something enormous, and the upper figure swayed and shaped itself into corresponding proportions, a great mass of corpulence, with a cadaverous and malignant face, and the furrows of a great old age, and colourless glassy eyes; and with these changes, which came indefinitely but rapidly as those of a sunset cloud, the fine regimentals faded away, and a loose, grey, wollen drapery, somehow, was there in its stead; and all seemed to be stained and rotten, for swarms of worms seemed creeping in and out, while the figure grew paler and paler, till my uncle, who liked his pipe, and employed the simile naturally, said the whole effigy grew to the colour of tobacco ashes, and the clusters of worms into little wriggling knots of sparks such as we see running over the residium of a burnt sheet of paper.

And so with the strong draught caused by the fire, and the current of air from the window, which was rattling in the storm, the feet seemed to be drawn into the fireplace, and the whole figure, light as ashes, floated away with them and disappeared with a whisk up the capacious old chimney.

It seemed to my uncle that the fire suddenly darkened and the air grew icy cold, and there came an awful roar and riot of tempest, which shook the old house from top to base, and sounded like the yelling of a blood-thirsty mob on receiving a new and long-expected victim.

Good Uncle Watson used to say: 'I have been in many situations of fear and danger in the course of my life, but never did I pray with so much agony before or

81

since; for then, as now, it was clear beyond a cavil that I had actually beheld the phantom of an evil spirit.'

Now there are two curious circumstances to be observed on this relation of my uncle's, who was, as I have said, a perfectly veracious man.

First: The wax candle which he took from the press in the parlour and burnt at his bedside on that horrible night was unquestionably, according to the testimony of the old deaf servant, who had been fifty years at Wauling, that identical piece of 'holy candle' which had stood in the fingers of the poor lady's corpse, and concerning which the old Irish crone, long since dead, had delivered the curious curse I have mentioned against the Captain.

Secondly: Behind the drawer under the looking-glass, he did actually discover a second but secret drawer, in which were concealed the identical papers which he had suspected the attorney of having made away with. There were circumstances, too, afterwards disclosed, which convinced my uncle that the old man had deposited them there preparatory to burning them, which he had nearly made up his mind to do.

Now, a very remarkable ingredient in this tale of my Uncle Watson was this, that so far as my father, who had never seen Captain Walshawe in the course of his life, could gather, the phantom had exhibited a horrible and grotesque, but unmistakable resemblance to that defunct scamp in the various stages of his long life.

Wauling was sold in the year 1837, and the old house shortly after pulled down, and a new one built nearer to the river. I often wondered whether it was rumoured to be haunted, and, if so, what stories were current about it. It was a commodious and staunch old house, and withall rather handsome; and its demolition was certainly suspicious.

LEGENDS OF WITCHES, FAIRIES AND LEPRECHAUNS

by Lady Wilde

LADY JANE FRANCISCA SPERANZA WILDE (1826-1896), now over-shadowed in literature by her son, Oscar, was nevertheless a distinguished and talented writer who for many years had the most famous salon in Dublin. Much of her life was devoted to collecting Irish folk tales and legends and these she published in numerous collections, the most notable being Ancient Legends, Mystic Charms and Superstitions of Ireland. *From this book I have taken three accounts of the most prevalent of all Irish fantasy figures—witches, fairies and leprechauns. Her retelling of these stories has provided invaluable source material for many writers, not least of these being Oscar Wilde, who follows with a tale of his own later in the book.*

The tales and legends told by the peasants in the Irish vernacular are often very weird and strange, and have much more of the old-world colouring than the ordinary fairy tales narrated in English by the people, as may be seen in the following tales, taken from the Irish, which date from a great many years ago.

THE HORNED WOMEN

A rich woman sat up late one night carding and preparing wool, while all the family and servants were asleep. Suddenly a knock was given at the door, and a voice called—'Open! open!'

83

'Who is there?' said the woman of the house.

'I am the Witch of the One Horn,' was answered.

The mistress, supposing that one of her neighbours had called and required assistance, opened the door, and a woman entered, having in her hand a pair of wool carders, and bearing a horn on her forehead, as if growing there. She sat down by the fire in silence, and began to card the wool with violent haste. Suddenly she paused and said aloud: 'Where are the women? They delay too long.'

Then a second knock came to the door, and a voice called as before—'Open! open!'

The mistress felt herself constrained to rise and open to the call, and immediately a second witch entered, having two horns on her forehead, and in her hand a wheel for spinning the wool.

'Give me place,' she said; 'I am the Witch of the Two Horns,' and she began to spin as quick as lightning.

And so the knocks went on, and the call was heard, and the witches entered, until at last twelve women sat round the fire—the first with one horn, the last with twelve horns. And they carded the thread, and turned their spinning wheels, and wound and wove, all singing together an ancient rhyme, but no word did they speak to the mistress of the house. Strange to hear, and frightful to look upon were these twelve women, with their horns and their wheels; and the mistress felt near to death, and she tried to rise that she might call for help, but she could not move, nor could she utter a word or a cry, for the spell of the witches was upon her.

Then one of them called to her in Irish and said—

'Rise, woman, and make us a cake.'

Then the mistress searched for a vessel to bring water from the well that she might mix the meal and make the cake, but she could find none. And they said to her—

84

'Take a sieve and bring water in it.'

And she took the sieve and went to the well; but the water poured from it, and she could fetch none for the cake, and she sat down by the well and wept. Then a voice came by her and said—

'Take yellow clay and moss and bind them together and plaster the sieve so that it will hold.'

This she did, and the sieve held the water for the cake. and the voice said again—

'Return, and when thou comest to the north angle of the house, cry aloud three times and say, "The mountain of the Fenian women and the sky over it is all on fire".'

And she did so.

When the witches inside heard the call, a great and terrible cry broke from their lips and they rushed forth with wild lamentations and shrieks, and fled away to Slieve-namon, where was their chief abode. But the Spirit of the Well bade the mistress of the house to enter and prepare her home against the enchantments of the witches if they returned again.

And first, to break their spells, she sprinkled the water in which she had washed her child's feet (the feet-water) outside the door on the threshold; secondly, she took the cake which the witches had made in her absence, of meal mixed with the blood drawn from the sleeping family. And she broke the cake in bits, and placed a bit in the mouth of each sleeper, and they were restored; and she took the cloth they had woven and placed it half in and half out of the chest with the padlock; and lastly, she secured the door with a great crossbeam fastened in the jambs, so that they could not enter. And having done these things she waited.

Not long were the witches in coming back, and they raged and called for vengeance.

'Open! open!' they screamed. 'Open, feet-water!'

85

'I cannot,' said the feet-water, 'I am scattered on the ground and my path is down to the Lough.'

'Open, open, wood and tree and beam!' they cried to to the door.

'I cannot,' said the door, 'for the beam is fixed in the jambs and I have no power to move.'

'Open, open, cake that we have made and mingled with blood,' they cried again.

'I cannot,' said the cake, 'for I am broken and bruised, and my blood is on the lips of the sleeping children.'

Then the witches rushed through the air with great cries, and fled back to Slieve-namon, uttering strange curses on the Spirit of the Well, who had wished their ruin; but the woman and the house were left in peace, and a mantle dropped by one of the witches in her flight was kept hung up by the mistress as a sign of the night's awful contest; and this mantle was in possession of the same family from generation to generation for five hundred years after.

THE FAIRY RACE

The *Sidhe,* or spirit race, called also the *Feadh-Ree,* or fairies, are supposed to have been once angels in heaven, who were cast out by Divine command as a punishment for their inordinate pride.

Some fell to earth, and dwelt there, long before man was created, as the first gods of the earth. Others fell into the sea, and they built themselves beautiful fairy palaces of crystal and pearl underneath the waves; but on moonlight nights they often come up on the land, riding their white horses, and they hold revels with their fairy kindred of the earth, who live in the clefts of the hills, and they dance together on the greensward under the ancient trees, and drink nectar from the cups of the flowers, which is the fairy wine.

86

Other fairies, however, are demoniacal, and given to evil and malicious deeds; for when cast out of heaven they fell into hell, and there the devil holds them under his rule, and sends them forth as he wills upon missions of evil to tempt the souls of men downward by the false glitter of sin and pleasure. These spirits dwell under the earth and impart their knowledge only to certain evil persons chosen of the devil, who gives them power to make incantations, and brew love potions, and to work wicked spells, and they can assume different forms by their knowledge and use of certain magical herbs.

The witch women who have been taught by them, and have thus become tools of the Evil One, are the terror of the neighbourhood; for they have all the power of the fairies and all the malice of the devil, who reveals to them secrets of times and days, and secrets of herbs, and secrets of evil spells; and by the power of magic they can effect all the purposes, whether for good or ill.

The fairies of the earth are small and beautiful. They passionately love music and dancing, and live luxuriously in their palaces under the hills and in the deep mountain caves; and they can obtain all things lovely for their fairy homes, merely by the strength of their magic power. They can also assume all forms, and will never know death until the last day comes, when their doom is to vanish away—to be annihilated for ever. But they are very jealous of the human race who are so tall and strong, and to whom has been promised immortality. And they are often tempted by the beauty of a mortal woman and greatly desire to have her as a wife.

The children of such marriages have a strange mystic nature, and generally become famous in music and song. But they are passionate, revengeful, and not easy to live with. Every one knows them to be of the Sidhe or spirit race, by their beautiful eyes and their bold, reckless temperament.

The fairy king and princes dress in green, with red caps bound on the head with a golden fillet. The fairy queen and the great court ladies are robed in glittering silver gauze, spangled with diamonds, and their long golden hair sweeps the ground as they dance on the greensward.

Their favourite camp and resting-place is under a hawthorn tree, and a peasant would die sooner than cut down one of the ancient hawthorns sacred to the fairies, and which generally stands in the centre of a fairy ring. But the people never offer worship to these fairy beings, for they look on the Sidhe as a race quite inferior to man. At the same time they have an immense dread and fear of the mystic fairy power, and never interfere with them nor offend them knowingly.

The Sidhe often strive to carry off the handsome children, who are then reared in the beautiful fairy palaces under the earth, and wedded to fairy mates when they grow up.

The people dread the idea of a fairy changeling being left in the cradle in place of their own lovely child; and if a wizened little thing is found there, it is sometimes take out at night and laid in an open grave till morning, when they hope to find their own child restored, although more often nothing is found save the cold corpse of the poor outcast.

Sometimes it is said the fairies carry off the mortal child for a sacrifice, as they have to offer one every seven years to the devil in return for the power he gives them. And beautiful young girls are carried off, also, either for sacrifice or to be wedded to the fairy king.

The fairies are pure and cleanly in their habits, and they like above all things a pail of water to be set for them at night, in case they may wish to bathe.

They also delight in good wines, and are careful to repay the donor in blessings, for they are truly upright and honest. The great lords in Ireland, in ancient times, used to leave a keg of the finest Spanish wine frequently at night out on the window-sill for the fairies, and in the morning it was all gone.

Fire is a great preventative against fairy magic, for fire is the most sacred of all created things, and man alone has power over it. No animal has ever yet attained the knowledge of how to draw out the spirit of fire from the stone or the wood, where it has found a dwelling-place. If a ring of fire is made round cattle or a child's cradle, or if fire is placed under the churn, the fairies have no power to harm. And the spirit of the fire is certain to destroy all fairy magic, if it exist.

THE LEPRECHAUNS

The Leprechauns are merry, industrious, tricksy little sprites, who do all the shoemaker's work and the tailor's and the cobbler's for the fairy gentry, and are often seen at sunset under the hedge singing and stitching. They know all the secrets of hidden treasure, and if they take a fancy to a person will guide him to the spot in the fairy rath where the pot of gold lies buried. It is believed that a family now living near Castlerea came by their riches in a strange way, all through the good offices of a friendly Leprechaun. And the legend has been handed down through many generations as an established fact.

There was a poor boy once, one of their forefathers, who used to drive his cart of turf daily back and forward, and make what money he could by the sale; but he was a strange boy, very silent and moody, and the people said he was a fairy changeling, for he joined in no sports and scarcely ever spoke to any one, but spent the nights reading all the old bits of books he picked up in his rambles. The one thing he longed for above all others was to get rich, and to be able to give up the old weary turf cart, and live in peace and quietness all alone, with nothing but books round him, in a beautiful house and garden all by himself.

Now he had read in the old books how the Leprechauns knew all the secret places where gold lay hid, and day by day he watched for a sight of the old cobbler, and listened for the click, click of his hammer as he sat under the hedge mending the shoes.

At last, one evening just as the sun set, he saw a little fellow under a dock leaf, working away, dressed all in green, with a cocked hat on his head. So the boy jumped down from the cart and seized him by the neck.

'Now, you don't stir from this,' he cried, 'till you tell me where to find the hidden gold.'

'Easy now,' said the Leprechaun, 'don't hurt me, and I will tell you all about it. But mind you, I could hurt you if I chose, for I have the power; but I won't do it, for we are cousins once removed. So as we are near relations I'll just be good, and show you the place of the secret gold that none can have or keep except those of fairy blood and race. Come along with me, then, to the old fort of Lipenshaw, for there it lies. But make haste, for when the last red glow of the sun vanishes the gold will disappear also, and you will never find it again.'

'Come off, then,' said the boy, and he carried the Leprechaun into the turf cart, and drove off. And in a second they were at the old fort, and went in through a door made in the stone wall.

'Now, look round,' said the Leprechaun; and the boy saw the whole ground covered with gold pieces, and there were vessels of silver lying about in such plenty that all the riches of all the world seemed gathered there.

'Now take what you want,' said the Leprechaun, 'but hasten, for if that door shuts you will never leave this place as long as you live.'

So the boy gathered up his arms full of gold and silver, and flung them into the cart; and was on his way back for more when the door shut with a clap like thunder, and all the place became dark as night. And he saw no more of the Leprechaun, and had not time even to thank him.

So he thought it best to drive home at once with his treasure, and when he arrived and was all alone by himself he counted his riches, and all the bright yellow gold pieces, enough for a king's ransom.

And he was very wise and told no one; but went off next day to Dublin and put all his treasures into the bank, and found that he was now indeed as rich as a lord.

So he ordered a fine house to be built with spacious gardens, and he had servants and carriages and books to his heart's content. And he gathered all the wise men round him to give him the learning of a gentleman; and he became a great and powerful man in the country, where his memory is still held in high honour, and his descendants are living to this day rich and prosperous; for their wealth has never decreased though they have ever given largely to the poor, and are noted above all things for the friendly heart and the liberal hand.

But the Leprechauns can be bitterly malicious if they are offended, and one should be very cautious in dealing with them, and always treat them with great civility, or they will take revenge and never reveal the secret of the hidden gold.

One day a young lad was out in the fields at work when he saw a little fellow, not the height of his hand, mending shoes under a dock leaf. And he went over, never taking his eyes off him for fear he would vanish away; and lifted him up and put him in his pocket.

Then he ran away home as fast as he could, and when

he had the Leprechaun safe in the house, he tied him by an iron chain to the hob.

'Now, tell me,' he said, 'where am I to find a pot of gold? Let me know the place or I'll punish you.'

'I know of no pot of gold,' said the Leprechaun; 'but let me go that I may finish mending the shoes.'

'Then I'll make you tell me,' said the lad.

And with that he made a great fire, and put the little fellow on it and scorched him.

'Oh, take me off, take me off!' cried the Leprechaun, 'and I'll tell you. Just there, under the dock leaf, where you found me, there is a pot of gold. Go; dig and find.'

So the lad was delighted, and ran to the door; but it so happened that his mother was just coming in with the pail of fresh milk, and in his haste he knocked the pail out of her hand, and all the milk was spilled on the floor.

Then, when the mother saw the Leprechaun, she grew very angry and beat him. 'Go away, you little wretch!' she cried. 'You have overlooked the milk and brought ill-luck.' And she kicked him out of the house.

But the lad ran off to find the dock leaf, though he came back very sorrowful in the evening, for he had dug and dug and dug nearly down to the middle of the earth; but no pot of gold was to be seen.

That same night the husband was coming home from his work, and as he passed the old fort he heard voices and laughter, and one said—

'They are looking for a pot of gold; but they little know that a crock of gold is lying down in the bottom of the old quarry, hid under the stones close by the garden wall. But whoever gets it must go on a dark night at twelve o'clock, and beware of bringing his wife with him.'

So the man hurried home and told his wife he would go that very night, for it was black dark, and she must stay at home and watch for him, and not stir from the house till he came back. Then he went out into the dark night alone.

'Now,' thought the wife, when he was gone, 'if I could only get to the quarry before him I would have the pot of gold all to myself; while if he gets it I shall have nothing.'

And with that she went out and ran like the wind until she reached the quarry, and then she began to creep down very quietly in the black dark. But a great stone was in her path, and she stumbled over it, and fell down and down till she reached the bottom, and there she lay groaning, for her leg was broken by the fall.

Just then her husband came to the edge of the quarry and began to descend. But when he heard the groans he was frightened.

'Cross of Christ about us!' he exclaimed; 'what is that down below? Is it evil, or is it good?'

'Oh, come down, come down and help me!' cried the woman. 'It's your wife is here, and my leg is broken, and I'll die if you don't help me.'

'And is this my pot of gold?' exclaimed the poor man. 'Only my wife with a broken leg lying at the bottom of the quarry.'

And he was at his wits' end to know what to do, for the night was so dark he could not see a hand before him. So he roused up a neighbour, and between them they dragged up the poor woman and carried her home, and laid her on the bed half dead from fright, and it was many a day before she was able to get about as usual; indeed she limped all her life long, so that the people said the curse of the Leprechaun was on her.

But as to the pot of gold, from that day to this not one of the family, father or son, or any belonging to them, ever set eyes on it. However, the little Leprechaun still sits under the dock leaf of the hedge and laughs at them as he mends the shoes with his little hammer—tick tack, tick tack—but they are afraid to touch him, for now they know he can take his revenge.

THE CANTERVILLE GHOST

by Oscar Wilde

OSCAR FINGALL O'FLAHERTIE WILLS WILDE *(1854-1900) enjoys, with the select circle of Joyce, O'Casey, Yeats, Behan and a few other Irish writers, the distinction of being read and acclaimed around the world. Like Charles Maturin before him, he lived flambuoyantly, never far from scandal and using his flashing wit to combat those who would ridicule or attack him. It has been said that he lived his genius, and that makes his few short stories such as* The Canterville Ghost *doubly valuable. That he had absorbed much of the climate of Ireland, its dark figures, superstitions and unseen forces, is very evident in this superb tale.*

I

When Mr. Hiram B. Otis, the American Minister, bought Canterville Chase, everyone told him he was doing a very foolish thing, as there was no doubt at all that the place was haunted. Indeed, Lord Canterville himself, who was a man of the most punctilious honour, had felt it his duty to mention the fact to Mr. Otis when they came to discuss terms.

'We have not cared to live in the place ourselves,' said Lord Canterville, 'since my grand-aunt, the Dowager

Duchess of Bolton, was frightened into a fit, from which she never really recovered, by two skeleton hands being placed on her shoulders as she was dressing for dinner, and I feel bound to tell you, Mr. Otis, that the ghost has been seen by several living members of my family, as well as by the rector of the parish, the Rev. Augustus Dampier, who is a Fellow of King's College, Cambridge. After the unfortunate accident to the Duchess, none of our younger servants would stay with us, and Lady Canterville often got very little sleep at night, in consequence of the mysterious noises that came from the corridor and the library.'

'My Lord,' answered the Minister, 'I will take the furniture and the ghost at a valuation. I come from a modern country, where we have everything that money can buy; and with all our spry young fellows painting the Old World red, and carrying off your best actresses and prima-donnas, I reckon that if there were such a thing as a ghost in Europe, we'd have it at home in a very short time in one of our public museums, or on the road as a show.'

'I fear that the ghost exists,' said Lord Canterville, smiling, 'though it may have resisted the overtures of your enterprising impresarios. It has been well known for three centuries, since 1584 in fact, and always makes its appearance before the death of any member of our family.'

'Well, so does the family doctor for that matter, Lord Canterville. But there is no such thing, sir, as a ghost, and I guess the laws of Nature are not going to be suspended for the British aristocracy.'

'You are certainly very natural in America,' answered Lord Canterville, who did not quite understand Mr. Otis's last observation, 'and if you don't mind a ghost in the house, it is all right. Only you must remember I warned you.'

A few weeks after this, the purchase was completed, and at the close of the season the Minister and his family went down to Canterville Chase. Mrs. Otis, who, as Miss Lucretia R. Tappan, of West 53rd Street, had been a celebrated New York belle, was now a very handsome, middle-aged woman, with fine eyes, and a superb profile. Many American ladies on leaving their native land adopt an appearance of chronic ill-health, under the impression that it is a form of European refinement, but Mrs. Otis had never fallen into this error. She had a magnificent constitution, and a really wonderful amount of animal spirits. Indeed, in many respects, she was quite English, and was an excellent example of the fact that we have really everything in common with America nowadays, except, of course, language. Her eldest son, christened Washington by his parents in a moment of patriotism, which he never ceased to regret, was a fair-haired, rather good-looking young man, who had qualified himself for American diplomacy by leading the German at the Newport Casino for three successive seasons, and even in London was well known as an excellent dancer. Gardenias and the peerage were his only weaknesses. Otherwise he was extremely sensible. Miss Virginia E. Otis was a little girl of fifteen, lithe and lovely as a fawn, and with a fine freedom in her large blue eyes. She was a wonderful amazon, and had once raced old Lord Bilton on her pony twice round the park, winning by a length and a half, just in front of the Achilles statue, to the huge delight of the young Duke of Cheshire, who proposed for her on the spot, and was sent back to Eton that very night by his guardians, in floods of tears. After Virginia came the twins, who were usually called 'The Stars and Stripes', as they were always getting swished. They were delightful boys, and with the exception of the worthy Minister the only true republicans of the family.

As Canterville Chase is seven miles from Ascot, the nearest railway station, Mr. Otis had telegraphed for a waggonette to meet them, and they started on their drive in high spirits. It was a lovely July evening, and the air was delicate with the scent of the pinewoods. Now and then they heard a wood pigeon brooding over its own sweet voice, or saw, deep in the rustling fern, the burnished breast of the pheasant. Little squirrels peered at them from the beech-trees as they went by, and the rabbits scudded away through the brushwood and over the mossy knolls, with their white tails in the air. As they entered the avenue of Canterville Chase, however, the sky became suddenly overcast with clouds, a curious stillness seemed to hold the atmosphere, a great flight of rooks passed silently over their heads, and, before they reached the house, some big drops of rain had fallen.

Standing on the steps to receive them was an old woman, neatly dressed in black silk, with a white cap and apron. This was Mrs. Umney, the housekeeper, whom Mrs. Otis, at Lady Canterville's earnest request, had consented to keep on in her former position. She made them each a low curtsey as they alighted, and said in a quaint, old-fashioned manner, 'I bid you welcome to Canterville Chase.' Following her, they passed through the fine Tudor hall into the library, a long, low room, panelled in black oak, at the end of which was a large stained-glass window. Here they found tea laid out for them, and, after taking off their wraps, they sat down and began to look round, while Mrs. Umney waited on them.

Suddenly Mrs. Otis caught sight of a dull red stain on the floor just by the fireplace and, quite unconscious of what it really signified, said to Mrs. Umney, 'I am afraid something has been spilt there.'

'Yes, madam,' replied the old housekeeper in a low voice, 'blood has been spilt on that spot.'

'How horrid,' cried Mrs. Otis; 'I don't at all care for bloodstains in a sitting-room. It must be removed at once.'

The old woman smiled, and answered in the same low, mysterious voice, 'It is the blood of Lady Eleanore de Canterville, who was murdered on that very spot by her own husband, Sir Simon de Canterville, in 1575. Sir Simon survived her nine years, and disappeared suddenly under very mysterious circumstances. His body has never been discovered, but his guilty spirit still haunts the Chase. The blood-stain has been much admired by tourists and others, and cannot be removed.'

'That is all nonsense,' cried Washington Otis; 'Pinkerton's Champion Stain Remover and Paragon Detergent will clean it up in no time,' and before the terrified housekeeper could interfere he had fallen upon his knees, and was rapidly scouring the floor with a small stick of what looked like a black cosmetic. In a few moments no trace of the blood-stain could be seen.

'I knew Pinkerton would do it,' he exclaimed triumphantly, as he looked round at his admiring family; but no sooner had he said these words than a terrible flash of lightning lit up the sombre room, a fearful peal of thunder made them all start to their feet, and Mrs. Umney fainted.

'What a monstrous climate!' said the American Minister calmly, as he lit a long cheroot. 'I guess the old country is so overpopulated that they have not enough decent weather for everybody. I have always been of opinion that emigration is the only thing for England.'

'My dear Hiram,' cried Mrs. Otis, 'what can we do with a woman who faints?'

'Charge it to her like breakages,' answered the Minister; 'she won't faint after that'; and in a few moments Mrs. Umney certainly came to. There was no doubt, however, that she was extremely upset, and she sternly warned Mr. Otis to beware of some trouble coming to the house.

'I have seen things with my own eyes, sir,' she said, 'that would make any Christian's hair stand on end, and many and many a night I have not closed my eyes in sleep for the awful things that are done here.' Mr. Otis, however, and his wife warmly assured the honest soul that they were not afraid of ghosts, and, after invoking the blessings of Providence on her new master and mistress, and making arrangements for an increase of salary, the old housekeeper tottered off to her own room.

II

The storm raged fiercely all that night, but nothing of particular note occurred. The next morning, however, when they came down to breakfast, they found the terrible stain of blood once again on the floor. 'I don't think it can be the fault of the Paragon Detergent,' said Washington, 'for I have tried it with everything. It must be the ghost.' He accordingly rubbed out the stain a second time, but the second morning it appeared again. The third morning also it was there, though the library had been locked up at night by Mr. Otis himself, and the key carried upstairs. The whole family were now quite interested; Mr. Otis began to suspect that he had been too dogmatic in his denial of the existence of ghosts, Mrs. Otis expressed her intention of joining the Psychical Society, and Washington prepared a long letter to Messrs. Myers and Podmore on the subject of the Permanence of Sanguineous Stains when connected with Crime. That night all doubts about the objective existence of phantasmata were removed for ever.

The day had been warm and sunny; and, in the cool of the evening, the whole family went out for a drive. They did not return home till nine o'clock, when they had a light supper. The conversation in no way turned upon ghosts, so there were not even those primary conditions of receptive expectation which so often precede the presentation of psychical phenomena. The subjects discussed, as I have since learned from Mr. Otis, were merely such as form the ordinary conversation of cultured Americans of the better class, such as the immense superiority of Miss Fanny Davenport over Sarah Bernhardt as an actress; the difficulty of obtaining green corn, buckwheat cakes, and hominy, even in the best English houses; the importance of Boston in the development of the world-soul; the advantages of the baggage check system in railway travelling; and the sweetness of the New York accent as compared to the London drawl. No mention at all was made of the supernatural, nor was Sir Simon de Canterville alluded to in any way. At eleven o'clock the family retired, and by half-past all the lights were out. Some time after, Mr. Otis was awakened by a curious noise in the corridor, outside his room. It sounded like the clank of metal, and seemed to be coming nearer every moment. He got up at once, struck a match, and looked at the time. It was exactly one o'clock. He was quite calm, and felt his pulse, which was not at all feverish. The strange noise still continued, and with it he heard distinctly the sound of footsteps. He put on his slippers, took a small oblong phial out of his dressing-case, and opened the door. Right in front of him he saw, in the wan moonlight, an old man of terrible aspect. His eyes were as red burning coals; long grey hair fell over his shoulders in matted coils; his garments, which were of antique cut, were soiled and ragged, and from his wrists and ankles hung heavy manacles and rusty gyves.

'My dear sir,' said Mr. Otis, 'I really must insist on your oiling those chains, and have brought you for that purpose a small bottle of the Tammany Rising Sun

Lubricator. It is said to be completely efficacious upon one application, and there are several testimonials to that effect on the wrapper from some of our most eminent native divines. I shall leave it here for you by the bedroom candles, and will be happy to supply you with more should you require it.' With these words the United States Minister laid the bottle down on a marble table, and, closing his door, retired to rest.

For a moment the Canterville ghost stood quite motionless in natural indignation; then, dashing the bottle violently upon the polished floor, he fled down the corridor, uttering hollow groans, and emitting a ghastly green light. Just, however, as he reached the top of the great oak staircase, a door was flung open, two little white-robed figures appeared, and a large pilow whizzed past his head! There was evidently no time to be lost, so, hastily adopting the Fourth Dimension of Space as a means of escape, he vanished through the wainscoting, and the house became quite quiet.

On reaching a small secret chamber in the left wing, he leaned up against a moonbeam to recover his breath, and began to try and realise his position. Never, in a brilliant and uninterrupted career of three hundred years, had he been so grossly insulted. He thought of the Dowager Duchess, whom he had frightened into a fit as she stood before the glass in her lace and diamonds; of the four housemaids, who had gone off into hysterics when he merely grinned at them through the curtains of one of the spare bedrooms; of the rector of the parish, whose candle he had blown out as he was coming late one night from the library, and who had been under the care of Sir William Gull ever since, a perfect martyr to nervous disorders; and of old Madame de Tremouillac, who, having wakened up one morning early and seen a skeleton seated in an arm-chair by the fire reading her diary, had been confined to her bed for six weeks with

101

an attack of brain fever, and, on her recovery, had become reconciled to the Church, and broken off her connection with that notorious sceptic Monsieur de Voltaire. He remembered the terrible night when the wicked Lord Canterville was found choking in his dressing-room, with the knave of diamonds halfway down his throat, and confessed, just before he died, that he had cheated Charles James Fox out of £50,000 at Crockford's by means of that very card, and swore that the ghost had made him swallow it. All his great achievements came back to him again, from the butler who had shot himself in the pantry because he had seen a green hand tapping at the window pane, to the beautiful Lady Stutfield, who was always obliged to year a black velvet band round her throat to hide the mark of five fingers burnt upon her white skin, and who drowned herself at last in the carp-pond at the end of the King's Walk. With the enthusiastic egotism of the true artist he went over his most celebrated performances, and smiled bitterly to himself as he recalled to mind his last appearance as 'Red Ruben, or the Strangled Babe', his *début* as 'Gaunt Gibeon, the Blood-sucker of Bexley Moor', and the *furore* he had excited one lovely June evening by merely playing ninepins with his own bones upon the lawn-tennis ground. And after all this, some wretched modern Americans were to come and offer him the Rising Sun Lubricator, and throw pillows at his head! It was quite unbearable. Besides, no ghost in history had ever been treated in this manner. Accordingly, he determined to have vengeance, and remained till daylight in an attitude of deep thought.

III

The next morning when the Otis family met at breakfast, they discussed the ghost at some length. The United

102

States Minister was actually a little annoyed to find that his present had not been accepted. 'I have no wish,' he said, 'to do the ghost any personal injury, and I must say that, considering the length of time he has been in the house, I don't think it is at all polite to throw pillows at him'—a very just remark, at which, I am sorry to say, the twins burst into shouts of laughter. 'Upon the other hand,' he continued, 'if he really declines to use the Rising Sun Lubricator, we shall have to take his chains from him. It would be quite impossible to sleep, with such a noise going on outside the bedrooms.'

For the rest of the week, however, they were undisturbed, the only thing that excited any attention being the continual renewal of the blood-stain on the library floor. This certainly was very strange, as the door was always locked at night by Mr. Otis, and the windows kept closely barred. The chameleon-like colour, also, of the stain excited a good deal of comment. Some mornings it was a dull (almost Indian) red, then it would be vermilion, then a rich purple, and once when they came down for family prayers, according to the simple rites of the Free American Reformed Episcopalian Church, they found it a bright emerald green. These kaleidoscopic changes naturally amused the party very much, and bets on the subject were freely made every evening. The only person who did not enter into the joke was little Virginia, who for some unexplained reason, was always a good deal distressed at the sight of the blood-stain, and very nearly cried the morning it was emerald-green.

The second appearance of the ghost was on Sunday night. Shortly after they had gone to bed they were suddenly alarmed by a fearful crash in the hall. Rushing downstairs, they found that a large suit of old armour had become detached from its stand, and had fallen on the stone floor, while, seated in a high-backed chair, was the Canterville ghost, rubbing his knees with an expression of acute agony on his face. The twins, having brought their peashooters with them, at once discharged two pellets on him. with that accuracy of aim which can only be attained by long and careful practice on a writing-master, while the United States Minister covered him with his revolver, and called upon him, in accordance with Californian etiquette, to hold up his hands! The ghost started up with a wild shriek of rage, and swept through them like a mist, extinguishing Washington Otis's candle as he passed, and so leaving them all in total darkness. On reaching the top of the staircase he recovered himself, and determined to give his celebrated peal of demoniac laughter. This he had on more than one occasion found extremely useful. It was said to have turned Lork Raker's wig grey in a single night, and had certainly made three of Lady Canterville's French governesses give notice before their month was up. He accordingly laughed his most horrible laugh, till the old vaulted roof rang and rang again, but hardly had the fearful echo died away when a door opened, and Mrs Otis came out in a light blue dressing-gown. 'I am afraid you are far from well,' she said, 'and have brought you a bottle of Dr. Dobell's tincture. If it is indigestion, you will find it a most excellent remedy.' The ghost glared at her in fury, and began at once to make preparations for turning himself into a large black dog, an accomplishment for which he was justly renowned, and to which the family doctor always attributed the permanent idiocy of Lord Canterville's uncle, the Hon. Thomas Horton. The sound of approaching footsteps, however, made him hesitate in his fell purpose, so he contented himself with becoming faintly phosphorescent, and vanished with a deep church-yard groan, just as the twins had come up to him.

On reaching his room he entirely broke down, and became a prey to the most violent agitation. The vulgarity of the twins, and the gross materialism of Mrs. Otis, were naturally extremely annoying, but what really distressed him most was, that he had been unable to wear the suit of mail. He had hoped that even modern Americans would be thrilled by the sight of a Spectre In Armour, if for no more sensible reason, at least out of respect for their national poet Longfellow, over whose graceful and attractive poetry he himself had whiled away many a weary hour when the Canterville's were up in town. Besides, it was his own suit. He had worn it with great success at the Kenilworth tournament, and had been highly complimented on it by no less a person than the Virgin Queen herself. Yet when he had put it on, he had been completely overpowered by the weight of the huge breastplate and steel casque, and had fallen heavily on the stone pavement, barking both his knees severely, and bruising the knuckles of his right hand.

For some days after this he was extremely ill, and hardly stirred out of his room at all, except to keep the blood-stain in proper repair. However, by taking great care of himself, he recovered, and resolved to make a third attempt to frighten the United States Minister and his family. He selected Friday, the 17th of August, for his appearance, and spent most of that day in looking over his wardrobe, ultimately deciding in favour of a large slouched hat with a red feather, a winding-sheet frilled at the wrists and neck, and a rusty dagger. Towards evening a violent storm of rain came on, and the wind was so high that all the windows and doors in the old house shook and rattled. In fact, it was just such weather as he loved. His plan of action was this. He was to make his way quietly to Washington Otis's room, gibber at him from the foot of the bed, and stab himself three times in the throat to the sound of slow music. He bore Washington a special grudge, being quite aware that it was he who was in the habit of removing the famous Canterville blood-stain, by means of Pinkerton's Paragon Detergent. Having reduced the reckless and foolhardy youth to a condition of abject terror, he was then to proceed to the room occupied by the United States Minister and his wife, and there to place a clammy hand on Mrs. Otis's forehead, while he hissed into her trembling husband's ear the awful secrets of the charnel-house. With regard to little Virginia, he had not quite made up his mind. She had never insulted him in any way, and was pretty and gentle. A few hollow groans from the wardrobe, he thought, would be more than sufficient, or, if that failed to wake her, he might grabble at the counterpane with palsy-twitching fingers. As for the twins, he was quite determined to teach them a lesson. The first thing to be done, was of course, to sit upon their chests, so as to produce the stifling sensation each other, to stand between them in the form of a green, icy-cold corpse, till they became paralysed with fear, and finally, to throw off the winding-sheet, and crawl round the room, with white bleached bones and one rolling eye-ball, in a character of 'Dumb Daniel, or the Suicide's Skeleton', a *rôle* in which he had on more than one occasion produced a great effect, and which he considered quite equal to his famous part of 'Martin the Maniac, or the Masked Mystery'.

At half-past ten he heard the family going to bed. For some time he was disturbed by wild shrieks of laughter from the twins, who, with the light-hearted gaiety of schoolboys, were evidently amusing themselves before they retired to rest, but at a quarter past eleven all was still, and as midnight sounded, he sallied forth. The owl beat against the window panes, the raven croaked from the old yew-tree, and the wind wandered moaning round the house like a lost soul; but the Otis family slept unconscious of their doom, and high above the rain and storm he could hear the steady snoring of the Minister for the United States. He stepped stealthily out of the wainscoting, with an evil smile on his cruel, wrinkled mouth, and the moon hid her face in a cloud as he stole past the great oriel window, where in his own arms and those of his murdered wife were blazoned in azure and gold. On and on he glided, like an evil shadow, the very darkness seeming to loathe him as he passed. Once he thought he heard something call, and stopped; but it was only the baying of a dog from the Red Farm, and he went on, muttering strange sixteenth-century curses, and ever and anon brandishing the rusty dagger in the midnight air. Finally he reached the corner of the passage that led to luckless Washington's room. For a moment he paused there, the wind blowing his long grey locks about his head, and twisting into grotesque and fantastic folds the nameless horror of the dead man's shroud. Then the clock struck the quarter, and he felt the time was come. He chuckled to himself, and turned the corner; but no sooner had he done so, than, with a piteous wail of terror, he fell back, and hid his blanched face in his long, bony hands. Right in front of him was standing a horrible spectre, motionless as a carved image, and monstrous as a madman's dream! Its head was bald and burnished; its face round, and fat, and white; and hideous laughter seemed to have writhed its features into an eternal grin. From the eyes streamed rays of scarlet light, the mouth was a wide well of fire, and a hideous garment, like to his own, swathed with its silent snows the Titan form. On its breast was a placard with strange writing in antique characters, some scroll of shame it seemed, some record of wild sins, some awful calendar of crime, and, with its right hand, it bore aloft a falchion of gleaming steel.

Never having seen a ghost before, he naturally was

107

terribly frightened, and, after a second hasty glance at the awful phantom, he fled back to his room, tripping up in his long winding-sheet as he sped down the corridor, and finally dropping the rusty dagger into the Minister's jack-boots, where it was found in the morning by the butler. Once in the privacy of his own apartment, he flung himself down on a small pallet-bed, and hid his face under the clothes. After a time, however, the brave old Canterville spirit asserted itself, and he determined to go and speak to the other ghost as soon as it was daylight. Accordingly, just as the dawn was touching the hills with silver, he returned towards the spot where he had first laid eyes on the grisly phantom, feeling that, after all, two ghosts were better than one, and that, by the aid of his new friend, he might safely grapple with the twins. On reaching the spot, however, a terrible sight met his gaze. Something had evidently happened to the spectre, for the light had entirely faded from his hollow eyes, the gleaming falchion had fallen from its hand, and it was leaning up against the wall in a strained and uncomfortable attitude. He rushed forward and seized it in his arms, when, to his horror, the head slipped off and rolled on the floor, the body assumed a recumbent posture, and he found himself clasping a white dimity bed-curtain, with a sweeping-brush, a kitchen cleaver, and a hollow turnip lying at his feet! Unable to understand this curious transformation, he clutched the placard with feverish haste, and there, in the grey morning light, he read these fearful words:

YE OTIS GHOSTE.
Ye Dulie True and Originale Spook.
Beware of Ye Imitationes.
All others are Counterfeite.

The whole thing flashed across him. He had been tricked, foiled, and outwitted! The old Canterville look came into his eyes; he ground his toothless gums together; and, raising his withered hands high above his head, swore, according to the picturesque phraseology of the antique school, that when Chanticleer had sounded twice his merry horn, deeds of blood would be wrought, and Murder walk abroad with silent feet.

Hardly had he finished this awful oath when, from the red-tiled roof of a distant homestead, a cock crew. He laughed a long, low, bitter laugh, and waited. Hour after hour he waited, but the cock, for some strange reason, did not crow again. Finally, at half-past seven, the arrival of the housemaids made him give up his fearful vigil, and he stalked back to his room, thinking of his vain hope and baffled purpose. There he consulted several books of ancient chivalry, of which he was exceedingly fond, and found that, on every occasion on which his oath had been used, Chanticleer had always crowed a second time. 'Perdition seize the naughty fowl,' he muttered, 'I have seen the day when, with my stout spear, I would have run him through the gorge, and made him crow for me as 'twere in death!' He then retired to a comfortable lead coffin, and stayed there till evening.

IV

The next day the ghost was very weak and tired. The terrible excitement of the last four weeks was beginning to have its effect. His nerves were completely shattered, and he started at the slightest noise. For five days he kept to his room and at last made up his mind to give up the point of the stain on the library floor. If the Otis family did not want it, they clearly did not deserve it. They were evidently people on a low, material plane of existence, and quite incapable of appreciating the symbolic value of sensuous phenomena. The question of phantasmic apparitions, and the development of astral bodies, was of course quite a different matter, and really not under his control. It was his solemn duty to appear in the corridor once a week, and to gibber from the large oriel window on the first and third Wednesday in every month, and he did not see how he could honour-ably escape from his obligations. It is quite true that his life had been very evil, but, upon the other hand, he was most conscious in all things connected with the supernatural. For the next three Saturdays, accordingly, he traversed the corridor as usual between midnight and three o'clock, taking every possible precaution against being either heard or seen. He removed his boots, trod as lightly as possible on the old worm-eaten boarrds, wore a large black velvet cloak, and was careful to use the Rising Sun Lubricator for oiling his chains. I am bound to acknowledge that it was with a good deal of difficulty that he brought himself to adopt this last mode of protection. However, one night, while the family were at dinner, he slipped into Mr. Otis's bedroom and carried off the bottle. He felt a little humiliated at first, but afterwards was sensible enough to see that there was a great deal to be said for the invention, and, to a certain degree, it served his purpose. Still, in spite of every-thing, he was not left unmolested. Strings were con-tinually being stretched across the corridor, over which he tripped in the dark, and on one occasion, while dressed for the part of 'Black Isaac, or the Huntsman of Hogley Woods', he met with a severe fall, through treading on a butter-slide, which the twins had con-structed from the entrance of the Tapestry Chamber to the top of the oak staircase. This last insult so enraged him, that he resolved to make one final effort to assert his dignity and social position, and determined to visit

110

the insolent young Etonians the next night in his celebrated character of 'Reckless Rupert, or the Headless
Earl'.

He had not appeared in this disguise for more than
seventy years; in fact, not since he had so frightened
pretty Lady Barbara Modish by means of it, that she
suddenly broke off her engagement with the present
Lord Canterville's grandfather, and ran away to Gretna
Green with handsome Jack Castleton, declaring that
nothing in the world would induce her to marry into a
family that allowed such a horrible phantom to walk
up and down the terrace at twilight. Poor Jack was
afterwards shot in a duel by Lord Canterville on Wands-
worth Common, and Lady Barbara died of a broken
heart at Tunbridge Wells before the year was out, so,
in every way, it had been a great success. It was, however, an extremely difficult 'make-up', if I may use such
a theatrical expression in connection with one of the
greatest mysteries of the supernatural, or, to employ a
more scientific term, the higher-natural world, and it
took him fully three hours to make his preparations. At
last everything was ready, and he was very pleased with
his appearance. The big leather riding-boots that went
with the dress were just a little too large for him, and
he could only find one of the two horse-pistols, but, on
the whole, he was quite satisfied, and at a quarter past
one he glided out of the wainscoting and crept down
the corridor. On reaching the room occupied by the
twins, which I should mention was called the Blue Bed
Chamber, on account of the colour of its hangings, he
found the door just ajar. Wishing to make an effective
entrance, he flung it wide open, when a heavy jug of
water fell right down on him, wetting him to the skin,
and just missing his left shoulder by a couple of inches.
At the same moment he heard stifled shrieks of laughter
proceeding from the four-post bed. The shock to his

111

nervous system was so great that he fled back to his room as hard as he could go, and the next day he was laid up with a severe cold. The only thing that at all consoled him in the whole affair was the fact that he had not brought his head with him, for had he done so, the consequences might have been very serious.

He now gave up all hope of ever frightening this rude American family, and contented himself, as a rule, with creeping about the passages in list slippers, with a thick red muffler round his throat for fear of draughts, and a small arquebuse, in case he should be attacked by the twins. The final blow he received occurred on the 19th of September. He had gone downstairs to the great entrance-hall, feeling sure that there, at any rate, he would be quite unmolested, and was amusing himself by making satirical remarks on the large Saroni photographs of the United States Minister and his wife, which had now taken the place of the Canterville family pictures. He was simply but neatly clad in a long shroud, spotted with churchyard mould, had tied up his jaw with a strip of yellow linen, and carried a small lantern impersonations, and one which the Cantervilles had every reason to remember, as it was the real origin of their quarrel with their neighbour, Lord Rufford. It was about a quarter past two o'clock in the morning, and, as far as he could ascertain, no one was stirring. As he was strolling towards the library, however, to see if there were any traces left of the blood-stain, suddenly there leaped out on him from a dark corner two figures, who waved their arms wildly above their heads, and shrieked out 'BOO!' in his ear.

Seized with a panic, which, under the circumstances, was only natural, he rushed for the staircase, but found Washington Otis waiting for him there with the big garden-syringe; and being thus hemmed in by his enemies on every side, and driven almost to bay, he

112

vanished into the great iron stove, which, fortunately for him, was not lit, and had to make his way home through the flues and chimneys, arriving at his own room in a terrible state of dirt, disorder, and despair.

After this he was not seen again on any nocturnal expedition. The twins lay in wait for him on several occasions, and strewed the passages with nutshells every night to the great annoyance of their parents and the servants, but it was of no avail. It was quite evident that his feelings were so wounded that he would not appear. Mr. Otis consequently resumed his great work on the history of the Democratic Party, on which he had been engaged for some years; Mrs. Otis organised a wonderful clam-bake, which amazed the whole county; the boys took to lacrosse, euchre, poker, and other American national games; and Virginia rode about the lanes on her pony, accompanied by the young Duke of Cheshire, who had come to spend the last week of his holidays at Canterville Chase. It was generally assumed that the ghost had gone away, and, in fact, Mr. Otis wrote a letter to that effect to Lord Canterville, who, in reply, expressed his great pleasure at the news, and sent his best congratulations to the Minister's worthy wife.

The Otises, however, were deceived, for the ghost was still in the house, and though now almost an invalid, was by no means ready to let matters rest, particularly as he heard that among the guests was the young Duke of Cheshire, whose grand-uncle, Lord Francis Stilton, had once bet a hundred guineas with Colonel Carbury that he would play dice with the Canterville ghost, and was found the next morning lying on the floor of the card-room in such a helpless paralytic state, that though he lived on to a great age, he was never able to say anything again but 'Double Sixes'. The story was well known at the time, though, of course, out of respect to the feelings of the two noble families, every attempt was made to hush it up; and a full account of all the circumstances connected with it will be found in the third volume of Lord Tattle's *Recollections of the Prince Regent and his Friends*. The ghost, then, was naturally very anxious to show that he had not lost his influence over the Stiltons, with whom, indeed, he was distantly connected, his own first cousin having been married *en secondes noces* to the Sieur de Bulkeley, from whom, as every one knows, the Dukes of Cheshire are lineally descended. Accordingly, he made arrangements for appearing to Virginia's little lover in his celebrated impersonation of 'The Vampire Monk, or, the Bloodless Benedictine', a performance so horrible that when old Lady Startup saw it, which she did on one fatal New Year's Eve, in the year 1764, she went off into the most piercing shrieks, which culminated in violent apoplexy, and died in three days, after disinheriting the Cantervilles, who were her nearest relations, and leaving all her money to her London apothecary. At the last moment, however, his terror of the twins prevented his leaving his room, and the little Duke slept in peace under the great feathered canopy in the Royal Bedchamber, and dreamed of Virginia.

V

A few days after this, Virginia and her curly-haired cavalier went out riding on Brockley meadows, where she tore her habit so badly in getting through a hedge, that, on her return home, she made up her mind to go up by the back staircase so as not to be seen. As she was running past the Tapestry Chamber, the door of which happened to be open, she fancied she saw someone inside, and thinking it was her mother's maid, who sometimes used to bring her work there, looked in to

114

ask her to mend her habit. To her immense surprise, however, it was the Canterville Ghost himself! He was sitting by the window, watching the ruined gold of the yellowing trees fly through the air, and the red leaves dancing madly down the long avenue. His head was leaning on his hand, and his whole attitude was one of extreme depression. Indeed, so folorn, and so much out of repair did he look, that little Virginia, whose first idea had been to run away and lock herself in her room, was filled with pity, and determined to try and comfort him. So light was her footfall, and so deep his melancholy, that he was not aware of her presence till she spoke to him.

'I am sorry for you,' she said, 'but my brothers are going back to Eton tomorrow, and then, if you behave yourself, no one will annoy you.'

'It is absurd asking me to behave myself,' he answered, looking round in astonishment at the pretty little girl who had ventured to address him, 'quite absurd. I must rattle my chains, and groan through keyholes, and walk about at night, if that is what you mean. It is my only reason for existing.'

'It is no reason at all for existing, and you know you have been very wicked. Mrs. Umney told us, the first day we arrived here, that you killed your wife.'

'Well, I quite admit it,' said the Ghost petulantly, 'but it was a purely family matter, and concerned no one else.'

'It is very wrong to kill anyone,' said Virginia, who at times had a sweet Puritan gravity, caught from some old New England ancestor.

'Oh, I hate the cheap severity of abstract ethics! My wife was very plain, never had my ruffs properly starched, and knew nothing about cookery. Why, there was a buck I had shot in Hogley Woods, a magnificent pricket, and do you know how she had it sent up to table? However, it is no matter now, for it is all over, and I don't think it was very nice of her brothers to starve me to death, though I did kill her.'

'Starve you to death? Oh, Mr. Ghost, I mean Sir Simon, are you hungry? I have a sandwich in my case. Would you like it?'

'No, thank you, I never eat anything now; but it is very kind of you, all the same, and you are much nicer than the rest of your horrid, rude, vulgar, dishonest family.'

'Stop!' cried Virginia, stamping her foot, 'it is you who are rude, and horrid, and vulgar, and as for dishonesty, you know you stole the paints out of my box to try and furbish up that ridiculous blood-stain in the library. First you took all my reds, including the vermilion, and I couldn't do any more sunsets, then you took the emerald-green and the chrome-yellow, and finally I had nothing left but indigo and Chinese white, and could only do moonlight scenes, which are always depressing to look at, and not at all easy to paint. I never told on you, though I was very much annoyed, and it was most ridiculous, the whole thing; for who ever heard of emerald-green blood?'

'Well, really,' said the Ghost, rather meekly, 'what was I to do? It is a very difficult thing to get real blood nowadays, and, as your brother began it all with his Paragon Detergent, I certainly saw no reason why I should not have your paints. As for colour, that is always a matter of taste: the Cantervilles have blue blood, for instance, the very bluest in England; but I know you Americans don't care for things of this kind.'

'You know nothing about it, and the best thing you can do is to emigrate and improve your mind. My father will be only too happy to give you a free passage, and though there is a heavy duty on spirits of every kind, there will be no difficulty about the Custom House, as the officers are all Democrats. Once in New York, you are sure to be a great success. I know lots of people there who would give a hundred thousand dollars to have a grandfather, and much more than that to have a family Ghost.'

'I don't think I should like America.'

'I suppose because we have no ruins and no curiosities,' said Virginia satirically.

'No ruins! no curiosities!' answered the Ghost; 'you have your navy and your manners.'

'Good evening; I will go and ask papa to get the twins an extra week's holiday.'

'Please don't go, Miss Virginia,' he cried; 'I am so lonely and so unhappy, and I really don't know what to do. I want to go to sleep and I cannot.'

'That's quite absurd! You have merely to go to bed and blow out the candle. It is very difficult sometimes to keep awake, especially at church, but there is no difficulty at all about sleeping. Why, even babies know how to do that, and they are not very clever.'

'I have not slept for three hundred years,' he said sadly, and Virginia's beautiful blue eyes opened in wonder; 'for three hundred years I have not slept, and I am so tired.'

Virginia grew grave, and her little lips trembled like rose-leaves. She came towards him, and kneeling down at his side, looked up into his old withered face.

'Poor, poor Ghost,' she murmured; 'have you no place where you can sleep?'

'Far away beyond the pine-woods,' he answered, in a low dreamy voice, 'there is a little garden. There the grass grows long and deep, there are the great white stars of the hemlock flower, there the nightingale sings all night long. All night long he sings, and the cold, crystal moon looks down, and the yew-tree spreads out its giant arms over the sleeper.'

Virginia's eyes grew dim with tears, and she hid her face in her hands.

'You mean the Garden of Death,' she whispered.

'Yes, Death. Death must be so beautiful. To lie in the soft brown earth, with the grasses waving above one's head, and listen to silence. To have no yesterday, and no tomorrow. To forget time, to forgive life, to be at peace. You can help me. You can open for me the portals of Death's house, for Love is always with you, and Love is stronger than Death is.'

Virginia trembled, a cold shudder ran through her, and for a few moments there was silence. She felt as if she was in a terrible dream.

Then the Ghost spoke again, and his voice sounded like the sighing of the wind.

'Have you ever read the old prophecy on the library window?'

'Oh, often,' cried the little girl, looking up; 'I know it quite well. It is painted in curious black letters, and it is difficult to read. There are only six lines:

> **When a golden girl can win**
> **Prayer from out the lips of sin,**
> **When the barren almond bears,**
> **And a little child gives away its tears,**
> **Then shall all the house be still**
> **And peace come to Canterville.**

But I don't know what they mean.'

'They mean,' he said sadly, 'that you must weep for me for my sins, because I have no tears, and pray with me for my soul, because I have no faith, and then, if you have always been sweet, and good, and gentle, the Angel of Death will have mercy on me. You will see fearful shapes in darkness, and wicked voices will whis-

118

per in your ear, but they will not harm you, for against the purity of a little child the powers of Hell cannot prevail.'

Virginia made no answer, and the Ghost wrung his hands in wild despair as he looked down at her bowed golden head. Souddenly she stood up, very pale, with a strange light in her eyes. 'I am not afraid,' she said firmly, 'and I will ask the Angel to have mercy on you.'

He rose from his seat with a faint cry of joy, and taking her hand bent over it with old-fashioned grace and kissed it. His fingers were as cold as ice, and his lips burned like fire, but Virginia did not falter, as he led her across the dusky room. On the faded green tapestry were embroidered little huntsmen. They blew their tasselled horns and with their tiny hands waved to her to go back. 'Go back! little Virginia,' they cried, go back!' but the Ghost clutched her hand more tightly and she shut her eyes against them. Horrible animals with lizard tails, and goggle eyes, blinked at her from the carved chimney-piece, and murmured 'Beware! little Virginia, beware! we may never see you again,' but the Ghost glided on more swiftly, and Virginia did not listen. When they reached the end of the room he stopped, and muttered some words she could not understand. She opened her eyes, and saw the wall slowly fading away like a mist, and a great black cavern in front of her. A bitter cold wind swept round them, and she felt something pulling at her dress. 'Quick, quick,' cried the Ghost, 'or it will be too late,' and, in a moment, the wainscoting had closed behind them, and the Tapestry Chamber was empty.

VI

About ten minutes later, the bell rang for tea, and, as Virginia did not come down, Mrs. Otis sent up one

119

of the footmen to tell her. After a little time he returned
and said that he could not find Miss Virginia anywhere.
As she was in the habit of going out to the garden every
evening to get flowers for the dinner-table, Mrs. Otis
was not at all alarmed at first, but when six o'clock
struck, and Virginia did not appear, she became really
agitated, and sent the boys out to look for her, while
she herself and Mr. Otis searched every room in the
house. At half-past six the boys came back and said that
they could find no trace of their sister anywhere. They
were all now in the greatest state of excitement, and
did not know what to do, when Mr. Otis suddenly remembered that, some few days before, he had given a
band of gypsies permission to camp in the park. He
accordingly at once set off for Blackfell Hollow, where
he knew they were, accompanied by his eldest son
and two of the farm-servants. The little Duke of
Cheshire, who was perfectly frantic with anxiety,
begged hard to be allowed to go too, but Mr. Otis
would not allow him, as he was afraid there might
be a scuffle. On arriving at the spot, however, he found
that the gypsies had gone, and it was evident that their
departure had been rather sudden, as the fire was
still burning, and some plates were lying on the
grass. Having sent off Washington and the two men to
scour the district, he ran home, and despatched tele-
grams to all the police inspectors in the county, telling
them to look out for a little girl who had been kidnapped
by tramps or gypsies. He then ordered his horse to be
brought round, and, after insisting on his wife and the
three boys sitting down to dinner, rode off down the
Ascot Road with a groom. He had hardly, however, gone
a couple of miles when he heard someone galloping after
him, and, looking round, saw the little Duke coming up
on his pony, with his face very flushed and no hat. 'I'm
awfully sorry, Mr. Otis,' gasped out the boy, 'but I

can't eat any dinner as long as Virginia is lost. Please, don't be angry with me; if you had let us be engaged last year, there would never have been all this trouble. You won't send me back, will you? I can't go! I won't go!'

The Minister could not help smiling at the handsome young scapegrace, and was a good deal touched at his devotion to Virginia, so leaning down from his horse, he patted him kindly on the shoulders, and said, 'Well, Cecil, if you won't go back I suppose you must come with me, but I must get you a hat at Ascot.'

'Oh, bother my hat! I want Virginia!' cried the little Duke, laughing, and they galloped on to the railway station. There Mr. Otis inquired of the station-master if anyone answering the description of Virginia had been seen on the platform, but could get no news of her. The station-master, however, wired up and down the line, and assured him that a strict watch would be kept for her, and, after having bought a hat for the little Duke from a linen-draper, who was just putting up his shutters, Hr. Otis rode off to Bexley, a village about four miles away, which he was told was a well-known haunt of the gypsies, as there was a large common next to it. Here they roused up the rural policeman, but could get no information from him, and, after riding all over the common, they turned their horses' heads homewards, and reached the Chase about eleven o'clock, dead tired and almost heart-broken. The found Washington and the twins waiting for them at the gate-house with lanterns as the avenue was very dark. Not the slightest trace of Virginia had been discovered. The gypsies had been caught on Brockley meadows, but she was not with them, and they had explained their sudden departure by saying that they had mistaken the date of Chorton Fair, and had gone off in a hurry for fear they might be late. Indeed, they had been quite distressed at hearing of

121

Virginia's disappearance, as they were very grateful to
Mr. Otis for having allowed them to camp in his park,
and four of their number had stayed behind to help in
the search. The carp-pond had been dragged, and the
whole Chase thoroughly gone over, but without any result.
It was evident that, for that night at any rate, Virginia
was lost to them; and it was in a state of the deepest
depression that Mr. Otis and the boys walked up to the
house, the groom following behind with the two horses
and the pony. In the hall they found a group of frightened servants, and lying on a sofa in the library was
poor Mrs. Otis, almost out of her mind with terror and
anxiety, and having her forehead bathed with eau-de-
cologne by the old housekeeper. Mr. Otis at once insisted on her having something to eat, and ordered up
supper for the whole party. It was a melancholy meal, as
hardly anyone spoke, and even the twins were awe-
struck and subdued, as they were very fond of their
sister. When they had finished, Mr. Otis, in spite of the
entreaties of the little Duke, ordered them all to bed, saying that nothing more could be done that night, and that
he would telegraph in the morning to Scotland Yard for
some detectives to be sent down immediately. Just as
they were passing out of the dining-room, midnight began to boom from the clock tower, and when the last
stroke sounded they heard a crash and a sudden shrill
cry; a dreadful peal of thunder shook the house, a
strain of unearthly music floated through the air, a panel
at the top of the staircase flew back with a loud noise,
and out on the landing, looking very pale and white,
with a little casket in her hand, stepped Virginia. In a
moment they had all rushed up to her. Mrs. Otis clasped
her passionately in her arms, the Duke smothered her
with violent kisses, and the twins executed a wild war-
dance round the group.

'Good heavens! child, where have you been?' said Mr.

Otis, rather angrily, thinking that she had been playing some foolish trick on them. 'Cecil and I have been riding all over the country looking for you, and your mother has been frightened to death. You must never play these practical jokes any more.'

'Except on the Ghost! except on the Ghost!' shrieked the twins, as they capered about.

'My own darling, thank God you are found; you must never leave my side again,' murmured Mrs. Otis, as she kissed the trembling child, and smoothed the tangled gold of her hair.

'Papa,' said Virginia quietly, 'I have been with the Ghost. He is dead, and you must come and see him. He had been very wicked, but he was really sorry for all that he had done, and he gave me this box of beautiful jewels before he died.'

The whole family gazed at her in mute amazement, but she was quite grave and serious; and, turning round, she led them through the opening in the wainscoting down a narrow secret corridor, Washington followed with a lighted candle, which he had caught up from the table. Finally, they came to a great oak door, studded with rusty nails. When Virginia touched it, it swung back on its heavy hinges, and they found themselves in a little low room, with a vaulted ceiling, and one tiny grated window. Imbedded in the wall was a huge iron ring, and chained to it was a gaunt skeleton, that was stretched out at full length on the stone floor, and seemed to be trying to grasp with its long fleshless fingers an old-fashioned trencher and ewer, that were placed just out of its reach. The jug had evidently been once filled with water, as it was covered inside with green mould. There was nothing on the trencher but a pile of dust. Virginia knelt down beside the skeleton, and, folding her little hands together, began to pray silently, while the rest of the party looked on in wonder at the terrible tragedy whose secret was now disclosed to them.

'Hallo!' suddenly exclaimed one of the twins, who had been looking out of the window to try and discover in what wing of the house the room was situated. 'Hallo! the old withered almond tree has blossomed. I can see the flowers quite plainly in the moonlight.'

'God has forgiven him,' said Virginia gravely, as she rose to her feet, and a beautiful light seemed to illumine her face.

'What an angel you are!' cried the young Duke, and he put his arm round her neck and kissed her.

VII

Four days after these curious incidents a funeral started from Canterville Chase about eleven o'clock at night. The hearse was drawn by eight black horses, each of which carried on its head a great tuft of nodding ostrich-plumes, and the leaden coffin was covered by a rich purple pall, on which was embroidered in gold the Canterville coat-of-arms. By the side of the hearse and the coaches walked the servants with lighted torches, and the whole procession was wonderfully impressive. Lord Canterville was the chief mourner, having come up specially from Wales to attend the funeral, and sat in the first carriage along with little Virginia. Then came the United States Minister and his wife, then Washington and the three boys, and in the last carriage was Mrs. Umney. It was generally felt that, as she had been frightened by the ghost for more than fifty years of her life, she had a right to see the last of him. A deep grave had been dug in the corner of the churchyard, just under the old yew-tree, and the service was read in the most impressive manner by the Rev. Augustus Dampier.

When the ceremony was over, the servants, according to an old custom observed in the Canterville family, extinguished their torches, and, as the coffin was being lowered into the grave, Virginia stepped forward and laid on it a large cross made of white and pink almond-blossoms. As she did so, the moon came out from behind a cloud, and flooded with its silent silver the little churchyard, and from a distant copse a nightingale began to sing. She thought of the ghost's description of the Garden of Death, her eyes became dim with tears, and she hardly spoke a word during the drive home.

The next morning, before Lord Canterville went up to town, Mr. Otis had an interview with him on the subject of the jewels the ghost had given to Virginia. They were perfectly magnificent, especially a certain ruby necklace with old Venetian setting, which was really a superb specimen of sixteenth-century work, and their value was so great that Mr. Otis felt considerable scruples about allowing his daughter to accept them.

'My lord,' he said, 'I know that in this country mortmain is held to apply to trinkets as well as to land, and it is quite clear to me that these jewels are, or should be, heirlooms in your family. I must beg you, accordingly, to take them to London with you, and to regard them simply as a portion of your property which has been restored to you under certain strange conditions. As for my daughter, she is merely a child, and has as yet, I am glad to say, but little interest in such appurtenances of idle luxury. I am also informed by Mrs. Otis, who, I may say, is no mean authority upon Art—having had the privilege of spending several winters in Boston when she was a girl—that these gems are of great monetary worth, and if offered for sale would fetch a tall price. Under these circumstances, Lord Canterville, I feel sure that you will recognise how impossible it would be for me to allow them to remain in the possession of any member of my family; and, indeed, all such vain gauds and toys, however suitable or necessary to the dignity of the British aristocracy, would be completely out of place among those who have been brought up on the severe and, I believe, immortal principles of republican simplicity. Perhaps I should mention that Virginia is very anxious that you should allow her to retain the box as a memento of your unfortunate but misguided ancestor. As it is extremely old, and consequently a good deal out of repair, you may perhaps think fit to comply with her request. For my own part, I confess I am a good deal surprised to find a child of mine expressing sympathy with mediaevalism in any form, and can only account for it by the fact that Virginia was born in one of your London suburbs shortly after Mrs. Otis had returned from a trip to Athens.'

Lord Canterville listened very gravely to the worthy Minister's speech, pulling his grey moustache now and then to hide an involuntary smile, and when Mr. Otis had ended, he shook him cordially by the hand, and said, 'My dear sir, your charming little daughter rendered my unlucky ancestor, Sir Simon, a very important service, and I and my family are much indebted to her for her marvellous courage and pluck. The jewels are clearly hers, and, egad, I believe that if I were heartless enough to take them from her, the wicked old fellow would be out of his grave in a fortnight, leading me the devil of a life. As for their being heirlooms, nothing is an heirloom that is not so mentioned in a will or legal document, and the existence of these jewels has been quite unknown. I assure you I have no more claim on them than your butler, and when Miss Virginia grows up I daresay she will be pleased to have pretty things to wear. Besides, you forget, Mr. Otis, that you took the furniture and the ghost at a valuation, and any-

126

thing that belonged to the ghost passed at once into your possession, as, whatever activity Sir Simon may have shown in the corridor at night, in point of law he was really dead, and you acquired his property by purchase.'

Mr. Otis was a good deal distressed at Lord Canterville's refusal, and begged him to reconsider his decision, but the good-natured peer was quite firm, and finally induced the Minister to allow his daughter to retain the present the ghost had given her, and when, in the spring of 1890, the young Duchess of Cheshire was presented at the Queen's first drawing-room on the occasion of her marriage, her jewels were the universal theme of admiration. For Virginia received the coronet, which is the reward of all good little American girls, and was married to her boy-lover as soon as he came of age. They were both so charming, and they loved each other so much, everyone was delighted at the match, except the old Marchioness of Dumbleton, who had tried to catch the Duke for one of her seven unmarried daughters, and had given no less than three expensive dinner-parties for that purpose, and, strange to say, Mr. Otis himself. Mr. Otis was extremely fond of the young Duke personally, but, theoretically, he objected to titles, and, to use his own words, 'was not without apprehension lest, amid the enervating influences of a pleasure-loving aristocracy, the true principles of republican simplicity should be forgotten.' His objections, however, were completely overruled, and I believe that when he walked up the aisle of St. George's, Hanover Square, with his daughter leaning on his arm, there was not a prouder man in the whole length and breadth of England.

The Duke and Duchess, after the honeymoon was over, went down to Canterville Chase, and on the day after their arrival they walked over in the afternoon to the lonely churchyard by the pine-woods. There had been a great deal of difficulty at first about the inscription on Sir Simon's tombstone, but finally it had been decided to engrave on it simply the initials of the old gentleman's name, and the verse from the library window. The Duchess had brought with her some lovely roses, which she strewed upon the grave, and after they had stood by it for some time they strolled into the ruined chancel of the old abbey. There the Duchess sat down on a fallen pillar, while her husband lay at her feet smoking a cigarette and looking up at her beautiful eyes. Suddenly he threw his cigarette away, took hold of her hand, and said to her, 'Virginia, a wife should have no secrets from her husband.'

'Dear Cecil! I have no secrets from you.'

'Yes, you have,' he answered, smiling, 'you have never told me what happened to you when you were locked up with the ghost.'

'I have never told anyone, Cecil,' said Virginia gravely.

'I know that, but you might tell me.'

'Please don't ask me, Cecil, I cannot tell you. Poor Sir Simon! I owe him a great deal. Yes, don't laugh, Cecil, I really do. He made me see what Life is, and what Death signifies, and why Love is stronger than both.'

The Duke rose and kissed his wife lovingly.

'You can have your secret as long as I have your heart,' he murmured.

'You have always had that, Cecil.'

'And you will tell our children some day, won't you?'

Virginia blushed.

THE BANSHEE'S WARNING

by Charlotte Riddell

CHARLOTTE ELIZA RIDDELL *(1832-1906), a prolific and popular Victorian novelist, was born in Carrick-fergus, but moved to London when still a young woman. She published her first book at twenty-six and wrote another forty during her lifetime. Strangely, she referred to Ireland very little in her work and* The Banshee's Warning *is a rarity both for this reason and for its story-line, which in some way parallels her own move from the Old Country, and perhaps an unconscious 'hearing' of voices from home. According to Sir Walter Scott,* Banshees *(women of the fairies) only haunt very ancient Irish families, and Elliott O'Donnel adds that they have been known to follow their people all over the world.*

Many a year, before chloroform was thought of, there lived in an old rambling house, in Gerrard Street, Soho, a clever Irishman called Hertford O'Donnell.

After Hertford O'Donnell he was entitled to write, M.R.C.S.. for he had studied hard to gain this distinction, and the older surgeons at Guy's (his hospital) considered him one of the most rising operators of the day.

Having said chloroform was unknown at the time this story opens, it will strike my readers that, if Hertford O'Donnell were a rising and successful operator in those days, of necessity he combined within himself a larger number of striking qualities than are by any means necessary to form a successful operator in these.

There was more than mere hand skill, more than even thorough knowledge of his profession, then needful for the man, who, dealing with conscious subjects, essayed to rid them of some of the diseases to which flesh is heir. There was greater courage required in the manipulator or old than is altogether essential at present. Then, as now, a thorough mastery of his instruments, a steady hand, a keen eye, a quick dexterity were indispensable to a good operator; but, added to all these things, there formerly required a pulse which knew no quickening, a mental strength which never faltered, a ready power of adaptation in unexpected circumstances, fertility of resource in difficult cases, and a brave front under all emergencies.

If I refrain from adding that a hard as well as a courageous heart was an important item in the programme, it is only out of deference to general opinion, which, amongst other strange delusions, clings to the belief that courage and hardness are antagonistic qualities.

Hertford O'Donnell, however, was hard as steel. He understood his work, and he did it thoroughly; but he cared no more for quivering nerves and shrinking muscles, for screams of agony, for faces white with pain, and teeth clenched in the extremity of anguish, than he did for the stony countenances of the dead, which so often in the dissecting room appalled younger and less experienced men.

He had no sentiment, and he had no sympathy. The human body was to him, merely an ingenious piece of mechanism, which it was at once a pleasure and a profit to understand. Precisely as Brunel loved the Thames Tunnel, or any other eingular engineering feat, so O'Donnell loved a patient on whom he had operated successfully, more especially if the ailment possessed by the patient were of a rare and difficult character.

130

And for this reason he was much liked by all who came under his hands, since patients are apt to mistake a surgeon's interest in their cases for interest in themselves; and it was gratifying to John Dicks, plasterer, and Timothy Regan, labourer, to be the happy possessors of remarkable diseases, which produced a cordial understanding between them and the handsome Irishman.

If he had been hard and cool at the moment of hacking them to pieces, that was all forgotten or remembered only as a virtue, when, after being discharged from hospital like soldiers who have served in a severe campaign, they met Mr. O'Donnell in the street, and were accosted by that rising individual just as though he considered himself nobody.

He had a royal memory, this stranger in a strange land, both for faces and cases; and like the rest of his countrymen, he never felt it beneath his dignity to talk cordially to corduroy and fustian.

In London, as a Calgillan, he never held back his tongue from speaking a cheery or a kindly word. His manners were pliable enough, if his heart were not; and the porters, and the patients, and the nurses, and the students at Guy's were all pleased to see Hertford O'Donnell.

Rain, hail, sunshine, it was all the same; there was a life and a brightness about the man which communicated itself to those with whom he came in contact. Let the mud in the Borough be a foot deep or the London fog as thick as pea-soup, Mr. O'Donnell never lost his temper, never muttered a surly reply to the gatekeeper's salutation, but spoke out blithely and cheerfully to his pupils and his patients, to the sick and to the well, to those below and to those above him.

And yet, spite of all these good qualities, spite of his

handsome face, his fine figure, his easy address, and his unquestionable skill as an operator, the dons, who acknowledged his talent, shook their heads gravely when two or three of them in private and solemn conclave, talked confidentially of their younger brother.

If there were many things in his favour, there were more in his disfavour. He was Irish—not merely by the accident of birth, which might have been forgiven, since a man cannot be held accountable for such caprices of Nature, but by every other accident and design which is objectionable to the orthodox and respectable and representative English mind.

In speech, appearance, manner, taste, modes of expression, habits of life, Hertford O'Donnell was Irish. To the core of his heart he loved the island which he declared he never meant to re-visit; and amongst the English he moved to all intents and purposes a foreigner, who was resolved, so said the great prophets at Guy's, to rush to destruction as fast as he could, and let no man hinder him.

'He means to go the whole length of his tether,' observed one of the ancient wiseacres to another; which speech implied a conviction that Hertford O'Donnell having sold himself to the Evil One, had determined to dive the full length of his rope into wickedness before being pulled to that shore where even wickedness is negative—where there are no mad carouses, no wild, sinful excitements, nothing but impotent wailing and gnashing of teeth.

A reckless, graceless, clever, wicked devil—going to his natural home as fast as in London anyone possibly speed thither; this was the opinion his superiors, held of the man who lived all alone with a housekeeper and her husband (who acted as butler) in his big house near Soho.

Gerrard Street—made famous by De Quincey, was not then an utterly shady and forgotten locality; carriage-patients found their way to the rising young surgeon—some great personages thought it not beneath them to fee an individual whose consulting rooms were situated on what was even then considered the wrong side of Regent Street. He was making money, and he was spending it; he was over head and ears in debt—useless, vulgar debt—senselessly contracted, never bravely faced. He had lived at an awful pace ever since he came to London, a pace which only a man who hopes and expects to die young can ever travel.

Life was good, was it? Death, was he a child, or a woman, or a coward, to be afraid of that hereafter? God knew all about the trifle which had upset his coach, better than the dons at Guy's.

Hertford O'Donnell understood the world pretty thoroughly, and the ways thereof were to him as roads often traversed; therefore, when he said that at the Day of Judgment he felt certain he should come off as well as many of those who censured him, it may be assumed, that, although his views of post-mortem punishment were vague, unsatisfactory and infidel, still his information as to the peccadilloes of his neighbours was such as consoled himself.

And yet, living all alone in the old house near Soho Square, grave thoughts would intrude into the surgeon's mind—thoughts which were, so to say, italicised by peremptory letters, and still more peremptory visits from people who wanted money.

Although he had many acquaintances he had no single friend, and accordingly these thoughts were receivel and brooded over in solitude—in those hours when, after returning from dinner, or supper, or congenial carouse, he sat in his dreary rooms, smoking his pipe and considering means and ways, chances and certainties.

In good truth he had started in London with some vague idea that as his life in it would not be of long continuance, the pace at which he elected to travel could be of little consequence; but the years since his first entry into the Metropolis were now piled one on the top of another, his youth was behind him, his chances of longevity, spite of the way he had striven to injure his constitution, quite as good as ever. He had come to that period in existence, to that narrow strip of table-land, whence the ascent of youth and the descent of age are equally discernible—when, simply because he has lived for so many years, it strikes a man as possible he may have to live for just as many more, with the ability for hard work gone, with the boom companions scattered, with the capacity for enjoying convivial meetings a mere memory, with small means perhaps, with no bright hopes, with the pomp and the circumstance and the fairy carriages, and the glamour which youth flings over earthly objects, faded away like the pageant of yesterday, while the dreary ceremony of living has to be gone through today and tomorrow and the morrow after, as though the gay cavalcade and the martial music, and the glittering helmets and the prancing steeds were still accompanying the wayfarer to his journey's end.

Ah! my friends, there comes a moment when we must all leave the coach, with its four bright bays, its pleasant outside freight, its cheery company, its guard who blows the horn so merrily through villages and along lonely country roads.

Long before we reach that final stage, where the black business claims us for its own special property, we have to bid goodbye to all easy, thoughtless journeying, and betake ourselves, with what zest we may, to traversing the common of reality. There is no royal road across it that ever I heard of. From the king on his throne to the

134

labourer who vaguely imagines what manner of being a king is, we have all to tramp across that desert at one period of our lives, at all events; and that period usually is when, as I have said, a man starts to find the hopes, and the strength, and the buoyancy of youth left behind, while years and years of life lie stretching out before him.

The coach he has travelled by drops him here. There is no appeal, there is no help; therefore, let him take off his hat and wish the new passengers good speed. without either envy or repining.

Behold, he has had his turn, and let whosoever will, mount on the box-seat of life again, and tip the coachman and handle the ribbons—he shall take that pleasant journey no more, no more for ever.

Even supposing a man's springtime to have been a cold and ungenial one, with bitter easterly winds and nipping frosts, biting the buds and retarding the blossoms, still it was spring for all that—spring with the young green leaves sprouting forth, with the flowers unfolding tenderly, with the songs of the birds and the rush of waters, with the summer before and the autumn afar off, and winter remote as death and eternity, but when once the trees have donned their summer foliage, when the pure white blossoms have disappeared, and the gorgeous red and orange and purple blaze of many-coloured flowers fills the gardens, then if there come a wet, dreary day, the idea of autumn and winter is not so difficult to realise. When once twelve o'clock is reached, the evening and night become facts, not possibilities; and it was of the afternoon, and the evening, and the night, Hertford O'Donnell sat thinking on the Christmas Eve, when I crave permission to introduce him to my readers.

A good-looking man ladies considered him. A tall, dark-complexioned, black-haired, straight-limbed, deeply divinely blue-eyed fellow, with a soft voice, with a pleasant brogue, who had ridden like a centaur over the loose stone walls in Connemara, who had danced all night at the Dublin balls, who had walked across the Bennebeola Mountains, gun in hand, day after day, without weariness, who had fished in every one of the hundred lakes you can behold from the top of that mountain near the Recess Hotel, who had led a mad, wild life in Trinity College, and a wilder, perhaps, while 'studying for a doctor'—as the Irish phrase goes—in Edinburgh, and who, after the death of his eldest brother left him free to return to Calgillan, and pursue the usual utterly useless, utterly purposeless, utterly pleasant life of an Irish gentleman possessed of health, birth, and expectations, suddenly kicked over the paternal traces, bade adieu to Calgillan Castle and the blandishments of a certain beautiful Miss Clifden, beloved of his mother, and laid out to be his wife, walked down the avenue without even so much company as a Gossoon to carry his carpet-bag, shook the dust from his feet at the lodge gates, and took his seat on the coach, never once looking back at Calgillan, where his favourite mare was standing in the stable, his greyhounds chasing one another round the home paddock, his gun at half-cock in his dressing-room and his fishing-tackle all in order and ready for use.

He had not kissed his mother, or asked for his father's blessing; he left Miss Clifden, arrayed in her brand-new riding-habit, without a word of affection or regret; he had spoken no syllable of farewell to any servant about the place; only when the old woman at the lodge bade him good morning and God-blessed his handsome face, he recommended her bitterly to look at it well for she would never see it more.

Twelve years and a half had passed since then, without either Miss Clifden or any other one of the Calgillan people having set eyes on Master Hertford's handsome face.

He had kept his vow to himself; he had not written home; he had not been indebted to mother or father for even a tenpenny-piece during the whole of that time; he had lived without friends; and he had lived without God—so far as God ever lets a man live without him.

One thing only he felt to be needful—money; money to keep him when the evil days of sickness, or age, or loss of practice came upon him. Though a spendthrift, he was not a simpleton; around him he saw men, who, having started with fairer prospects that his own, were, nevertheless, reduced to indigence; and he knew that what had happened to others might happen to himself.

An unlucky cut, slipping on a piece of orange-peel in the street, the merest accident imaginable, is sufficient to change opulence to beggary in the life's programme of an individual, whose income depends on eye, on nerve, on hand; and, besides the consciousness of this fact, Hertford O'Donnell knew that beyond a certain point in his profession, progress was not easy.

It did not depend quite on the strength of his own bow and shield whether he counted his earnings by hundreds or thousands. Work may achieve competence; but mere work cannot, in a profession, at all events, compass fortune.

He looked around him, and he perceived that the majority of great men—great and wealthy—had been indebted for their elevation, more to the accident of birth, patronage, connection, or marriage, than to personal ability.

Personal ability, no doubt, they possessed; but then, little Jones, who lived in Frith Street, and who could barely keep himself and his wife and family, had ability, too, only he lacked the concomitants of success.

He wanted something or someone to puff him into

notoriety—a brother at Court—a lord's leg to mend—a rich wife to give him prestige in Society; and in his absence of this something or someone, he had grown grey-haired and faint-hearted while labouring for a world which utterly despises its most obsequious servants.

'Clatter along the streets with a pair of fine horses, snub the middle classes, and drive over the commonalty —that is the way to compass wealth and popularity in England,' said Hertford O'Donnell, bitterly; and as the man desired wealth and popularity, he sat before his fire, with a foot on each hob, and a short pipe in his mouth, considering how he might best obtain the means to clatter along the streets in his carriage, and splash plebeians with mud from his wheels like the best.

In Dublin he could, by means of his name and connection, have done well; but then he was not in Dublin, neither did he want to be. The bitterest memories of his life were inseparable from the very name of the Green Island, and he had no desire to return to it.

Besides, in Dublin, heiresses are not quite so plentiful as in London; and an heiress, Hertford O'Donnell had decided, would do more for him than years of steady work.

A rich wife could clear him of debt, introduce him to fashionable practice, afford him that measure of social respectability which a medical bachelor invariably lacks, deliver him from the loneliness of Gerrard Street, and the domination of Mr. and Mrs. Coles.

To most men, deliberately bartering away their independence for money seems so prosaic a business that they strive to gloss it over even to themselves, and to assign every reason for their choice, save that which is really the influencing one.

Not so, however, with Hertford O'Donnell. He sat beside the fire scoffing over his proposed bargain— thinking of the lady's age, her money bags, her desirable house in town, her seat in the country, her snobbishness, her folly.

'It could be a fitting ending,' he sneered, 'and why I did not settle the matter tonight passes my comprehension. I am not a fool, to be frightened with old women's tales; and yet I must have turned white. I felt I did, and she asked me whether I were ill. And then to think of my being such an idiot as to ask her if she had heard anything like a cry, as though she would be likely to hear *that*, she with her poor parvenu blood, which I often imagine must have been mixed with some of her father's strong pickling vinegar. What a deuce could I have been dreaming about? I wonder what it really was.' And Hertford O'Donnell pushed his hair back off his forehead, and took another draught from the too familiar tumbler, which was placed conveniently on the chimney-piece.

'After expressly making up my mind to propose, too!' he mentally continued. 'Could it have been conscience—that myth, which somebody, who knew nothing about the matter, said, "Makes cowards of us all"? I don't believe in conscience; and even if there be such a thing capable of being developed by sentiment and cultivation, why should it trouble me? I have no intention of wronging Miss Janice Price Ingot, not the least. Honestly and fairly I shall marry her; honestly and fairly I shall act by her. An old wife is not exactly an ornamental article of furniture in a man's house; and I do not know that the fact of her being well gilded makes her look any handsomer. But she shall have no cause for complaint; and I will go and dine with her tomorrow, and settle the matter.'

Having arrived at which resolution, Mr. O'Donnell arose, kicked down the fire—burning hollow—with the heel of his boot, knocked the ashes out of his pipe, emptied his sumbler, and bethought him it was time to

139

go to bed. He was not in the habit of taking his rest so early as a quarter to twelve o'clock; but he felt unusually weary—tired mentally and bodily—and lonely beyond all power of expression.

'The fair Janet would be better than this,' he said, half aloud; and then, with a start and a shiver, and a blanched face, he turned sharply round, whilst a low, sobbing, wailing cry echoed mournfully through the room. No form of words could give an idea of the sound. The plaintiveness of the Æolian harp—that plaintiveness which so soon affects and lowers the highest spirits— would have seemed wildly gay in comparison with the sadness of the cry which seemed floating in the air. As the summer wind comes and goes amongst the trees, so that mournful wail came and went—came and went. It came in a rush of sound, like a gradual crescendo managed by a skilful musician, and died away in a lingering note, so gently that the listener could scarcely tell the exact moment when it faded into utter silence.

I say faded, for it disappeared as the coast line disappears in the twilight, and there was total stillness in the apartment.

Then, for the first time, Hertford O'Donnell looked at his dog, and beholding the creature crouched into a corner beside the fireplace, called upon him to come out.

His voice sounded strange even to himself, and apparently the dog thought so too, for he made no effort to obey the summons.

'Come here, sir,' his master repeated, and then the animal came crawling reluctantly forward with his hair on end, his eyes almost starting from his head, trembling violently, as the surgeon, who caressed him, felt.

'So you heard it, Brian?' he said to the dog. 'And so your ears are sharper than Miss Ingot's, old fellow. It's a mighty queer thing to think of, being favoured with a visit from a Banshee in Gerrard Street; and as the lady has travelled so far, I only wish I knew whether there is any sort of refreshment she would like to take after her long journey.'

He spoke loudly, and with a certain mocking defiance, seeming to think the phantom he addressed would reply; but when he stopped at the end of his sentence, no sound came through the stillness. There was a dead silence in the room—a silence broken only by the falling of cinders on the hearth and the breathing of his dog.

'If my visitor would tell me,' he proceeded, 'for whom this lamentation is being made, whether for myself, or for for some member of my illustrious family, I should feel immensely obliged. It seems too much honour for a poor surgeon to have such attention paid him. Good Heavens! What is that?' he exclaimed, as a ring, loud and peremptory, woke all the echoes in the house, and brought his housekeeper, in a state of distressing dishabille, 'out of her warm bed', as she subsequently stated, to the head of the staircase.

Across the hall Hertford O'Donnell strode, relieved at the prospect of speaking to any living being. He took no precaution of putting up the chain, but flung the door wide. A dozen burglars would have proved welcome in comparison with that ghostly intruder he had been interviewing; therefore, as has been said, he threw the door wide, admitting a rush of wet, cold air, which made poor Mrs. Coles' few remaining teeth chatter in her head.

'Who is there? What do you want?' asked the surgeon, seeing no person, and hearing no voice. 'Who is there? Why the devil can't you speak?'

When even this polite exhortation failed to elicit an answer, he passed out into the night and looked up the

141

street and down the street, to see nothing but the driving rain and the blinking lights.

'If this goes on much longer I shall soon think I must be either mad or drunk,' he muttered, as he re-entered the house and locked and bolted th door once more.

'Lord's sake! What is the matter, sir?' asked Mrs. Coles, from the upper flight, careful only to reveal the borders of her night-cap to Mr. O'Donnell's admiring gaze. 'Is anybody killed? Have you to go out, sir?'

'It was only a run-away ring,' he answered, trying to reassure himself with an explanation he did not in his heart believe.

'Run-away—I'd run away them!' murmured Mrs. Coles, as she retired to the conjugal couch, where Coles was, to quote her own expression, 'snoring like a pig through it all'.

Almost immediately afterwards she heard her master ascend the stairs and close his bedroom door.

'Madam will surely be too much of a gentlewoman to intrude here,' thought the surgeon, scoffing even at his own fears; but when he lay down he did not put out his light, and made Brian leap up and crouch on the coverlet beside him.

The man was fairly frightened, and would have thought it no discredit to his manhood to acknowledge as much. He was not afraid of death, he was not afraid of trouble, he was not afraid of danger; but he was afraid of the Banshee; and as he lay with his hand on the dog's head, he recalled the many stories he had been told concerning this family retainer in the days of his youth.

He had not thought about her for years and years. Never before had he heard her voice himself. When his brother died she had not thought it necessary to travel up to Dublin and give him notice of the impending catastrophe. 'If she had, I would have gone down to

142

Calgillan, and perhaps saved his life,' considered the surgeon. 'I wonder who this is for? If for me, that will settle my debts and my marriage. If I could be quite certain it was either of the old people, I would start tomorrow.'

Then vaguely his mind wandered on to think of every Banshee story he had ever heard in his life. About the beautiful lady with the wreath of flowers, who sat on the rocks below Red Castle, in the County Antrim, crying till one of the sons died for love of her; about the Round Chamber at Dunluce, which was swept clean by the Banshee every night; about the bed in a certain great house in Ireland, which was slept in constantly, although no human being ever passed in or out after dark; about that General Officer who, the night before Waterloo, said to a friend, 'I have heard the Banshee, and shall not come off the field alive tomorrow; break the news gently to poor Carry'; and who, nevertheless, coming safe off the field, had subsequently news about poor Carry broken tenderly and pitifully to him; about the lad, who, aloft in the rigging, hearing through the night a sobbing and wailing coming over the waters, went down to the captain and told him he was afraid they were somehow out of their reckoning, just in time to save the ship, which, when morning broke, they found but for his warning would have been on the rocks. It was blowing great guns, and the sea was all in a fret and turmoil, and they could sometimes see in the trough of the waves, as down a valley, the cruel black reefs they had escaped.

On deck the captain stood speaking to the boy who had saved them, and asking how he knew of their danger; and when the lad told him, the captain laughed, and said her ladyship had been outwitted that time.

But the boy answered, with a grave shake of his head, that the warning was either for him or his, and that if he got safe to port there would be bad tidings waiting for him from home; whereupon the captain bade him go below, and get some brandy and lie down.

He got the brandy, and he lay down, but he never rose again; and when the storm abated—when a great calm succeeded to the previous tempest—there was a very solemn funeral at sea; and on their arrival at Liverpool the captain took a journey to Ireland to tell a widowed mother how her only son died, and to bear his few effects to the poor desolate soul.

And Hertford O'Donnell thought again about his own father riding full-chase across country, and hearing, as he galloped by a clump of plantation, something like a sobbing and wailing. The hounds were in full cry, but he still felt, as he afterwards expressed it, that there was something among those trees he could not pass; and so he jumped off his horse, and hung the reins over the branch of a Scotch fir, and beat the cover well, but not a thing could he find in it.

Then, for the first time in his life, Miles O'Donnell turned his horse's head *from* the hunt, and, within a mile of Calgillan, met a man running to tell him his brother's gun had burst, and injured him mortally.

And he remembered the story also, of how Mary O'Donnell, his great aunt, being married to a young Englishman, heard the Banshee as she sat one evening waiting for his return; and of how she, thinking the bridge by which he often came home unsafe for horse and man, went out in a great panic, to meet and entreat him to go round by the main road for her sake. Sir Edward was riding along in the moonlight, making straight for the bridge, when he beheld a figure dressed all in white crossing it. Then there was a crash, and the figure disappeared.

The lady was rescued and brought back to the hall; but next morning there were two dead bodies within its

144

walls—those of Lady Eyreton and her still-born son.

Quicker than I write them, these memories chased one another through Hertford O'Donnell's brain; and there was one more terrible memory than any, which would recur to him, concerning an Irish nobleman who, seated alone in his great town-house in London, heard the Banshee, and rushed out to get rid of the phantom, which wailed in his ear, nevertheless, as he strode down Piccadilly. And then the surgeon remembered how that nobleman went with a friend to the Opera, feeling sure that there no Banshee, unless she had a box, could find admittance, until suddenly he heard her singing up amongst the highest part of the scenery, with a terrible mournfulness, and a pathos which made the prima donna's tenderest notes seem harsh by comparison.

As he came out, some quarrel arose between him and a famous fire-eater, against whom he stumbled; and the result was that the next afternoon there was a new Lord —— vice Lord ——, killed in a duel with Captain Bravo.

Memories like these are not the most enlivening possible; they are apt to make a man fanciful, and nervous, and wakeful; but as time ran on, Hertford O'Donnell fell asleep, with his candle still burning, and Brian's cold nose pressed against his hand.

He dreamt of his mother's family—the Hertfords of Artingbury, Yorkshire, far-off relatives of Lord Hertford—so far off that even Mrs. O'Donnell held no clue to the genealogical maze.

He thought he was at Artingbury, fishing; that it was a misty summer morning, and the fish rising beautifully. In his dreams he hooked one after another, and the boy who was with him threw them into the basket.

At last there was one more difficult to land than the others; and the boy, in his eagerness to watch the sport, drew nearer and nearer to the brink, while the fisher, intent on his prey, failed to notice his companion's danger.

Suddenly there was a cry, a splash, and the boy disappeared from sight.

Next instance he rose again, however, and then, for the first time, Hertford O'Donnell saw his face.

It was one he knew well.

In a moment he plunged into the water, and struck out for the lad. He had him by the hair, he was turning to bring him back to land, when the stream suddenly changed into a wide, wild, shoreless sea, where the billows were chasing one another with a mad demoniac mirth.

For a while O'Donnell kept the lad and himself afloat. They were swept under the waves, and came up again, only to see larger waves rushing towards them; but through all, the surgeon never loosened his hold, until a tremendous billow, engulfing them both, tore the boy from his grasp.

With the horror of his dream upon him he awoke, to hear a voice quite distinctly:

'Go to the hospital—go at once!'

The surgeon started up in bed, rubbing his eyes, and looked around. The candle was flickering faintly in its socket. Brian, with his ears pricked forward, had raised his head at his master's sudden movement.

Everything was quiet, but still those words were ringing in his ear:

'Go to the hospital—go at once!'

The tremendous peal of the bell over night, and this sentence, seemed to be simultaneous.

That he was wanted at Guy's—wanted imperatively—came to O'Donnell like an inspiration. Neither sense nor reason had anything to do with the conviction that roused him out of bed, and made him dress as speedily

146

as possible, and grope his way down the staircase, Brian following.

He opened the front door, and passed out into the darkness. The rain was over, and the stars were shining as he pursued his way down Newport Market, and thence, winding in and out in a south-easterly direction, through Lincoln's Inn Fields and Old Square to Chancery Lane, whence he proceeded to St. Paul's.

Along the deserted streets he resolutely continued his walk. He did not know what he was going to Guy's for. Some instinct was urging him on, and he neither strove to combat nor control it. Only once did the thought of turning back cross his mind, and that was the archway leading into Old Square. There he had paused for a moment, asking himself whether he were not gone stark, staring mad; but Guy's seemed preferable to the haunted house in Gerrard Street, and he walked resolutely on, determined to say, if any surprise were expressed at his appearance, that he had been sent for.

Sent for?—yea, truly; but by whom?

On through Cannon Street; on over London Bridge, where the lights flickered in the river, and the sullen splash of the water flowing beneath the arches, washing the stone piers, could be heard, now the human din was hushed and lulled to sleep. On, thinking of many things: of the days of his youth; of his dead brother; of his father's heavily-encumbered estate; of the fortune his mother had vowed she would leave to some charity rather than to him, if he refused to marry according to her choice; of his wild life in London; of the terrible cry he had heard over-night—that unearthly wail which he could not drive from his memory even when he entered Guy's, and confronted the porter, who said:

'You have been sent for, sir; did you meet the messenger?'

Like one in a dream, Hertford O'Donnell heard him;

147

like one in a dream, also, he asked what was the matter.

'Bad accident, sir; fire; fell off a balcony—unsafe—old building. Mother and child—a son; child with compound fracture of thigh.'

This, the joint information of porter and house-surgeon, mingled together, and made a boom in Mr. O'Donnell's ears like the sound of the sea breaking on a shingly shore.

Only one sentence he understood properly—'Immediate amputation necessary.' At this point he grew cool; he was the careful, cautious, successful surgeon, in a moment.

'The child you say?' he answered. 'Let me see him.'

The Guy's Hospital of today may be different to the Guy's Hertford O'Donnell knew so well. Railways have, I believe, swept away the old operating room; railways may have changed the position of the former accident ward, to reach which, in the days of which I am writing, the two surgeons had to pass a staircase leading to the opper stories.

On the lower step of this staircase, partially in shadow, Hertford O'Donnell beheld, as he came forward, an old woman seated.

An old woman with streaming grey hair, with attenuated arms, with head bowed forward, with scanty clothing, with bare feet; who never looked up at their approach, but sat unnoticing, shaking her head and wringing her hands in an extremity of despair.

'Who is that?' asked Mr. O'Donnell, almost involuntarily.

'Who is what?' demanded his companion.

'That—that woman,' was the reply.

'What woman?'

'There—are you blind?—seated on the bottom step of the staircase. What is she doing?' persisted Mr. O'Donnell.

148

'There is no woman near us,' his companion answered, looking at the rising surgeon very much as though he suspected him of seeing double.

'No woman!' scoffed Hertford. 'Do you expect me to disbelieve the evidence of my own eyes?' and he walked up to the figure, meaning to touch it.

But as he assayed to do so, the woman seemed to rise in the air and float away, with her arms stretched high up-over her head, uttering such a wail of pain, and agony, and distress, as caused the Irishman's blood to curdle.

'My God! Did you hear that?' he said to his companion.

'What?' was the reply.

Then, although he knew the sound had fallen on deaf ears, he answered:

'The wail of the Banshee! Some of my people are doomed!'

'I trust not,' answered the house-surgeon, who had an idea, nevertheless, that Hertford O'Donnell's Banshee lived in a whisky bottle, and would at some remote day make an end to the rising and clever operator.

With nerves utterly shaken, Mr. O'Donnell walked forward to the accident ward. There with his face shaded from the light, lay his patient—a young boy, with a compound fracture of the thigh.

In that ward, in the face of actual danger or pain capable of relief the surgeon had never known faltering or fear; and now he carefully examined the injury, felt the pulse, inquired as to the treatment pursued, and ordered the sufferer to be carried to the operating room.

While he was looking out his instruments he heard the boy lying on the table murmur faintly:

'Tell her not to cry so—tell her not to cry.'

'What is he talking about?' Hertford O'Donnell inquired.

149

'The nurse says he has been speaking about some woman crying ever since he came in—his mother, most likely,' answered one of the attendants.

'He is delirious then?' observed the surgeon.

'No, sir,' pleaded the boy, excitedly, 'no; it is that woman—that woman with the grey hair. I saw her looking from the upper window before the balcony gave way. She has never left me since, and she won't be quiet, wringing her hands and crying.'

'Can you see her now?' Hertford O'Donnell inquired, stepping to the side of the table. 'Point out where she is.'

Then the lad stretched forth a feeble finger in the direction of the door, where clearly, as he had seen her seated on the stairs, the surgeon saw a woman standing —a woman with grey hair and scanty clothing, and upstretched arms and bare feet.

'A word with you, sir,' O'Donnell said to the house-surgeon, drawing him back from the table. 'I cannot perform this operation: send for some other person. I am ill; I am incapable.'

'But,' pleaded the other, 'there is no time to get anyone else. We sent for Mr. West, before we troubled you, but he was out of town, and all the rest of the surgeons live so far away. Mortification may set in at any moment and——'.

'Do you think you require to teach me my business?' was the reply. 'I know the boy's life hangs on a thread, and that is the very reason I cannot operate. I am not fit for it. I tell you I have seen tonight that which unnerves me utterly. My hand is not steady. Send for someone else without delay. Say I am ill—dead!—what you please. Heavens! There she is again, right over the boy! Do you hear her?' and Hertford O'Donnell fell fainting on the floor.

150

How long he lay in that death-like swoon I cannot say; but when he returned to consciousness, the principal physician of Guy's was standing beside him in the cold grey light of the Christmas morning.

'The boy?' murmured O'Donnell, faintly.

'Now, my dear fellow, keep yourself quiet,' was the reply.

'The boy?' he repeated, irritably. 'Who operated?'

'No one,' Dr. Lanson answered. 'It would have been useless cruelty. Mortification had set in and—'

Hertford O'Donnell turned his face to the wall, and his friend could not see it.

'Do not distress yourself,' went on the physician, kindly. 'Allington says he could not have survived the operation in any case. He was quite delirious from the first, raving about a woman with grey hair and—'

'I know,' Hertford O'Donnell interrupted; 'and the boy had a mother, they told me, or I dreamt it.'

'Yes, she was bruised and shaken, but not seriously injured.'

'Has she blue eyes and fair hair—fair hair all rippling and wavy? Is she white as a lily, with just a faint flush of colour in her cheek? Is she young and trusting and innocent? No; I am wandering. She must be nearly thirty now. Go, for God's sake, and tell me if you can find a woman you could imagine having once been as a girl such as I describe.'

'Irish?' asked the doctor; and O'Donnell made a gesture of assent.

'It is she then,' was the reply, 'a woman with the face of an angel.'

'A woman who should have been my wife,' the surgeon answered; 'whose child was my son.'

'Lord help you!' ejaculated the doctor. Then Hertford O'Donnell raised himself from the sofa where they had laid him, and told his companion the story of his life

151

—how there had been bitter feud between his people and her people—how they were divided by old animosities and by difference of religion—how they had met by stealth, and exchanged rings and vows, all for naught— how his family had insulted hers, so that her father, wishful for her to marry a kinsman of his own, bore her off to a far-away land, and made her write him a letter of eternal farewell—how his own parents had kept all knowledge of the quarrel from him till she was utterly beyond his reach—how they had vowed to discard him unless he agreed to marry according to their wishes— how he left home, and came to London, and sought his fortune. All this Hertford O'Donnell repeated; and when he had finished, the bells were ringing for morning service—ringing loudly, ringing joyfully, 'Peace on earth, goodwill towards men'.

But there was little peace that morning for Hertford O'Donnell. He had to look on the face of his dead son, wherein he beheld, as though reflected, the face of the boy in his dream.

Afterwards, stealthily he followed his friend, and beheld, with her eyes closed, her cheeks pale and pinched, her hair thinner but still falling like a veil over her, the love of his youth, the only woman he had ever loved devotedly and unselfishly.

There is little space left her to tell of how the two met at last—of how the stone of the years seemed suddenly rolled away from the tomb of their past, and their youth arose and returned to them, even amid their tears.

She had been true to him, through persecution, through contumely, through kindness, which was more trying; through shame, and grief, and poverty, she had been loyal to the lover of her youth; and before the New Year dawned there came a letter from Calgillan, saying that the Banshee's wail had been heard there, and praying Hertford, if he were still alive, to let bygones be bygones, in consideration of the long years of estrangement—the anguish and remorse of his afflicted parents.

More than that. Hertford O'Donnell, if a reckless man, was honourable; and so, on the Christmas Day when he was to have proposed for Miss Ingot, he went to that lady, and told her how he had wooed and won, in the years of his youth, one who after many days was miraculously restored to him; and from the hour in which he took her into his confidence, he never thought her either vulgar or foolish, but rather he paid homage to the woman who, when she had heard the whole tale repeated, said, simply, 'Ask her to come to me till you can claim her—and God bless you both!'

THE LEGEND OF FIN M'COUL

by William Carleton

WILLIAM CARLETON *(1794-1869) rose from a humble background—he was one of a poor farmer's fourteen children—to a position of pre-eminence in Irish letters. Dogged for much of his life by money troubles, he nevertheless wrote widely on Irish life and customs; of his famous collection,* Traits and Stories of the Irish Peasantry, *a contemporary critic said 'there is nothing in Irish literature within reasonable distance of them for completeness, variety, character-drawing, humour, pathos and dramatic power'. The story here of the legendary Irish hero, Fin M'Coul, is taken from another of Carleton's collections and admirably demonstrates his ability to recreate the climates of ancient fantasy and myth.*

What Irish man, woman, or child has not heard of our renowned Hibernian Hercules, the great and glorious Fin M'Coul? Not one, from Cape Clear to the Giant's Causeway, nor from that back again to Cape Clear. And, by-the-way, speaking of the Giant's Causeway brings me at once to the beginning of my story. Well, it so happened that Fin and his gigantic relatives were all working at the Causeway, in order to make a bridge, or what was still better, a good stout pad-road, across to Scotland; when Fin, who was very fond of his wife Oonagh, took it into his head that he would go home and see how the poor woman got on in his absence. To be sure, Fin was a true Irishman, and so the sorrow

154

thing in life brought him back, only to see that she was snug and comfortable, and, above all things, that she got her rest well at night; for he knew that the poor woman, when he was with her, used to be subject to nightly qualms and configurations, and kept him very anxious, decent man, striving to keep her up to the good spirits and health that she had when they were first married. So, accordingly, he pulled up a firtree, and, after lopping off the roots and branches, made a walking stick of it, and set out on his way to Oonagh.

Oonagh, or rather Fin, lived at this time on the very tip-tip of Knockmany Hill, which faces a cousin of its own called Cullamore, that rises up, half-hill, half-mountain, on the opposite side—east-east by south, as the sailors say, when they wish to puzzle a landsman.

Now, the truth is, for it must come out, that honest Fin's affection for his wife, though cordial enough in itself, was by no manner of means the real cause of his journey home. There was at that time another giant, named Cucullin—some say he was Irish, and some say he was Scotch—but whether Scotch or Irish, sorrow doubt of it but he was a *targer*. No other giant of the day could stand before him; and such was his strength, that when well vexed, he could give a stamp that shook the country about him. The fame and name of him went far and near; and nothing in the shape of a man, it was said, had any chance with him in a fight. Whether the story is true or not, I cannot say, but the report went that, by one blow of his fists he flattened a thunderbolt, and kept it in his pocket, in the shape of a pancake, to show to all his enemies, when they were about to fight him. Undoubtedly he had given every giant in Ireland a considerable beating, barring Min W'Coul himself; and he swore, by the solemn contents of Moll Kelly's Primer, that he would never rest, night or day, winter or summer, till he would serve Fin with the same sauce, if he could catch him. Fin, however, who no doubt was the cock of the walk on his own dunghill, had a strong disinclination to meet a giant who could make a young earthquake, or flatten a thunderbolt when he was angry; so he accordingly kept dodging about from place to place, not much to his credit as a Trojan, to be sure, whenever he happened to get the hard word that Cucullin was on the scent of him. This, then, was the marrow of the whole movement, although he put it on his anxiety to see Oonagh; and I am not saying but that there was some truth in that too. However, the short and long of it was, with reverence be it spoken, that he heard Cucullin was coming to the Causeway to have a trial of strength with him; and he was naturally enough seized, in consequence, with a very warm and sudden fit of affection for his wife, poor woman, who was delicate in her health, and leading, besides, a very lonely, uncomfortable life of it (he assured them) in his absence. He accordingly pulled up the fir tree, as I said before, and having *snedded* it into a walking-stick, set out on his affectionate travels to see his darling Oonagh on the top of Knockmany, by the way.

In truth, to state the suspicions of the country at the time, the people wondered very much why it was that Fin selected such a windy spot for his dwelling-house, and they even went so far as to tell him as much.

'What can you mean, Mr. M'Coul,' said they, 'by pitching your tent upon the top of Knockmany, where you never are without a breeze, day or night, winter or summer, and where you're often forced to take your nightcap without either going to bed or turning up your little finger; ay, an' where, besides this, there's the sorrow's own want of water?'

'Why,' said Fin, 'ever since I was the height of a round tower, I was known to be fond of having a good prospect of my own; and where the dickens, neighbours,

156

could I find a better spot for a good prespect than the top of Knockmany? As for water, I am sinking a pump, and, please goodness, as soon as the Causeway's made, I intend to finish it.'

Now, this was more of Fin's philosophy; for the real state of the case was, that he pitched upon the top of Knockmany in order that he might be able to see Cucullin coming towards the house, and, of course, that he himself might go to look after his distant transactions in other parts of the country, rather than—but no matter —we do not wish to be too hard on Fin. All we have to say is, that if he wanted a spot from which to keep a sharp look-out—and between ourselves, he did want it grievously—barring Slieve Croob, or Slieve Donard, or its own cousin, Cullamore, he could not find a neater or more convenient situation for it in the sweet and sagacious province of Ulster.

'God save all here!' said Fin, good-humouredly, on putting his honest face into his own door.

'Musha, Fin, avick, an' you're welcome home to your own Oonagh, you darlin' bully.' Here followed a smack that is said to have made the water of the lake at the bottom of the hill curl, as it were, with kindness and sympathy.

'Faith,' said Fin, 'beautiful; an' how are you, Oonagh and how did you sport your figure during my absence, my bilberry?'

'Never a merrier—as bouncing a grass widow as ever there was in swett "Tyrone among the bushes".'

Fin gave a short, good-humoured cough, and laughed most heartily, to show her how much he was delighted that she made herself happy in his absence.

'An' what brought you home so soon, Fin?' said she.

'Why, avourneen,' said Fin, putting in his answer in the proper way, 'never the thing but the purest of love

157

and affection for yourself. Sure you know that's truth, anyhow, Oonagh.'

Fin spent two or three happy days with Oonagh, and felt himself very comfortable, considering the dread he had of Cucullin. This, however, grew upon him so much that his wife could not but perceive something lay on his mind which he kept altogether to himself. Let a woman alone, in the meantime, for ferreting or wheedling a secret out of her good man, when she wishes. Fin was a proof of this.

'It's this Cucullin,' said he, 'that's troubling me. When the fellow gets angry, and begins to stamp, he'll shake you a whole townland; and it's well known that he can stop a thunderbolt, for he always carries one about him in the shape of a pancake, to show to anyone that might misdoubt it.'

As he spoke, he clapped his thumb in his mouth, which he always did when he wanted to prophesy, or to know anything that happened in his absence; and the wife, who knew what he did it for, said, very sweetly:

'Fin, darling, I hope you don't bite your thumb at me, dear?'

'No,' said Fin; 'but I bite my thumb, acushla,' said he.

'Yes, jewel; but take care and don't draw blood,' said she. 'Ah, Fin! don't, my bully—don't.'

'He's coming,' said Fin; 'I see him below Dungannon.'

'Thank goodness, darling, dear! an' who is it, avick? Glory be to God!'

'That baste, Cucullin,' replied Fin; 'and how to manage I don't know. If I run away, I am disgraced; and I know that sooner or later I must meet him, for my thumb tells me so.'

'When will he be here?' said she.

'Tomorrow, about two o'clock,' replied Fin, with a

groan.

'Well, my bully, don't be cast down,' said Oonagh; 'depend on me, and maybe I'll bring you better out of this scrape than ever you could bring yourself, by your rule o'thumb.'

This quietened Fin's heart very much, for he knew that Oonagh was hand and glove with the fairies; and, indeed, to tell the truth, she was supposed to be a fairy herself. If she was, however, she must have been a kind-hearted one, for by all accounts, she never did anything but good in the neighbourhood.

Now it so happened that Oonagh had a sister named Granua, living opposite them, on the very top of Cullamore, which I have mentioned already, and this Granua was quite as powerful as herself. The beautiful valley that lies between them is not more than about three or four miles broad, so that of a summer's evening, Granua and Oonagh were able to hold many an agreeable conversation across it, from the one hill-top to the other. Upon this occasion Oonagh resolved to consult her sister as to what was best to be done in the difficulty that surrounded them.

'Granua,' said she, 'are you at home?'

'No,' said the other; 'I'm picking bilberries in Althadhawan' (*Anglicé*, the Devil's Glen).

'Well,' said Oonagh, 'get up to the top of Cullamore, look about you and then tell us what you see.'

'Very well,' replied Granua; after a few minutes, 'I am there now.'

'What do you see?' asked the other.

'Goodness be about us!' exclaimed Granua, 'I see the biggest giant that ever was known coming up from Dungannon.'

'Ay,' said Oonagh, 'there's our difficulty. That giant is the great Cucullin; and he's now comin' up to leather Fin. What's to be done?'

159

'I'll call to him,' she replied, 'to come up to Cullamore and refresh himself, and maybe that will give you and Fin time to think of some plan to get yourselves out of the scrape. But,' she proceeded, 'I'm short of butter, having in the house only a half-a-dozen firkins, and as I'm to have a few giants and giantesses to spend the evenin' with me, I'd feel thankful, Oonagh, if you'd throw me up fifteen or sixteen tubs, or the largest miscaun you have got, and you'll oblige me very much.'

'I'll do that with a heart and a-half,' replied Oonagh; 'and, indeed, Granua, I feel myself under great obligations to you for your kindness in keeping him off of us till we see what can be done; for what would become of us all if anything happened to Fin, poor man.'

She accordingly got the largest miscaun of butter she had—which might be about the weight of a couple of dozen millstones, so that you may easily judge of its size—and calling up to her sister, 'Granua,' said she, 'are you ready? I'm going to throw you up a miscaun, so be prepared to catch it.'

'I will,' said the other; 'a good throw now, and take care it does not fall short.'

Oonagh threw it; but, in consequence of her anxiety about Fin and Cucullin, she forgot to say the charm that was to send it up, so that, instead of reaching Cullamore, as she expected, it fell about half-way between the two hills, at the edge of the Broad Bog near Augher.

'My curse upon you!' she exclaimed; 'you've disgraced me. I now change you into a grey stone. Lie there as a testimony of what has happened; and may evil betide the first living man that will ever attempt to remove or injure you!'

And, sure enough, there it lies to this day, with the mark of the four fingers and thumb imprinted in it, exactly as it came out of her hand.

'Never mind,' said Granua, 'I must only do the best

160

I can with Cucullin. If all fail, I'll give him a cast of
heather broth to keep the wind out of his stomach, or
a panada of oak-bark to draw it in a bit; but, above all
things, think of some plan to get Fin out of the scrape
he's in, otherwise he's a lost man. You know you used
to be sharp and ready-witted; and my own opinion,
Oonagh, is, that it will go hard with you, or you'll outdo
Cucullin yet.'

She then made a high smoke on the top of the hill,
after which she put her finger in her mouth, and gave
three whistles, and by that Cucullin knew he was invited to Cullamore—for this was the way that the Irish
long ago gave a sign to all strangers and travellers, to
let them know they were welcome to come and take
share of whatever was going.

In the meantime, Fin was very melancholy, and did
not know what to do, or how to act at all. Cucullin was
an ugly customer, no doubt, to meet with; and, moreover, the idea of the confounded 'cake' aforesaid flattened the very heart within him. What chance could he
have, strong and brave though he was, with a man who
could, when put in a passion, walk the country into
earthquakes and knock thunderbolts into pancakes?
The thing was impossible; and Fin knew not on what
hand to turn him. Right or left—backward or forward—
where to go he could form no guess whatsoever.

'Oonagh,' said he, 'can you do nothing for me?
Where's all your invention? Am I to be skivered like
a rabbit before your eyes, and to have my name disgraced forever in the sight of all my tribe, and me the
best man among them? How am I to fight this man-
mountain—this huge cross between an earthquake and
a thunderbolt?—with a pancake in his pocket that was
once—'

'Be easy, Fin,' replied Oonagh; 'troth, I'm ashamed
of you. Keep your toe in your pump, will you? Talking

of pancakes, maybe we'll give him as good as any he brings with him—thunderbolt or otherwise. If I don't treat him to as smart feeding as he's got this many a day, never trust Oonagh again. Leave him to me, and do just as I bid you.'

This relieved Fin very much; for, after all, he had great confidence in his wife, knowing, as he did, that she had got him out of many a quandry before. The present, however, was the greatest of all; but still he began to get courage, and was able to eat his victuals as usual. Oonagh then drew the nine woollen threads of different colours, which she always did to find out the best way of succeeding in anything of importance she went about. She then platted them into three plaits with three colours in each, putting one on her right arm, one round her heart, and the third round her right ankle, for then she knew that nothing could fail with her that she undertook.

Having everything now prepared, she went round to the neighbours and borrowed one-and-twenty iron griddles, which she took and kneaded into the hearts of one-and-twenty cakes of bread, and these she baked on a fire in the usual way, setting them aside in the cupboard according as they were done. She then put down a large pot of new milk, which she made into curds and whey, and gave Fin due instructions how to use the curds when Cucullin should come. Having done all this, she sat down quite contented, waiting for his arrival on the next day about two o'clock, that being the hour at which he was expected—for Fin knew as much by the sucking of his thumb. Now, this was a curious property that Fin's thumb had; but, notwithstanding all the wisdom and logic he used, to suck out of it, it could never have stood to him here were it not for the wit of his wife. In this very thing, moreover, he was very much resembled by his great foe, Cucullin, for it was well known that the huge strength he possessed all lay in the middle finger of his right hand, and that, if he happened by any mischance to lose it, he was no more, notwithstanding his bulk, than a common man.

At length, the next day, he was seen coming across the valley, and Oonagh knew that it was time to commence operations. She immediately made the cradle, and desired Fin to lie down in it, and cover himself up with the clothes.

'You must pass for your own child,' she said; 'so just lie there snug, and say nothing, but be guided by me.' This, to be sure, was wormwood to Fin—I mean going into the cradle in such a cowardly manner—but he knew Oonagh well; and finding that he had nothing else for it, with a very rueful face he gathered himself into it, and lay snug, as she had desired him.

About two o'clock, as he had been expected, Cucullin came in. 'God save all here!' said he; 'is this where the great Fin M'Coul lives?'

'Indeed it is, honest man,' replied Oonagh; 'God save you kindly—won't you be sitting?'

'Thank you, ma'am,' says he, sitting down; 'you're Mrs. M'Coul, I suppose?'

'I am,' said she; 'and I have no reason, I hope, to be ashamed of my husband.'

'No,' said the other, 'he has the name of being the strongest and bravest man in Ireland; but for all that, there's a man not far from you that's very desirous of taking a shake with him. Is he at home?'

'Why, then, no,' she replied; 'and if ever a man left his house in a fury, he did. It appears that someone told him of a big basthoon of a giant called Cucullin being down at the Causeway to look for him, and so he set out there to try if he could catch him. Troth, I hope, for the poor giant's sake, he won't meet with him, for if he does, Fin will make paste of him at once.'

'Well,' said the other, 'I am Cucullin, and I have been seeking him these twelve months, but he always kept clear of me; and I will never rest night or day till I lay my hands on him.'

At this Oonagh set up a loud laugh, of great contempt, by-the-way, and looked at him as if he was only a mere handful of a man.

'Did you ever see Fin?' said she changing her manner all at once.

'How could I?' said he; 'he always took care to keep his distance.'

'I thought so,' she replied; 'I judged as much; and if you take my advice, you poor-looking creature, you'll pray night and day that you may never see him, for I tell you it will be a black day for you when you do. But, in the meantime, you perceive that the wind's on the door, and as Fin himself is from home, maybe you'd be civil enough to turn the house, for it's always what Fin does when he's here.'

This was a startler even to Cucullin; but he got up, however, and after pulling the middle finger of his right hand until it cracked three times, he went outside, and getting his arms about the house, completely turned it as she had wished. When Fin saw this, he felt a certain description of moisture, which shall be nameless, oozing out through every pore of his skin; but Oonagh, depending upon her woman's wit, felt not a whit daunted.

'Arrah, then,' said she, 'as you are so civil, maybe you'd do another obliging turn for us, as Fin's not here to do it himself. You see, after this long stretch of dry weather we've had, we feel very badly off for want of water. Now, Fin says there's a fine spring-well somewhere under the rocks behind the hill here below, and it was his intention to pull them asunder; but having heard of you he left the place in such a fury, that he never thought of it. Now, if you try to find it, troth I'd

164

feel it a kindness.'

She then brought Cucullin down to see the place, which was then all one solid rock; and, after looking at it for some time, he cracked his right middle finger nine time, and, stooping down, tore a cleft about four hundred feet deep, and a quarter of a mile in length, which has since been christened by the name of Lumford's Glen. This feat nearly threw Oonagh herself off her guard; but what won't a woman's sagacity and presence of mind accomplish?

'You'll now come in,' said she, 'and eat a bit of such humble fare as we can give you. Fin, even although he and you are enemies, would scorn not to treat you kindly in his own house; and, indeed, if I didn't do it even in his absence, he would not be pleased with me.'

She accordingly brought him in, and placing half-a-dozen of the cakes we spoke of before him, together with a can or two of butter, a side of boiled bacon, and a stack of cabbage, she desired him to help himself—for this, be it known, was long before the invention of potatoes. Cucullin, who, by the way, was a glutton as well as a hero, put one of the cakes in his mouth to take a huge whack out of it, when both Fin and Oonagh were stunned with a noise that resembled something between a growl and a yell. 'Blood and fury!' he shouted; 'how is this? Here are two of my teeth out! What kind of bread is this you gave me?'

'What's the matter?' said Oonagh coolly.

'Matter!' shouted the other again; 'why, here are the two best teeth in my head gone.'

'Why,' said she, 'that's Fin's bread—the only bread he ever eats when at home; but, indeed, I forgot to tell you that nobody can eat it but himself, and that child in the cradle there. I thought, however, that, as you were reported to be rather a stout little fellow of your size, you might be able to manage it, and I did not wish to affront a man that thinks himself able to fight Fin. Here's another cake—maybe it's not so hard as that.'

Cucullin at the moment was not only hungry, but ravenous, so he accordingly made a fresh set at the second cake, and immediately another yell was heard twice as loud as the first. 'Thunder and giblets!' he roared, 'take your bread out of this, or I will not have a tooth in my head; there's another pair of them gone!'

'Well, honest man,' replied Oonagh, 'if you're not able to eat the bread, say so quietly, and don't be wakening the child in the cradle there. There, now, he's awake upon me.'

Fin now gave a skirl that startled the giant, as coming from such a youngster as he was represented to be. 'Mother,' said he, 'I'm hungry—get me something to eat.' Oonagh went over, and putting into his hand a cake *that had no griddle in it*, Fin, whose appetite in the meantime was sharpened by what he saw going forward, soon made it disappear. Cucullin was thunderstruck, and secretly thanked his stars that he had the good fortune to miss meeting Fin, for, as he said to himself, I'd have no chance with a man who could eat such bread as that, which even his son that's but in his cradle can munch before my eyes.

'I'd like to take a glimpse at the lad in the cradle,' said he to Oonagh; 'for I can tell you that the infant who can manage that nutriment is no joke to look at, or to feed of a scarce summer.'

'With all the veins of my heart,' replied Oonagh; 'get up, acushla, and show this decent little man something that won't be unworthy of your father, Fin M'Coul.'

Fin, who was dressed for the occasion as much like a boy as possible, got up, and bringing Cucullin out, 'Are you strong?' said he.

'Thunder an' ounds!' exclaimed the other, 'what a voice in so small a chap!'

166

'Are you strong?' said Fin again; 'are you able to squeeze water out of that white stone?' he asked, putting one into Cucullin's hand. The latter squeezed and squeezed the stone, but to no purpose; he might pull the rocks of Lumford's Glen asunder, and flatten a thunderbolt, but to squeeze water out of a white stone was beyond his strength. Fin eyed him with great contempt, as he kept straining and squeezing and squeezing and straining, till he got black in the face with the efforts.

'Ah, you're a poor creature!' said Fin. 'You a giant! Give me the stone here, and when I'll show you what Fin's little son can do; you may then judge of what my daddy himself is.'

Fin then took the stone, and slyly exchanging it for the curds, he squeezed the latter until the whey, as clear as water, oozed out in a little shower from his hand.

'I'll now go in,' said he, 'to my cradle; for I scorn to lose my time with anyone that's not able to eat my daddy's bread, or squeeze water out of a stone. Bedad, you had better be off out of this before he comes back; for if he catches you, it's in flummery he'd have you in two minutes.'

Cucullin, seeing what he had seen, was of the same opinion himself; his knees knocked together with the terror of Fin's return, and he accordingly hastened in to bid Oonagh farewell, and to assure her, that from that day out, he never wished to hear of, much less to see, her husband. 'I admit fairly that I'm not a match for him,' said he, 'strong as I am; tell him I will avoid him as I would the plague, and that I will make myself scarce in this part of the country while I live.'

Fin, in the meantime, had gone into the cradle, where he lay very quietly, his heart at his mouth with delight that Cucullin was about to take his departure, without discovering the tricks that had been played off on him.

167

'It's well for you,' said Oonagh, 'that he doesn't happen to be here, for it's nothing but hawk's meat he'd make of you.'

'I know that,' says Cucullin; 'devil a thing else he'd make of me; but before I go, will you let me feel what kind of teeth they are that can eat griddle-bread like *that*?'—and he pointed to it as he spoke.

'With all pleasure in life,' said she, 'only they're far back in his head, you must put your finger a good way in.'

Cucullin was surprised to find such a powerful set of grinders in one so young; but he was still much more so on finding, when he took his hand from Fin's mouth, that he had left the very finger upon which his whole strength depended, behind him. He gave one loud groan, and fell down at once with terror and weakness. This was all Fin wanted, who now knew that his most powerful and bitterest enemy was completely at his mercy. He instantly started out of the cradle, and in a few minutes the great Cucullin, that was for such a length of time the terror of him and all his followers, lay a corpse before him. Thus did Fin, through the wit and invention of Oonagh, his wife, succeed in overcoming his enemy by strategem, which he never could have done by force: and thus also is it proved that the women, if they bring us *into* many an unpleasant scrape, can sometimes succeed in getting us *out* of others that are as bad.

JULIA CAHILL'S CURSE

by George Moore

GEORGE MOORE (1852–1933), the son of landed gentry in County Mayo, spent his youth in Paris as a dilettante· artist and writer. Later he settled in London and came under the influence of the work of Emile Zola. This was to shape his entire life, and he was a prime mover in introducing the 'naturalist' style of writing to English letters. On the outbreak of the Boer War, Moore returned to Ireland and there produced some of his best work on contemporary Irish life. His obvious knowledge of his countrymen's superstitions is very evident in this story of a curse and the blight it put on a small community. Curses are still known in Ireland today —so the people will tell you—and it is a brave person who will risk incurring the anger of a 'wise' man or woman.

As we were journeying along, the driver of the coach and I fell into conversation about various people we knew in the locality and all at once we hit on the name of Julia Cahill. I had never heard the full story of this woman and asked my companion to recount it to me.

'Wasn't it Father Madden who had her put out of the parish?' he began, 'but she put a curse on it, and it's on it to this day.'

'Do you believe in curses?' I asked. 'Bedad I do, sir. It's a terrible thing to put a curse on a man, and the curse that Julia put on Father Madden's parish was a bad one, the divel a worse. The sun was up at the time, and she on the hilltop raising both her hands. And the curse she put on the parish was that every year a roof must fall in and a family go to America. That was the curse, your honour, and every word of it has come true. You'll see for yourself as soon as we cross the mearing.'

'And what has become of Julia's baby?'

'I never heard she had one, sir.'

He flicked his horse pensively with his whip, and it seemed to me that the disbelief I had expressed in the power of the curse disinclined him for further conversation.

'But,' I said, 'who is Julia Cahill, and how did she get the power to put a curse upon the village?'

'Didn't she go into the mountains every night to meet the fairies, and who else could've given her the power to put a curse upon the village?'

'But she couldn't walk so far in one evening.'

'Them that's in league with the fairies can walk that far and much farther in an evening, your honour. A shepherd saw her; and you'll see the ruins of the cabins for yourself as soon as we cross the mearing, and I'll show you the cabin of the blind woman that Julia lived with before she went away.'

'And how long is it since she went?'

'About twenty year, and there hasn't been a girl the like of her in these parts since. I was only a gossoon at the time, but I've heard tell she was as tall as I'm myself, and as straight as a poplar. She walked with a little swing in her walk, so that all the boys used to be looking after her, and she had fine black eyes, sir, and she was nearly always laughing. Father Madden had just come to the parish; and there was courting in these parts then, for aren't we the same as other people—we'd like to go out with a girl well enough if it was the custom of the country. Father Madden put down the ball alley because he said the boys stayed there instead of going into Mass, and he put down the cross-road dances because he said dancing was the cause of many a bastard, and he wanted none in his parish. Now there was no dancer like Julia; the boys used to gather about to see her dance, and whoever walked with her under the hedges in the summer could never think about another woman. The village was cracked about her. There was fighting, so I suppose the priest was right: he had to get rid of her. But I think he mightn't have been as hard on her as he was.

'One evening he went down to the house. Julia's people were well-to-do people, they kept a grocery-store in the village; and when he came into the shop who should be there but the richest farmer in the country, Michael Moran by name, trying to get Julia for his wife. He didn't go straight to Julia, and that's what swept him. There are two counters in that shop, and Julia was at the one on the left as you go in. And many's the pound she had made for her parents at that counter. Michael Moran says to the father, 'Now, what fortune are you going to give with Julia?' And the father says there was many a man who would take her without any; and that's how they spoke, and Julia listening quietly all the while at the opposite counter. For Michael didn't know what a spirited girl she was, but went on arguing till he got the father to say fifty pounds, and thinking he had got him so far he said, 'I'll never drop a flap to her unless you give the two heifers.' Julia never said a word, she just sat listening. It was then that the priest came in. And over he goes to Julia. 'And now,' says he, 'aren't you proud to hear that you'll have such a fine fortune, and it's I that'll be glad to see you married, for I can't have any more of your goings-on in my parish. You're the encouragement of the dancing and courting here, but I'm going to put an end to it.' Julia didn't answer a word, and he went over to them that were arguing about

171

the sixty pounds. 'Now, why not make it fifty-five?'
says he. So the father agreed to that, since the priest had
said it, and all three of them thought the marriage was
settled. 'Now what will you be taking, Father Tom?'
says Cahill, 'and you Michael?' Sorra one of them
thought of asking her if she was pleased with Michael;
but little did they know what was passing in her mind,
and when they came over to the counter to tell her what
they had settled, she said, 'Well, I've just been listening
to you, and 'tis well for you to be wasting your time
talking about me,' and she tossed her head, saying she
would just pick the boy out of the parish that pleased
her best. And what angered the priest most of all was
her way of saying it—that the boy that would marry her
would be marrying herself and not the money that
would be paid when the book was signed or when the
first baby was born. Now it was agin girls marrying
according to their fancy that Father Madden had set
himself. He had said in his sermon the Sunday before
that young people shouldn't be allowed out by themselves at all, but that the parents should make up the
marriages for them. And he went fairly wild when Julia
told him the example she was going to set. He tried to
keep his temper, sir, but it was getting the better of him
all the while. And Julia said, 'My boy isn't in the parish
now, but maybe he is on his way here, and he may be
here tomorrow or the next day.' And when Julia's
father heard her speak like that he knew that no one
would turn her from what she was saying, and he said,
'Michael Moran, my good man, you may go your way:
you will never get her.' Then he went back to hear what
Julia was saying to the priest, but it was the priest that
was talking. 'Do you think,' says he, 'I am going to let
you go on turning the head of every boy in the parish?
Do you think,' says he, 'I'm going to see you gallivanting
with one and then with the other? Do you think I am

going to see fighting and quarrelling for your like? Do you think I am going to hear stories like I heard last week about poor Patsy Carey, who has gone out of his mind, they say, on account of your treatment? No,' says he, 'I'll have no more of that. I'll have you out of my parish, or I'll have you married.' Julia didn't answer the priest; she tossed her head, and went on making up parcels of tea and sugar, and getting the steps and taking down candles, though she didn't want them, just to show the priest that she didn't mind what he was saying. And all the while her father trembling, not knowing what would happen, for the priest had a big stick, and there was no saying that he wouldn't strike her. Cahill tried to quiet the priest, he promising him that Julia shouldn't go out any more in the evenings, and bedad, sir, she was out the same evening with a young man and the priest saw them, nor was she minded at the end of the month to marry any of them. Then the priest went down to the shop to speak to her a second time, and he went down again a third time, though what he said the third time no one knows, no one being there at the time. And next Sunday he spoke out, saying that a disobedient daughter would have the worst devil in hell to attend to her. I've heard tell that he called her the evil spirit that sent men mad. But most of the people that were there are dead or gone to America, and no one rightly knows what he did say, only that the words came out of his mouth, and the people when they saw Julia crossed themselves, and even the boys that were most mad after Julia were afraid to speak to her. Cahill had to put her out.'

'Do you mean to say that the father put his daughter out?'

'Sure, didn't the priest threaten to turn him into a rabbit if he didn't, and no one in the parish would speak to Julia, they were so afraid of Father Madden, and if it

173

hadn't been for the blind woman that I was speaking about a while ago, sir, it is to the Poor House she'd have to go. The blind woman has a little cabin at the edge of the bog—I'll point it out to you, sir; we do be passing it by—and she was with the blind woman for nearly two years disowned by her own father. Her clothes wore out, but she was as beautiful without them as with them. The boys were told not to look back, but sure they couldn't help it.

'Ah, it was a long while before Father Madden could get shut of her. The blind woman said she wouldn't see Julia thrown out on the roadside, and she was as good as her word for well-night two years, till Julia went to America, so some do be saying, sir, whilst others do be saying she joined the fairies. But 'tis for sure, sir, that the day she left the parish Pat Quinn heard a knocking at his window and somebody asking if he would lend his cart to go to the railway station. Pat was a heavy sleeper and he didn't get up, and it is thought that it was Julia who wanted Pat's cart to take her to the station; it's a good ten mile; but she got there all the same!'

'You said something about a curse?'

'Yes, sir. You'll see the hill presently. And a man who was taking some sheep to the fair saw her there. The sun was just getting up and he saw her cursing the village, raising both her hands, up to the sun, and since that curse was spoken every year a roof has fallen in, sometimes two or three.'

I could see he believed the story, and for the moment I, too, believed in an outcast Venus becoming the evil spirit of a village that would not accept her as divine.

'Look, sir, the woman coming down the road is Bridget Coyne. And that's her house,' he said, and we passed a house built of loose stone without mortar, but a little better than the mud cabins I had seen in Father MacTurnan's parish.

'And now, sir, you will see the loneliest parish in Ireland.'

And I noticed that though the land was good, there seemed to be few people on it, and, what was more significant than the untilled fields were the ruins, for they were not the cold ruins of twenty, or thirty, or forty years ago when the people were evicted and their tillage turned into pasture—the ruins I saw were the ruins of cabins that had been lately abandoned, and I said:

'It wasn't the landlord who evicted these people.'

'Ah, it's the landlord who would be glad to have them back, but there's no getting them back. Everyone here will have to go, and 'tis said that the priest will say Mass in an empty chapel, sorra a one will be there but Bridget, and she'll be the least he'll give communion to. It's said, your honour, that Julia has been seen in America, and I'm going there this autumn. You may be sure I'll keep a lookout for her.'

'But all this is twenty years ago. You won't know her. A woman changes a good deal in twenty years.'

'There will be no change in her, your honour. Sure, hasn't she been with the fairies?'

THE CRUCIFIXION OF THE OUTCAST

by W. B. Yeats

WILLIAM BUTLER YEATS *(1865-1939) was winner of the Nobel Prize and Ireland's greatest poet and dramatist. The son of a renowned Dublin artist, he was educated partly in Ireland and partly in London and during this time formed an interest in occultism. Later, drawing on his experiences with his relatives in Sligo, he began to write on folklore, the first results being published in 1893 as* The Celtic Twilight. *This title was subsequently used to label a school of writing that attempted a renaissance of ancient Irish culture. Yeats' style in prose—like in his poetry—is gloriously varied: from light, beautiful tales of unworldly fantasy to grim and horrifying parables of death and cruelty.* The Crucifixion of the Outcast *is a horror story in the tradition of Poe and Blackwood, and when published in 1898 its effect on readers was stunning. The years have taken away little of its power or meaning.*

A man, with thin brown hair and a pale face, half ran, half walked, along the road that wound from the south to the town of Sligo. Many called him Cumhal, the son of Cormac, and many called him the Swift, Wild Horse; and he was a gleeman, and he wore a short particoloured doublet, and had pointed shoes, with a bulging wallet. Also he was of the blood of the Ernaans, and his birthplace was the Field of Gold; but his eating and sleeping places were in the five kingdoms of Eri, and his abiding place was not upon the ridge of the earth. His eyes strayed from the tower of what was later the Abbey of the White Friars to a row of crosses which stood out against the sky upon a hill a little to the eastward of the town, and he clenched his fist, and shook it at the crosses. He knew they were not empty, for the birds were fluttering about them; and he thought how, as like as not, just such another vagabond as himself had been mounted on one of them; and he muttered: 'If it were hanging or bow-stringing, or stoning or beheading, it would be bad enough. But to have the birds pecking your eyes and the wolves eating your feet! I would that the red wind of the Druids had withered in his cradle the soldier of Dathi, who brought the tree of death out of barbarous lands, or that the lightning, when it smote Dathi at the foot of the mountain, had smitten him also, or that his grave had been dug by the green-haired and green-toothed merrows deep at the roots of the deep sea.'

While he spoke, he shivered from head to foot, and the sweat came out upon his face, and he knew not why, for he had looked upon many crosses. He passed over two hills and under the battlemented gate, and then round by a left-hand way to the door of the Abbey. It was studded with great nails, and when he knocked at it he roused the lay brother who was the porter, and of him he asked a place in the guest-house. Then the lay brother took a glowing turf on a shovel, and led the way to a big and naked outhouse strewn with very dirty rushes; and lighted a rush-candle fixed between two of the stones of the wall, and set the glowing turf upon the hearth and gave him two unlighted sods and a wisp of straw, and showed him a blanket hanging from a nail, and a shelf with a loaf of bread and a jug of water, and a tub in a far corner. Then the lay brother left him and went back to his place by the door. And Cumhal the son of Cormac began to blow upon the glowing turf that he might light the two sods and the wisp of straw; but the sods and the straw would not light, for they were damp. So he took off his pointed shoes, and drew the tub out of the corner with the thought of washing the dust of the highway from his feet; but the water was so dirty that he could not see the bottom. He was very hungry, for he had not eaten all that day, so he did not waste much anger upon the tub, but took up the black loaf, and bit into it, and then spat out the bite, for the bread was hard and mouldy. Still he did not give way to his anger, for he had not drunken these many hours; having a hope of heath beer or wine at his day's end, he had left the brooks untasted, to make his supper the more delightful. Now he put the jug to his lips, but he flung it from him straightway, for the water was bitter and ill-smelling. Then he gave the jug a kick, so that it broke against the opposite wall, and he took down the blanket to wrap it about him for the night. But no sooner did he touch it than it was alive with skipping fleas. At this, beside himself with anger, he rushed to the door of the guest-house, but the lay brother, being well accustomed to such outcries, had locked it on the outside; so he emptied the tub and began to beat the door with it, till the lay brother came to the door and asked what ailed him, and why he woke him out of sleep. 'What ails me!' shouted Cumhal; 'are not the sods as wet as the sands of the Three Rosses? and are not the fleas in the blanket as many as the waves of the sea and as lively? and is not the bread as hard as the heart of a lay brother who has forgotten God? and is not the water in the jug as bitter and as ill-smelling as his soul? and is not the foot-water the colour that shall be upon him when he has been charred in the Undying Fires?' The lay brother saw that the lock was fast, and went back to his niche, for he was too sleepy to talk with comfort. And Cumhal went on beating at the door, and presently he heard the lay brother's foot once more, and cried out at him, 'O

cowardly and tyrannous race of monks, persecutors of
the bard and the gleeman, haters of life and joy! O
race that does not draw the sword and tell the truth!
O race that melts the bones of the people with cowardice
and with deceit!'

'Gleeman,' said the lay brother, 'I also makes rhymes;
I make many while I sit in my niche by the door, and I
sorrow to hear the bards railing upon the monks.
Brother, I would sleep, and therefore I make known to
you that it is the head of the monastery, our gracious
abbot, who orders all things concerning the lodging of
travellers.'

'You may sleep,' said Cumhal, 'I will sing a bard's
curse on the abbot.' And he set the tub upside down
under the window, and stood upon it, and began to sing
in a very loud voice. The singing awoke the abbot, so
that he sat up in bed and blew a silver whistle until the
lay brother came to him. 'I cannot get a wink of sleep
with that noise,' said the abbot. 'What is happening?'

'It is a gleeman,' said the lay brother, 'who complains
of the sods, of the bread, of the water in the jug, of the
foot-water, and of the blanket. And now he is singing a
bard's curse upon you, O brother abbot, and upon your
father and your mother, and your grandfather and your
grandmother, and upon all your relations.'

'Is he cursing in rhyme?'

'He is cursing in rhyme, and with two assonances in
every line of his curse.'

The abbot pulled his night-cap off and crumpled it in
his hands, and the circular grey patch of hair in the
middle of his bald head looked like the cairn upon
Knocknarea, for in Connaught they had not yet abandoned the ancient tonsure. 'Unless we do somewhat,' he
said, 'he will teach his curses to the children in the street,
and the girls spinning at the doors, and to the robbers
upon Ben Bulben.'

'Shall I go, then,' said the other, 'and give him dry sods, a fresh loaf, clean water in a jug, clean foot-water, and a new blanket, and make him swear by the blessed Saint Benignus, and by the sun and moon, that no bond be lacking, not to tell his rhymes to the children in the street, and the girls spinning at the doors, and the robbers upon Ben Bulben?'

'Neither our Blessed Patron nor the sun and moon would avail at all,' said the abbot; 'for tomorrow or the next day the mood to curse would come upon him, or a pride in those rhymes would move him, and he would teach his lines to the children, and the girls, and the robbers. Or else he would tell another of his craft how he fared in the guest-house, and he in his turn would begin to curse, and my name would wither. For learn there is no steadfastness of purpose upon the roads, but only under roofs and between four walls. Therefore I bid you go and awaken Brother Kevin, Brother Dove, Brother Little Wolf, Brother Bald Patrick, Brother Bald Brandon, Brother James, and Brother Peter. And they shall take the man, and bind him with ropes, and dip him in the river that he shall cease to sing. And in the morning, lest this but make him curse the louder, we will crucify him.'

'The crosses are all full,' said the lay brother.

'Then we must make another cross. If we do not make and end to him another will, for who can eat and sleep in peace while men like him are going about the world? We would stand shamed indeed before blessed Saint Benignus, and sour would be his face when he comes to judge us at the Last Day, were we to spare an enemy of his when we had him under our thumb! Brother, there is not one of these bards and gleemen who has not scattered his bastards through the five kingdoms, and if they slit a purse or a throat, and it is always one or the other, it never comes into their heads to confess and do penance. Can you name one that is not heathen at heart, always longing after the Son of Lir, and Aengus, and Bridget, and the Dagda, and Dana the Mother, and all the false gods of the old days; always making poems in praise of those kings and queens of the demons, Finvaragh, whose home is under Cruachmaa, and Red Aodh of Cnocna-Sidhe, and Cleena of the Wave, and Aoibhell of the Grey Rock, and him they call Donn of the Vats of the Sea; and railing against God and Christ and the blessed Saints.' While he was speaking he crossed himself, and when he had finished he drew the nightcap over his ears to shut out the noise, and closed his eyes and composed himself to sleep.

The lay brother found Brother Kevin, Brother Dove, Brother Little Wolf, Brother Bald Patrick, Brother Bald Brandon, Brother James, and Brother Peter sitting up in bed, and he made them get up. Then they bound Cumhal, and they dragged him to the river, and they dipped him in it at the place which was afterwards called Buckley's Ford.

'Gleeman,' said the lay brother, as they led him back to the guest-house, 'why do you ever use the wit which God has given you to make blasphemous and immoral tales and verses? For such is the way of your craft. I have, indeed, many such tales and verses wellnigh by rote, and so I know that I speak true! And why do you praise with rhyme those demons, Finvaragh, Red Aodh, Cleena, Aoibhell and Donn? I, too, am a man of great wit and learning, but I ever glorify our gracious abbot, and Benignus our Patron, and the princes of the province. My soul is decent and orderly, but yours is like the wind among the salley gardens. I said what I could for you, being also a man of many thoughts, but who could help such a one as you?'

'Friend,' answered the gleeman, 'my soul is indeed like the wind, and it blows me to and fro, and up and down, and puts many things into my mind and out of my mind, and therefore am I called the Swift, Wild Horse.' And he spoke no more that night, for his teeth were chattering with the cold.

The abbot and the monks came to him in the morning, and bade him get ready to be crucified, and led him out of the guest-house. And while he still stood upon the step a flock of great grass-barnacles passed high above him with clanking cries. He lifted his arms to them and said, 'O great grass-barnacles, tarry a little, and mayhap my soul will travel with you to the waste places of the shore and to the ungovernable sea!' At the gate a crowd of beggars gathered about them, being come there to beg from any traveller or pilgrim who might have spent the night in the guest-house. The abbot and the monks led the gleeman to a place in the woods at some distance, where many straight young trees were growing, and they made him cut one down and fashion it to the right length, while the beggars stood round them in a ring, talking and gesticulating. The abbot then bade him cut off another and shorter piece of wood, and nail it upon the first. So there was his cross for him, and they put it upon his shoulder, for his crucifixion was to be on the top of the hill where the others were. A half-mile on the way he asked them to stop and see him juggle for them; for he knew, he said, all the tricks of Aengus and Subtlehearted. The old monks were for pressing on, but the young monks would see him: so he did many wonders for them, even to the drawing of live frogs out of his ears. But after a while they turned on him, and said his tricks were dull and a little unholy, and set the cross on his shoulders again. Another half-mile on the way and he asked them to stop and hear him jest for them, for he knew, he said, all the jests of Conan the Bald, upon whose back a sheep's wool grew. And the young monks, when they had heard his merry tales, again bade him take up his cross, for it ill became them to listen to such follies. Another half-mile on the way, he asked them to stop and hear him sing the story of White-breasted Deirdre, and how she endured many sorrows, and how the sons of Usna died to serve her. And the young monks were mad to hear him, but when he had ended they grew angry, and beat him for waking for-gotten longings in their hearts. So they set the cross upon his back and hurried him to the hill.

When he was come to the top, they took the cross from him, and began to dig a hole for it to stand in, while the beggars gathered round, and talked among themselves. 'I ask a favour before I die,' says Cumhal.

'We will grant you no more delays,' says the abbot.

'I ask no more delays, for I have drawn the sword, and told the truth, and lived my dream, and am content.'

'Would you, then, confess?'

'By sun and moon, not I; I ask but to be let eat the food I carry in my wallet. I carry food in my wallet whenever I go upon a journey, but I do not taste of it unless I am wellnigh starved. I have not eaten now these two days.'

'You may eat, then,' says the abbot, and he turned to help the monks dig the hole.

The gleeman took a loaf and some strips of cold fried bacon out of his wallet and laid them upon the ground. 'I will give a tithe to the poor,' says he, and he cut a tenth part from the loaf and the bacon. 'Who among you is the poorest?' And thereupon was a great clamour, for the beggars began the history of their sor-rows and their poverty, and their yellow faces swayed like Gara Lough when the floods have filled it with water from the bogs.

He listened for a little, and, says he, 'I am myself the poorest, for I have travelled the bare road, and by the edges of the sea; and the tattered doublet of parti-

183

coloured cloth upon my back and the torn pointed shoes upon my feet have ever irked me, because of the towered city full of noble raiment which was in my heart. And I have been the more alone upon the roads and by the sea because I heard in my heart the rustling of the rose-bordered dress of her who is more subtle than Aengus the Subtlehearted, and more full of the beauty of laughter than Conan the Bald, and more full of wisdom of tears than White-breasted Deirdre, and more lovely than a bursting dawn to them that are lost in the darkness. Therefore, I award the tithe to myself; but yet, because I am done with all things, I give it unto you.'

So he flung the bread and the strips of bacon among the beggars, and they fought with many cries until the last scrap was eaten. But meanwhile the monks nailed the gleeman to his cross, and set it upright in the hope, and shovelled the earth into the hole, and trampled it level and hard. So then they went away, but the beggars stayed on, sitting round the cross. But when the sun was sinking, they also got up to go, for the air was getting chilly. And as soon as they had gone a little way, the wolves, who had been showing themselves on the edge of a neighbouring coppice, came nearer, and the birds wheeled closer and closer. 'Stay, outcasts, yet a little while,' the crucified one called in a weak voice to the beggars, 'and keep the beasts and the birds from me.' But the beggars were angry because he had called them outcasts, so they threw stones and mud at him, and one that had a child held it up before his eyes and said that he was its father, and cursed him, and thereupon they left him. Then the wolves gathered at the foot of the cross, and the birds flew lower and lower. And presently the birds lighted all at once upon his head and arms and shoulders, and began to peck at him, and the

184

wolves began to eat his feet. 'Outcasts,' he moaned, 'have
you all turned against the outcast?'

THE MAN FROM KILSHEELAN

by A. E. Coppard

ALFRED EDGAR COPPARD *(1878–1957) is justifiably
regarded as one of the finest chroniclers of English
country life and character; his exactly observed
situations and easy style make him a writer to be
savoured and admired. With a formal education
lasting only until he was nine, Coppard was ill-
equipped for business life, and after a brief and
unsuccessful career as an accountant turned to writing for a living. Where many others had failed, he
succeeded, and in 1921 enjoyed a major triumph
with his novel,* Adam and Eve and Pinch Me. *This
was followed by several collections of short stories,
notably* The Black Dog *from which this tale is
taken. He had a very real love and understanding
of the Irish and this is rarely seen to better advantage than in the magical life of* The Man from
Kilsheelan.

I

If you knew the Man from Kilsheelan it was no use
saying you did not believe in fairies and secret powers;
believe it or no, but believe it you should—there he
was! It is true he was in an asylum for the insane, but
he was a man with age upon him so he didn't mind;
and besides, better men than himself have been in such
places, or they ought to be, and if there is justice in the
world they will be.

185

'A cousin of mine,' he said to old Tom Tool one night, 'is come from Ameriky. A rich person.'

He lay in the bed next to him, but Tom Tool didn't answer, so he went on again: 'In a ship,' he said.

'I hear you,' answered Tom Tool.

'I see his mother with her bosom open once, and it stuffed with diamonds, bags full.'

Tom Tool kept kept.

'If,' said the Man from Kilsheelan, 'if I'd the trusty comrade I'd make a break from this and go seek him.'

'Was he asking you to do that?'

'How could he an' all and he in a ship?'

'Was he writing fine letters to you, then?'

'How could he, under the Lord? Would he give them to a savage bird or a herring to bring to me so?'

'How did he let on to you?'

'He did not let on,' said the Man from Kilsheelan.

Tom Tool lay long silent in the darkness; he had a mistrust of the Man, knowing him to have a forgetful mind; everything slipped through it like rain through the nest of a pigeon. But at last he asked him: 'Where is he now?'

'He'll be at Ballygoveen.'

'You to know that and you with no word for him?'

'Oh, I know it, I know; and if I'd a trusty comrade I'd walk out of this and to him I would go. Bags of diamonds!'

Then he went to sleep, sudden; but the next night he was at Tom Tool again: 'If I'd a trusty comrade,' said he; and all that and a lot more.

' 'Tis not convenient to me now,' said Tom Tool, 'but tomorrow night I might go wid you.'

The next night was a wild night, and a dark night, and he would not go to make a break from the asylum, he said: 'Fifty miles of journey, and I with no heart for great walking feats! It is not convenient, but tomorrow

186

night I might go wid you.'

The night after that he said: 'Ah, whisht wid your diamonds and all! Why would you go from the place that is snug and warm into a world that is like a wall for cold dark, and but the thread of a coat to divide you from its mighty clasp, and only one thing blacker under the heaven of God and that's the road you walk on, and only one thing more shy than your heart and that's your two feet worn to a tissue tramping in dung and ditches . . .'

'If I'd a trusty comrade,' said the Man from Kilsheelan, 'I'd go seek my rich cousin.'

'. . . stars gaping at you a few spans away, and the things that have life in them, but cannot see or speak, begin to breathe and bend. If ever your hair stood up it is then it would be, though you've no more than would thatch a thimble, God help you.'

'Bags of gold he has,' continued the Man, 'and his pockets stuffed with the tobacca.'

'Tobacca!'

'They were large pockets and well stuffed.'

'Do you say, now!'

'And the gold! large bags and rich bags.'

'Well, I might do it tomorrow.'

And the next day Tom Tool and the Man from Kilsheelan broke from the asylum and crossed the mountains and went on.

Four little nights and four long days they were walking: slow it was, for they were oldish men and lost they were, but the journey was kind and the weather was good weather. On the fourth day Tom Tool said to him: 'The Dear knows what way you'd be taking me! Blind it seems, and dazed I am. I could do with a skillet of good soup to steady me and to soothe me.'

'Hard it is, and hungry it is,' sighed the Man; 'starved daft I am for a taste of nourishment, a blind man's dog

187

would pity me. If I see a cat I'll eat it; I could bite the nose off a duck.'

They did not converse any more for a time, not until Tom Tool asked him what was the name of his grand cousin, and then the Man from Kilsheelan was in a bedazement, and he was confused.

'I declare, on my soul, I've forgot his little name. Wait now while I think of it.'

'Was it McInerney then?'

'No, not it at all.'

'Kavanagh? the Grogans? or the Duffys?'

'Wait, wait while I think of it now.'

Tom Tool waited; he waited and all until he thought he would burst.

'Ah, what's astray wid you? Was it Phelan—or O'Hara—or Clancy—or Peter Mew?'

'No, not it at all.'

'The Murphys—the Sweeneys—the Moores.'

'Divil a one. Wait while I think of it now.'

And the Man from Kilsheelan sat holding his face as if it hurt him, and his comrade kept saying at him: 'Duhy, then? Coman? McGrath?' driving him distracted with his O this and O that, his Mc he's and Mc she's.

Well, he could not think of it; but when they walked on they had not far to go, for they came over a twist of the hills and there was the ocean, and the neat little town of Ballygoveen in a bay of it below, with the wreck of a ship lying sunk near the strand. There was a sharp cliff at either horn of the bay, and between them some bullocks stravaiging on the beach.

'Truth is a fortune,' cried the Man from Kilsheelan, 'this is it!'

They went down the hill to the strand near the wreck, and just on the wing of the town they saw a paddock

188

full of hemp stretched drying, and a house near it, and a man weaving a rope. He had a great cast of hemp around his loins, and a green apron. He walked backwards to the sea, and a young girl stood turning a little wheel as he went away from her.

'God save you,' said Tom Tool to her, 'for who are you weaving this rope?'

'For none but God himself and the hangman,' said she.

Turning the wheel she was, and the man going away from it backwards, and the dead wreck in the rocky bay; a fine sweet girl of good dispose and no ways drifty.

'Long life to you then, young woman,' says he. 'But that's a strong word, and a sour word, the Lord spare us all.'

At that the ropewalker let a shout to her to stop the wheel; then he cut the rope at the end and tied it to a black post. After that he came throwing off his green apron and said he was hungry.

'Denis, avick!' cried the girl. 'Come, and I'll get your food.' And the two of them went away into the house.

'Brother and sister they are,' said the Man from Kilsheelan, 'a good appetite to them.'

'Very neat she is, and clean she is, and good and sweet and tidy she is,' said Tom Tool. They stood in the yard watching some white fowls parading and feeding and conversing in the grass; scratch, peck, peck, ruffle, quarrel, scratch, peck, peck, cock-a-doodle-doo.

'What will we do now, Tom Tool? My belly has a scroop and a screech in it. I could eat the full of Isknagahiny Lake and gape for more, or the Hill of Bawn and not get my enough.'

Beyond them was the paddock with the hemp drying across it, long heavy strands, and two big stacks of it beside, dark and sodden, like seaweed. The girl came to the door and called: 'Will ye take a bite?' They said

189

they would, and that she should eat with spoons of gold in the heaven of God and Mary. 'You're welcome,' she said, but no more she said, for while they ate she was sad and silent.

The young man Denis let on that their father, one Horan, was away on his journeys peddling a load of ropes, a long journey, days he had been gone, and he might be back today, or tomorrow, or the day after.

'A great strew of hemp you have,' said the Man from Kilsheelan. The young man cast down his eyes; and the young girl cried out: ' 'Tis foul hemp, God preserve us all!'

'Do you tell me of that now,' he asked; but she would not, and her brother said: 'I will tell you. It's a great misfortune, mister man. 'Tis from the wreck in the bay beyant, a good stout ship, but burst on the rocks one dark terror of a night and all the poor sailors tipped in the sea. But the tide was low and they got ashore, ten strong sailor men, with a bird in a cage that was dead drowned.'

'The Dear rest its soul,' said Tom Tool.

'There was no rest in the ocean for a week, the bay was full of storms, and the vessel burst, and the big bales split, and the hemp was scattered and torn and tangled on the rocks, or it did drift. But at last it soothed, and we gathered it and brought it to the field here. We brought it, and my father did buy it off the salvage man for a price; a Mexican valuer he was, but the deal was bad, and it lies there; going rotten it is, the rain wears it, and the sun's astray, and the wind is gone.'

'That's a great misfortune. What is on it?' said the Man from Kilsheelan. 'It is a great misfortune, mister man. Laid out it is, turned it is, hackled it is, but faith it will not dry or sweeten, never a hank of it worth a pig's eye.'

' 'Tis the devil and all his injury,' said Kilsheelan.

190

The young girl, her name it was Christine, at grieving. One of her beautiful long hands rested on her knee, and she kept beating it with the other. Then she began to speak.

'The captain of that ship lodged in this house with us while the hemp was recovered and sold; a fine handsome sport he was, but fond of the drink and very friendly with the Mexican man, very hearty they were, a great greasy man with his hands covered with rings that you'd not believe. Covered! My father had been gone travelling a week or a few days when a dark raging gale came off the bay one night till the hemp was lifted all over the field.'

'It would have lifted a bullock,' said Denis, 'great lumps of it, like trees.'

'And we sat waiting the captain, but he didn't come home and we went sleeping. But in the morning the Mexican man was found dead murdered on the strand below, struck in the skull, and the two hands of him gone. 'Twas not long when they came to the house and said he was last seen with the captain, drunk quarrelling; and where was he? I said to them that he didn't come home at all and was away from it. "We'll take a peep at his bed," they said, and I brought them there, and my heart gave a strong twist in me when I see'd the captain stretched on it, snoring to the world, and his face and hands smeared with the blood. So he was brought away and searched, and in his pocket they found one of the poor Mexican's hands, just the one, but none of the riches. Everything to be so black against him and the assizes just coming on in Cork! So they took him there before the judge, and he judged him and said it's to hang he was. And if they asked the captain how he did it, he said he did not do it at all.'

'But there was a bit of iron pipe beside the body,' said Denis.

191

'And if they asked him hewer was the other hand, the one with the rings and the mighty jewels on them, and his budget of riches, he said he knew nothing of that nor how the one hand got into his pocket. Placed there it was by some schemer. It was all he could say, for the drink was on him and nothing he knew.

' "You to be so drunk," they said, "how did you get home to your bed and nothing heard?"

' "I don't know," says he. Good sakes, the poor lamb, a gallant strong sailor he was! His mind was a blank, he said. " 'Tis blank," said the judge, "if it's as blank as the head of himself with a gap like that in it, God rest him!" '

'You could have put a pound of cheese in it,' said Denis.

'And Peter Corcoran cried like a loony man, for his courage was gone, like a stream of water. To hang him, the judge said, and to hang him well, was their intention. It was a pity, the judge said, to rob a man because he was foreign, and destroy him for riches and the drink on him. And Peter Corcoran swore he was innocent of this crime. "Put a clean shirt to me back," says he, "for it's to heaven I'm going." '

'And,' added Denis, 'the peeler at the door said "Amen".'

'That was a week ago,' said Christine, 'and in another he'll be stretched. A handsome sporting sailor boy.'

'What—what did you say was the name of him?' gasped the Man from Kilsheelan.

'Peter Corcoran, the poor lamb,' said Christine.

'Begod,' he cried out as if he was choking, ' 'tis me grand cousin from Ameriky!'

True it was, and the grief on him so great that Denis was after giving the two of them a lodge till the execution was over. 'Rest here, my dad's away,' said he, 'and he knowing nothing of the murder, or the robbery, or the hanging that's coming, nothing. Ah, what will we tell him an' all? 'Tis a black story on this house.'

'The blessing of God and Mary on you,' said Tom Tool. 'Maybe we could do a hand's turn for you; me comrade's a great wonder with the miracles, maybe he could do a stroke would free an innocent man.'

'Is it joking you are?' asked Christine sternly.

'God deliver him, how would I joke on a man going to his doom and destruction?'

The next day the young girl gave them jobs to do, but the Man from Kilsheelan was destroyed with trouble and he shook like water when a pan of it is struck.

'What is on you?' said Tom Tool.

'Vexed and waxy I am,' says he, 'in regard of the great journeys we's took, and sorra a help in the end of it. Why couldn't he do his bloody murder after we had done with him?'

'Maybe he didn't do it at all.'

'Ah, what are you saying now, Tom Tool? Wouldn't anyone do it, a nice, easy, innocent crime? The cranky gosoon to get himself stretched on the head of it, 'tis the drink destroyed him! Sure there's no more justice in the world than you'd find in the craw of a sick pullet. Vexed and waxy I am for me careless cousin. Do it! Who wouldn't do it?'

He went up to the rope that Denis and Christine were weaving together and he put his finger on it.

'Is that the rope,' says he, 'that will hang my grand cousin?'

'No,' said Denis, 'it is not. His rope came through the post office yesterday. For the prison master it was, a long new rope—saints preserve us—and Jimmy Fallon, the postman, getting roaring drunk showing it to the scores of creatures who'd give him a drink for the sight of it. Just coiled it was, and no way hidden, with a label on it, "O.H.M.S.".'

193

'The wind's rising, you," said Christine. 'Take a couple of forks now and turn the hemp in the field. Maybe 'twill scour the Satan out of it.'

'Stormy it does be, and the bay has darkened in broad noon,' said Tom Tool.

'Why wouldn't the whole world be dark and a man to be hung?' said she.

They went to the hemp, so knotted and stinking, and begun raking it and raking it. The wind was roaring from the bay, the hulk twitching and tottering; the gulls came off the wave, and Christine's clothes stretched out from her like the wings of a bird. The hemp heaved upon the paddock like a great beast bursting a snare that was on it, and a strong blast drove a heap of it up on the Man from Kilsheelan, twisting and binding him in its clasp till he thought he would not escape from it and he went falling and yelping. Tom Tool unwound him from it and he sat in the lew of the stack till he got his strength again, and then he began to moan of his misfortune.

'Stint your shouting,' said Tom Tool, 'isn't it as hard to cure as a wart on the back of a hedgehog?'

But he wouldn't stint it. ' 'Tis large and splendid talk I get from you, Tom Tool, but divil a deed of strength. Vexed and waxy I am. Why couldn't he do his murder after we'd done with him? What a cranky cousin! What a foolish creature! What a silly man, the devil take him!'

'Let you be aisy,' the other said, 'to heaven he is going.'

'And what's the gain of it, he to go with his neck stretched?'

'Indeed, I did know a man went to heaven once,' began Tom Tool, 'but he did not care for it.'

'That's queer,' said the Man, 'for it couldn't be anything you'd not want, indeed to glory.'

'Well, he came back to Ireland on the head of it. I forget what was his name.'

'Was it Corcoran, or Tool, or Horan?'

'No, none of those names. He let on it was a lonely place, not fit for living people or dead people, he said; nothing but trees and streams and beasts and birds.'

'What beasts and birds?'

'Rabbits and badgers, the elephant, the dromedary, and all those ancient races; eagles and hawks and cuckoos and magpies. He wandered in a thick forest for nights and days like a flea in a great beard, and the beasts and the birds setting traps and hooks and dangers for a poor feller; the worst villains of all was the sheep.'

'The sheep! What could a sheep do, then?' asked Kilsheelan.

'I don't know the right of it, but you'd not believe me if I told you at all. If you went for the little swim you was not seen again.'

'I never heard the like of that in Roscommon.'

'Not another holy soul was in it but himself, and if he was taken with the thirst he would dip his hand in a stream that flowed with rich wine and put it to his lips, but if he did, it turned into air at once and twisted up in a blue cloud. But grand wine to look at, he said. If he took oranges from a tree, he could not bite them, they were chiny oranges, hard as a plate. But beautiful oranges to look at they were. To pick a flower it burst on you like a gun. What was cold was too cold to touch, and what was warm was too warm to swallow, you must throw it up or die.'

'Faith, it's no region for a Christian soul, Tom Tool. Where is it at all?'

'High it may be, low it may be, it may be here, it may be there.'

195

'What could the like of a sheep do? A sheep!'

'A devouring savage creature it is there, the most hard to come at, the most difficult to conquer, with the teeth of a lion and a tiger, the strength of a bear and a half, the deceit of two foxes, the run of a deer, the—'

'Is it heaven you call it! I'd not look twice at a place the like of that.'

'No, you would not, no.'

'Ah, but wait now,' said Kilsheelan, 'wait till the Day of Judgment.'

'Well, I will not wait then,' said Tom Tool sternly. 'When the sinners of the world are called to their judgment, scatter they will all over the face of the earth, running like hares till they come to the sea, and there they will perish.'

'Ah, the love of God on the world!'

They went raking and raking, till they came to a great stiff hump of it that rolled over, and they could see sticking from the end of it two boots.

'Oh, what is it, in the name of God?' asks Kilsheelan.

'Sorra and all, but I'd not like to look,' says Tom Tool, and they called the girl to come see what was it.

'A dead man!' says Christine in a thin voice with a great tremble coming on her, and she white as a tooth. 'Unwind him now.' They began to unwind him like a tailor with a bale of tweed, and at last they came to a man black in the face. Strangled he was. The girl let a great cry out of her. 'Queen of heaven, 'tis my dad; choked he is, the long strands have choked him, my good, pleasant dad!' and she went with a run to the house crying.

'What has he there in his hand?' asked Kilsheelan.

' 'Tis a chopper,' says he.

'Do you see what is on it, Tom Tool?'

'Sure I see, and you see, what is on it; blood is on it,

196

and murder is on it. Go fetch a peeler and I'll wait while you bring him.'

When his friend was gone for the police Tom Tool took a little squint around him and slid his hand into the dead man's pocket. But as he did so he was nearly struck man from his senses, for he pulled out a loose dead hand that had been chopped off as neat as the foot of a pig. He looked at the dead man's arms, and there was a hand to each; so he looked at the hand again. The fingers were covered with rings of gold and diamonds. Covered!

'Glory be to God!' said Tom Tool, and he put his hand in another pocket and fetched a budget full of papers and banknotes.

'Glory be to God!' he said again, and put the hand and the budget back in the pockets and turned his back and said prayers until the peelers came and took them all off to the court.

It was not long, two days or three, until an inquiry was held; grand it was and its judgement was good. And the bigwig asked: 'Where is the man that found the body?'

'There are two of him,' says the peeler.

'Swear 'em,' says he, and Kilsheelan stepped up to a great murdering joker of a clerk, who gave him a book in his hand and roared at him: 'I swear by Almighty God—'

'Yes,' says Kilsheelan.

'Swear it,' says the clerk.

'Indeed I do.'

'You must repeat it,' says the clerk.

'I will, sir.'

'Well, repeat it then,' says he.

'And what will I repeat?'

So he told him again and he repeated it. Then the clerk goes on: '—that the evidence I give—'

'Yes,' says Kilsheelan.

'Say those words, if you please.'

'The words! Och, give me the head of 'em again!'

So he told him again and he repeated it. Then the clerk goes on: '—shall be the truth—'

'It will,' says Kilsheelan.

'—and nothing but the truth—'

'Yes, begod, indeed!'

'Say "nothing but the truth",' roared the clerk.

'No!' says Kilsheelan.

'Say "nothing".'

'All right,' says Kilsheelan.

'Can't you say "nothing but the truth"?'

'Yes,' he says.

'Well, say it!'

'I will so,' says he, 'the scrapings of sense on it all!'

So they swore them both, and their evidence they gave.

'Very good,' his lordship said, 'a most important and opportune discovery, in the nick of time, by the tracing of God. There is a reward of fifty pounds offered for the finding of this property and jewels; fifty pounds you will get in due course.'

They said they were obliged to him, though sorra a one of them knew what he meant by a due course, nor where it was.

Then a lawyer man got the rights of the whole case; he was the cunningest man ever lived in the city of Cork; no one could match him, and he made it straight and he made it clear.

Old Horan must have returned from his journey unbeknown on the night of the gale when the deed was done. Perhaps he had made a poor profit on his toil, for there was little of his own coin found on his body. He saw the two drunks staggering along the bay—he clove in the head of the one with a bit of pipe—he hit the other a good whack to still or stiffen him—he got an

198

axe from the yard—he shore off the Mexican's two hands, for the rings were grown tight and wouldn't be drawn from his fat fingers. Perhaps he dragged the captain home to bed—you couldn't be sure of that—but put the hand in the captain's pocket he did, and then went to the paddock to bury the treasure. But a blast of wind whipped and wove some of the hemp strand around his limbs, binding him sudden. He was all huffled and hogled and went mad with the fear struggling, the hemp rolling him and binding him till he was strangled or smothered.

And that is what happened to him, believe it or no, but believe it you should. It was the tracing of God on him for his dark crime.

Within a week of it Peter Corcoran was away out of jail, a stout walking man again, free in Ballygoveen. But on the day of his release he did not go near the rope-walker's house. The Horans were there waiting, and the two old silly men, but he did not go next or near them. The next day Kilsheelan said to her: 'Strange it is my cousin not to seek you, and he a sneezer for gallantry.'

' 'Tis no wonder at all,' replied Christine, 'and he with him in his black misfortune,' said Tom Tool.

'Well, he will not come then,' Christine said in her soft voice, 'in regard of the red murder on the soul of my dad. And why should be put a mark on his family, and he the captain of a ship?'

In the afternoon Tom Tool and the other went walking to try if they should see him, and they did see him at a hotel, but he was hurrying from it; he had a frieze coat on him and a bag in his hand.

'Well, who are you at all?' asks Peter Corcoran.

'You are my cousin from Ameriky,' says Kilsheelan.

'Is that so? And I never heard it,' says Peter. 'What's your name?'

The Man from Kilsheelan hung down his old head and couldn't answer him, but Tom Tool said: 'Drifty he is, sir, he forgets his little name.'

'Astray is he? My mother said I've cousins in Roscommon, d'ye know 'em? the Twingeings—'

'Twingeing! Owen Twingeing it is!' roared Kilsheelan. ' 'Tis my name! 'Tis my name! 'This my name!' and he danced about squawking like a parrot in a frenzy.

'If it's Owen Twingeing you are, I'll bring you to my mother in Manhattan.' The captain grabbed up his bag. 'Haste now, come along out of it. I'm going from the cunning town this minute, bad sleep to it for ever and a month! There's a cart waiting to catch me the boat train to Queenstown. Will you go? Now?'

'Holy God contrive it,' said Kilsheelan; his voice was wheezy as an old goat, and he made to go off with him. 'Good day to you, Tom Tool, you'll get all the reward and endure a rich life from this out, fortune on it all, a fortune on it all!'

And the two of them were gone in a twink.

Tom Tool went back to the Horans then; night was beginning to dusk and to darken. As he went up the ropewalk Christine came to him from her potato gardens and gave him signs, he to be quiet and follow her down to the strand. So he followed her down to the strand and told her all that happened, till she was vexed and full of tender words for the old fool.

'Aren't you the spit of misfortune! It would daunt a saint, so it would, and scrape a tear from silky Satan's eye. Those two deluders, they've but the drainings of a half a heart between 'em. And he not willing to lift the feather of a thought on me? I'd not forget him till there's ten days in a week and every one of 'em lucky. But—but —isn't Peter Corcoran the nice name for a captain man, the very pattern?'

She gave him a little bundle into his hands. 'There's a

loaf and a cut of meat. You'd best be stirring from here.'

'Yes,' he said, and stood looking stupid, for his mind was in a dream. The rock at one horn of the bay had a red glow on it like the shawl on the neck of a lady, but the other was black now. A man was dragging a turf boat up the beach.

'Listen, you,' said Christine. 'There's two upstart men in the house now, seeking you and the other. There's trouble and damage on the head of it. From the asylum they are. To the police they have been, to put an embargo on the reward, and sorra a sixpence you'll receive of the fifty pounds of it: to the expenses of the asylum it must go, they say. The treachery! Devil and all, the blood sweating on every coin of it would rot the palm of a nigger. Do you hear me at all?'

She gave him a little shaking, for he was standing stupid, gazing at the bay, which was dying into grave darkness except for the wash of its broken waves.

'Do you hear me at all? It's quit now you should, my little old man, or they'll be taking you.'

'Ah, yes, sure, I hear you, Christine; thank you kindly. Just looking and listening I was. I'll be stirring from it now, and I'll get on and I'll go. Just looking and listening I was, just a wee look.'

'Then goodbye to you, Mr. Tool,' said Christine Horan, and turning from him she left him in the darkness and went running up the ropewalk to her home.

THE DEAD SMILE

by Francis Marion Crawford

FRANCIS MARION CRAWFORD *(1854–1901) had few connections with Ireland, yet with* The Dead Smile *he has written one of the most famous and highly regarded of all Irish fantasy tales. Son of the distinguished American sculptor, Thomas Crawford, he devoted much of his youth to travelling and to the study of Sanskrit. He wrote a number of novels on the occult—including the much under-valued* The Witch of Prague—*but rarely exceeded the brilliance of this tale in terms of atmosphere, growing tension and chilling denouncement. Here in one story is the essence of so many Irish legends; and if some readers claim, because of its undoubted popularity, that they have read the work before, I make no excuse for bringing it back into print again.* The Dead Smile *is a classic of the supernatural, and this collection would be incomplete without it.*

I

Sir Hugh Ockram smiled as he sat by the open window of his study, in the late August afternoon, and just then a curiously yellow cloud obscured the low sun, and the clear summer light turned lurid, as if it had been suddenly poisoned and polluted by the foul vapours of a plague. Sir Hugh's face seemed, at best, to be made of fine parchment drawn skin-tight over a wooden mask, in which two eyes were sunk out of sight, and peered from far within through crevices under the slanting, wrinkled lids, alive and watchful like two toads in their

202

holes, side by side and exactly alike. But as the light changed, then a little yellow glare flashed in each. Nurse Macdonald said once that when Sir Hugh smiled he saw the faces of two women in hell—two dead women he had betrayed. (Nurse Macdonald was a hundred years old.) And the smile widened, stretching the pale lips across the discoloured teeth in an expression of profound self-satisfaction, blended with the most unforgiving hatred and contempt for the human doll. The hideous disease of which he was dying had touched his brain. His son stood beside him, tall, white, and delicate as an angel in a primitive picture, and though there was deep distress in his violet eyes as he looked at his father's face, he felt the shadow of that sickening smile stealing across his own lips and parting them and drawing them against his will. And it was like a bad dream, for he tried not to smile and smiled the more. Beside him, strangely like him in her wan, angelic beauty, with the same shadowy golden hair, the same sad violet eyes, the same luminously pale face, Evelyn Warburton rested one hand upon his arm. And as she looked into her uncle's eyes, and could not turn her own away, she knew that the deathly smile was hovering on her own red lips, drawing them tightly across her little teeth, while two bright tears ran down her cheeks to her mouth, and dropped from the upper to the lower lip while she smiled—and the smile was like the shadow of death and the seal of damnation upon her pure, young face.

'Of course,' said Sir Hugh very slowly, and still looking out at the trees, 'if you have made up your mind to be married, I cannot hinder you, and I don't suppose you attach the smallest importance to my consent—'

'Father!' exclaimed Gabriel reproachfully.

'No, I do not deceive myself,' continued the old man, smiling terribly. 'You will marry when I am dead, though there is a very good reason why you had better not—why you had better not,' he repeated very emphatically, and he slowly turned his toad eyes upon the lovers.

'What reason?' asked Evelyn in a frightened voice.

'Never mind the reason, my dear. You will marry just as if it did not exist.' There was a long pause. 'Two gone,' he said, his voice lowering strangely, 'and two more will be four—all together—for ever and ever, burning, burning, burning bright.'

At the last words his head sank slowly back, and the little glare of the toad eyes disappeared under the swollen lids, and the lurid cloud passed from the westering sun, so that the earth was green again and the light pure. Sir Hugh had fallen asleep, as he often did in his last illness, even while speaking.

Gabriel Ockram drew Evelyn away, and from the study they went out into the dim hall, softly closing the door behind them, and each audibly drew breath, as though some sudden danger had been passed. They laid their hands each in the others, and their strangely-alike eyes met in a long look, in which love and perfect understanding were darkened by the secret terror of an unknown thing. Their pale faces reflected each other's fear.

'It is his secret,' said Evelyn at last. 'He will never tell us what it is.'

'If he dies with it,' answered Gabriel, 'let it be on his own head!'

'On his head!' echoed the dim hall. It was a strange echo, and some were frightened by it, for they said that if it were a real echo it should repeat everything and not give back a phrase here and there, now speaking, now solent. But Nurse Macdonald said that the great hall would never echo a prayer when an Ockram was to die, though it would give back curses ten for one.

'On his head!' it repeated quite softly, and Evelyn

started and looked round.

'It is only the echo,' said Gabriel, leading her away.

They went out into the late afternoon light, and sat upon a stone seat behind the chapel, which was built across the end of the east wing. It was very still, not a breath stirred, and there was no sound near them. Only far off in the park a song-bird was whistling the high prelude to the evening chorus.

'It is very lonely here,' said Evelyn, taking Gabriel's hand nervously, and speaking as if she dreaded to disturb the silence. 'If it were dark, I should be afraid.'

'Of what? Of me?' Gabriel's sad eyes turned to her.

'Oh no! How could I be afraid of you? But of the old Ockrams—they say they are just under our feet here in the north vault outside the chapel, all in their shrouds, with no coffins, as they used to bury them.'

'As they always will—as they will bury my father, and me. They say an Ockram will not lie in a coffin.'

'But is cannot be true—these are fairy tales—ghost stories!' Evelyn nestled nearer to her companion, grasping his hand more tightly, and the sun began to go down.

'Of course. But there is a story of old Sir Vernon, who was beheaded for treason under James II. The family brought his body back from the scaffold in an iron coffin with heavy locks, and they put it in the north vault. But even afterwards, whenever the vault was opened to bury another of the family, they found the coffin wide open, and the body standing upright against the wall, and the head rolled away in a corner, smiling at it.'

'As Uncle Hugh smiles?' Evelyn shivered.

'Yes, I suppose so,' answered Gabriel, thoughtfully. 'Of course I never saw it, and the vault has not been opened for thirty years—none of us have died since then.'

205

'And if—if Uncle Hugh dies—shall you—' Evelyn stopped, and her beautiful thin face was quite white.

'Yes. I shall see him laid there too—with his secret, whatever it is.' Gabriel sighed and pressed the girl's little hand.

'I do not like to think of it,' she said unsteadily. 'O Gabriel, what can the secret be? He said we had better not marry—not that he forbade it—but he said it so strangely, and he smiled—ugh!' Her small white teeth chattered with fear, and she looked over her shoulder while drawing still closer to Gabriel. 'And, somehow, I felt it in my own face—'

'So did I,' answered Gabriel in a low, nervous voice. 'Nurse Macdonald—' He stopped abruptly.

'What? What did she say?'

'Oh—nothing. She has told me things— they would frighten you, dear. Come, it is growing chilly.' He rose, byt Evelyn held his hand in both of hers, still sitting and looking up into his face.

'But we shall be married, just the same—Gabriel! Say that we shall!'

Of course, darling—of course. But while my father is so very ill, it is impossible—'

'O Gabriel, Gabriel dear! I wish we were married now!' cried Evelyn in sudden distress. 'I know that something will prevent it and keep us apart.'

'Nothing shall!'

'Nothing?'

'Nothing human,' said Gabriel Ockram, as she drew him down to her.

And their faces, that were so strangely alike, met and touched—and Gabriel knew that the kiss had a marvellous savour of evil, but on Evelyn's lips it was like the cool breath of a sweet and mortal fear. And neither of them understood, for they were innocent and young. Yet she drew him to her by her lightest touch, as a

sensitive plant shivers and waves its thin leaves, and
bends and closes softly upon what it wants, and he let
himself be drawn to her willingly, as he would if her
touch had been deadly and poisonous; for she strangely
loved that half voluptuous breath of fear and he passionately desired the nameless evil something that lurked
in her maiden lips.

'It is as if we loved in a strange dream,' she said.

'I fear the waking,' he murmured.

'We shall not wake, dear—when the dream is over it
will have already turned into death, so softly that we
shall not know it. But until then—'

She paused, and her eyes sought his, and their faces
slowly came nearer. It was as if they had thoughts in
their red lips that foresaw and foreknew the deep kiss
of each other.

'Until then—' she said again, very low, and her mouth
was nearer to his.

'Dream—till then,' murmured his breath.

II

Nurse Macdonald was a hundred years old. She used
to sleep sitting all bent together in a great old leathern
arm-chair with wings, her feet in a bag footstool lined
with sheepskin, and many warm blankets wrapped about
her, even in summer. Beside her a little lamp always
burned at night by an old silver cup, in which there
was something to drink.

Her face was very wrinkled, but the wrinkles were
so small and fine and near together that they made
shadows instead of lines. Two thin locks of hair, that
was turning from white to a smoky yellow again, were
drawn over her temples from under her starched white
cap. Every now and then she woke, and her eyelids were
drawn up in tiny folds like little pink silk curtains, and

her queer blue eyes looked straight before her through doors and walls and worlds to a far place beyond. Then she slept again, and her hands lay one upon the other on the edge of the blanket, the thumbs had grown longer than the fingers with age, and the joints shone in the low lamplight like polished crab-apples.

It was nearly one o'clock in the night, and the summer breeze was blowing the ivy branch against the panes of the window with a hushing caress. In the small room beyond, with the door ajar, the girl-maid who took care of Nurse Macdonald was fast asleep. All was very quiet. The old woman breathed regularly, and her indrawn lips trembled each time as the breath went out, and her eyes were shut.

But outside the closed window there was a face, and violet eyes were looking steadily at the ancient sleeper, for it was like the face of Evelyn Warburton, though there were eighty feet from the sill of the window to the foot of the tower. Yet the cheeks were thinner than Evelyn's, and as white as a gleam, and her eyes stared, and the lips were not red with life, they were dead and painted with new blood.

Slowly Nurse Macdonald's wrinkled eyelids folded themselves back, and she looked straight at the face at the window while one might count ten.

'Is it time?' she asked in her little old, far-away voice.

While she looked the face at the window changed, for the eyes opened wider and wider till the white glared all round the bright violet, and the bloody lips opened over gleaming teeth, and stretched and widened and stretched again, and the shadow golden hair rose and streamed against the window in the night breeze. And in answer to Nurse Macdonald's question came the sound that freezes the living flesh.

That low moaning voice that rises suddenly, like the scream of storm, from a moan to a wail, from a wail to a howl, from a howl to the fear-shriek of the tortured dead—he who had heard knows, and he can bear witness that the cry of the banshee is an evil cry to hear alone in the deep night. When it was over and the face was gone, Nurse Macdonald shook a little in her great chair, and still she looked at the black square of the window, but there was nothing more there, nothing but the night, and the whispering ivy branch. She turned her head to the door that was ajar, and there stood the girl in her white gown, her teeth chattering with fright.

'It is time, child,' said Nurse Macdonald. 'I must go to him, for it is the end.'

She rose slowly, leaning her withered hands upon the arms of the chair, and the girl brought her a woollen gown and a great mantle, and her crutch-stick, and made her ready. But very often the girl looked at the window and was unjointed with fear, and often Nurse Macdonald shook her head and said words which the maid could not understand.

'It was like the face of Miss Evelyn,' said the girl at last, trembling.

But the ancient woman looked up sharply and angrily, and her queer blue eyes blared. She held herself by the arm of the great chair with her left hand, and lifted up her crutch-stick to strike the maid with all her might. But she did not.

'You are a good girl,' she said, 'but you are a fool. Pray for wit, child, pray for wit—or else find service in another house than Ockram Hall. Bring the lamp and help me under my left arm.'

The crutch-stick clacked on the wooden floor, and the low heels of the woman's slippers clappered after her in slow triplets, as Nurse Macdonald got toward the door. And down the stairs each step she took was a labour in itself, and by the clacking noise the waking servants knew that she was coming, very long before, they saw her.

No one was sleeping now, and there were lights and whisperings and pale faces in the corridors near Sir Hugh's bedroom, and now someone went in, and now someone came out, but everyone made way for Nurse Macdonald, who had nursed Sir Hugh's father more than eighty years ago.

The light was soft and clear in the room. There stood Gabriel Ockram by his father's bedside, and there knelt Evelyn Warburton, her hair lying like a golden shadow down her shoulders, and her hands clasped nervously together. And opposite Gabriel, a nurse was trying to make Sir Hugh drink. But he would not, and though his lips were parted, his teeth were set. He was very, very thin and yellow now, and his eyes caught the light sideways and were as yellow coals.

'Do not torment him,' said Nurse Macdonald to the woman who held the cup. 'Let me speak to him, for his hour is come.'

'Let her speak to him,' said Gabriel in a dull voice.

So the ancient woman leaned to the pillow and laid the feather-weight of her withered hand, that was like a brown moth, upon Sir Hugh's yellow fingers, and she spoke to him earnestly, while only Gabriel and Evelyn were left in the room to hear.

'Hugh Ockram,' she said, 'this is the end of your life; and as I saw you born, and saw your father born before you, I am come to see you die. Hugh Ockram, will you tell me the truth?'

The dying man recognised the little far-away voice he had known all his life, and he very slowly turned his yellow face to Nurse Macdonald; but he said nothing. Then she spoke again.

'Hugh Ockram, you will never see the daylight again. Will you tell the truth?'

210

His toad-like eyes were not dull yet. They fastened themselves on her face.

'What do you want of me?' he asked, and each word struck hollow on the last. 'I have no secrets. I have lived a good life.'

Nurse Macdonald laughed—a tiny, cracked laugh, that made her old head bob and tremble a little, as if her neck were on a steel spring. But Sir Hugh's eyes grew red, and his pale lips began to twist.

'Let me die in peace,' he said slowly.

But Nurse Macdonald shook her head, and her brown, moth-like hand left his and fluttered to his forehead.

'By the mother that bore you and died of grief for the sins you did, tell me the truth!'

Sir Hugh's lips tightened on his discoloured teeth.

'Not on earth,' he answered slowly.

'By the wife who bore your son and died heart-broken, tell me the truth!'

'Neither to you in life, nor to her in eternal death.'

His lips writhed, as if the words were coals between them, and a great drop of sweat rolled across the parchment of his forehead. Gabriel Ockram bit his hand as he watched his father die. But Nurse Macdonald spoke a third time.

'By the woman whom you betrayed, and who waits for you this night, Hugh Ockram, tell me the truth!'

'It is too late. Let me die in peace.'

The writhing lips began to smile across the set yellow teeth, and the toad eyes glowed like evil jewels in his head.

'There is time,' said the ancient woman. 'Tell me the name of Evelyn Warburton's father. Then I will let you die in peace.'

Evelyn started back, kneeling as she was, and stared at Nurse Macdonald, and then at her uncle.

'The name of Evelyn's father?' he repeated slowly, while the awful smile spread upon his dying face.

The light was growing strangely dim in the great room. As Evelyn looked, Nurse Macdonald's crooked shadow on the wall grew gigantic. Sir Hugh's breath came thick, rattling in his throat, as death crept in like a snake and choked it back. Evelyn prayed aloud, high and clear.

Then something rapped at the window, and she felt her hair rise upon her head in a cool breeze, as she looked around in spite of herself. And when she saw her own white face looking in at the window, and her own eyes staring at her through the glass, wide and fearful, and her own hair streaming against the pane, and her own lips dashed with blood, she rose slowly from the floor and stood rigid for one moment, till she screamed once and fell back into Gabriel's arms. But the shriek that answered hers was the fear-shriek of the tormented corpse, out of which the soul cannot pass for shame of deadly sins, though the devils fight in it with corruption, each for their due share.

Sir Hugh Ockram sat upright in his death-bed, and saw and cried aloud:

'Evelyn!' His harsh voice broke and rattled in his chest as he sank down. But still Nurse Macdonald tortured him, for there was a little life left in him still.

'You have seen the mother as she waits for you, Hugh Ockram. Who was this girl Evelyn's father? What was his name?'

For the last time the dreadful smile came upon the twisted lips, very slowly, very surely now, and the toad eyes glared red, and the parchment face glowed a little in the flickering light. For the last time words came.

'They know it in hell.'

Then the glowing eyes went out quickly, the yellow face turned waxen pale, and a great shiver ran through

212

the thin body as Hugh Ockram died.

But in death he still smiled, for he knew his secret and kept it still, on the other side, and he would take it with him, to lie with him for ever in the north vault of the chapel where the Ockrams lie uncoffined in their shrouds—all but one. Though he was dead, he smiled, for he had kept his treasure of evil truth to the end, and there was none left to tell the name he had spoken, but there was all the evil he had not undone left to bear fruit.

As they watched—Nurse Macdonald and Gabriel, who held Evelyn still unconscious in his arms while he looked at the father—they felt the dead smile crawling along their own lips—the ancient crone and the youth with the angel's face. Then they shivered a little, and both looked at Evelyn as she lay with her head on his shoulder, and, though she was very beautiful, the same sickening smile was twisting her mouth too, and it was like the foreshadowing of a great evil which they could not understand.

But by and by they carried Evelyn out, and she opened her eyes and the smile was gone. From far away in the great house the sound of weeping and crooning came up the stairs and echoed along the dismal corridors, for the women had begun to mourn the dead master, after the Irish fashion, and the hall had echoes of its own all that night, like the far-off wail of the banshee among forest trees.

When the time was come they took Sir Hugh in his winding-sheet on a trestle bier, and bore him to the chapel and through the iron door and down the long descent to the north vault, with tapers, to lay him by his father. And two men went in first to prepare the place and came back staggering like drunken men, and white, leaving their lights behind them.

But Gabriel Ockram was not afraid, for he knew. And he went in alone and saw that the body of Sir Vernon Ockram was leaning upright against the stone wall, and that his head lay on the ground near by with the face turned up, and the dried leathern lips smiled horribly at the dried-up corpse, while the iron coffin, lined with black velvet, stood open on the floor.

Then Gabriel took the thing in his hands, for it was very light, being quite dried by the air of the vault, and those who peeped in from the door saw him lay it in the coffin again, and it rustled a little, like a bundle of reeds, and sounded hollow as it touched the sides and the bottom. He also placed the head upon the shoulders and shut down the lid, which fell to with a rusty spring that snapped.

After that they laid Sir Hugh beside his father, with the trestle bier on which they had brought him, and they went back to the chapel.

But when they saw one another's faces, master and men, they were all smiling with the dead smile of the corpse they had left in the vault, so that they could not bear to look at one another until it had faded away.

III

Gabriel Ockram became Sir Gabriel, inheriting the baronetcy with the half-ruined fortune left by his father, and still Evelyn Warburton lived at Ockham Hall, in the south room that had been hers ever since she could remember anything. She could not go away, for there were no relatives to whom she could have gone, and besides there seemed to be no reason why she should not stay. The world would never trouble itself to care what the Ockrams did on their Irish estates, as it was long since the Ockrams had asked anything of the world.

So Sir Gabriel took his father's place at the dark old

214

table in the dining-room, and Evelyn sat opposite to him, until such time as their mourning should be over, and they might be married at last. And meanwhile their lives went on as before, since Sir Hugh had been a hopeless invalid during the last year of his life, and they had seen him but once a day for the little while, spending most of their time together in a strangely perfect companionship.

But though the late summer saddened into autumn, and autumn darkened into winter, and storm followed storm, and rain poured on rain through the short days and the long nights, yet Ockram Hall seemed less gloomy since Sir Hugh had been laid in the north vault beside his father. And at Christmastide Evelyn decked the great hall with holly and green boughs, and huge fires blazed on every hearth. Then the tenants were all bidden to a New Year's dinner, and they ate and drank well, while Sir Gabriel sat at the head of the table. Evelyn came in when the port wine was brought, and the most respected of the tenants made a speech to propose her health.

It was long, he said, since there had been a Lady Ockram. Sir Gabriel shaded his eyes with his hand and looked down at the table, but a faint colour came into Evelyn's transparent cheeks. But, said the grey-haired farmer, it was longer still since there had been a Lady Ockram so fair as the next was to be, and he gave the health of Evelyn Warburton.

Then the tenants all stood up and shouted for her, and Sir Gabriel stood up likewise, beside Evelyn. And when the men gave the last and loudest cheer of all there was a voice not theirs, above them all, higher, fiercer, louder—a scream not earthly, shrieking for the bride of Ockram Hall. And the holly and the green boughs over the great chimney-piece shook and slowly waved as if a cool breeze were blowing over them. But the men turned very pale, and many of them sat down their glasses, but others let them fall upon the floor for fear. And looking into one another's faces, they were all smiling strangely, a dead smile, like dead Sir Hugh's. One cried out words in Irish, and the fear of death was suddenly upon them all so that they fled in panic, falling over one another like wild beasts in the burning forest, when the thick smoke runs along the flame, and the tables were overset, and drinking glasses and bottles were broken in heaps, and the dark red wine crawled like blood upon the polished floor.

Sir Gabriel and Evelyn stood alone at the head of the table before the wreck of the feast, not daring to turn to see each other, for each knew that the other smiled. But his right arm held her and his left hand clasped her right as they stared before them, and but for the shadows of her hair one might not have told their two faces apart. They listened long, but the cry came not again, and the dead smile faded from their lips, while each remembered that Sir Hugh Ockram lay in the north vault, smiling in his winding-sheet, in the dark, because he had died with his secret.

So ended the tenant's New Year's dinner. But from that time on Sir Gabriel grew more and more silent, and his face grew even paler and thinner than before. Often without warning and without words, he would rise from his seat, as if something moved him against his will, and he would go out into the rain or the sunshine to the north side of the chapel, and sit on the stone bench, staring at the ground as if he could see through it, and through the vault below, and through the white winding-sheet in the dark, to the dead smile that would not die.

Always when he went out in that way Evelyn came out presently and sat beside him. Once, too, as in summer, their beautiful faces came suddenly near, and their lids drooped, and their red lips were almost joined together. But as their eyes met, they grew wide and wild, so that the white showed in a ring all round the deep violet, and their teeth chattered, and their hands were like hands of corpses, each in the other's for the terror of what was under their feet, and of what they knew but could not see.

Once, also, Evelyn found Sir Gabriel in the Chapel alone, standing before the iron door that led down to the place of death, and in his hand there was the key to the door, but he had not put it in the lock. Evelyn drew him away, shivering, for she had also been driven in waking dreams to see that terrible thing again, and to find out whether it had changed since it had lain there.

'I'm going mad, Sir,' said Gabriel, covering his eyes with his hand as he went with her. 'I see it in my sleep, I see it when I am awake—it draws me to it, day and night—and unless I see it I shall die!'

'I know,' answered Evelyn, 'I know. It is as if threads were spun from it, like a spider's, drawing us down to it.' She was silent for a moment, and then she stared violently and grasped his arm with a man's strength, and almost screamed the words she spoke. 'But we must not go there!' she cried. 'We must not go!'

Sir Gabriel's eyes were half shut, and he was not moved by the agony on her face.

'I shall die, unless I see it again,' he said, in a quiet voice not like his own. And all that day and that evening he scarcely spoke, thinking of it, always thinking, while Evelyn Warburton quivered from head to foot with a terror she had never known.

She went alone, on a grey winter's morning, to Nurse Macdonald's room in the tower, and sat down beside the great leathern easy-chair, laying her thin white hand upon the withered fingers.

'Nurse,' she said, 'what was it that Uncle Hugh should have told you, that night before he died? It must have

217

been an awful secret—and yet, though you asked him, I feel somehow that you know it, and that you know why he used to smile so dreadfully.'

The old woman's head moved slowly from side to side.

'I only guess—I shall never know,' she answered slowly in her cracked little voice.

'But what do you guess? Who am I? Why did you ask who my father was? You know I am Colonel Warburton's daughter, and my mother was Lady Ockram's sister, so that Gabriel and I are cousins. My father was killed in Afghanistan. What secret can there be?'

'I do not know. I can only guess.'

'Guess what?' asked Evelyn imploringly, and pressing the soft withered hands, as she leaned forward. But Nurse Macdonald's wrinkled lids dropped suddenly over her queer blue eyes, and her lips shook a little with her breath, as if she were asleep.

Evelyn waited. By the fire the Irish maid was knitting fast, and the needles clicked like three or four clocks ticking against each other. And the real clock on the wall solemnliy ticked alone, checking off the seconds of the woman who was a hundred years old, and had not many days left. Outside the ivy branch beat the window in the wintry blast, as it had beaten against the glass a hundred years ago.

Then as Evelyn sat there she felt again the waking of a horrible desire—the sickening wish to go down, down to the thing in the north vault, and to open the winding-sheet, and see whether it had changed, and she held Nurse Macdonald's hands as if to keep herself in her place and fight against the appalling attraction of the evil dead.

But the old cat that kept Nurse Macdonald's feet warm, lying aways on the bag footstool, got up and stretched itself, and looked up into Evelyn's eyes, while its back arched, and its tail thickened and bristled, and its ugly pink lips drew back in a develish grin, showing its sharp teeth. Evelyn stared at it, half fascinated by its ugliness. Then the creature suddenly put out one paw with all its claws spread, and spat at the girl, and all at once the grinning cat was like the smiling corpse far down below, so that Evelyn shivered down to her small feet and covered her face with her free hand lest Nurse Macdonald should wake and see the dead smile there, for she could feel it.

The old woman had already opened her eyes again, and she touched her cat with the end of her crutch-stick, whereupon its back went down and its tail shrunk, and it sidled back to its place in the bag footstool. But its yellow eyes looked up sideways at Evelyn, between the slits of its lids.

'What is it that you guess, nurse?' asked the young girl again.

'A bad thing—a wicked thing. But I dare not tell you, lest it might not be true, and the very thought should blast your life. For if I guess right, he meant that you should not know, and that you two should marry, and pay for his old sin with your souls.'

'He used to tell us that we ought not to marry—'

'Yes—he told you that, perhaps—but it was as if a man put poisoned meat before a starving beast, and said "do not eat" but never raised his hand to take the meat away. And if he told you that you should not marry, it was because he hoped you would, for of all men living or dead, Hugh Ockram was the falsest man that ever told a cowardly lie, and the cruellest that ever hurt a weak woman, and the worst that ever loved a sin.'

'But Gabriel and I love each other,' said Evelyn very sadly.

Nurse Macdonald's old eyes looked far away, at sights seen long ago, and that rose in the grey winter air amid the mists of an ancient youth.

'If you love, you can die together,' she said very slowly. 'Why should you live, if it is true? I am a hundred years old. What has life given me? The beginning is fire, the end is a heap of ashes, and between the end and the beginning lies all the pain in the world. Let me sleep, since I cannot die.'

Then the old woman's eyes closed again, and her head sank a little lower upon her breast.

So Evelyn went away and left her asleep, with the cat asleep on the bag footstool; and the young girl tried to forget Nurse Macdonald's words, but she could not, for she heard them over and over again in the wind, and behind her on the stairs. And as she grew sick with fear of the frightful unknown evil to which her soul was bound, she felt a bodily something pressing her, and pushing her, and forcing her on, and from the other side she felt the threads that drew her mysteriously, and when she shut her eyes, she saw in the chapel behind the altar, the low iron door through which she must pass to go to the thing.

And as she lay awake at night, she drew the sheet over her face, lest she should see shadows on the wall beckoning her and the sound of her own warm breath made whisperings in her ears, while she held the mattress with her hands, to keep from getting up and going to the chapel. It would have been easier if there had not been a way thither through the library, by a door which was never locked. It would be fearfully easy to take her candle and go softly through the sleeping house. And the key of the vault lay under the altar behind a stone that turned. She knew the little secret. She could go alone and see.

But when she thought of it, she felt her hair rise on

her head, and first she shivered so that the bed shook, and then the horror went through her in a cold thrill that was agony again, like myriads of icy needles, boring into her nerves.

IV

The old clock in Nurse Macdonald's tower struck midnight. From her room she could hear the creaking chains and weights in their box in the corner of the stair-case, and overheard the jarring of the rusty lever that lifted the hammer. She had heard it all her life. It struck eleven strokes clearly and then came the twelfth, with a dull half stroke, as though the hammer were too weary to go on, and had fallen asleep against the bell.

The old cat got up from the bag footstool and stretched itself, and Nurse Macdonald opened he ancient eyes and looked slowly round the room by the dim light of the night lamp. She touched the cat with her crutch-stick, and it lay down upon her feet. She drank a few drops from her cup and went to sleep again.

But downstairs Sir Gabriel sat straight up as the clock struck, for he had dreamed a fearful dream of horror, and his heart stood still, till he awoke at its stopping, and it beat again furiously with his breath, like a wild thing set free. No Ockram had ever known fear waking, but sometimes it came to Sir Gabriel in his sleep.

He pressed his hands on his temples as he sat up in bed, and his hands were icy cold, but his head was hot. The dream faded far, and in its place there came the sick twisting of his lips in the dark that would have been a smile. Far off, Evelyn Warburton dreamed that the dead smile was on her mouth, and awoke, starting with a little moan, her face in her hands shivering.

But Sir Gabriel struck a light and got up and began to walk up and down his great room. It was midnight, and he had barely slept an hour, and in the north of Ireland the winter nights are long.

'I shall go mad,' he said to himself, holding his forehead. He knew that it was true. For weeks and months the possession of the thing had grown upon him like a disease, till he could think of nothing without thinking first of that. And now all at once it outgrew his strength, and he knew that he must be its instrument or lose his mind—that he must do the deed he hated and feared, if he could fear anything, or that something would snap in his brain and divide him from life while he was yet alive. He took the candlestick in his hand, the old-fashioned heavy candlestick that had always been used by the head of the house. He did not think of dressing, but went as he was, in his silk nightclothes and his slippers, and he opened the door. Everything was very still in the great old house. He shut the door behind him and walked noiselessly on the carpet through the long corridor. A cool breeze blew over his shoulder and blew the flame of his candle straight out from him. Instinctively he stopped and looked round, but all was still, and the upright flame burned steadily. He walked on, and instantly a strong draught was behind him, almost extinguishing the light. It seemed to blow him on his way, ceasing whenever he turned, coming again when he went on—invisible, icy.

Down the great staircase to the echoing hall he went, seeing nothing but the flame of the candle standing away from him over the guttering wax, while the cold wind blew over his shoulder and through his hair. On he passed through the open door into the library, dark with old books and carved bookcases, on through the door in the shelves, with painted shelves on it, and the imitated backs of books, so that one needed to know where to find it—and it shut itself after him with a soft click. He entered the low-arched passage, and though the door was shut behind him and fitted tightly in its frame, still the cold breeze blew the flame forward as he walked. And he was not afraid, but his face was very pale, and his eyes were wide and bright, looking before him, seeing already in the dark air the picture of the thing beyond. But in the chapel he stood still, his hand on the little turning stone tablet in the back of the stone altar. On the tablet were engraved words, *'Clavis sepulchri Clarissimorum Dominorum De Ockram'*—('the key to the vault of the most illustrious lord of Ockram.') Sir Gabriel paused and listened. He fancied that he heard a sound far off in the great house where all had been so still, but it did not come again. Yet he waited at the last, and looked at the low iron door. Beyond it, down the long descent, lay his father uncoffined, six months dead, corrupt, terrible in his clinging shroud. The strangely preserving air of the vault could not yet have done its work completely. But on the thing's ghastly features, with their half-dried, open eyes, there would still be the frightful smile with which the man had died—the smile that haunted—

As the thought crossed Sir Gabriel's mind, he felt his lips writhing, and he struck his own mouth in wrath with the back of his hand so fiercely that a drop of blood ran down his chin and another, and more, falling back in the gloom upon the chapel pavement. But still his bruised lips twisted themselves. He turned the tablet by the simple secret. It needed no safer fastening, for had each Ockram been confined in pure gold, and had the door been wide, there was not a man in Tyrone brave enough to go down to the place, saving Gabriel Ockram himself, with his angel's face and his thin, white hands, and his sad unflinching eyes. He took the great gold key and set it into the lock of the iron door, and the heavy, rattling noise echoed down the descent beyond like footsteps, as if a watcher had stood behind the iron

223

and were running away within, with heavy dead feet. And though he was standing still, the cool wind was from behind him, and blew the flame of the candle against the iron panel. He turned the key.

Sir Gabriel saw that his candle was short. There were new ones on the altar, with long candlesticks and he lit one, and left his own burning on the floor. As he set it down on the pavement his lip began to bleed again, and another drop fell upon the stones.

He drew the iron door open and pushed it back against the chapel wall, so that it should not shut of itself, while he was within, and the horrible draught of the sepulchre came up out of the depths in his face, foul and dark. He went in, but though the fetid air met him, yet the flame of the tall candle was blown straight from him against the wind while he walked down the easy incline with steady steps, his loose slippers slapping the pavement as he trod.

He shaded the candle with his hand, and his fingers seemed to be made of wax and blood as the light shone through them. And in spite of him the unearthly draught forced the flame forward, till it was blue over the black wick, and it seemed as if it must go out. But he went straight on, with shining eyes.

The downward passage was wide, and he could not always see the walls by the struggling light, but he knew when he was in the place of death by the larger, drearier echo of his steps in the greater space and by the sensation of a distant blank wall. He stood still, almost enclosing the flame of the candle in the hollow of his hand. He could see a little, for his eyes were growing used to the gloom. Shadowy forms were outlined in the dimness, where the biers of the Ockrams stood crowded together, side by side, each with its straight, shrouded corpse, strangely preserved by the dry air, like the empty shell that the locust sheds in summer. And a few steps before

224

him he saw clearly the dark shape of headless Sir Vernon's iron coffin, and he knew that nearest to it lay the thing he sought.

He was as brave as any of those dead men had been, and they were his fathers, and he knew that sooner or later he should lie there himself, beside Sir Hugh, slowly drying to a parchment shell. But he was still alive, and he closed his eyes a moment, and three great drops stood on his forehead.

Then he looked again, and by the whiteness of the winding-sheet he knew his father's corpse, for all the others were brown with age; and, moreover, the flame of the candle was blown towards it. He made four steps till he reached it, and suddenly the light burned straight and high, shedding a dazzling yellow glare upon the fine linen that was all white, save over the face, and where the joined hands were laid on the breast. And at those places ugly stains had spread, darkened with outlines of the features and of the tight-clasped fingers. There was a frightful stench of drying death.

As Sir Gabriel looked down, something stirred behind him, softly at first, then more noisily, and something fell to the stone floor with a dull thud and rolled up to his feet; he started back, and saw a withered head lying almost face upward on the pavement, grinning at him. He felt the cold sweat standing on his face, and his heart beat painfully.

For the first time in all his life that evil thing which men call fear was getting hold of him, checking his heart-strings as a cruel driver checks a quivering horse, clawing at his backbone with icy hands, lifting his hair with freezing breath climbing up and gathering in his midriff with leaden weight.

Yet presently he bit his lip and bent down, holding the candle in one hand, to lift the shroud back from the head of the corpse with the other. Slowly he lifted it.

Then it clove to the half-dried skin of the face, and his hand shook as if someone had struck him on the elbow, but half in fear and half in anger at himself, he pulled it, so that it came away with a little ripping sound. He caught his breath as he held it, not yet throwing it back, and not yet looking. The horror was working in him. and he felt that old Vernon Ockram was standing up in his iron coffin, headless, yet watching him with the stump of his severed neck.

While he held his breath he felt the dead smile twisting his lips. In sudden wrath at his own misery, he tossed the death-stained linen backward, and looked at last. He ground his teeth lest he should shriek aloud.

There it was, the thing that haunted him, that haunted Evelyn Warburton, that was like a blight on all that came near him.

The dead face was blotched with dark stains, and the thin, grey hair was matted about the discoloured forehead. The sunken lids were half open, and the candle light gleamed on something foul where the toad eyes had lived.

But yet the dead thing smiled, as it had smiled in life; the ghastly lips were parted and drawn wide and tight upon the wolfish teeth, cursing still, and still defying hell to do its worst—defying, cursing, and always and for ever smiling alone in the dark.

Sir Gabriel opened the winding-sheet where the hands were, and the blackened, withered fingers were closed upon something stained and mottled. Shivering from head to foot, but fighting like a man in agony for his life, he tried to take the package from the dead man's hold. But as he pulled at it the claw-like fingers seemed to close more tightly, and when he pulled harder the shrunken hands and arms rose from the corpse with a horrible look of life following his motion—then as he wrenched the sealed packet loose at last, the hands fell back into their place still folded.

He set down the candle on the edge of the bier to break the seals from the stout paper. And, kneeling on one knee, to get a better light, he read what was within, written long ago in Sir Hugh's queer hand.

He was no longer afraid.

He read how Sir Hugh had written it all down that it might perchance be a witness of evil and of his hatred; how he had loved Evelyn Warburton, his wife's sister; and how his wife had died of a broken heart with his curse upon her, and how Warburton and he had fought side by side in Afghanistan, and Warburton had fallen; but Ockram had brought his comrade's wife back a full year later, and little Evelyn, her child, had been born in Ockram Hall. And next, how he had wearied of the mother, and she had died like her sister with his curse on her. And then, how Evelyn had been brought up as his niece, and how he had trusted that his son Gabriel and his daughter, innocent and unknowing, might love and marry, and the souls of the women he had betrayed might suffer another anguish before eternity was out. And, last of all, he hoped that some day, when nothing could be undone, the two might find his writing and live on, not daring to tell the truth for their children's sake and the world's word, man and wife.

This he read, kneeling beside the corpse in the north vault, by the light of the altar candle; and when he had read it all, he thanked God aloud that he had found the secret in time. But when he rose to his feet and looked down at the dead face it was changed, and the smile was gone from it for ever, and the jaw had fallen a little, and the tired, dead lips were relaxed. And then there was a breath behind him and close to him, not cold like that which had blown the flame of the candle as he came, but warm and human. He turned suddenly.

There she stood, all in white, with her shadowy golden hair—for she had risen from her bed and had followed him noiselessly, and had found him reading, and had herself read over his shoulder. He started violently when he saw her, for his nerves were unstrung—and then he cried out her name in the still place of death:

'Evelyn!'

'My brother!' she answered, softly and tenderly, putting out both hands to meet his.

HELL FIRE

by James Joyce

JAMES JOYCE *(1882–1941) is the most famous of all Irish literary figures, author of* Ulysses *and* Finegan's Wake. *He spent much of his life away from Ireland but none the less captured the mean existence of a section of the people in several works of unquestioned genius. He knew a great deal about Irish fantasy, and his adventures of Shem and Shaun are an object lesson to any writer who would wish to use his language in a new way. Because of his strict Roman Catholic upbringing, Joyce saw religion in harsh shades, as is demonstrated in this account of a preacher describing the (imaginary) tortures of hell. Extravagant and unbelievable though the man's words are, to many people of the period when Joyce was writing they had a very real meaning and warning.*

The preacher's voice sank. He paused, joined his palms for an instant, parted them. Then he resumed: Now let us try for a moment to realise as far as we can, the nature of that abode of the damned which the justice of an offended God has called into existence for the eternal punishment of sinners. Hell is a strait and dark and foul-smelling prison, an abode of demons and lost souls, filled with fire and smoke. The straitness of this prison is expressly designed by God to punish those who refused to be bound by his laws. In earthy prisons the poor captive has at least some liberty of movement, were it only within the four walls of his cell or in the gloomy yard of his prison. Not so in hell. There, by reason of the great number of the damned, the prisoners are heaped together in their awful prison, the walls of which are said to be four thousand miles thick: and the damned are so utterly bound and helpless that, as a blessed saint, Saint Anselm, write in his book on similitudes, they are not even able to remove from the eye a worm that gnaws it.

They lie in exterior darkness. For, remember, the fire of hell gives forth no light. As, at the command of God, the fire of the Babylonian furnace lost its heat but not its light, so, at the command of God, the fire of hell, while retaining the intensity of its heat, burns eternally in darkness. It is a never-ending storm of darkness, dark flames and dark smoke of burning brimstone amid which the bodies are heaped one upon another, without even a glimpse of air. Of all the plagues with which the land of the Pharaohs were smitten one plague alone, that of darkness, was called horrible. What name, then, shall we give to the darkness of hell which is to last not for three days alone but for all eternity?

The horror of this strait and dark prison is increased by its awful stench. All the filth of the world, all the offal and scum of the world, we are told, shall run there as to a vast reeking sewer when the terrible conflagration of the last day has purged the world. The brimstone, too, which burns there in such prodigious quantity fills all hell with its intolerable stench; and the bodies of the

229

damned themselves inhale such a pestilential odour that, as Saint Bonaventure says, one of them alone would suffice to infect the whole world. The very air of this world, that pure element, becomes foul and unbreathable when it has been long enclosed. Consider then what must be the foulness of the air of hell. Imagine some foul and putrid corpse that has lain rotting and decomposing in the grave, a jelly-like mass of liquid corruption. Imagine such a corpse a prey to flames, devoured by the fire of burning brimstone and giving off dense choking fumes of nauseous loathsome decomposition. And then imagine this sickening stench, multiplied a millionfold and a millionfold again from the millions upon millions of fetid carcasses massed together in the reeking darkness, a huge and rotting human fungus. Imagine all this, and you will have some idea of the horror of the stench of hell.

But this stench is not, horrible though it is, the greatest physical torment to which the damned are subjected. The torment of fire is the greatest torment to which the tyrant has ever subjected his fellow-creatures. Place your finger for a moment in the flame of a candle and you will feel the pain of fire. But our earthly fire was created by God for the benefit of man, to maintain in him the spark of life and to help him in the useful arts, whereas the fire of hell is of another quality and was created by God to torture and punish the unrepentant sinner. Our earthly fire also consumes more or less rapidly according to the object which it attacks being more or less combustible, so that human ingenuity has even succeeded in inventing chemical preparations to check or frustrate its action. But the sulphurous brimstone which burns in hell is a substance which is specially designed to burn for ever and ever with unspeakable fury.

Moreover, our earthly fire destroys at the same time as it burns, so that the more intense it is the shorter its duration; but the fire of hell has this property, that it preserves that which it burns, and, though it rages with incredible intensity, it rages for ever.

Our earthly fire again, no matter how fierce or widespread it may be, is always of a limited extent; but the lake of fire in hell is boundless, shoreless and bottomless. It is on record that the devil himself, when asked the question by a certain soldier, was obliged to confess that if a whole mountain were thrown into the burning ocean of hell it would be burned up in an instant like a piece of wax. And this terrible fire would not afflict the bodies of the damned only from without, but each lost soul will be hell unto itself, the boundless fire raging in its very vitals. O how terrible is the lot of those wretched beings! The blood seethes and boils in the veins, the brains are boiling in the skull, the heart in the breast glowing and burning, the bowels a red-hot mass of burning pulp, the tender eyes flaming like molten balls.

And yet what I have said as to the strength and quality and boundlessness of this fire is as nothing when compared to its intensity, an intensity which it has as being the instrument chosen by divine design for the punishment of soul and body alike. It is a fire which proceeds directly from the ire of God, working not of its own activity but as an instrument of Divine vengeance. As the waters of baptism cleanse the soul with the body, so do the fire of punishment torture the spirit with the flesh. Every sense of the flesh is tortured and every faculty of the soul therewith: the eyes with impenetrable utter darkness, the nose with noisome odours, the ears with yells and howls and execrations, the taste with foul matter, leprous corruption, nameless suffocating filth, the touch with red-hot goads and spikes, with cruel tongues of flame. And through the several torments of the senses the immortal soul is tortured eternally in its very essence amid the leagues upon leagues of glowing

231

fires kindled in the abyss of the offended majesty of the Omnipotent God and fanned into everlasting and ever increasing fury by the breath of the anger of the God-head.

Consider finally that the torment of this infernal prison is increased by the company of the damned themselves. Evil company on earth is so noxious that the plants, as if by instinct, withdraw from the company of whatsoever is deadly or hurtful to them. In hell all laws are over-turned—there is no thoughts of family or country, of ties, of relationships. The damned howl and scream at one another, their torture and rage intensified by the presence of beings tortured and raging like themselves. All sense of humanity is forgotten. The yells of the suffering sinners fill the remotest corners of the vast abyss. The mouths of the damned are full of blasphemies against God and of hatred for their fellow sufferers and of curses against those souls which were their accomplices in sin. In olden times it was the custom to punish the parricide, the man who had raised his murderous hand against his father, by casting him into the depths of the sea in a sock in which were placed a cock, a monkey and a serpent. The idea was to punish the criminal by the company of hurtful and hateful beasts. what is the fury of those dumb beasts compared with the fury of execration which bursts from the parched lips and aching throats of the damned in hell when they behold in their companions in misery those who aided and abetted them in sin, those whose words sowed the first seeds of evil thinking and evil living in their minds, those whose immodest suggestions led them on to sin, those whose eyes tempted and allured them from the path of virtue. They turn upon those accomplices and upbraid them and curse them. But they are helpless and hopeless: it is too late now for repentance.

Last of all consider the frightful torment to those

damned souls, tempters and tempted alike, of the company of the devils. These devils will afflict the damned in two ways, by their presence and by their reproaches. We can have no idea of how horrible these devils are. Saint Catherine of Siena once saw a devil and she has written that, rather than look again for one single instant on such a frightful monster, she would prefer to walk until the end of her life along a track of red coals. These devils, who were once beautiful angels, have become as hideous and ugly as they once were beautiful. They mock and jeer at the lost souls whom they dragged down to ruin. It is they, the foul demons, who are made in hell the voices of conscience. Why did you sin? Why did you lend an ear to the temptings of friends? Why did you turn aside from your pious practices and good works? Why did you not shun the occasions of sin? Why did you not leave that evil companion? Why did you not give up that lewd habit, that impure habit? Why did you not, even after you had fallen the first or the second or the third or the fourth of the hundredth time, repent of your evil ways and turn to God who only waited for your repentance to absolve you of your sins? Now the time for repentance has gone by. This is, time was, but time shall be no more? Time was sin in secrecy, to indulge in that sloth and pride, to covet the unlawful, to yield to the promptings of your lower nature, to live like the beasts of the field, nay worse than the beasts of the field, for they, at least are but brutes and have not reason to guide them: time was, but time shall be no more. God spoke to you by so many voices, but you would not hear. You would not crush out that pride and anger in your heart, you would not restore those ill-gotten goods, you would not obey the precepts of your holy church nor attend to your religious duties, you would not abandon these wicked companions, you would not avoid those dangerous temptations. Such is the language of those fiendish tormentors, words of taunting and reproach, and hatred and of disgust. Of disgust, yes! For even they, the very devils, when they sinned, sinned by such a sin as alone was compatible with such angelical natures, a rebellion of the intellect; and they, even they, the foul devils must turn away; revolted and disgusted, from the contemplation of those unspeakable sins by which degraded man outrages and defiles the temple of the Holy Ghost, defiles and pollutes himself.

WITCH WOOD

by Lord Dunsany

EDWARD J. M. DRAX PLUNKETT DUNSANY, *18th Baron (1875–1957), was a soldier with a leaning for literature. Educated at Eton and Sandhurst, he served first with the Coldstream Guards in the Boer War and later as an officer in the Inniskilling Fusiliers during World War One. His absorption with the written word had, however, already resulted in the first of many books* (The Gods of Pegana *in 1905) and he eventually broke away from Army life completely to become Byron Professor of English Literature at Athens. At the invitation of W. B. Yeats he began writing plays for the Abbey Theatre and simultaneously developed a unique kind of fantasy tale of legendary gods and warlords. Today, these tales are somewhat neglected, but Dunsany's other stories of the tale-teller Jorkens and his experiences with the occult still find their way into the occasional anthology. I am particularly pleased, therefore, to continue this trend by bringing back into print this little-known episode of Jorkens and a small copse which is cursed by the malignant spell of an old witch . . .*

'I think there are more witches in Ireland than in any other land that I know,' said Jorkens.

Nobody was talking of witches that day at the Billiards Club. On the other hand our general conversation was at rather a low ebb, so far as interest was concerned, and not really sufficiently full of even reliable

235

fact for me to pass it on to my readers; and Jorkens's
remark was little more than an attempt, which was fortunately successful to turn our talk from speculations
about technicalities of which we were not very fully
informed to the story of some fragment of his own life.
Jorkens is no scientist, nor does he pretend to be, and
yet I believe that when I shall have been able to fit
together all the stories of his I have heard, until the end
of one touches the beginning of another all the way
through, his life will be found to be full of material that
will be new to science, and which scientists must explain
as they may. But now to his story, for his opening
remark was, as my reader may have guessed, no more
than a prelude to one he is intended to tell. I think somebody said, 'Ah, yes, I suppose there are.' But it is not
important.

'I remember a man named Twohey,' said Jorkens. 'I
think he had once been some kind of a general, but he
was a nice quiet fellow when I knew him. I was walking
along a road in Ireland, when first I saw him, which ran
through a nice estate, with little clumps of trees in it
here and there, and looking over a hedge I chanced to
see him slipping a ferret into a rabbit-hole; and he
looked up rather sharply, as if he thought I might be
someone that was going to interfere with him; and when
he saw that I wasn't, however he saw that, he gave me
a charming smile, and said "I thought you were one of
those— But never mind. I'm just getting a bit of a
rabbit for my old mother. Sure, no one could object to
a man doing that."

'I agreed that nobody could. And from that we got
talking of other things. And presently he told me about
one of the clumps quite near us. It was a hazel wood,
about a hundred yards long, and in breadth a little less,
and it was called Witch Wood, because a witch had once

cursed it, he said, so that anybody out in it at night would lose his way and be lost.

' "But it is only a clump," I said.

' "And so it is, by day," said Twohey.

' "And what is it by night?" I asked.

' "Sure, the curse works, then," he said.

' "What does it do?" I asked.

' "It's as I said," replied Twohey, "You lose your way."

' "In a little wood like that?" I asked.

' "Aye," said Twohey, "Sure, that's what it looks. And so it does."

'Well, it isn't any use arguing about witchcraft. The only thing was to test it. And so I said to Twohey.

' "Look here," I said, "I'll walk through that clump at any time of night. I'll go in by the far side and come out by the road."

' "Any time after dark will do," said Twohey.

' "Then I'll do it," I said, "witch or no witch."

' "Very well," said Twohey. "There's no one to stop you, unless Lord Monaghan's keeper. And he doesn't be sitting up late these days, the way he used to when he was younger. Time was he was a bit wicked, but he'd not bother you now."

' "Well then I'll try it," I said, "If you think no one will mind."

' "Sorra a mind," said Twohey.

' "I'll try it tonight," I said.

' "Then you'll be lost," said Twohey.

' "What did she curse it for?" I asked when that was settled.

' "Ah, there was a bad Lord Monaghan in the old days." Twohey said, "and he turned her out of her cottage where this wood is, and he planted birch-trees all over her garden, and hazels all the way round."

237

'I saw the birches standing all white in the wood and a few Scotch firs beyond them. And all the rest was hazels.'

' "What did he do it for?" I asked.

' "For no reason at all," said Twohey, "only that the poor old woman wouldn't pay her rent. And, sure, I don't blame her."

'And then a rabbit bolted into a little net that Twohey had waiting for it over a hole.

' "Excuse me a moment," said Twohey.

'And it was really no more than a moment before he had snapped its neck. "It's only for my old mother," he said, "Sure no one in the world could grudge her a rabbit."

'I entirely agreed with Twohey, and promised not to say a word about the rabbit to anybody, for fear it should come to ears that Twohey said had nothing better to do than to listen for that kind of talk, which was not properly their concern at all. And we arranged a meeting next morning in the little neighbouring village, outside a door within which Twohey said one could get a drink of some sort, though it was nothing like the drink that it used to be in the old days. And I was to tell Twohey just how I got through Witch Wood. And I looked forward to doing so, for I didn't think much of his witch, and I felt pretty sure that I could walk through that wood in less time and with less exertion than it would take me to explain that a witch had not the powers with which Twohey appeared to credit her. For I could see that he was a decent fellow and would believe whatever I told him. Very unlike the more suspicious kind of devil who will never believe a straight account of anything, if he has not been there himself and seen the whole thing with his own eyes.'

And I made some little interruption, such as I make from time to time to forestall any unmannerly discussion that might arise in the Club. I think such interruptions are a good thing.

'Well,' said Jorkens, 'we parted then, and I remember my words to Twohey, "I don't think it will take me more than three or four minutes, even in the dark, to do the longest part of the wood."

"Well," said Twohey, "the last man I knew that tried it allowed himself three or four hours."

' "Three or four hours!" I exclaimed.

' "Aye, and it wasn't long enough," said Twohey. "Dawn didn't come up for another two hours after that. But maybe your honour will do it, being fresh from London and all, and with the help of your Oxford-and-Cambridge education."

'He was a polite and pleasant fellow, though pig-headed about the witch.

'Well, I was staying at a little inn, where they made me very comfortable, and I spent a holiday of a week there and got a bit of fishing.'

'A holiday from what?' asked Terbut, who happened to be in the Club.

'Oh, from one thing and another,' said Jorkens. 'From one thing and another. Various little things, including a bit of work. You may have tried it once, only don't let's talk about it. No, I was on my holiday. Well, I told them I was going out for a short walk after supper. I wasn't a quarter of an hour's walk from the wood, so I told them I would be back in about half an hour; and they said they would let me in any time, up to eleven o'clock. It was in the early summer, after the mayfly had gone down, and the corncrake had just arrived from the South; I heard its voice as I went in over the fields. There was a line of distant mountains low in the sky; I never knew the names of them; and I waited till they had wholly disappeared, and everything got dim, though some luminous trace of day was still overhead and a glimmer shone on the fields.

'As I left the road I heard the bark of one dog, and then an intense stillness, that was broken after a while by the voice of the corncrake. A dim white moth flew low above the tops of the grasses, bringing a gleam of light that was noticeable and welcome in the huge area of darkness that was gaining upon the world, and somehow gained on one's spirits, so that one felt all through one the unreasonable awe of the night, an awe that one tried to avoid by keeping away from trees, and out in the open spaces where the last of the daylight lingered. It is not a feeling that I can explain, because reason has no concern with it. Nor was there any sense in avoiding trees in the fields, when the purpose of my journey was to enter a wood. Soon I saw a huge shape standing behind an ash-tree, watching me. It turned out to be a horse. It scarcely moved as I went by. Movement, it seemed to feel, was for the day-time, and everything was too hushed and still for it to move now. I went on from the silent figure and came to still cattle, some standing, some lying down, all equally still. The hush had deepened, and now held everything.

'Over the sleeping fields not far away, I saw one light that was all alone in the dimness, glittering at the top of a little hill, a golden radiance that seemed, small though it was, to be perhaps the first flash of the rising moon; but the moon was in another part of the sky, and I saw it later, a blurred mass of fine gold, nearly hidden in mist. This light, then, which did not increase, was the bright light of a window, the one light in all the valley, when all else was curtained. I wondered for a while at the glare of it. Then it occurred to me that it must be the house of the priest, and that perhaps he kept that light shining so late as a kind of warning that he was there, to whomever might be wandering at such an hour.

Again a moth passed by me, and then I came to the wood. At the edge of it somebody had lately cut an ash tree, and the stump of it shone white; that and the gleam of the moth and the far-off glow from the hill were the last lights I saw for some time.

'As I entered the little wood I saw at once, what is obvious to anyone who has seen a wood after dark, that the little clump was different to what it had been in the day. It looked larger, for one thing, and, besides that, it looked menacing. But then, for some reason or other, woods at night always do. I don't quite know why. I suppose that it is just the way they are made.

'Well, I didn't think much of that, and for a while I got on very well. The only thing that was troubling me was the faint glow in the sky, which I was afraid might possibly make it an unfair test, as it could be argued that it was not entirely night while any light was there. But I thought I would go on and then run through the wood again later, so as to make quite sure. I was among large leaves of cow-parsnip at first, growing underneath hazels; then a faint glow came from the white trunks of birches; but very soon, as I got deeper into the wood, I was unable to tell them from the grey trunk of an occasional oak, except by feeling the bark, and that was not much use to me, as, from what I had seen of the little grove in the distance, I did not know that there were any oak trees there, so that they did not help to show me where I was. The birches that stood in what was the witch's garden were close to the point at which I had entered the wood, and I expected to go through them and then through the hazels, and so come to the road. But soon I saw no more the glow of the birches, and there were hazels all round me, as I could tell by their shapes. I was surprised at seeing no birches, but I knew the direction of the road and I aimed to come out

241

exactly at a gate that I knew there was on the roadside, leading into the wood.

'Perhaps I may offer a suggestion to anyone who may at any time be lost in a wood at night, or at any time anywhere, and that is that, however sure one may think one is of the right direction, yet, if one does not recognise landmarks that are close beside one, one's direction also is wrong. Mistake North for East, and the other points of the compass will come out wrong too. So I went on through the wood, thinking I knew the way. Of course I kept straight on in so small a wood, but I got diverted by water. Whether it was the same long strip appearing again and again I do not know, but it prevented my going straight; and not only that, but it was no guide to me whatever, for I knew nothing of any stream that entered the wood, and could not make out what water was doing there. Perhaps it was a deep marshy ditch that guarded one side of Witch Wood, or there may have been four of them and I may have come on them all; whatever it was, I was continually being turned by it. Not that it seemed at first to matter, as I still thought I knew where the road was, but it made my journey slower, because the water often turned me from clearer spaces, through which I intended to walk, into thicker parts of the wood, and some of these were so thick that I had to vary my direction again.

'I went on and on for a very long while through the wood, and the night grew darker, and any glimmer of light that still remained was where it was no use to me up overhead, except where it suddenly flashed in patches of water; and the cow-parsnip had ceased, as though I had changed my climate. There had been a kind of hush when I first entered Witch Wood, as though everything had suddenly held its breath; no dog barked, the corn-crake had ceased, there was no sound from the cattle; and this silence continued the whole time that I was in the wood. If I could have heard any sounds I had heard before, they might have given me some direction, but the curse didn't seem to allow that. That was what I wanted, direction; any direction at all. For I was beginning now to see that my idea of the direction of the road was all wrong. Birches by now had taken the place of hazels, and there was an occasional dark pine: I was in an entirely different country.

'My theory that I knew the way, my knowledge that I was in a little grove, my belief that I could cross it in three minutes, all had to go by the board, and I had to acknowledge the fact that I was lost in a forest. I knew that some forests went for a thousand miles, that some of them ran right into the Arctic. It was no use arguing with myself any longer that I knew where I was. The most important thing for me to do then was to start all over again, unhindered by any theory that I could get out of the wood and, looking at things in an entirely new light, to try and find out where I was. The birches somehow seemed to suggest Russia. You may think that mistaken of me, but I had recognised by now that I knew nothing of my whereabouts whatever and that I might just as likely be in one place as any other.

'That is how I felt when my cocksureness was gone. I had thought I could stroll through that wood and that the witch's curses were nothing, and now I was in her garden with dark forest all around me. And, if any vestige of my confidence remained, any reliance whatever on any preconceived thing, all that was swept away by finding those birches at the end of an hour's walk, when I had expected to find them in the first few yards. Obviously they could not be the same birches, and might be any forest whatever. What I mean is that by clinging to the belief that I was in a small grove in Ireland I could not get any further; my only chance was to give up the idea that was doing me no good, and to get as

243

far away from it as I could. That is why I examined the possibility of being lost in a birch-forest somewhere in Russia. The wrong idea perhaps, but better than the one that I clung to so long and that had left me all that time completely lost in the wood.

'Well, I travelled on through the forest a very long way, through the faint gleam of the birches. And at last I said, "Wherever this forest is, I am obviously lost in it, and I've nothing to guide me. What's the use of going on?" A man who has travelled as much as I have is never helpless, especially if he has water somewhere near and has got a box of matches—and a man who's travelled at all always has matches—so I decided to make myself comfortable for the night. Nothing burns better than birch-bark, and I stripped off a good lot of it and soon I had a fire that would burn anything I threw down on it; and I piled on branches that I broke from the trees, and logs and sticks that I found in the dark of the weeds, for I fancied a big fire would be necessary to keep me warm in those latitudes, where those dense birch-forests grew, as soon as the night should settle down to grow colder. I felt no cold as yet, on account of my long hard walk, but I was glad of the warmth of the fire and glad of the rest.

'The fire was soon burning well, brilliantly lighting up the birches around me, but it did not show me my way, for, bright though it made the ground that had been so dark to my footsteps, a circle of darkness seemed to draw in round it that was even blacker than it had been before. For a moment the clear bright ground for a few paces all round me tempted me to try to look for my way again, but I had the sense to look at the darkness that hung so close all around and to accept the obvious fact that I was lost, and to make it no worse by wandering. After that I was really quite comfortable, lying on a few handfuls of twigs that kept off most of

the wet and getting all the warmth that I wanted from
the fire, and warmth is one of the first of our necessities.
The bright light of the flames added cheerfulness and I
settled down to wait for the dawn, which is early at
that time of year, when the curse, as I gathered from
Twohey, usually lifted, apart from which I should be
able to see my way. The great hush continued, and I
heard no sound at all from outside the wood. I got
another damp log or two and threw them on to the fire,
which was doing too well to be harmed by their being
damp, and then I settled down to try to sleep, with the
fire on my face and a cool wind on my neck. But I could
not get to sleep for a long time; and, just as I thought
that I was going to do so, I heard my first sound from
outside, the sound of a cock crowing from some cottage
far over the fields, as early as that in the night, for at
any rate in the wood, there was yet no trace of dawn.
I listened for a while, and it crowed again.

'And then I got the idea that, whatever Twohey had
said, it was not so much the dawn that abated curses, as
the cock-crow that usually accompanied it, and came
often a little before. So I threw a bit more stuff down
on the fire, for it had now sunk low, and as soon as ever
I had it blazing well I started off again on my journey
through Witch Wood. And this time, though I still had
no point to make for, and had quite given up my futile
belief that I knew the way to go, I had, as I had not had
before, a point from which I was able to move away, and
this at least was a help to prevent me moving in circles.
So I set out, looking often over my shoulder, to see that
the fire behind me was receding as it should. And in a
surprisingly short time I saw another light, that was
shining through the branches of the hazels before me, a
pale golden light. It was the light of the priest's window
shining over the fields. What it was doing at such an
hour I could have no idea, but that of course was no

245

affair of mine. There it shone and I walked through Witch Wood towards it, and soon was out in the field where the cattle were, still lying or standing motionless. And I heard the corncrake again. And I went back past the same horse, that was standing still by his tree, and back through the hush of the night.

'I came to the inn before there was as yet any sign of the dawn. For a moment I wondered what excuse to give, and then the right idea came to me; I threw pebbles up at the window and, when it opened, I gave them the bare truth: I said I was lost in Witch Wood. And they understood me at once. All people are suspicious of strangers, and any excuse that I gave for being so late would have been examined very thoroughly, and it might have been a long time before they opened the door, but the bare truth about Witch Wood went straight to their hearts and they let me in at once.

'Next day I saw Twohey and told him straight out that his witch had won.

' "Ah, and so she would," said Twohey.

' "Are there many other curses like that," I asked him, "being laid down hereabouts now?"

' "Ah," said Twohey, "there are not."

' "Why is that?" I asked.

' "Ah," he said, "I don't know what's come over the country. The witches are no good any longer. The wickedness has gone out of them. I don't know what's wrong at all. But it's not like what it was in the old days." '

THE HOUSE AMONG THE LAURELS

by William Hope Hodgson

WILLIAM HOPE HODGSON (1877–1918), though well-known as a writer of ghost stories, made his literary reputation with a series of novels about the sea— this being due in no small measure to the fact that he had served before the mast as a young man. Born the son of a clergyman and brought up in the witch-haunted county of Essex, he naturally developed a 'feel' for the supernatural, and when he began introducing the occult into his tales he was soon earning comparison with the greatest names in the genre. His most outstanding creation was Carnacki, The Ghost-Finder, *a most determined and adventurous man who battled with the forces of the unseen through many dramatic stories. In* The House Among The Laurels *Carnacki encounters not only the forces of evil, but some human terror and a mystery which needs to be solved by ritual ...*

'This is a curious yarn that I am going to tell you,' said Carnacki, as after a quiet little dinner we made ourselves comfortable in his cosy dining-room.

'I have just got back from the West of Ireland,' he continued. 'Wentworth, a friend of mine, has lately had rather an unexpected legacy, in the shape of a large estate and manor, about a mile and a half outside of the village of Korunton. The place is named Gannington Manor, and has been empty a great number of years; as you will find is so often the case with houses reputed to be haunted.

'It seems that when Wentworth went over to take possession, he found the place in very poor repair, and the estate totally uncared for, and, as I know, looking very desolate and lonesome generally. He went through the big house by himself, and he admitted to me that it had an uncomfortable feeling about it; but, of course, that might be nothing more than the natural dismalness of a big, empty house, which has been long uninhabited, and through which one is wandering alone.

'When he had finished his look round, he went down to the village, meaning to see the one-time Agent of the Estate, and arrange for someone to go in as caretaker. The Agent, who proved, by the way, to be a Scotsman, was very willing to take up the management of the Estate once more; but he assured Wentworth that they would get no one to go in as caretaker; and that his— the Agent's—advice was to have the house pulled down, and a new one built.

'This, naturally, astonished my friend, and, as they went down to the village, he managed to get a kind of explanation from the man. It seems that there had always been curious stories told about the place, which in the early days was called Landru Castle, and that within the last seven years there had been two extraordinary deaths there. In each case they had been tramps, who were ignorant of the reputation of the house, and had probably thought the big empty place suitable for a night's free lodging. There had been absolutely no signs of violence to indicate the method by which death was caused, and on each occasion the body had been found in the great entrance hall.

'By this time they had reached the inn where Wentworth had put up, and he told the Agent that he would prove that it was all rubbish about the haunting, by staying a night or two in the Manor himself. The death of the tramps was certainly curious; but did not prove

248

that any supernatural agency had been at work. They were but isolated incidents, spread over a large number of years by the memory of the villagers, which was natural enough in a little place like Korunton. Tramps had to die some time, and in some place, and it proved nothing that two, out of possibly hundreds who had slept in the enemy house, had happened to take the opportunity to die under its shelter.

'But the Agent took his remark very seriously, and both he and Dennis, the Landlord of the inn, tried their best to persuade him not to go. For his "sowl's sake", Irish Dennis begged him to do no such thing; and because of his "life's sake", the Scotsman was equally in earnest.

'It was late afternoon at the time, and as Wentworth told me, it was warm and bright, and it seemed such utter rot to hear those two talking seriously about the Impossible. He felt full of pluck, and he made up his mind he would smash the story of the haunting, at once, by staying that very night in the Manor. He made this quite clear to them, and told them that it would be more to the point and to their credit, if they offered to come up along with him, and keep him company. But poor old Dennis was quite shocked, I believe, at the suggestion; and though Tabbit, the Agent, took it more quietly, he was very solemn about it.

'It appears that Wentworth did go; though, as he said to me, when the evening began to come on, it seemed a very different sort of thing to tackle.

'A whole crowd of the villagers assembled to see him off; for by this time they all knew of his intention. Wentworth had his gun with him, and a big packet of candles; and he made it clear to them all that it would not be wise for anyone to play any tricks; as he intended to shoot "at sight". And then, you know, he got a hint of how serious they considered the whole thing; for one of them came up to him, leading a great bull-mastiff, and offered it to him, to take to keep him company. Wentworth patted his gun; but the old man who owned the dog, shook his head and explained that the brute might warn him in sufficient time for him to get away from the castle. For it was obvious that he did not consider the gun would prove of any use.

'Wentworth took the dog, and thanked the man. He told me that, already, he was beginning to wish that he had not said definitely that he would go; but, as it was, he was simply forced to. He went through the crowd of men, and found suddenly that they all turned in a body and were keeping him company. They stayed with him all the way to the Manor, and then went right over the whole place with him.

'It was still daylight when this was finished, though turning to dusk; and, for a little, the men stood about, hesitating, as if they felt ashamed to go away and leave Wentworth there all alone. He told me that, by this time, he would gladly have given fifty pounds to be going back with them. And then, abruptly, an idea came to him. He suggested that they should stay with him, and keep him company through the night. For a time they refused, and tried to persuade him to go back with them; but finally he made a proposition that got home to them all. He planned that they should go back to the inn, and there get a couple of dozen bottles of whisky, a donkey-load of turf and wood and some more candles. Then they could come back, and make a great fire in the big fireplace, light all the candles, and put them round the place, open the whisky and make a night of it. And, by Jove! he got them to agree.

'They set off back, and were soon at the inn, and there, whilst the donkey was being loaded, and the candles and whisky distributed, Dennis was doing his best to keep Wentworth from going back; but he was a sensible man in his way; for when he found that it was no use, he stopped. I believe, he did not want to frighten the others from accompanying Wentworth.

'"I tell ye, sorr," he told him, "'tis no use at all at all thryin' to reclaim ther castle. 'Tis curst with innocent blood, an' ye'll be betther pullin' it down, an' buildin' a fine new wan. But if ye be intendin' to shtay this night, kape the big dhoor open whide, an' watch for the bhlood-dhrip. If so much as a single dhrip falls, don't shtay though all the gold in the world were offered ye."

'Wentworth asked him what he meant by the blood-drip.

'"Shure," he said, "'tis the bhlood av thim as ould Black Mick, 'way back in the ould days, kilt in their shlape. 'Twas a feud as he pretendid to patch up, an' he invited thim—the O'Haras they was—sivinty av thim. An' he fed thim, an' sphoke soft to thim, an' thim thrustin' him, shtayed to shlape with him. Thin, he an' thim with him, stharted in an' mhurdered thim wan an' all as the slep'. 'Tis from me father's grandfather ye have the sthory. An' sence thin 'tis death to any, so they say, to pass the night in the castle whin the bhlood-drip comes. 'Twill put out candle an' fire, an' thin in the darkness the Virgin Herself would be powerless to protect ye."

'Wentworth told me he laughed at this; chiefly because, as he put it: One always must laugh at that sort of yarn, however it makes you feel inside. He asked old Dennis whether he expected him to believe it.

'"Yes, Sorr," said Dennis, "I do mane ye to b'lieve it; an', please God, if ye'll b'lieve, ye may be back safe befor' mornin'." The man's serious simplicity took hold of Wentworth, and he held out his hand. But, for all that, he went; and I must admire his pluck.

'There were now about forty men, and when they got back to the Manor—or castle as the villagers always

251

call it—they were not long in getting a big fire going, and lighted candles all round the great hall. They had all brought sticks; so that they would have been a pretty formidable lot to tackle by anything simply physical; and, of course, Wentworth had his gun. He kept the whisky in his own charge; for he intended to keep them sober; but he gave them a good strong tot all round first, so as to make things cheerful; and to get them yarning. If you once let a crowd of men like that grow silent, they begin to think, and then to fancy things.

'The big entrance door had been left wide open, by his orders; which shows that he had taken some notice of Dennis. It was a quiet night, so this did not matter, for the lights kept steady, and all went on in a jolly sort of fashion for about three hours. He had opened a second lot of bottles, and everyone was feeling cheerful; so much so that one of the men called out aloud to the ghosts to come out and show themselves. And then, you know, a very extraordinary thing happened; for the ponderous main door swung quietly and steadily to, as if pushed by an invisible hand, and shut with a sharp click.

'Wentworth stared, feeling suddenly rather chilly. Then he remembered the men, and looked round at them. Several had ceased their talk, and were staring in a frightened way at the big door; but the greater number had never noticed, and were talking and yarning. He reached for his gun, and the following instant the great bull-mastiff set up a tremendous barking, which drew the attention of the whole company.

'The hall I should tell you is oblong. The south wall is all windows; but the north and the east have rows of doors leading into the house, while the west wall is occupied by the great entrance. The rows of doors leading into the house were all closed, and it was towards one of these in the north wall that the big dog ran; yet he would not go very close; and suddenly the door

252

began to move slowly open, until the blackness of the passage beyond was shown. The dog came back among the men, whimpering, and for perhaps a minute there was an absolute silence.

'Then Wentworth went out from the men a little, and aimed his gun at the doorway.

' "Whoever is there, come out, or I shall fire," he shouted; but nothing came, and he blazed both barrels into the dark. As though the report had been a signal, all the doors along the north and east walls moved slowly open, and Wentworth and his men were staring, frightened, into the black shapes of the empty doorways.

'Wentworth loaded his gun quickly, and called to the dog; but the brute was burrowing away in among the men; and this fear on the dog's part frightened Wentworth more, he told me, than anything. Then something else happened. Three of the candles over in the corner of the hall went out; and immediately about half a dozen in different parts of the place. More candles were put out, and the hall had become quite dark in the corners.

'The men were all standing now, holding their clubs, and crowded together. And no one said a word. Wentworth told me he felt positively ill with fright. I know the feeling. Then, suddenly, something splashed on to the back of his left hand. He lifted it, and looked. It was covered with a great splash of red that dripped through his fingers. An old Irishman near to him, saw it, and croaked out in a quavering voice: "The bhlood-dhrip!" When the old man called out, they all looked, and in the same instance others felt it upon them. There was frightened cries of: "The bhlood-dhrip! The bhlood-dhrip!" And then, about a dozen candles went out simultaneously, and the hall was suddenly almost dark. The dog let out a great, mournful howl, and there was a horrible little silence, with everyone standing rigid. Then the tension broke, and there was a mad rush for the main door. They wrenched it open, and tumbled out into the dark; but something slammed it with a crash after them, and shut the dog in; for Wentworth heard it howling as they raced through the drive. Yet no one had the pluck to go back and let it out, which does not surprise me.

'Wentworth sent for me the following day. He had heard of me in connection with that Steeple Monster Case. I arrived by the night mail, and put up with him at the inn. The next day he went up to the old manor, which certainly lies in rather a wilderness; though what struck me most was the extraordinary number of laurel bushes about the house. The place was smothered with them; so that the house seemed to be growing up out of a sea of green laurel. These, and the grim, ancient look of the old building, made the place look a bit dank and ghostly, even by daylight.

'The hall was a big place, and well lit by daylight; for which I was not sorry. You see, I had been rather wound-up by Wentworth's yarn. We found one rather funny thing, and that was the great bull-mastiff, lying stiff with its neck broken. This made me feel very serious; for it showed that whether the cause was supernatural or not, there was present in the house some force dangerous to life.

'Later, whilst Wentworth stood guard with his shotgun, I made an examination of the hall. The bottles and mugs from which the men had drunk their whisky were scattered about; and all over the place were the candles, stuck upright in their own grease. But in that somewhat brief and general search, I found nothing; and decided to begin my usual exact examination of every square foot of the place—not only of the hall, in this case, but of the whole interior of the castle.

'I spent three uncomfortable weeks, searching; but without result of any kind. And, you know, the care I take at this period is extreme; for I have solved hundreds of cases of so-called "hauntings" at this early stage, simply by the most minute investigation, and the keeping of a perfectly open mind. But, as I have said, I found nothing. During the whole of the examination, I got Wentworth to stand guard with his loaded shot-gun; and I was very particular that we were never caught there after dusk.

'I decided now to make the experiment of staying a night in the great hall, of course "protected". I spoke about it to Wentworth; but his own attempt had made him so nervous that he begged me to do no such thing. However, I thought it well worth the risk, and I managed in the end to persuade him to be present.

'With this in view, I went to the neighbouring town of Gaunt, and by an arrangement with the Chief Constable I obtained the services of six policemen with their rifles. The arrangement was unofficial, of course, and the men were allowed to volunteer, with a promise of payment.

'When the constables arrived early that evening at the inn, I gave them a good feed; and after that we all set out for the manor. We had four donkeys with us, loaded with fuel and other matters; also two great boar-hounds, which one of the police led. When we reached the house, I set the men to unload the donkeys; whilst Wentworth and I set-to and sealed all the doors, except the main entrance, with tape and wax; and if the doors were really opened, I was going to be sure of the fact. I was going to run no risk of being deceived either by ghostly hallucination, or mesmeric influence.

'By the time that we had sealed the doors, the policemen had unloaded the donkeys, and were waiting, looking about them, curiously. I set two of them to lay a fire in the big grate, and the others I used as I required them. I took one of the boar hounds to the end of the hall furthest from the entrance, and there I drove a staple into the floor, to which I tied the dog with a short tether. Then, round him, I drew upon the floor the figure of a pentacle, in chalk. Outside of the pentacle, I made a circle with garlic. I did exactly the same thing with the other hound; but over in the north-east corner of the big hall, where the two rows of doors made the angle.

'When this was done, I cleared the whole centre of the hall, and put one of the policemen to sweep it; after which I had all my apparatus carried into the cleared space. Then I went over to the main door, and hooked it open, so that the hook would have to be lifted out of the hasp, before the door could be closed.

'After that, I placed lighted candles before each of the sealed doors, and one in each corner of the big room; and then I lit the fire. When I saw that it was properly alight, I got all the men together, by the pile of things in the centre of the room, and took their pipes from them; for, as the Sigsand MS. has it: "They're must noe lyght come from wythin the barryier". And I was going to make sure.

'I got my tape-measure then, and measured out a circle ninety-nine feet in circumference, and immediately began to chalk it out. The police and Wentworth were tremendously interested, and I took the opportunity to warn them that this was no piece of silly mumming on my part, but done with a definite intention of erecting a barrier between us and any ab-human thing that the night might show to us. I warned them that, as they valued their lives (and more than their lives it might be), no one must on any account whatever pass beyond the limits of the barrier I was making.

'After I had drawn the circle, I took a bunch of garlic, and smudged it right round the chalk circle, a little outside of it. When this was complete, I called for

256

candles from my stock of material. I set the police to lighting them, and as they were lit I took them and sealed them down on the floor, just along the chalk circle, five inches apart. Each candle measured one inch in diameter and it took one hundred and ninety-eight candles to complete the circle. I need hardly say that every number and measurement has a significance.

'Then, from candle to candle, I took a "gayrd" of human hair, entwining it alternatively to the left and to the right, until the circle was completed, and the ends of the final hairs shod with silver, were pressed into the wax of the one hundredth and ninety eighth candle.

'It had now been dark some time, and I made haste to get the "Defence" complete. To this end I got the men well together, and began to fit the Electric Pentacle right around us, so that the five points of the Defensive Star came just within the Hair-Circle. This did not take me long, and a few minutes later I had connected up the batteries, and the weak blue glare of the intertwining vacuum tubes shone all round us.

'I felt happier then; for this Pentacle is, as you all know, a wonderful "Defence". I have told you before how the idea came to me, after reading Professor Gardor's "Experiments with a Medium". He found that a current, of a certain number of vibrations, *in vacuo*, "insulated" the Medium. It is difficult to suggest an explanation non-technically, and if you are really interested you should read Gardor's lecture on "Astral Vibrations Compared with Matero-involuted Vibrations Below The Six Billion Limit".

'As I stood up from my work, I could hear outside in the night a constant drip from the laurels, which, as I have said, come right up around the house very thick. By the sound, I knew that a "soft" rain had set in, and there was absolutely no wind, as I could tell by the steady flames of the candles.

'I stood a moment or two, listening, and then one of the men touched my arm, and asked me in a low voice what they should do. By his tone I could tell that he was feeling something of the strangeness of it all; and the other men, including Wentworth, were so quiet that I was afraid they were beginning to get nervy.

'I set-to, then, and arranged them with their backs to one common centre, so that they were sitting flat upon the floor, with their feet radiating onwards. Then, by compass, I laid their legs to the eight point chief points, and afterwards I drew a "circle" with chalk round them; and opposite to their feet, I made the Eight Signs of the Saaamaaa Ritual. The eighth place was, of course, empty; but ready for me to occupy at any moment; for I had omitted to make the Sealing Sign to that point, until I had finished all my preparations, and could enter the "Inner Star".

'I took a last look round the great hall, and saw that the two big hounds were lying quietly, with their noses between their paws. The fire was big and cheerful, and the candles before the two rows of doors, burnt steadily, as well as the solitary ones in the corners. Then I went round the little star of men, and warned them not to be frightened whatever happened; but to trust to the "Defence", and to let *nothing* tempt to drive them to cross the Barriers. Also, I told them to watch their movements, and to keep their feet strictly to their places. For the rest, there was to be no shooting, unless I gave the word.

'And now at last, I went to my place, and, sitting down, made the Eighth Sign just beyond my feet. Then I arranged my camera and flashlight handy, and examined my revolver.

'Wentworth sat behind the First Sign, and as the numbering went round reversed, that put him next to me on my left. I asked him, in a low voice, how he felt;

and he told me, rather nervous; but that he had confidence in my knowledge, and was resolved to go through with the matter, whatever happened.

'We settled down then to wait. There was no talking, except that, once or twice, the police bent towards one another, and whispered odd remarks concerning the hall .. their whispers being queerly audible in the intense silence. But in a while there was not even a word from anyone, and only the monotonous drip, drip of the quiet rain without the great entrance, and the low, dull sound of the fire in the big fireplace.

'It was a queer group that we made sitting there, back to back, with our legs starred outwards; and all round us the strange, weak blue glow of the intertwining Pentacle, and beyond that the brilliant shining of the great ring of lighted candles. Outside of the glare of the candles, the large empty hall looked a little gloomy, by contrast, except where the lights shone before the sealed doors and in the corners; whilst the blaze of the big fire made a good honest mass of flame on the monster hearth. And the feeling of mystery! Can you picture it all?

'It might have been an hour later that it came to me suddenly that I was aware of an extraordinary sense of dreeness, as it were, come into the air of the place. Not the nervous feeling of mystery that had been with us all the time; but a new feeling, as if there were something going to happen any moment.

'Abruptly, there came a slight noise from the east end of the hall, and I felt the start of men move suddenly. "Steady! Keep steady!" I said sharply, and they quietened. I looked up the hall, and saw that the dogs were upon their feet, and staring in an extraordinary fashion towards the great entrance. I turned and stared, also, and felt the men move as they craned their heads to look. Suddenly the dogs set up a tremendous barking, and I glanced across to them, and found they were still "pointing" for the big doorway. They ceased their noise just as quickly and seemed to be listening. In the same instant I heard a faint chink of metal to my left, that set me staring at the hook which held the great door wide. It moved, even as I looked. Some invisible thing was meddling with it. A queer, sickening thrill went through me, and I felt all the men about me stiffen and go rigid with intensity. I had a certainty of something impending; as it might be the impression of an invisible, but over-whelming, Presence. The hall was full of a queer silence, and not a sound came from the dogs. *Then, I saw the hook slowly raised from out of its hasp, without any visible thing touching it.* A sudden power of movement came to me. I raised my camera, with the flashlight fixed, and snapped it at the door. There came the great blare of the flashlight, and a simultaneous roar of barking from the two dogs.

'The intensity of the flash made all the place seem dark for some moments after, and in that time of darkness, I heard a jingle in the direction of the door, and that made me strain to look. The effect of the bright light passed, and I could see clearly again. The great entrance door was being slowly closed. It shut with a sharp snick, and there followed a long silence, broken only by the whimpering of the dogs.

'I turned suddenly, and looked at Wentworth. He was looking at me.

' "Just as it did before," he whispered.

' "Most extraordinary," I said, and he nodded and looked round, nervously.

'The policemen were pretty quiet, and I judged that they were feeling rather worse than Wentworth; though, for that matter, you must not think that I was altogether natural; yet I have seen so much that is extraordinary, that I daresay I can keep my nerves steady longer than

260

most people; at any rate, in that kind of thing.

'I looked over my shoulder at the men, and cautioned them, in a low voice, not to move outside the Barriers, *whatever happened;* not even though the house should seem to be rocking and about to tumble on them; for I knew well enough what some of the great Forces are capable of doing. Yet, unless it should prove to be one of the cases of the more terrible Saiitii Manifestations, we were almost certain of safety, so long as we kept to our order within the Pentacle.

'Perhaps an hour and a half passed, quietly, except when, once in a way, the dogs would whine distressfully. Presently, however, they ceased from this, and I could see them lying on the floor with their paws over their noses, in a most peculiar fashion, and shivering visibly. The sight made me feel more serious, as you can understand.

'Suddenly, the candle in the corner furthest from the main door, went out. An instant later, Wentworth jerked my arm, and I saw that a candle before one of the sealed doors had been put out. I held my camera ready. Then, one after another, every candle about the hall was put out, and with such speed and irregularity, that I could never catch one in the actual act of being extinguished. Yet, for all that, I took a flashlight of the hall in general.

'There was a time in which I sat half-blinded by the great glare of the flash, and I blamed myself for not having remembered to bring a pair of smoked goggles, which I have sometimes used at these times. I had felt the men jump, at the sudden light, and I called out loud to them to sit quiet, and to keep their feet exactly to their proper places. My voice, as you can imagine, sounded rather horrid and frightening in the great empty room, and altogether it was a beastly moment.

'Then, I was able to see again, and I stared round and

round the hall; but there was nothing showing unusual; only, of course, it was dark now over in the corners.

'Suddenly, I saw that the great fire was blackening. It was going out visibly, as I looked. If I said some monstrous, invisible, impossible Force sucked the life from it, I could best explain my impression of the way the light and flame went out of it. It was most extraordinary to watch. In the time that I stared at it, every vestige of fire disappeared, and there was no light outside of the ring of candles around the Pentacle.

'The deliberateness of the thing troubled me more than I can make clear to you. It conveyed to me such a sense of a calm, Deliberate Force present in the hall. The steadfast intention to "make a darkness" was horrible. The *extent* of the Power to affect the Material was now the one constant, anxious questioning in my brain. You can understand?

'Behind me, I heard the policemen moving again, and I knew they were getting thoroughly frightened. I turned half round, and told them, quietly but plainly, that they were safe only so long as they stayed within the Pentacle, in the position in which I had put them. If they once broke, and went outside of the Barrier, no knowledge of mine could state the full extent or dreadfulness of the danger.

'I steadied them up, by this quiet, straight reminder; but if they had known, as I knew, that there is no *certainty* in any "Protection", they would have suffered a great deal more, and probably have broken the "Defence" and made a mad, foolish run for an impossible safety.

'Another hour passed, after this, in an absolute quietness. I had a sense of awful strain and oppression, as if I were an infinitely insignificant spirit in the company of some invisible, brooding monster of the unseen world, who, as yet, was scarcely conscious of us. I leant across to Wentworth, and asked him in a whisper whether he had a feeling as if Something were in the room. He looked very pale, and his eyes kept always on the move. He glanced just once at me, and nodded; then stared away round the hall again.

'Abruptly, as though a hundred unseen hands had snuffed them, every candle in the barrier went dead out, and we were left in a darkness that seemed, for a little, absolute; for the light from the Pentacle was too weak and pale to penetrate far across the great hall.

'I tell you, for a moment, I just sat there as though I had been frozen solid. I felt the "creep" go all over me, and seem to stop in my brain. I felt all at once to be given a power of hearing that was far beyond the normal. I could hear my own heart thudding most extraordinarily loud. I began, however, to feel better, after a little; but I simply had not the pluck to move. You can understand?

'Presently, I began to get my courage back. I gripped at my camera and flashlight, and waited. My hands were simply soaked with sweat. I glanced once at Wentworth. I could see him only dimly. His shoulders were hunched a little, his head forward; but though it was motionless, I knew that his eyes were not. It is queer how one knows that sort of thing at times. The police were just as silent. And in this way a while passed.

'A sound broke across the silence. From two sides of the room there came faint noises. I recognised them at once, as the breaking of the sealing-wax. *The sealed doors were opening.* I raised the camera and flashlight, and it was a peculiar mixture of fear and courage that helped me to press the button. As the great belch of light lit up the hall, I felt the men all baout me, jump. The darkness fell like a clap of thunder, if you can understand, and seemed tenfold. Yet, in the moment of

263

brightness, I had seen that all the sealed doors were wide open.

'Suddenly, all round us, there sounded a drip, drip, drip, upon the floor of the great hall. I thrilled with a queer, realising emotion, and a sense of a very real and present danger—*imminent*. The "blood-drip" had commenced. And the grim question was now whether the Barriers could save us from whatever had come into the huge room.

'Through some awful minutes the "blood-drip" continued to fall in an increasing rain, and presently some began to fall within the Barriers. I saw several great drops splash and star upon the pale glowing intertwining tubes of the Electric Pentacle; but, strangely enough, I could not trace that any fell among us.

'Beyond the strange horrible noise of the 'drip", there was no other sound. And then, abruptly, from the boarhound over in the far corner, there came a terrible yelling howl of agony, followed instantly by a sickening, breaking noise, and an immediate silence. If you have ever, when out shooting, broken a rabbit's neck, you will know the sound that I mean—in miniature! Like lightning, the thought sprang into my brain: *IT has crossed the pentacle*. For you will remember that I had made one about each of the dogs. I thought instantly, with a sick apprehension, of our own Barriers. There was something in the hall with us that had passed the barrier of the pentacle about one of the dogs. In the awful succeeding silence, I positively quivered. And suddenly, one of the men behind me, gave out a scream, like any woman, and bolted for the door. He fumbled, and had it open in a moment. I yelled to the others not to move; but they followed like sheep, and I heard them kick the candles flying, in their panic. One of them stepped on the Electric Pentacle, and smashed it, and there was an utter darkness. In an instant, I realised

264

that I was defenceless against the powers of the Unknown World, and with one savage leap I was out of the useless Barriers, and instantly through the great doorway, and into the night. I believe I yelled with sheer funk.

'The men were a little ahead of me, and I never ceased running, and neither did they. Sometimes, I glanced back over my shoulder; and I kept glancing into the laurels which grew all along the drive. The beastly things kept rustling, rustling in a hollow sort of way, as though something was keeping parallel with me, among them. The rain had stopped, and a dismal little wind kept moaning through the grounds. It was disgusting.

'I caught Wentworth and the police at the lodge gate. We got outside and ran all the way to the village. We found old Dennis up, waiting for us, and half the villagers to keep him company. He told us that he had known in his "sowl" that we should come back—that is, if we came back at all; which is not a bad rendering of his remark.

'Fortunately, I had brought my camera away from the House—possibly because the strap had happened to be over my head. Yet, I did not go straight away to develop; but sat with the rest in the bar, where we talked for some hours, trying to be coherent about the whole horrible business.

'Later, however, I went up to my room, and proceeded with my photography. I was steadier now, and it was just possible, so I hoped, that the negatives might show something.

'On two of the plates, I found nothing unusual; but on the third, which was the first one I snapped, I saw something that made me quite excited. I examined it very carefully with a magnifying glass; then I put it to wash, and slipped a pair of rubber half shoes over my boots.

265

'The negative had shown me something very extraordinary, and I had made up my mind to test the truth of what it seemed to indicate, without losing another moment. It was no use telling anything to Wentworth and the police, until I was certain; and also, I believed that I stood a greater chance to succeed by myself; though, for that matter, I do not suppose anything would have got them up to the Manor again that night.

'I took my revolver, and went quietly downstairs, and into the dark. The rain had commenced again; but that did not bother me. I walked hard. When I came to the lodge gates, a sudden queer instinct stopped me from going through, and I climbed the wall into the park. I kept away from the drive, and approached the building from the dismal, dripping laurels. You can imagine how beastly it was. Every time a leaf rustled, I jumped.

'I made my way round to the back of the big House, and got in through a little window which I had taken note of during my search; for, of course, I knew the whole place now from roof to cellars. I went silently up the kitchen stairs, fairly quivering with funk; and at the top, I stepped to the left, and then into a long corridor that had opened through one of the doors we had sealed into the big hall. I looked up it, and saw a faint flicker of light away at the end; and I tip-toed silently towards it, holding my revolver ready. As I came near to the open door, I heard men's voices, and then a burst of laughing. I went on, until I could see into the hall. There were several men there, all in a group. They were well dressed, and one, at least, I saw was armed. They were examining my "barriers" against the Supernatural, with a good deal of unkind laughter. I never felt such a fool in my life.

'It was plain to me that they were a gang of men who had made use of the empty Manor, perhaps for years, for some purpose of their own; and now that Wentworth was attempting to take possession, they were acting up to the traditions of the place, with the view of driving him away, and keeping so useful a place still at their disposal. But what they were, I mean whether coiners, thieves, inventors, or what—I could not imagine.

'Presently, they left the Pentacle and gathered round the living boarhound, which seemed curiously quiet as if it were half-drugged. There was some talk as to whether to let the poor brute live or not; but finally they decided it would be good policy to kill it. I saw two of them force a twisted loop of rope into its mouth, and the two bights of the loop were brought together at the back of the hound's neck. Then a third man thrust a thick walking-stick through the two loops. The two men with the rope stooped to hold the dog so that I could not see what was done; but the poor beast gave a sudden awful howl, and immediately there was a repetition of the uncomfortable breaking sound as I had heard earlier in the night, as you will remember.

'The men stood up, and left the dog lying there— quiet enough now, as you may suppose. For my part, I fully appreciated the calculated remorselessness which had decided upon the animal's death, and the cold determination with which it had been afterwards executed so neatly. I guessed that a man who might get into the "light" of these particular men, would be likely to come to quite as uncomfortable an ending.

'A minute later, one of them called out to the rest that they should "shift the wires". One of them came towards the doorway of the corridor in which I stood, and I ran quickly back into the darkness of the upper end. I saw the man reach up, and I heard the slight, ringing jangle of steel-wire.

When he had gone, I ran back again, and saw the men passing, one after another, through an opening in the stairs, formed by one of the marble steps being

267

raised. When the last man had vanished, the slab that made the step was shut down, and there was not a sign of the secret door. It was the seventh step from the bottom, as I took care to count; and a splendid idea, for it was so solid that it did not ring hollow, even to a fairly heavy hammer, as I found later.

'There is little more to tell. I got out of the House as quickly and quietly as possible, and back to the inn. The police came without any coaxing, when they knew the "ghosts" were normal flesh and blood. We entered the Park and Manor in the same way that I had done. Yet, when we tried to open the step, we failed, and had finally to smash it. This must have warned the haunters; for when we descended to a secret room which we found at the end of a long and narrow passage in the thickness of the walls, we found no one.

'The police were horribly disgusted, as you can imagine; for they seemed tolerably certain that I had dropped on the meeting-place of a certain "political" club much wanted by the authorities; but for my part, I did not care either way. I had "laid the ghost", as you might say, and that was what I set out to do. I was not particularly afraid of being laughed at by the others; for they had all been thoroughly "taken in"; and in the end, I had scored, without their help.

'We searched right through the secret ways, and found that there was an exit, at the end of a long tunnel, which opened in the side of a well, out in the grounds. The ceiling of the hall was hollow, and reached by a little secret stairway inside of the big staircase. The "blood-drip" was merely coloured water, dropped through the minute crevices of the ornamented ceiling. How the candles and fire were put out, I do not know; for the haunters certainly did not act quite up to tradition, which held that the lights were put out by the "blood-drip". Perhaps it was too difficult to direct the fluid, without positively squirting it, which might have given the whole thing away. The candles and the fire may possibly have been extinguished by the agency of carbonic acid gas; but how suspended, I have no idea.

'The secret hiding places were, of course, ancient. There was also (did I tell you?) a bell which they had rigged up to ring, when anyone entered the gates at the end of the drive. If I had not climbed the wall, I should have found nothing for my pains; for the bell would have warned them, had I gone in through the gateway.'

'What was on the negative?' I asked, with much curiosity.

'A picture of the fine wire with which they were grappling for the hook that held the entrance door open. They were doing it from one of the crevices in the ceiling. They had evidently made no preparations for lifting the hook. I suppose they never thought that anyone would make use of it, and so they had to improvise a grapple. The wire was too fine to be seen by the amount of light we had in the hall; but the flashlight "picked it out". Do you see?

'The opening of the inner doors was managed by wires, as you will have guessed, which they unshipped after use, or else I should have found them, when I made my search.

'I think I have now explained everything. The hound was killed, of course, by the men direct. You see they made the place as dark as possible, first. Of course, if I had managed to take a flashlight just at that instant, the whole secret of the haunting would have been exposed. But Fate just ordered it the other way.'

'And the tramps?' I asked.

'O, you mean the two tramps who were found dead in the Manor,' said Carnacki. 'Well, of course it is impossible to be sure, one way or the other. Perhaps they happened to find out something, and were given a hypodermic. Or it is quite as probable that they had come to the time of their dying, and just died naturally. It is conceivable that a great many tramps had slept in the old house, at one time or another.'

Carnacki stood up, and knocked out his pipe. We rose also, and went for our coats and hats.

'Out you go!' said Carnacki, genially, using the recognised formula. And we went on to the Embankment, and presently through the darkness to our various houses.

THE COONIAN GHOST

by Shane Leslie

SHANE LESLIE (1885–1971) was one of Ireland's great collectors of ghost stories and a man whose painstaking and thorough research into phenomena has given his writing real merit and conviction. A devout Roman Catholic and friend of many high churchmen, he travelled extensively to visit the sights of alleged hauntings and never allowed himself to be easily swayed or convinced. This dedication has produced a number of highly documented accounts of which The Coonian Ghost is, in my opinion, the best. According to Irish tradition the Thevshi (ghosts) live on the borderland of reality and unreality having been drawn there, on death, by the fairies. They are retained in this nether world either by love for some earthly being, a duty to fulfil, or a vengeance to inflict . . .

The poltergeist at Coonian near Brookborough, County Fermanagh, dates from 1913-14. Father Hugh Benson, the writer, had promised to come and investigate but died before this was possible. However, it was at different times investigated by three priests, from whom I collected the following notes.

And in so many cases of this kind, it was bewildered and innocent young girls, just reaching puberty, who became unconscious mediums enabling mischievous forms of spirit life to manifest themselves.

There was really no ghost-origin dating from real life except a rumour that an old pensioner had been murdered there on the day he drew his pension. This may have opened the way for the poltergeist, but the only ghost described was very unlike an old pensioner. A man had entered the house over-early in the morning and while waiting at the fire saw a ghost 'come down like a ball of wool in a black bag by the trapdoor and coast round the floor.'

The house had passed from Burnsides to Corrigans, to Sherry and Murphys, under whom troubles began. The Sherrys occupied it one night only, but kept quiet and sold it six months later.

When the Miss Murphys lay by the fireside, the pillows were torn from under their heads. A priest told me that he heard *it* snoring in the dark, and sitting on the bed *it* felt like snakes moving under him, and when a light was lit, a human bulk was seen to collapse under the sheets and then develop a new swelling while the snoring started afresh.

It showed Protestant hostility to holy water which seemed to infuriate *it* for it played back the tune of 'Boyne Water'. He placed the sacred Pyx where there was a noise, which sank underground but still sounded from the depths.

He investigated more than fifty times. *It* came down like the sound of straw in the air. *It* operated on a bed with testers in a corner, where three or four young

271

girls up to eighteen slept. Once he saw a human form raised under the sheets of an empty bed until *it* collapsed. He described *it* as like an animal moving underneath. He felt fear when *it* was spitting at him or lapping like a dog or escaping under him on the bed. He always addressed *it* as 'Johnny'. When *it* was asked to play 'The Soldiers' Song', the tune came in taps.

Another priest described going there one night and finding a mother and two girls sleeping on pallets round the fire away from the haunted room. The moment the children returned to bed, there was a sound like a kicking horse. The bedclothes were thrown across the room. He held the children by their hands with one hand and laid the other over their feet. When the phenomena continued, he was convinced the children could not have produced them. At the suggestion he made that *it* came from a far distance—from Hell—there was a big hiss. He stood with his hand on the bed and challenged *it*. There was clearly something like a rat moving around his hand under the clothes. He had a shock and the feeling of an eel twisting round his wrist but no farther. *It* did not dare touch his *consecrated hand!* He remained there till four in the morning.

A canon of the diocese told me he went about sixteen times. Once he heard a musical noise in the ceiling. He said: 'Perhaps *it* will whistle'. *It* did whistle. There was certainly an intelligence working behind and he was as certain of the ghost as of his being alive. 'It fooled us as *it* was contradictory and gave nothing definite about itself. Holy water was used copiously. *It* was vexed and fled more and more along the wall while the knocking became more pronounced. Mass was said in the kitchen where henceforth relief and sleep became possible for the Murphys. When the children sat on a stool, the noise continued round them. When I cracked my thumb, it cracked louder. We asked for nine raps for *yes* and they

272

came. They tried it in Irish and Latin successfully. They asked: 'How many of us were born in County Monaghan?' Answer correct. They asked: 'Could you put the dog from under the bed?' The collie came out dancing mad, with fire from his eyes.

A famous horse-dealer invoked *it* in the presence of visitors from England. *It* answered accurately with raps how many of them had been born in Ireland. 'How many horse-dealers present?' *It* thumped under his chair. The first time he investigated he left a pony trap outside. The lights were mysteriously put out and the pony was terrified. The driver said someone had passed several times in the same direction but never returned. Later a teacher had his bicycle lights mysteriously put out.

'Well, what was the end of it all?'

The Parish Priest was weak and nervous about the ghost. The clergy were divided in opinion. The old ones kept away, but the young curates leaped in where the angels might fear to tread. The girls were expected to produce results every time and did so, for two curates believed they had caught them in fraud, when the ghost was not sounding. The girls were avoided at crochet class for no one would sit by them. When they took refuge in neighbours' houses, *it* always followed them. As the Parish Priest would not believe them, they marched to his house and after that he believed, for *it* came down his back!

The canon later wrote to me that as I was writing a book on the subject I should have all this information following (12th November 1944):

It was noised about that the children themselves, three of them, ranging from 9 to 13 years, were making the noises on the wood at the head and bottom of the bed. On this particular evening there were nine or ten in the room, the knocking all around fairly

273

vigorous, and although none of us there believed that
the children were knocking, I suggested that two men
in the room should come over and hold the hands
and feet of the children so that false rumour should
be disproved. They did so. I sat on the bed-stock also.
The knocking continued as usual but more vigorously,
for ten minutes, when suddenly the two men rushed
away saying they were being punched and pushed off
the bed. They would not return. I was not pushed
away from the bed, but something moved close to
my back up and down the length of the bed. I was not
afraid, and remained for five minutes or longer. This
killed the rumour that the children were making the
noises. It was also rumoured that some of the family
read bad books and had the 'Black Art', etc. This
was quite untrue.

I think it was the same night that a sheep dog belonging to the family came into the room. I put him
under the bed and said something like this. 'Whatever
is there, I would ask you, if you have the power, to
put this dog out'. Suddenly such noises, all round the
bed, as never were heard, burst out and frightened
us all, with the result that the dog rushed out, nearly
knocking me down on his way. No inducement could
get him, freely, to come into the room afterwards.

Now I am going to relate the most remarkable incident I experienced during the whole time I spent
in Mrs. Murphy's.

Our usual course, whether Father S. and I went
together or singly, was to go before the family retired.
You may remember that I told you when the first
'manifestations' were made, the Bishop, Dr. McKenna,
was notified about them. He told Father S. to say
Mass in the house. There were three apartments in
the house. He said Mass in the kitchen, which was
the middle one, as this was done at a very early

period, the children could, from time to time, sleep undisturbed in the kitchen. When Father S. and myself visited the house we usually had the children put in their own bed, which was in the room to the right as you entered. Sometimes the knocking, etc., would commence vigorously as soon as they would go to bed; otherwise less vigorously, perhaps very mildly, or perhaps not at all. Sometimes it did not start for about an hour after they went to bed.

On this particular night there was no noise in the children's room although they had been in bed for more than an hour. The rest of us were sitting around the kitchen fire chatting when I asked James, unknown to the others (he was an intelligent boy of about 25 years), to get a candle and matches. We went to the other room on the ground floor where no one was sleeping. This was a fairly large room; two windows with blinds drawn, a bed covered with a white quilt, also some chairs. We stood in the middle of the room in almost complete darkness, and listened. For five minutes all was silence. Suddenly we heard the tramp diagonally across the room upstairs, of something like the footfall of a fairly large dog or sheep. It continued. We listened. James said there was nothing in the room above but some chaff and a bundle of straw. The room was being used as a barn and was reached by stone steps on the outside of the gable end. Leaving James where he was, I took the candle and matches, went out, up the steps and stood at the door for a few minutes. I then walked round the room three times. The barn was as James described it. I heard or saw nothing. I returned to James who told me that the 'tramp of the dog' had continued all the time. James then went to the barn, and I remained below. It had the same result. Nothing above and 'the tramp' of the dog heard below.

275

Very soon after we were standing together in the middle of the room. Something that I cannot describe and did not see, rushed down, practically touching us, and went into the earth. For the first time we were really frightened, but soon we immediately noticed that the tramping above had ceased. I then said to James that it was breaking day and to pull up the blinds. He did so. Day was dawning, as it was summer time. We clearly saw the room and immediately noticed, although there was no wind blowing in the room, that the bed clothes were moving up and down fairly fast, especially in the centre of the bed. I actually went and held my hand over the bed and tested the matter for two or three minutes. After that, we went to the kitchen, where the family, Mrs. Murphy, her two grown-up daughters and I think Father S. or possibly some neighbour were chatting. We had been absent about half an hour. We told them what had happened. They wondered, took their chairs and stools, came to the room. The movements of the bed-clothes were gradually getting more pronounced, vigorous, and defined. The whole thing resembled the form of a person lying diagonally across the bed in his or her death agony. The centre where the clothes were heaving most was where the chest would be. Soon we could hear the heavy breathing, the gurgling in the throat, the symptoms of pain. It resembled what country people would call 'a hard death'. From the time they came from the kitchen the whole death scene occupied ten minutes at least. Finally, the movements and death-symptoms ceased and the room was as silent as the grave. I only saw this scene once, but heard that there were further such manifestations later on, but I can't vouch for their truth.

Soon after this scene I was transferred from Maguiresbridge to Fintona. But I heard afterwards that old people from the locality said that in the 'olden days' an occupant of the house hanged himself in that room. I cannot vouch for this.

Now I come to item No. 3 which is as strange in its way as anything else recorded. Some time near the end of my time as Curate of Maguiresbridge I took it into my head that *possibly* other members of the family were 'affected' as people said, and that *possibly* one of the full-grown daughters, Annie aged about 20, or Mary about 22 years, was affected. So I went in the middle of the day, alone, saw Mrs. Murphy and asked her to tell the whole truth about the matter. She told me that Annie was 'affected' and that it did not develop until Mass had been said in the kitchen. Being a big girl, the mother said, and I agreed, that we should not let it be known publicly. The mother sent to the field where she was working. She came in. I brought Mrs. Murphy and herself to the bedroom on the right where there were so many 'manifestations'. I told her to stretch herself out on the bed and then threw a rug over her. To my great surprise from the ceiling above the door which led into the room from the kitchen, a peculiar *rush* immediately came, until it reached half-way down the wall and then turned at right angles until it reached the head of the bed where the girl was and then the knocking commenced most vigorously. I asked her to rise. She arose, and immediately the same rush, distinctly audible, rushed back, turned at right angles and into the ceiling.

I then asked Mrs. Murphy to get into the bed. She did so and there were no manifestations. I asked Annie to go again. She did so, and whatever came, came by the same route and departed as before. I tried Annie twice more with the same result, and also Mrs. Murphy with a negative result. This to my mind

277

was very strange indeed. Any person in the room could hear the comings and goings as distinctly as the ticking of a Grandfather's clock, but the noises were five times louder on this occasion.

The final item is—soon after the manifestations commenced Fr —— was out on a sick call. He was passing Murphy's, on returning, and had the Blessed Sacrament with him. The noises were great around the bed that night. Fr —— and some of the neighbours were in the room. So, after lowering the light, Fr —— took out the Pyx and made the Sign of the Cross with it, over the bed unknown to the others. He had no sooner done so than all the noises imaginable were made before the evil spirits departed, and did not return that night. The people in the room threw themselves on their faces and were terrified thinking Fr —— was about to be attacked.

I heard the story of the terrible noises afterwards, and of what they believed was an attack on Fr —— from some of the people who were present. They did not know he had used the Pyx.

This is a summary of all my experiences.

It remains to be added that the family retreated to America, where they were no more troubled.

The gallant clergy, who made such constant efforts on their behalf, seem to have been the worse for it. One priest had a nervous break-down, another spinal meningitis and the third facial paralysis.

So much was said and rumoured that I am glad to have interviewed the three priests and obtained the most trustworthy evidence concerning the 'Coonian Ghost'. In my opinion it was no mere ghost but a poltergeist obsessed by truly Demoniacal powers.

278

THE HAUNTED SPINNEY

by Elliott O'Donnell

ELLIOTT O'DONNELL *(1872-1968) was descended from one of the oldest and most honoured families in Ireland. It is not surprising, therefore that he should have devoted his life to exploring and explaining the many facets of Irish ghost and legend lore. The subject matter of his many books ranges from poltergeists and phantoms to vampires, werewolves and even secret societies. The O'Donnell family have themselves suffered from the attentions of spirits—notably* Banshees—*and Elliott himself underwent a number of strange and inexplicable personal experiences with unseen forces. This probably accounts for the quite remarkable feeling of terror he manages to build up in the following story.*

I

It was a cold night. Rain had been falling steadily not only for hours but days, the ground was saturated. As I walked along the country lane the slush splashed over my boots and trousers. To my left was a huge stone wall, behind which I could see the nodding heads of firs, and through them the wind was rushing, making a curious whistling sound, now loud, now soft, roaring and gently murmuring. The sound fascinated me. I fancied it might be the angry voice of a man and the plaintive pleading of a woman, and then a weird chorus of unearthly beings, of grotesque things that stalked along the moors, and crept from behind huge boulders.

Nothing but the wind was to be heard. I stood and listened to it. I could have listened for hours, for I felt in harmony with my surroundings, lonely. The moon showed itself at intervals from behind the scudding clouds, and lighted up the open landscape to my left.

A gaunt hill covered with rocks, some piled up pyramidically, others strewn here and there; a few trees with naked arms tossing about and looking distressfully slim beside the more stalwart boulders; a sloping field or two, a couple of level ones, crossed by a tiny path, and the lane where I stood. The scenery was desolate, not actually wild, but sad and forlorn, and the spinney by my side lent an additional weird aspect to the place, which was pleasing to me.

Suddenly I heard a sound, a familiar sound enough at other times, but at this hour and in this place everything seemed different. A woman was coming along the road, a woman in a dark cloak with a basket under her arm, and the wind was blowing her skirts about her legs. I looked at the trees. One singularly gaunt and fantastic one appalled me. It had long, gnarled arms, and two of them ended in bunches of twigs like hands— huge, murderous-looking hands, with bony fingers. The moonlight played over and around me. I had no business to be on the earth; my poor place was in the moon; I no longer thought it, I knew it. The woman was close at hand. She stopped at a little wicket gate leading into the lane skirting the north walls of the spinney. I felt angry; what right had she to be there, interrupting my musings with the moon? The tree with the human hands appeared to agree. I saw anger in the movements of its branches, anger which soon blazed into fury, as they gave a mighty bend towards her as if longing to rend her to pieces.

I followed the woman, and the wind howled louder and louder through those rustling leaves. How long I scrambled on I do not know. As soon as the moonlight left me I fell into a kind of slumber, a delicious trance, broken by nothing save the murmurings of the wind and the sighing and groaning of the wind, sweeter music I never heard. Then came a terrible change. The charm of my thought was broken. I woke from my reverie. A terrific roar broke on my ears, and a perfect hurricane of rain swept through the woods. I crept cold and shivering beneath the shelter of the trees.

To my surprise a hand fell on my shoulder; it was a man and, like myself, he shivered. 'Who are you?' he whispered, in a strangely hoarse voice. 'Who are you? Why are you here?'

'You wouldn't believe me if I told you,' I replied, shaking off his grasp.

'Well, tell me, for God's sake, sir.' He was frightened, trembling with fright. Could it be the storm, or was it, was it those trees? I told him then and there why I had trespassed; I was fascinated, the wind and the trees had led me thither.

'So am I,' he whispered, 'I am fascinated. It is a long word, but it describes my sentiments. What did the wind sound like?'

I told him. He was a poor, common man, and had no poetical ideas. The wildly romantic had never interested him. He was an ignorant labouring man.

'Sounded like sighing, groaning, and so on?' he asked, shifting uneasily from one foot to another. He was cold, horribly cold. 'Was that all?'

'Yes, of course! Why ask?' I replied. Then I laughed. This stupid, sturdy son of toil had been scared; to him the sounds had been those of his Cornish bogies, things he had dreaded in his infancy. I told him so. He didn't like to hear me make fun of him; he didn't like my laugh, and he persisted 'Was that all you heard?'

Then I grew impatient and asked him to explain what he meant.

'Well,' he said, 'I thought I heard a scream, a cry. Just as if someone had jumped out on someone else and taken them unawares. Maybe it was the wind, only the wind, but it had an eerie sound.' This man was nervous. The storm had frightened away whatever wits he may have possessed.

'Come, let us be going,' I said, moving away in the direction of the wall. I wanted to find a new exit, I was tired of paths. The man kept close to me. I could hear his teeth chatter. Accidentally I felt his hand brush against mine; his flesh was icy cold. He gave a cry as if a snake had bitten him. Then the truth flashed through me, the man was mad. His terror, his strange manner of showing it, and now his sudden shrinking from me, revealed it all. He was mad. The moon and the trees had done their work.

'I'm not going that way,' he said. 'Come along with me; I want to see which of the trees it was that cried.' His voice was changed, he seemed suddenly to have grown stronger. There was no insanity in his tone now, but I knew the cunning of the insane, and I feared to anger him. So I acquiesced. What an idea! One of the trees had cried; did he mean the wind? He grew sullen when I jeered at him. He led me to a little hollow in the ground, and I noticed the prints of several feet in the wet mud; then I saw something which sent the cold blood to my heart, a woman lay before me bathed in blood. Somehow she was familiar to me. I looked again, then again. Yes, there was the dark shawl, the basket, broken it was true, with the contents scattered, but it was the same basket; it was the woman I had seen coming down the road.

'My God, whatever is this?' the man by his side spoke. He swayed backwards and forwards on his feet, white and awful in the moonlight. He was sick with terror. 'Oh, God, it is horrible, horrible!' Then, with a sudden earnestness and a crafty look in his eyes, he bent over her. 'Who is it?' he cried. 'Who is the poor wretch?'

I saw him peer into her face, but he didn't touch her, he dreaded the blood, Then he started back, his eyes filled with such savage fury as I had never seen in any man's before. He looked a devil, he was a devil. 'It's my wife!' he shrieked. 'My wife!' His voice fell and turned into what sounded like a sob. 'It's Mary! She was coming back to St. Meave. It was her cry. There, see it, confound you. You have it on your arm, your coat, it is all over you!' He raised his hand to strike me; the moonlight fell on it, a great, coarse hand, and I noticed with a thrill of horror a red splash on it. Blood! The man was a murderer! He had killed her, and with all the cunning of the madman was trying to throw the guilt on me.

I sprang at him with a cry of despair. He kicked, bit and tried to tear my arms from his neck; but somehow I seemed to have ten times my usual strength. And all the while we struggled a sea of faces waved to and fro, peering down at us from the gaunt trees above.

He gave in at length; I held him no longer with the iron grip, and help came in the shape of a policeman. The constable seemed to grasp the situation easily. There had been a murder, the man whom I secured was known to him. He was a labouring man, of unsteady habits; he had been drinking, had met and quarrelled with his wife. The rest was to be seen in the ghastly heap before us.

The wretch had no defence; he seemed bewildered, and eyed the bloodstains on his face and clothes in a dazed kind of way.

I slipped five shillings into the policeman's hand when he parted. He thanked me and pocketed the money; he knew his position and mine.

283

I was a gentleman and a very plucky one at that. So I thought as I walked back to my rooms, yet I lay awake and shuddered as visions of the nodding heads of the trees rose before me, and from without, across the silent rows of houses, lanes and fields, there rose and fell again the wailing of a woman, of a woman in distress.

II

The murder in the spinney was an event in the neighbourhood; the people were unused to such tragedies, and it afforded them conversation for many weeks. The evidence against the husband was conclusive. He had been caught red-handed, he was an habitual drunkard; and he paid the penalty for his crime in the usual manner. I left Cornwall, I had seen enough of it and thirsted for life in London once more. Yet, often at night, the sighing of the wind in the trees sounded in my ears and bid me visit them once more. One day, as I was sitting by my fire with a pile of magazines by my side, taking life easily, for I had nothing to do but kill time, my old friend, Frank Widmore, looked me up.

We had been at Sefton together, and he was the only friend of the old set of whom I had lost sight. He had not altered so much, in spite of a moustache and a fair sprinkling of white hairs. I should have known him had I met him anywhere. He was wearing a new overcoat, and looked very spruce and smart. His face was red with healthy exercise. 'How are you, old chap?' he exclaimed, shaking hands in the hearty fashion of true friendship.

I winced, for he had strong hands. 'Oh, fit enough,' I said, 'but a bit bored. But you, well. You look just the same, and fresh as a daisy.' I gave him the easy chair.

'Oh, I'm first-rate, plenty of work. I'm a journalist, you know. Plenty of grind, but I'm taking a bit of a holiday. You look pale. Your eyes are bad.'

I told him they got strained if I read much.

'I daresay you will think me mad,' he went on, 'but I'm going to ask you a rather curious question. I remember you used to be fond of ghosts and all sorts of queer things.'

I nodded. We had many such discussions in my study at school.

'Well, I'm a member of the New Occult Research Society.'

I smiled doubtfully 'You can't say they have discovered much,' I sneered. 'The name is high-sounding but nothing beyond.'

'Never mind,' he retorted, 'some day, perhaps, we shall show the Public that at present Occult Research is only in the embryo stage.'

Widmore lit a cigarette, puffed away in silence for a few seconds, and then went on: 'I am undertaking work for the Society now.'

'Where?' I asked.

'In Cornwall. Ever been there?'

I nodded. Widmore was very much at his ease.

'Been to St. Meave?' he inquired.

I knew by instinct he would mention the place. He thought I looked ill, and told me I had been overdoing it.

'It is merely a case of the 'flu,' I assured him. 'I had it six weeks ago, and still feel the effects.' The woman in the hollow was before me. I saw again her shabby shawl and the blood round her throat.

'There was a murder down there a short time ago.'

'I heard of it,' I remarked casually. 'It was a wife murder, I believe.'

'Yes, just a common wife murder, and the fellow was caught and hanged.'

'Then, why the ghost?' I commented.

'Well, that is the odd part of it,' Widmore said slowly, leaning back in his chair, his long legs stretched out. 'I have heard from two St. Meave artists that screams have been heard in the spinney there just about twelve o'clock at night. Not the time for practical jokers, and the Cornish are too superstitious to try their pranks in unsavoury spots. And from what I heard the spot is singularly uncanny.'

'They haven't seen anything?' I said.

Widmore shook his grey head. 'No, only heard the cries, and they are so appalling that no one cares to pass the place at night; indeed, it is utterly banned. I mentioned the case to old Potters, you may have heard of him. He is the author of *When the Veil is Cleared Away*, and he pressed me to go down to St. Meave and investigate. I agreed. Then I thought of you. Just the man to accompany me. Do you remember your pet aversion in the way of ghosts?'

I nodded. 'Yes, and I still have the aversion. I think locality exercises strange influence over some minds. The peaceful meadow-scenery holds no lurking horrors in its bosom, but in the lonesome moorlands, full of curiously-moulded boulders, grotesque fancies must assail one there. Creatures seem to come, odd and ill-defined as their surroundings. As a child I had a peculiar horror of those tall, odd-shaped boulders, with seeming faces, featureless, it is true, but sometimes strangely resembling humans and animals. I believe the spinney may be haunted by something of this nature, terrible as the trees.'

'You know the spinney?'

'I do. And I know the trees.' Again in my ears the wind rushed as it had on the night in question.

'Will you come with me?' Widmore eyed me eagerly. The same old affection he had once entertained for me was ripening in his eyes; indeed, it had always remained there. Should I go? An irresistible impulse seized me, a morbid craving to look once more at the blood-stained hollow, to hear once more the wind. I looked out of the window, the sky was cold and grey. There were rows and rows of chimneys everywhere, a sea of chimneys, an ocean of dull, uninviting smoke. I began to hate London and to long for the wide expanse of the Atlantic, and the fresh resin-laden air of the woods. I assented, when better judgment should have led me to refuse. 'Yes, I will go,' I said. 'As for the ghost, it may be there, but it is not as you apparently think, it is not the apparition of a man or woman. It may be in part like a human, but it is one of those cursed nightmares I have always had. I shall see it, hear it, shriek, and if I drop dead from fright, you, old man, will be to blame.'

Widmore was an enthusiast, psychial adventure always allured him, and he would run the risk of my weak heart, and have me with him. A thousand times I prepared to go back on my word, a thousand tumultuous emotions of some impending disaster rushed through me. I felt on the border of an abyss, dark and hopeless. I was pushed on by invisible and unfriendly hands. I knew I must fall, knew that the black depths in front would engulf me eternally. I took the plunge. We talked over school-days and arranged our train to the West.

Widmore looked very boyish, I thought, as he rose to go, and stood smiling his good-bye in the doorway. He was all kindness, I liked him more than ever. I felt my heart go out to him, and yet, somehow, as we stood looking at one another, a grey shadow swept around him, and an icy pang shot through my heart.

· III

It was night once more, and the moonlight poured in floods from over the summit of the knoll where the uncanny boulders lay. Every obstacle was silhouetted against the dark background. A house with its white walls stood there grim and silent, and the paths running in various directions up and alongside the hill were made doubly clear in the whiteness of the beams that fell on them. There were no swift clouds, nothing to hide the brilliance of the stars, and it was nearly midnight. The air was cold, colder than was usual in St. Meave.

The lights of many boats twinkled in the bay and Godrevy stood out boldly away to the right, looking not more than a mile away. There were no lights to be seen in St. Meave itself. The town was absolutely still and dark; not a voice, not a sound, not even the baying of a dog. It was very ghostly. I shivered.

Widmore stood by my side. I glanced apprehensively at him. Why did he stand in the moonlight? What business had he there? I laughed, but I fear there was little mirth in the sound.

'I wish you would stop that infernal noise,' he said. 'I am pretty nervous as it is.'

'All right,' I whispered. 'I won't do it again.' But I did, and he edged sharply away from me. I looked over his head; there was the gaunt tree with the great hands. I fancied the branches were once again fingers. I told him so. 'For God's sake, man, keep quiet,' he said, 'you are enough to upset anyone's nerves.' He pulled out his watch for the hundredth time. 'It's close on the hour.'

I again looked at the trees and listened. Suddenly, although there had been absolute silence before, I heard a faint breathing sound, a very gentle murmur. It came from over the knoll. Very soft and low, but gradually louder and louder, and then, as it rushed past us into the spinney beyond, I saw once more the great trees rock beneath it, and again came those voices, those of the woman and the man. Widmore looked ill, I thought. I touched him on the arm. 'You are frightened,' I said.

288

'You a member of the New Occult Research Society, you afraid!'

'Something is going to happen,' he gasped. 'I feel it, I know it, we shall see the murder. We shall know the secret of her death. What is that?'

Away in the distance the tapping of shoes came through the now still night air. Tap, tap, tap, down the path from the knoll. I clutched Widmore by the arm. 'You think you will see the murder, do you? And the murderer?' Widmore didn't answer, his breath came in gasps. He looked about him like a man at bay.

'And the murderer! Ha! It comes from there! See, it is looking at us from those trees. It is all arms and legs. It has no human face. It will drop to the ground, and then we shall see what happens.'

Tap, tap, tap. The steps grew louder. Nearer and nearer they came. The great shadows from the trees stole down one by one to meet them.

I looked at Widmore. He was fearfully expectant; so was I.

A woman came tripping along the white path, her black shadow keeping pace with her. I knew her in an instant; there was the shabby shawl, the basket on her arm.

It was the same person. She approached the wicket. I looked at Widmore. He was spellbound with fear. I touched his arm. I dragged him with me. 'Come!' I whispered. 'We shall see which of us is right. You think the ghostly murderer will resemble some man, some human. It won't. Come! I dragged him forward. Had it not been for me, he would have fled. He, a member of the learned New Occult Research Society. I laughed. I could not help myself. It was so comical. Such fear! We passed through the gate. We followed the figure as it silently glided on. We turned to the left. The place grew

289

very dark as the trees met overhead. I heard the trickling of water and knew we were close to the ditch.

I gazed intently at the trees. When would the horror drop from them? A sickly terror laid hold of me. I turned to fly.

To my surprise Widmore stopped me. He had recovered, pulled himself together, and he was all excitement now. 'Wait,' he hissed, 'wait. It is you who are afraid. Hark! It is twelve o'clock.'

And as he spoke the clock of St. Meave Parish Church slowly boomed midnight. Then the end came. An awful scream rang out, so piercing and so full of terror that I felt all the blood in my body turn to ice.

My heart stood still. But no figure dropped from the trees. Not from the trees. From behind the woman a form darted forward and seized her round the neck. It tore at her throat with its white, curved fingers. It dragged and hurried her into the moonlight, and then, oh God! I saw its face. It was my own!

THE MOON-BOG

by H. P. Lovecraft

HOWARD PHILLIPS LOVECRAFT (1890–1937), a master in the ranks of modern horror story writers, lived and worked in almost total obscurity at Providence, Rhode Island and received little recognition for his work until after his death. Today he is rarely missing from any new anthology of the macabre, and many of his tales are familiar to people with only a passing interest in the genre. Although he never visited Ireland he was familiar with many of the towns and cities of America where the Irish had settled, and brought this knowledge to bear when writing The Moon-Bog. *It is interesting to note that he wrote this story virtually to order when attending a gathering of amateur writers on St. Patrick's Day. The group were all invited to devise a tale about Ireland; this was Lovecraft's contribution, full of myth, mystery and doom.*

Somewhere, to what remote and fearsome region I know not, Denys Barry has gone. I was with him the last night he lived among men, and heard his screams when the thing came to him; but all the peasants and police in County Meath could never find him, or the others, though they searched long and far. And now I shudder when I hear the frogs piping in swamps, or see the moon in lonely places.

I had known Denys Barry well in America, where he had grown rich, and had congratulated him when he bought back the old castle by the bog at sleepy Kilderry. It was from Kilderry that his father had come, and it was there that he wished to enjoy his wealth among ancestral scenes. Men of his blood had once ruled over Kilderry and built and dwelt in the castle, but those days were very remote, so that for generations the castle had been empty and decaying. After he went to Ireland Barry wrote me often, and told me how under his care the grey castle was rising tower by tower to its ancient splendour, how the ivy was climbing slowly over the restored walls as it had climbed so many centuries ago, and how the peasants blessed him for bringing back the old days with his gold from over the sea. But in time there came troubles, and the peasants ceased to bless him, and fled away instead as from a doom. And then he sent a letter and asked me to visit him, for he was lonely in the castle with no one to speak to save the new servants and labourers he had brought from the North.

The bog was the cause of all these troubles, as Barry told me the night I came to the castle. I had reached Kilderry in the summer sunset, as the gold of the sky lighted the green of the hills and groves and the blue of the bog, where on a far islet a strange olden ruin glistened spectrally. That sunset was very beautiful, but the peasants at Ballylough had warned me against it and said that Kilderry had become accursed, so that I almost shuddered to see the high turrets of the castle gilded with fire. Barry's motor had met me at the Ballylough station, for Kilderry is off the railway. The villagers had shunned the car and the driver from the North, but had whispered to me with pale faces when they saw I was going to Kilderry. And that night, after our reunion, Barry told me why.

The peasants had gone from Kilderry because Denys Barry was to drain the great bog. For all his love of

292

Ireland, America had not left him untouched, and he hated the beautiful wasted space where the peat might be cut and land opened up. The legends and superstitions of Kilderry did not move him, and he laughed when the peasants first refused to help, and then cursed him and went away to Ballylough with their few belongings as they saw his determination. In their place he sent for labourers from the North, and when the servants left he replaced them likewise. But it was lonely among strangers, so Barry had asked me to come.

When I heard the fears which had driven the people from Kilderry I laughed as loudly as my friend had laughed, for these fears were of the vaguest, wildest, and most absurd character. They had to do with some preposterous legend of the bog, and of a grim guardian spirit that dwelt in the strange olden ruin on the far islet I had seen in the sunset. There were tales of dancing lights in the dark of the moon, and of chill winds when the night was warm; of wraiths in white hovering over the waters, and of an imagined city of stone deep down below the swampy surface. But foremost among the weird fancies, and alone in its absolute unanimity, was that of the curse awaiting him who should dare to touch or drain the vast reddish morass. There were secrets, said the peasants, which must not be uncovered; secrets that had lain hidden since the plague came to the children of Partholan in the fabulous years beyond history. In the *Book of Invaders* it is told that these sons of the Greeks were all buried at Tallaght, but old men in Kilderry said that one city was overlooked, saved by its patron moon-goddess; so that only the wooded hills buried it when the men of Nemed swept down from Scythia in their thirty ships.

Such were the idle tales which had made the villagers leave Kilderry, and when I heard them I did not wonder

that Denys Barry had refused to listen. He had, however, a great interest in antiquities, and proposed to
explore the bog thoroughly when it was drained. The
white ruins on the islet he had often visited, but though
their age was plainly great, and their contour very little
like that of most ruins in Ireland, they were too dila-
pidated to tell the days of their glory. Now the work of
drainage was ready to begin, and the labourers from the
North were soon to strip the forbidden bog of its green
moss and red heather, and kill the tiny shell-paved
streamlets and quiet blue pools fringed with rushes.

After Barry had told me these things I was very
drowsy, for the travels of the day had been wearying and
my host had talked late into the night. A man-servant
showed me to my room, which was in a remote tower
overlooking the village, and the plain at the edge of the
bog, and the bog itself; so that I could see from my
windows in the moonlight the silent roofs from which
the peasants had fled and which now sheltered the
labourers from the North, and too, the parish church
with its antique spire, and far out across the brooding
bog the remote olden ruin on the islet gleaming white
and spectral. Just as I dropped to sleep I fancied I heard
faint sounds from the distance; sounds that were wild
and half musical, and stirred me with a weird excitement
which coloured my dreams. But when I awaked next
morning I felt it had all been a dream, for the visions
I had seen were more wonderful than any sound of wild
pipes in the night. Influenced by the legends that Barry
had related, my mind had in slumber hovered around
a stately city in a green valley, where marble streets and
statues, villas and temples, carving and inscriptions, all
spoke in certain tones the glory that was Greece. When
I told this dream to Barry we both laughed; but I
laughed the louder, because he was perplexed about his
labourers from the North. For the sixth time they had

all overslept, waking very slowly and dazedly, and acting as if they had not rested, although they were known to have gone early to bed the night before.

That morning and afternoon I wandered alone through the sun-gilded village and talked now and then with idle labourers, for Barry was busy with the final plans for beginning his work of drainage. The labourers were not as happy as they might have been, for most of them seemed uneasy over some dream which they had had, yet which they tried in vain to remember. I told them of my dream, but they were not interested till I spoke of the weird sounds I thought I had heard. Then they looked oddly at me, and said that they seemed to remember weird sounds, too.

In the evening Barry dined with me and announced that he would begin the drainage in two days. I was glad, for although I disliked to see the moss and the heather and the little streams and lakes depart, I had a growing wish to discern the ancient secrets the deep-matted peat might hide. And that night my dreams of piping flutes and marble peristyles came to a sudden and disquieting end; for upon the city in the valley I saw a pestilence descend, and then a frightful avalanche of wooded slopes that covered the dead bodies in the streets and left unburied only the temple of Artemis on the high peak, where the aged moon-priestess Cleis lay cold and silent with a crown of ivory on her silver head.

I have said that I awaked suddenly and in alarm. For some time I could not tell whether I was waking or sleeping, for the sound of flutes still rang shrilly in my ears; but when I saw on the floor the icy moonbeams and the outlines of a latticed gothic window I decided I must be awake and in the castle of Kilderry. Then I heard a clock f om some remote landing below strike the hour of two, and knew I was awake. Yet still there came that monotonous piping from afar; wild, weird airs that made me think of some dance of fauns on distant Maenalus. It would not let me sleep, and in impatience I sprang up and paced the floor. Only by chance did I go to the north window and look out upon the silent village and the plain at the edge of the bog. I had no wish to gaze abroad, for I wanted to sleep; but the flutes tormented me, and I had to do or see something. How could I have suspected the thing I was to behold?

There in the moonlight that flooded the spacious plain was a spectacle which no mortal, having seen it, could ever forget. To the sound of reedy pipes that echoed over the bog there glided silently and eerily a mixed throng of swaying figures, reeling through such a revel as the Sicilians may have danced to Demeter in the old days under the harvest moon beside the Cyane. The wide plain, the golden moonlight, the shadowy moving forms, and above all the shrill monotonous piping, produced an effect which almost paralysed me; yet I noted amidst my fear that half of these tireless, mechanical dancers were the labourers whom I had thought asleep, whilst the other half were strange airy beings in white, half-indeterminate in nature, but suggesting pale wistful naiads from the haunted fountains of the bog. I do not know how long I gazed at this sight from the lonely turret window before I dropped suddenly in a dreamless swoon, out of which the high sun of morning aroused me.

My first impulse on awaking was to communicate all my fears and observations to Denys Barry, but as I saw the sunlight glowing through the latticed east window I became sure that there was no reality in what I thought I had seen. I am given to strange fantasms, yet am never weak enough to believe in them; so on this occasion contented myself with questioning the labourers, who slept very late and recalled nothing of the previous night save misty dreams of shrill sounds. This matter of the spectral piping harassed me greatly, and I wondered if the crickets of autumn had come before their time to vex the night and haunt the visions of men. Later in the day I watched Barry in the library poring over his plans for the great work which was to begin on the morrow, and for the first time felt a touch of the same kind of fear that had driven the peasants away. For some unknown reason I dreaded the thought of disturbing the ancient bog and its sunless secrets, and pictured terrible sights lying black under the unmeasured depth of age-old peat. That these secrets should be brought to light seemed injudicious, and I began to wish for an excuse to leave the castle and the village. I went so far as to talk casually to Barry on the subject, but did not dare continue after he gave his resounding laugh. So I was silent when the sun set gently over the far hills, and Kilderry blazed all red and gold in a flame that seemed a portent.

Whether the events of that night were of reality or ilusion I shall never ascertain. Certainly they transcend anything we dream of in nature and the universe; yet in no normal fashion can I explain those disappearances which were known to all men after it was over. I retired early and full of dread, and for a long time could not sleep in the uncanny silence of the tower. It was very dark, for although the sky was clear the moon was now well in the wane, and would not rise till the small hours. I thought as I lay there of Denys Barry, and of what would befall that bog when the day came, and found myself almost frantic with an impulse to rush out into the night, take Barry's car, and drive madly to Ballylough out of the menaced lands. But before my fears could crystallise into action I had fallen asleep, and gazed in dreams upon the city in the valley, cold and dead under a shroud of hideous shadow.

Probably it was the shrill piping that awaked me, yet that piping was not what I noticed first when I opened my eyes. I saw lying with my back to the east window overlooking the bog, where the waning moon would rise, and therefore expected to see light cast on the opposite wall before me; but I had not looked for such a sight as now appeared. Light indeed glowed on the panels ahead, but it was not any light that the moon gives. Terrible and piercing was the shaft of ruddy refulgence that streamed through the gothic window, and the whole chamber was brilliant with a splendour intense and unearthly. My immediate actions were peculiar for such a situation, but it is only in tales that a man does the dramatic and foreseen thing. Instead of looking out across the bog toward the source of the new light, I kept my eyes from the window in panic fear, and clumsily drew on my clothing with some dazed idea of escape. I remember seizing my revolver and hat, but before it was over I had lost them both without firing the one or donning the other. After a time the fascination of the red radiance overcame my fright, and I crept to the east window and looked out whilst the maddening, incessant piping whined and reverberated through the castle and over all the village.

Over the bog was a deluge of flaring light, scarlet and sinister, and pouring from the strange olden ruin on the far islet. The aspect of that ruin I cannot describe—I must have been mad, for it seemed to rise majestic and undecayed, splendid and column-cinctured, the flame-reflecting marble of its entablature piercing the sky like the apex of a temple on a mountain-top. Flutes shrieked and drums began to beat, and as I watched in awe and terror I thought I saw dark saltant forms silhouetted grotesquely against the vision of marble and effulgence. The effect was titanic—altogether unthinkable—and I might have stared indefinitely had not the sound of the

piping seemed to grow stronger at my left. Trembling
with a terror oddly mixed with ecstasy. I crossed the
circular room to the north window from which I could
see the village and the plain at the edge of the bog.
There my eyes dilated again with a wild wonder as
great as if I had just turned from a scene beyond the
pale of nature, for on the ghastly red-litten plain was
moving a procession of beings in such a manner as none
ever saw before save in nightmares.

Half gliding, half floating in the air, the white-clad
bog-wraiths were slowly retreating toward the still
waters and the island ruin in fantastic formations
suggesting some ancient and solemn ceremonial dance.
Their waving translucent arms, guided by the detestable
piping of those unseen flutes, beckoned in uncanny
rhythm to a throng of lurching labourers who followed
doglike with blind, brainless, floundering steps as if
dragged by a clumsy but resistless demon-will. As the
naiads neared the bog, without altering their course, a
new line of stumbling stragglers zigzagged drunkenly out
of the castle from some door far below my window,
groped sightlessly across the courtyard and through the
intervening bit of village, and joined the floundering
column of labourers on the plain. Despite their distance
below me I at once knew they were the servants brought
from the North, for I recognised the ugly and unwieldly
form of the cook, whose very absurdness had now become unutterably tragic. The flutes piped horribly, and
again I heard the beating of the drums from the direction of the island ruin. Then silently and gracefully the
naiads reached the water and melted one by one into
the ancient bog; while the line of followers, never checking their speed, splashed awkwardly after them and
vanished amidst a tiny vortex of unwholesome bubbles
which I could barely see in the scarlet light. And as the
last pathetic straggler, the fat cook, sank heavily out of

sight in that sullen pool, the flutes and the drums grew silent, and the blinding red rays from the ruins snapped instantaneously out, leaving the village of doom lone and desolate in the wan beams of a new-risen moon.

My condition was now one of indescribable chaos. Not knowing whether I was mad or sane, sleeping or waking, I was saved only by a merciful numbness. I believe I did ridiculous things such as offering prayers to Artemis, Latona, Demeter, Persephone, and Plouton. All that I recalled of a classic youth came to my lips as the horrors of the situation roused my deepest superstitions. I felt that I had witnessed the death of a whole village, and knew I was alone in the castle with Denys Barry, whose boldness had brought down a doom. As I thought of him new terrors convulsed me, and I fell to the floor; not fainting, but physically helpless. Then I felt the icy blast from the east window where the moon has risen, and began to hear the shrieks in the castle far below me. Soon those shrieks had attained a magnitude and quality which cannot be written of, and which make me faint as I think of them. All I can say is that they came from something I had known as a friend.

At some time during this shocking period the cold wind and the screaming must have roused me, for my next impression is of racing madly through inky rooms and corridors and out across the courtyard into the hideous night. They found me at dawn wandering mindless near Ballylough, but what unhinged me utterly was not any of the horrors I had seen or heard before. What I muttered about as I came slowly out of the shadows was a pair of fantastic incidents which occurred in my flight: incidents of no significance, yet which haunt me unceasingly when I am alone in certain marshy places or in the moonlight.

As I fled from the accursed castle along the bog's edge I heard a new sound: common, yet unlike any I had heard before at Kilderry. The stagnant waters, lately quite devoid of animal life, now teemed with a horde of slimy enormous frogs which piped shrilly and incessantly in tones strangely out of keeping with their size. They glistened bloated and green in the moonbeams, and seemed to gaze up at the fount of light. I followed the gaze of one very fat and ugly frog, and saw the second of the things which drove my senses away.

Stretching directly from the strange olden ruin on the far islet to the waning moon, my eyes seemed to trace a beam of faint quivering radiance having no reflection in the waters of the bog. And upward along that pallid path my fevered fancy pictured a thin shadow slowly writhing; a vague contorted shadow struggling as if drawn by unseen demons. Crazed as I was, I saw in that awful shadow a monstrous resemblance—a nauseous, unbelievable caricature—a blasphemous effigy of him who had been Denys Barry.

THE FAIRIES' REVENGE

by Sinead De Valera

SINEAD DE VALERA (1889–1974) was the wife of the President of Eire and one of the very few really outstanding tellers of fantasy tales in the country today. Her husband's heroic rise to fame from gunman to leader of the country has brought her close to the people, and it is their overheard stories which she delights to retell. Much of her work is aimed at the younger generation, explaining the legends of the countryside and encouraging a love of the Irish heritage. In this tale she advises caution where the Sheehogue (fairies) are concerned, for these little people are—according to some legends—the Pagan Gods who, no longer being worshipped and fed with offerings, have dwindled in size to their present stature. True or not, they are capricious beings as likely to do good as evil, as this story indicates.

'Oh don't step inside that fairy ring, Nuala.'

'Nonsense, Conn. The fairies do not come out until midnight and they will never know I have been inside the ring.'

'I tell you, Nuala, they know everything.'

'Well, I am sure they will not see any trace of my footsteps on the soft grass. Look at those lovely white voilets. I will pull a bunch of them. The "good people" would not grudge them to me.'

'Oh, Nuala, there are just as beautiful flowers growing at the other end of the field.'

'Perhaps, but I like these and will have some.'

'You are foolish, Nuala. The fairies will have revenge for this.'

'It is you who are foolish, Conn, even though you are twelve years old. Though I am two years younger I have more sense than you.'

Conn and Nuala lived with their parents in a remote place in the West of Ireland. Near their homes there were many places where the fairies were said to have their dwellings. Every hill, mound and lios was said to be under their sway. The children had been constantly warned not to interfere with these places.

'These are lovely violets, Nuala,' said the mother as the children came into the house. 'Where did you gather them?'

Nuala hesitated.

'Where did you gather them? Tell me,' said her father.

'At the Fainne Si (the fairy ring),' stammered Nuala.

'How often have you been told not to take anything from the fairy ring? Indeed, I hope no harm will come to us for this.'

Nuala loved flowers. She put the violets in a cup of water and placed the cup beside her bed.

When she went to her room that night to undress she saw that all the violets had disappeared. The cup was quite empty.

Conn was almost asleep when he heard screams from Nuala's room. He and the parents ran to see what was the matter. They found Nuala torn and bleeding. When they looked at the bed they saw that it was full of sharp thorns. The mother lifted Nuala out. The thorns immediately disappeared. Nuala lay down again. The thorns returned.

'This is the fairies' revenge,' said the mother, 'Nuala can never sleep in a bed again.'

'Let her get into mine,' said Conn.

303

'I fear that will not be any better,' said the father.

Nuala got into Con's bed, but what the father said was true. The thorns were there as long as she was in the bed, but when she left it they at once disappeared.

'Oh,' said the mother, 'until the fairies' spell is broken she can never sleep in a bed again.'

There was great trouble in the house that night. Poor Nuala had to sleep on a blanket near the fire.

While the family were at breakfast next morning Sorcha, a neighbouring woman, came in.

'I came to ask for a few eggs,' she said, 'my own hens are not laying.'

'Oh! Sorcha, we are in great trouble,' said the mother.

'What is it?' asked Sorcha.

When she heard what had happened she shook her head and said:

'This is a bad case. It is very hard to get free from the spell of the fairies. The only thing you can do is to try to please them in some way.'

'Do you know any way in which we could please them?' asked the father.

'Well, I believe they love music. If anyone could play for them while they are dancing they would grant any request.'

'There is no musician anywhere about here,' said the mother.

'No,' said Sorcha. 'It is a pity you, yourself, Sive, never learned music. You have a lovely singing voice. And where is there a whistler like Conn? Well, I must be going now. Thanks, Sive, for the eggs. I am sorry for Nuala, but we all know it is dangerous to interfere with the fairies.'

Conn had been listening attentively to all that was said.

'Mother, isn't it a pity that there is no one here that could play music for the fairies? I wish I could have

304

learned to play some instrument,' he said.

'What about whistling for them, Conn,' asked the mother, laughing.

Conn could whistle any tune he heard. His whistling was so clear and sweet that the blackbirds, thrushes and other birds answered his notes. He laughed when his mother said he could whistle for the fairies but decided he would try. He waited till all the family were asleep that night. He then stole quietly out and went to the fairy ring.

The night was dark but round the ring were little glittering lights shining out like stars from the flowers in the grassy ring.

One fairy was playing on a little instrument like a flute. Conn hid behind a tree. He listened for some time to the music in order to learn the air of the tune. The fairies danced round merrily.

After a time the little musician laid down his flute as if he were tired. Conn saw that the dancers was disappointed. They called out!

'We want to continue our dance.'

Conn from behind the tree began to whistle the dance tune. The fairies seemed delighted.

One of them called out!

'Who is the mortal that knows our fairy music?'

Conn, still whistling, came from behind the tree. The fairies danced and danced while he continued to whistle. At last they ceased and the Queen addressing Conn said:

'As a reward of your music we will grant any request you ask.'

'Oh,' said Conn, 'I want my sister to be released from a spell.'

'Spells are placed on those only who interfere with our dwellings,' said the Queen.

305

'I know that,' said Conn. 'My sister took some flowers from the ring yesterday.'

'Yes,' said the Queen, 'and by our powers the flowers turned into thorns. She pulled the white violets which are our special possession. We will not allow any mortal to take anything from the Ring without inflicting punishment on the human who does such an act.'

'Is there any way in which the spell can be removed?' asked Conn.

'There is and you have pleased us so much by whistling our fairy tune we will tell you how it can be done. However, it will be a hard task.'

'I will do anything to help my sister.'

'Very well. Take this basket.'

She gave him a beautiful little basket made of reeds and lined with soft green moss.

'Do not allow any mortal eye to rest on it. When you have finished your work, place it among the tall reeds on the lake side where no one will see it. We will take it away in the darkness of the night. To brighten your way take one of these lights. Put it in the basket when you are returning it.

'Now go to the end of the field and take the winding road that leads to the black mountain.'

'Is that the mountain where the black witch has her home?'

'Yes, the witch is very wicked but we have power to protect you from harm. She sleeps from midnight till dawn. Be sure you get your work done before she awakes.

'Here is what you have to do. Climb the mountain on the side that faces you as you approach it. There is a lake at the top. Round it is a row of small trees and creeping round these you will see the *dreimire gorm* (night shade, bitter sweet). Gather as many of the leaves as you can into the basket. Hurry home and put the

306

leaves in your sister's bed and place the bedclothes over them. The leaves will disappear. The spell will be broken and your sister's sleep will be sweet and peaceful.

'You must act quickly for if the witch hears you she will make a hole in the mountain and the water will rush down and form a cataract so that you cannot descend from that side.'

'What about the other side?' asked Conn.

'The other side is very steep and as slippery as ice, but near the top there is a large flat stone. Rub your bare feet to that stone and you will be able to get safely down.

'One thing more. You must not tell any mortal about this. Keep it all as a strict secret. *Slán leat*. Good luck.'

Conn followed all the fairy's directions.

Just as he had nearly finished gathering the leaves the day began to break.

He heard a harsh grating voice and the sound of rushing water. He hastened to the far side of the mountain. He had barely reached the stone when he saw the witch followed him. She would have caught him only she stumbled and fell over a bush. Conn quickly rubbed his feet on the big stone and began to descend the mountain. As he reached the foot he heard the voice of the witch close behind him. He ran as quickly as he could but she was gaining on him. Just as she was about to catch hold of his coat he reached a stream. Witches cannot cross running water. Conn jumped across. He looked back to see her dancing and prancing with rage on the other side.

He reached home while the family was still in bed. Nuala was asleep in the blanket. Conn slipped into her room and placed the leaves in her bed and covered them with the bedclothes. Then he hurried off and put the basket back among the reeds.

When he came home breakfast was ready.

307

'You got up very early this morning,' said the mother.

The father who knew Conn was fond of work said:

'I am sure the lad was doing something useful.'

Conn said nothing. He thought how happy all of them would be when they knew that the cruel spell was broken. That night at bed time he said to Nuala:

'You ought to try if the thorns are still in your bed.'

'Indeed,' said the father, 'they will surely be there for how can we break the cruel spell?'

'My poor back is sore from lying on the blanket, but I know the thorns are still there,' said Nuala.

'Well,' said Conn, 'just try if they are gone.'

'Have sense,' said the mother, 'and don't bother the poor child.'

'Well, just to please me, Nuala,' urged Conn, 'lie down in the bed for a moment.'

'All right, Conn, just to please you.'

She turned down the bedclothes and lay down. There were no thorns there. The bed was soft and comfortable and through the room there was a fragrant perfume of flowers.

'How did all this happen?' asked the father.

'Who broke the spell?' asked the mother.

Conn smiled. 'That is my secret,' he said.

'If it is a secret, my boy,' said the father, 'keep it to yourself no matter what may happen.'

And Conn kept his secret for ever.

A WILD NIGHT IN GALWAY

by Ray Bradbury

*RAYMOND BRADBURY (1920–   ) is the greatest of
living fantasy writers, an endlessly inventive man of
words, completely at home in the realms of witches,
fairies and leprechauns, and with more of the Irishman's unique story-telling ability in him than many
of those actually born in the country. His style, so
patiently evolved and now so envied, was developed
in the face of discouragement, non-publication and
even ridicule. Today he treads with words where
others fear to go. He first came to Ireland in 1953 to
write the script for John Huston's film 'Moby Dick'.
By his own admission his senses were soon bewitched by the land and its people, and from the
confrontation of the Master of Fantasy and the
Home of Fantasy came a series of short stories: not
the least of these being* A Wild Night in Galway.
*Ray Bradbury did me the honour of introducing
this collection, and it is now my pleasure to close
it with his words—which will undoubtedly help
carry the Irish fantasy tale into the seventies; and
who can tell how far beyond that?*

We were far out at the tip of Ireland, in Galway, where
the weather strikes from its bleak quarters in the Atlantic
with sheets of rain and gusts of cold and still more sheets
of rain. You go to bed and wake in the middle of the
night thinking you heard someone cry, thinking you
yourself were weeping and feel at your face and find it
dry. Then you look at the window and think, why, yes,

it's just rain, the rain, always the rain, and turn over, sadder still, and fumble about for your dripping sleep and try to get it back on.

We were out, as I said, in Galway, which is grey stone with green beards on it, a rock town, and the sea coming in and the rain falling down and we had been there a month solid working with our film director on a script which was, with immense irony, to be shot in the warm yellow sun of Mexico some time in January. The pages of the script were full of fiery bulls and hot tropical flowers and burning eyes, and I typed it with chopped-off frozen fingers in my grey hotel room where the food was criminal's gruel and the weather a beast at the window.

On the 31st night, a knock at the door, at seven. The door opened, my film director stepped nervously in.

'Let's get the hell out and find some wild life in Ireland and forget this damn rain!' he said, all in a rush.

'What rain?' I said, sucking my fingers to get the ice out. 'The concussion here under the roof is so steady I'm shell-shocked and have quite forgot the stuff's coming down!'

'Four weeks here and you're talking Irish,' said the director.

'Hand me my clay pipe,' I said.

And we ran from the room.

'Where?' said I.

'Johnny Murphy's pub!' said he.

And we blew along the stony street in the dark that rocked gently as a boat on a black flood because of the tilty-dancing streetlights above which made the shadows tear and fly, uneasy.

Then, sweating rain, faces pearled, we struck through the pub door and it was warm as a sheepfold because there were the townsmen pressed in a great compost heap at the bar and Johnny Murphy yelling jokes and foaming up drinks.

'Johnny!' cried the director. 'We're here for a wild night!'

'A wild night we'll make it!' said Johnny, and in a moment a slug of John Jamieson was burning lace patterns in our stomachs, to let new light in.

I exhaled fire. 'That's a start!' I said.

We had another and listened to the rollicking jests and the jokes that were less than half-clean, or so we guessed, for the brogue made it difficult, and the whisky poured on the brogue and thus combined made it double-difficult. But we knew when to laugh, because when a joke was finished, the men hit their knees and then hit us. They'd give their limb a great smack and then bang us on the arm or thump us in the chest. As our breath exploded, we'd shape the explosion to hilarity and squeeze our eyes tight. Tears ran down our cheeks not from joy but from the exquisite torture of the drink scalding our throats. Thus pressed like shy flowers in a huge warm-mouldy book, the director and I lingered on, waiting for some vast event.

At last my director's patience thinned. 'Johnny!' he called across the seethe. 'It's been wild, so far, all right, but we want it wilder, I mean, the biggest night Ireland ever saw!'

Whereupon Johnny whipped off his apron, shrugged his meat-cleaver shoulders into a tweed coat, jumped up in the air and slid down inside his raincoat, slung on his beardy cap and thrust us at the door.

'Nail everything down till I get back!' he advised his crew. 'I'm taking these gents to the damnedest evening ever! Little do they know what waits for them out there!'

He opened the door and pointed. The wind threw half a ton of ice-water on him. Taking this as no more than an additional spur to rhetoric, Johnny, not wiping his face, added in a roar, 'Out with you! Here we go!'

'Do you think we should?' I said, doubtful now that things seemed really letting go.

'What do you mean?' cried the director. 'What do you want to do? Go freeze in your room? Rewrite that scene you did so lousily today?'

'No, no!' I said, and slung on my own cap.

I was first outside thinking, I've a wife and three loud but lovely children, what am I doing here, eight thousand miles gone from them on the off side of God's behind? Do I *really* want to do this?

Then, like Ahab, I thought on my bed, a damp box with its pale cool winding-sheets and the window dripping next to it like a conscience all night through. I groaned. I opened the door of Johnny Murphy's car, took my legs apart to get in, and in no time we shot down the town like a ball in a bowling alley.

Johnny Murphy at the wheel talked fierce, half hilarity, half sobering King Lear.

A wild night, is it? You'll have the grandest night ever!' he said. 'You'd never guess, would you, to walk through Ireland, so much could go on under the skin?'

'I knew there must be an outlet somewhere,' I yelled.

The speedometer was up to one-hundred kilometres an hour. Stone walls raced by on the right, stone walls raced by on the left. It was raining the entire dark sky down on the entire dark land.

'Outlet indeed!' said Johnny. 'If the church knew, but it don't! or then maybe it does but figures—the poor buggars! and let's us be!'

'Where, what—?'

'You'll see!' said Murphy.

The speedometer read 110. My stomach was stone like the stone walls rushing left and right. Up over a hill, down into a valley. Does the car have brakes? I won-

dered. Death on an Irish road, I thought, a wreck, and
before anyone found us strewn we'd melt away in the
pounding rain and be part of the turf by morn. What's
Death, anyways? better than hotel food.

'Can't we go a bit faster?' I asked.

'It's done!' said Johnny, and made it 120.

'That will do it nicely,' I said, in a faint voice, wondering what lay ahead. Behind all the slatestone weeping walls of Ireland, what happened? Somewhere in this
drizzling land were there hearth-fleshed peach-fuzz
Renoir women bright as lamps you could hold your
hands out to and warm your palms? Beneath the rain-
drenched sod, the flinty rocks, at the numbed core of
living was there one small seed of fire which, fanned,
might break volcanoes free and boil the rains to steam?
Was there then somewhere a Baghdad harem, nests
awriggle and aslither with silk and tassel the absolute
perfect tint of women unadorned? We passed a church.
No. We passed a convent. No. We passed a village
slouched under its old men's thatch. No. Stone walls to
left. Stone walls to right. No. Yet ...

I glanced over at Johnny Murphy. We could have
switched off our lights and driven by the steady piercing
beams of his forward-directed eyes snatching at the
dark, flickering away the rain.

Wife, I thought, to myself, children, forgive me for
what I do this night, terrible as it might be, for this is
Ireland in the rain of an ungodly time and way out in
Galway where the dead must go to die.

The brakes were hit. We slid a good ninety feet, my
nose mashed on the windshield. Johnny Murphy was out
of the car.

'We're here!' He sounded like a man drowning deep
in the rain.

I looked left. Stone walls. I looked right. Stone walls.

'Where is it?' I shouted.

'Where, indeed!' He pointed, mysteriously. 'There!'

I saw a hole in the wall, a tiny gate flung wide.

The director and I followed at a plunge. We saw other cars in the dark now, and many bikes. But not a light anywhere. A secret, I thought, oh it *must* be wild to be *this* secret. What am I doing here? I yanked my cap lower. Rain crawled down my neck.

Through the hole in the wall we stumbled, Johnny clenching our elbows. 'Here!' he husked. 'Stand here. It'll be a moment. Swig on this to keep your blood high!'

I felt a flask knock my fingers. I got the fire into my boilers and let the steam up the flues.

'It's a lovely rain,' I said.

'The man's mad,' said Murphy, and drank after the director, a shadow among shadows in the dark.

I squinted about. I had an impression of midnight sea upon which men like little boats passed on the murmurous tides. Heads down, muttering, in twos and threes, a hundred men stirred out beyond.

It has an unholy air. Good God, what's it all about? I asked myself, incredibly curious now.

'Johnny—?' said the director.

'Wait!' whispered Johnny. 'This is *it*!'

What did I expect? Perhaps some scene like those old movies where innocent sailing ships suddenly flap down cabin walls and guns appear like magic to fire on the foe. Or a farmhouse falls apart like a cereal box, Long Tom rears up to blast a projectile five hundred miles to target Paris. So here, maybe I thought, the stones will spill away each from the others, the walls of that house will curtain back, rosy lights will flash forth and from a monstrous cannon six, a dozen, ten dozen pink pearly women, not dwarf-Irish but willowy French, will be shot out over the heads and down into the waving arms of

314

the grateful multitude. Benison indeed! What's more—manna!

The lights came on.

I blinked.

For I saw the entire unholy thing. There it was, laid out for me under the drizzling rain.

The lights came on. The men quickened, turned, gathered, and we with them.

A mechanical rabbit popped out of a little box at the far end of the stony yard and ran. Eight dogs, let free from gates, yelping, ran after in a great circle. There was not one yell or a murmur from the crowd of men. Their heads turned slowly, watching. The rain rained down on the illuminated scene. The rain fell upon tweed caps and thin cloth coats. The rain dripped off thick eyebrows and thin noses. The rain beat on hunched shoulders. I stared. The rabbit ran. The dogs ran. At the finish, the rabbit popped into its electric hatch. The dogs collided on each other, barking. The lights went out.

In the dark I turned to stare at the director as I knew he must be turning to stare at me.

I was thankful for the dark, the rain, so Johnny Murphy could not see our faces.

'Come on, now!' he shouted. 'Place your bets!'

We were back in Galway, speeding, at ten o'clock. The rain was still raining, the wind was still blowing. The ocean was smashing the shore with titanic fists. The highway was a river working to erase the stone beneath as we drew up in a great tidal spray before the pub.

'Well, now!' said Johnny Murphy, not looking at us, but at the windshield wiper beating, palpitating there. 'Well.'

The directors and I had bet on five races and had lost, between us, two or three pounds. It worried Johnny.

'I won a great deal,' he said, 'and some of it, I keep telling you, over and over, I put down in your names,

315

both of you. That last race, I swear to God, I bet and won for all of us. Let me pay you!'

'No, Johnny, thanks,' I said.

'But you lost, what? in the States? nine dollars?'

'It's all right, Johnny,' I said, my numb lips moving.

He took my hand and pressed two shillings into it. I didn't fight him. 'That's better!' he said. 'Now, one last drink on me!'

We had the drink and walked back to my hotel. My director saw me to the door, before going on his way to his house, alone. Wringing out his cap in the hotel lobby he looked at me and said, 'It was a wild Irish night, wasn't it?'

'A wild night,' I said.

He left.

I hated to go up to my room. So I sat for another hour in the reading lounge of the damp hotel and took the traveller's privilege, a glass and a bottle provided by the dazed hallporter. I sat alone listening to the rain, and the rain on the cold hotel roof, thinking of Ahab's coffin-bed waiting for me up there under the drumbeat weather. I thought of the only warm thing in the hotel, in the town, in all the land of Eire this night, the script in my typewriter this moment, with its sun of Mexico, its hot winds blowing from the Pacific, its mellow papayas, its yellow lemons, its fiery sands and its women with dark charcoal-burning eyes.

And I thought of the darkness beyond the town, the light flashing on, the electric rabbit running, the dogs running, and the rabbit gone and the light going out and the rain falling down on the dank shoulders and the soaked caps and trickling off the noses and seeping through the tweeds.

Going upstairs I glanced out of a steaming window. There, on the road, riding by under a street light, was a man on a bicycle. He was terribly drunk, for the bike

316

weaved back and forth across the road, as the man vomited. He did not stop the bike to do this. He kept pumping unsteadily, blearily, as he threw up. I watched him go off down the road into raining dark.

Then I went on up to die in my room.